NO WAY HOME

Andrew Coburn

▶▶▶▶▶▶▶▶▶▶▶▶▶▶▶▶▶

NO WAY

◀◀◀◀◀◀◀◀◀◀◀◀◀◀◀◀

HOME

▶▶▶▶▶▶▶▶▶▶▶▶▶▶▶▶▶

A DUTTON BOOK

DUTTON
Published by the Penguin Group
Penguin Books USA Inc., 375 Hudson Street,
New York, New York 10014, U.S.A.
Penguin Books Ltd, 27 Wrights Lane,
London W8 5TZ, England
Penguin Books Australia Ltd, Ringwood,
Victoria, Australia
Penguin Books Canada Ltd, 10 Alcorn Avenue,
Toronto, Ontario, Canada M4V 3B2
Penguin Books (N.Z.) Ltd, 182–190 Wairau Road,
Auckland 10, New Zealand

Penguin Books Ltd, Registered Offices:
Harmondsworth, Middlesex, England

First published by Dutton, an imprint of New American Library,
a division of Penguin Books USA Inc.
Distributed in Canada by McClelland & Stewart Inc.

First Printing, July, 1992
10 9 8 7 6 5 4 3 2 1

 REGISTERED TRADEMARK—MARCA REGISTRADA

LIBRARY OF CONGRESS CATALOGING-IN-PUBLICATION DATA:
Coburn, Andrew.
  No way home / by Andrew Coburn.
    p.   cm.
  ISBN 0-525-93470-7
  PS3553.O23N6   1992
  813'.54—dc20   91-40036
                                                  CIP

Printed in the United States of America
Set in Janson
Designed by Eve L. Kirch

PUBLISHER'S NOTE
This is a work of fiction. Names, characters, places, and incidents either are the
products of the author's imagination or are used fictitiously, and any resemblance
to actual persons, living or dead, events, or locales is entirely coincidental.

For my wife, Bernadine Casey Coburn, and our four daughters; my sister, Julie Coburn Masera; and to the memory of my mother, Georgiana (Dolly) Coburn Ford; and my great-grandmother, Georgiana Burnham McLane. And, of course, for my friend and agent, Nikki Smith.

1

The sun lay warm on Flo Lapham's shoulders and colored the woodlot bordering the back lawn. The woodlot was home to rabbits, raccoons, weasels, squirrels, and a family of red foxes. A pair of hooters, along with peepers, kept nights alive. Jays and robins vied for the bird bath. For Flo, each spring was the first ever. She could find newness in anything, even her rumpled husband, whose bottom teeth were in his shirt pocket.

A gray curl dangled irrelevantly over Earl Lapham's forehead. He was ensconced in a lawn chair with a cup of coffee beside him and the local weekly in his lap. With affection he watched Flo stoop to yank a weed from the tulip bed. A dicky heart, which had forced him from the insurance business, made him more aware of her. He watched intently as she straightened with a smile that brought out the little cracks in her face but in no way lessened her appeal. The flaws complemented the design.

Their heads turned in unison when their daughter emerged from the house to say good-bye before leaving for work. Lydia was a hospital nurse, second shift. In her uniform, the whitest white, she could have been a bride without the fancies.

Lydia strode to her father first and kissed his cheek. She

was thirty years old. At home she was still the child. At the hospital she was a respected professional, with something swift and vague about her and little that was public. One would have been hard put to explain her, not least of all doctors who were rotten to the other nurses but held their tongues with her.

"How are you doing, Dad?" She rested a hand on the curve of his shoulder.

"Fine," he said, the warmth of her touch pressing through his shirt.

"Honest?"

"Honest."

He saw not the high-strung woman in lipstick but, in the watercolors of memories, the little girl in pigtails who had thrilled to the workmanship of a spider's web, the harmony of music given the wind, and the aura of mystery surrounding a common cat.

Flo, watching her daughter move smoothly toward her, relished the sight of her: the hasty, boyish figure and soft, straight hair that seemed to be brown. The tones were assorted. In childhood the hair had held the hue and scent of hay. Flo extended an arm.

"Are you seeing Matthew later?"

Lydia's voice had a husk of irony. "I'm probably the only gal in town who gets courted in a police cruiser."

"When are you going to make an honest man of him, my dear?"

"Soon as we grow up."

"If you wait that long, you might lose him."

"I doubt it, Mom."

Flo smiled indulgently. She and her only child had a good relationship. She could ask questions and not feel left out, and she could render advice without fear of rebuff. She had hoped that Lydia might marry a doctor, but she no longer had objections to Matthew MacGregor, despite his look of an overgrown schoolboy.

Earl reached for his coffee, wistful eyes on his wife. Memory resurrected her enormously pregnant, her belly a globe of the world, his young ear pressed to it. Then he shifted his gaze to the burgeoning woodlot where, rustling their leaves, maples and oaks spoke a language he was almost beginning to understand. Insects sang, reaffirming the sweetness of life. Lowering his eyes, he sipped his coffee. The gilt around the mouth of the cup was vanishing, as all things do.

"Gotta go," Lydia said cheerily.

Flo heard movements in the woodlot and glimpsed bits of color, sparks. A breeze sweeping through the branches seemed to have something to say but slurred the words. Lydia, who had taken two strides, turned and looked back.

"Did you hear something?"

Earl, as if nudged by an invisible hand, rose too fast and spilled coffee. His teeth fell from his shirt. Flo, with a warning from the oldest part of her brain, started toward her daughter. That was when the report of a high-powered rifle obliterated every other sound.

The shot disturbed leaves, scattered birds, and tore through the back of Flo's neck. Earl disbelieved his eyes. Stumbling toward his wife, he suddenly clutched his chest and felt the final pain he always knew would come. Lydia, poised between her mother and father, both on the ground, froze.

Inside the house the telephone rang and rang.

At the police station, which was snugged into the rear of the Bensington Town Hall, Meg O'Brien, the daytime dispatcher, answered an outside call. The voice on the other end, a woman's, was abrupt, peremptory, and scathingly sweet: "Chief Cock, please."

"Cut the crap, Mrs. Bowman." Meg spoke without taking the cigarette from her mouth, so that the cigarette gave flutter and fire to each word. "Chief's not in—and don't call again." She slammed the receiver down. "The gall of that woman!"

Eugene Avery, who wore his sergeant stripes with pride, said, "I won't ask what that was all about."

"Best you don't." Spilling ash, Meg took a final puff on her cigarette and smashed it out. She was a stringy woman, somewhere in her fifties, with the face of a pony. Her mouth was a rupture of heavy teeth.

"I won't even ask where he is," Sergeant Avery said, though his whole face posed the question. When the chief was away from the office, the sergeant was nominally in charge but took direction from Meg, seldom diplomatic in rendering it.

"Tuck your shirt in, Eugene."

He was short and squarish and did not wear his uniform well. The shirt was baggy, unlike the trousers meant for a trimmer man. Before joining the police department some twenty-five years ago, he had driven a laundry truck, which had put him through McIntosh Business School, now defunct. Stuffing in a side of his shirt, he said, "But I could make some guesses."

"So you don't bother your brain, go get us some root beer."

He picked up his cap, the perforated summer one, and pushed it flat down on his head. "Who's paying?"

"Who always pays?" Meg dug into her bag, which held a snub-nose revolver, though her civilian status did not necessitate her carrying one. She reduced her eyes to kernels as Sergeant Avery approached in an uneasy gait with his hand out.

"What's the matter?" he asked.

"Those pants are so tight I doubt you got any balls left."

"Don't worry about my balls," he said, offended. "Just worry about yourself."

She came up with a dollar bill so worn it felt like silk, but before she could surrender it the telephone shrilled in their ears. Her teeth erupted. "If it's that bitch again I'm swearing out a warrant."

James Morgan entered the private air of Christine Poole's bedroom, which gave out significant hints of her husband, as if he might be lurking in the closet or under the bed. Jeweled cuff links glinted like eyes. A shaft of light shot through a half-used flask of aftershave, giving it new meaning and a life of its own. A glance in the mirror made Morgan feel vaguely like a fugitive.

"Relax, James."

Christine spoke from the bathroom. Then she appeared, without her robe. She had a strikingly intelligent face, at once pronounced and refined, and a nonchalant body with swooning breasts and a belly she did not try to gulp in. Morgan, who considered a woman's nakedness a sacred image, reached for her head, loaded his hands with her hair, and kissed her.

"I haven't seen you in a while," she said.

"I always come when you call."

"Sometimes it might be rewarding for *you* to call."

He sat on her husband's side of the bed and slipped off his loafers and socks. Once, scrambling for his clothes, he had retrieved one sock but failed to find its fellow, and Christine had lent him a pair of her husband's, not yet returned. Now he laid his own neatly in view, one on top of the other, and stripped off his narrow-legged chinos. His Jockey shorts were tangerine, a gift from another woman, her joke. When he lifted his shirt, Christine traced a finger across the small of his back. He was lean and long, with the hint of a roll around his middle that occasional tennis, swimming, and other activities kept from spreading. He had all his hair, which refused to gray.

Under the covers his hand went to her.

"Don't hurry it, James. At this stage of the game the warmth is more important than the thrill."

She was Morgan's age, forty-six. Mr. Poole, much older, was her second husband, an unfortunate placement, for she gauged all men by romantic memories of her first husband. Morgan apparently measured close.

"May is not a good month for me," she said, and he could guess the reason. Everything was connected with that first husband of hers, while Mr. Poole, out of sight, failed to matter, perhaps even ceased to exist. She counted Morgan's ribs. "We've both been disappointed, haven't we, James? No, that's too weak a word. *Struck down* is more like it."

He would not argue that, nor would he discuss it. What

she sought to recapture, he tried to keep in perspective, with probably no more success than she achieved. But he had come a long way, he liked to remind himself. He had survived that solitary drive ten years before when the speedometer jittered past ninety and would have crept to a hundred if the hand of God or that of his dead wife had not touched him in a way that woke him. The skid marks ran wild, but he missed the tree.

Christine spread her fingers over his chest hair. "Seems we've known each other forever."

Six months, that was all, but she had revealed so much about herself that it was like forever. And she was always probing to learn more about him, occasionally assigning traits that had never been his. Some he assumed.

"Your other women are younger than I, aren't they?" Her voice was curiously neutral, yet still warm. "I imagine you're the magic bullet in their lives. Are you, James?"

"There's no such bullet," he said.

"Are they married like me, divorced, what?"

"What," he said.

She leaned sideways to scratch her bottom, then rolled back to him with eyes that were ready. A kiss held them together, and in moments they were immersed in each other. Always in her lovemaking was a blazing touch of theatrics. She kicked hard and high, moaned dramatically, and dug her nails too fiercely into his flesh. His back bloody, he always felt entitled to a Purple Heart.

Later, the bedside phone rang, a subdued tinkling, like chimes, but loud enough for him to come awake as if water had been flung in his face.

Her eyes remained closed. "I don't intend to answer it."

"It might be for me," he said.

"How could it be for you?"

"They know I'm here."

"Oh, that's nice, James. Really nice." She blindly flung out an arm, snatched up the receiver, and spoke clearly into it. An instant later she dangled it over to him. Her voice was wryly formal. "Miss O'Brien wants to speak to Chief Morgan."

"Yes, Meg," he said, rising with the phone clamped to his ear. As she spoke, his entire jaw tightened. "Christ," he said, catapulting to his feet and tripping over his loafers. The cord stretched precariously. When he grabbed his chinos with his free hand, loose change spilled from a pocket. "I didn't hear that, Meg. Say it again."

"What is it, James?" Christine asked in a harsh whisper and was shushed.

Quarters and nickels felt like ice under his soles. A breeze burned his body. "Make the calls, Meg. Bakinowski last, I want to be there first."

They wanted her to stay inside the house, to sit down, to lie down if possible, but nothing was possible. Matthew MacGregor's arm was a weight, not a comfort, and she avoided it. He was her sweetheart but seemed a stranger. At the front window her hair slumped over half her face, which gave her only one eye to look out of, more than enough. Police cars, local and state, some with doors left open, clogged the street. Horrified neighbors lined the far sidewalk. She pulled back when she realized they could see her as well.

"Tell me this hasn't happened," she said, and MacGregor's face went helpless.

"Lydia . . ." His voice faded into frustration. He wanted to squeeze her in his arms and show her that the strength of his love would sustain her, but she gazed through him as if he were no longer a presence.

"I can't stay inside," she said and walked woodenly toward the back door through rooms that now seemed alien. Outside, the sun pounced at her. Rambunctious hornets flew like stunt pilots over the shocking pink of a rhododendron. MacGregor hovered, useless, unwanted.

"You don't want to be out here," he said and was ignored.

Lieutenant Bakinowski of the state police was reconnoitering, eyes fastened on the grass, as if he were tracking somebody's spoor. Troopers were scouring the woodlot for evidence, footprints, a casing from a shell. So far they had come upon only poison ivy and woodchuck holes. One of the troopers, a bird lover, paused to observe the flight of an oriole.

"Please, Lydia."

The bodies were still on the ground, for Lieutenant Bakinowski, deaf to Chief Morgan's protest, did not want them removed yet.

Sergeant Avery had taken pictures with an old Speed Graphic, but Bakinowski had then assigned his own man to do the job. To the chief he said, "Your guy comes up with blanks, where does that leave me?"

Morgan, unwilling to wait for the county medical examiner, had summoned nearby Dr. Skinner, semiretired, who pronounced the victims dead—Flo Lapham of the bullet that had torn through an artery and Earl of an apparent coronary, most likely massive. Morgan had then covered them with blankets, one from the sergeant's car and the other from his.

Lydia stood rigid from an inner spring that had tightened. Had it tightened more her head would have snapped back. From the distance the chief was staring. Clearly he did not want her out here, but he made no move. He had known Earl and Flo Lapham all his life and Lydia since she was a child knock-kneed in a ruffled dress, her father showing her off at a Memorial Day ceremony on the green, shots fired into the air, which scared her. She bolted to her mother. After all these years he remembered that and tried to catch MacGregor's eye, a signal to get her back into the house, but MacGregor was staring at the ground.

Turning her face, Lydia gazed at a loose drain pipe her father would never fix and at a bed of Alpine strawberries her mother would not see ripen. At the hospital, where she was accustomed to terminal illnesses, to pain and suffering, death was often only a breath away. Here it had been less than that, without warning, without rhyme, leaving only the riveting weight of loss.

Lieutenant Bakinowski finished his reconnoitering and approached the chief. He wore a blue business suit and had deep-set eyes that came out of their cages when he spoke. "Think I've figured out the line of fire." With a shout and a strenuous wave, he redirected the troopers in the woodlot.

"Could've been a stray shot, some kid playing around. What d'you know about the family?"

"Good people," Morgan said.

"But these little towns are funny. You were born here, weren't you?"

"And I've lived here all my life," Morgan said with loyalty and pride but with less force than usual, his voice sharp but sad. Tragedy, he firmly believed, is bred into every triumph. The stunning loss of his wife and the scattering of his father in the final victory blasts of a war had proved that. Happiness has nowhere to settle except in sadness. That, he felt, was a given.

"Something the matter, Chief?"

"I just wish to hell you'd get the bodies out of here, make it easier on the daughter."

"Not yet."

"Why not?"

"They keep the scene real."

"This isn't a stage set."

"That's exactly what it is," Bakinowski said with authority and a deep-fixed impatience with local cops, whom he considered unprofessional, incompetent, and obstructive. Over Morgan's head he also hung a cloud of moral laxity, for he had heard stories about the chief's personal life. "Look here, Chief, I don't care if you're not a help, just don't be a hindrance."

The minister from the Congregational church appeared. Lydia was not a churchgoer, but her parents had been faithful ones. "Please don't say anything," she said with a raw awareness of his presence. His well-intended face was solemnly set and his gray hair smartly combed as if in celebration of saintly thoughts. Officer MacGregor, in deference to him, had slipped away.

"I just want you to know I'm here," the minister said. "And to help if I can."

"Nothing will bring them back," she said in a hollow voice.

"But we know where they are."

"Yes," she said. "Somewhere in the nowhere."

A trooper scratching his bug bites came out of the woodlot. He was sweating; his skin poured through his shirt. "Look what I got, Lieutenant." He laid open a broad hand and showed a shell casing, which Bakinowski eyed closely. "I know what it's from," said the trooper, a sharpshooter who once had picked off a deranged man holding hostages. "So do you, Lieutenant."

Bakinowski turned to Chief Morgan. "Know anyone in town owns an F-1 sniper rifle?"

Meg O'Brien stayed at the station past her shift to help answer telephones that did not stop ringing. As soon as she put her phone down it would jangle in her hand, the sound vibrating into her arm. There had not been this much excitement since two youths from out of town had held up the Sunoco station, shot the owner in the leg, pistol-whipped the attendant, and were apprehended in the woods two miles from where their car broke down. That night the chief took her and Eugene Avery to a restaurant in Lawrence, where they ate scampi and drank wine, and the waiter, his fly not properly zipped, sang a little song in Italian.

On the lighted steps of the town hall, overlooking the green, Lieutenant Bakinowski fielded questions from the media, including reporters from Boston's three major television stations. In Boston, scarcely twenty miles away, a killing was simply part of a count that rose each year, but in a hamlet like Bensington it was an event. Unremarkable in their sockets, Bakinowski's eyes emerged electric for the cameras. The eyes of the man beside him stirred soupy blue under brows in need of a trim. Randolph Jackson, his family Bensington's oldest, was chairman of the selectmen and a former state legislator. He was losing some of his sandy hair, one sizable bite on the crown, and with a freckled hand he smoothed strands over the spot. Sotto voce, he said, "Where's the chief?"

"Who the hell knows?" Bakinowski whispered back. Then the same query was posed by a reporter from the Lawrence paper, whose circulation included Bensington. "Probably having his supper," Bakinowski offered in his public voice and went on to the next question.

Sergeant Avery, on the chief's orders, sat in a cruiser outside a white frame house flanked by lilacs with a scent that pervaded the growing dark. Beside him was a twelve-gauge Mossberg shotgun and the wrapping from a sandwich he had consumed. On the dash was a can of root beer. An empty mayonnaise jar awaited his need to relieve his bladder. His head was tipped and his eyes focused on the porch light, which was collecting moths at a rapid rate. The house belonged to Lydia Lapham's unmarried aunt. Lydia was spending the night there, perhaps many nights.

Matthew MacGregor stood with Chief Morgan in the half-lit parking lot of the library, which had closed at eight. Morgan's car was unmarked except for the town seal on each side and a noticeable scrape that had defaced one of the seals. MacGregor said, "It must've happened when I was trying to call her. I wanted to catch her before she left for work. Christ, Chief, I should've gone there instead."

Ten years his senior, Morgan regarded him somewhat paternally. With certain expressions MacGregor looked like a schoolboy fitted into a policeman's uniform. The sidearm he carried could have been a heavy toy. A pug nose caricatured wholesome looks, and a muscular build evoked days he played three sports at the regional high school, a letter earned in each.

"She saw them drop." He snapped his fingers. "Like *that*, they were gone!" He snapped his fingers again, so hard they must have hurt. "Like *that!*"

"Take it easy," Morgan said with a strong sense of connection. Each had lost his father young. MacGregor was ten when, without warning, without even an explanation, his father abandoned the family, simply walked out the door with a packed bag, and was never heard from again.

"I know what she's going through, Chief."

"I know you do."

"I want the son of a bitch who did it."

A mosquito whined between, and both batted it away,

MacGregor with the faster hand. Morgan spoke quietly. "I've been mulling over what Lydia told us. I don't think her mother was the target. I think she got in the way."

MacGregor's face faltered, and the boy in it vanished. "You're saying Lydia."

"Makes more sense, doesn't it?"

MacGregor agreed without speaking, without moving a muscle. Then he disagreed. "Makes no sense at all. Who'd want to hurt her? Christ, no one. At the hospital she puts doctors in their place, but they respect her. Patients love her, everybody loves her. *I* love her, Chief. She's the world to me."

"Exactly," Morgan said in a slow voice meant to drive home the meaning, which MacGregor resisted.

"I don't know what you're telling me."

"Yes, you do."

"Then say it plain."

"It's like I always said. Somebody wants to hurt a cop, he goes after the family." Morgan averted his head and sneezed. Oaks and birches were disseminating their pollen. "Or a person just as close," he added.

The driver stopped, idled the motor, and squinted through the windshield. Pitched high, the headlights burned a tunnel through the dark of the steel bridge spanning the Merrimack River, which was muscular from recent rains. The driver dimmed the lights and squeezed a smile he did not know was there. His breathing, like the motor, ran rough. "Give it here," he said, and the sleek pieces of a dismantled rifle tumbled weightily into his hands. The stink of the shot was still in the barrel. Then he pushed open his door.

The night air was rife with the taste and smell of the river, and from everywhere came the racket of peepers. Walking along the rail to the middle of the bridge, he reassembled the weapon with amazing dexterity and speed. He wanted to see it whole again. A fearsome piece of workmanship, it had proved a rewarding instrument of business.

He pricked an ear when he thought he heard the sound of a car coming, but it was merely the rumble of the river, which brought up more of its taste and a deeper odor. For a moment he was struck by the thought that the river had a voice and was saying things to him. But he had no time to listen. Stepping back, he gripped the rifle by the barrel and with a whirl threw it over the rail.

The splash was insignificant.

◄ ◄ ◄ 2 ► ► ►

The morning broke bright over the town, which had wakened early. Crows scavenged residential streets to feast on the remains of unlucky woodlot animals. A boy on a bicycle slung yesterday's news over lawns still moist from the night. Here and there front doors opened tentatively. A woman in a robe rushed to pick up her paper, and across the street a man in an undershirt retrieved his. A bread truck, on its way to Tuck's General Store, rumbled around the green, where a few souls had already gathered as if expecting a show. They trained their eyes on the police sign protruding from the far side of the town hall.

The Blue Bonnet restaurant opened at seven and filled by quarter-past. The breakfast menu, chalked on a blackboard screwed into a wall of knotty pine, offered muffins straight from the baking tins, doughnuts hot from the oven, and eggs fresh from Tish Hopkins's chickens. A communal table of regulars ate with their eyes aimed out the windows. Mitch Brown, preparing a dozen orders at once, turned from the grill and scanned the faces at every table. "I don't see the chief," he declared.

The chief, usually there, was not, which surprised no one.

At an hour when most men were leaving for work, a number of wives made their husbands stay home. The school bus ran half empty. At eight-fifteen Fred Fossey, commander of the local VFW, lowered the flag at the town hall to half mast. He and Earl Lapham had fought in the Korean War, and Flo Lapham, née Westerly, on whom he had had a crush since childhood, was a third or fourth cousin. Entering the town hall, where he held the part-time position of veterans affairs officer, he bumped into the Congregational minister and grabbed the man's upper arm. "Something we have to ask ourselves, Reverend. Is God always on duty?"

Meg O'Brien, with little sleep, was back in the station, with a mug of coffee at her elbow. Sergeant Avery, arriving late, peeked into the chief's office, which was vacant. "Not in yet?" he asked.

"Been and gone," Meg O'Brien said.

"Say where?"

"You want him, you can reach him on the radio. You want him?"

Sergeant Avery shook his head, poured coffee from the Silex, and had an unwanted memory of Chief Morgan gently draping a blanket over Flo Lapham's body. For a stunning moment he had thought the chief, for the comfort of each, might shift her closer to her husband. His voice went small. "Doesn't make sense, does it, Meg?"

"World sort of made sense once, but I was a kid then," said Meg, who had suffered her own losses.

At nine o'clock, Lieutenant Bakinowski assigned troopers to requisition neighbors of the Laphams'. Hours leading to the shooting, had they noticed anything unusual, no matter how insignificant? Think hard. Some, desperate to help, made up things, citing strangers on the street and noises in the yard, figures fleeing in the woods beyond.

Near noon, Bakinowski spoke with Randolph Jackson in the front seat of Jackson's Audi, a replacement for one cracked up a month before. "You must have a few hunters in this town," Bakinowski said, and Jackson immediately challenged the inference.

"What would a hunter have been doing in that little woodlot?"

"He could've been testing his weapon. Could've fired it accidentally." Bakinowski's eyes came forward. "Let me remind you of something, sir. Fellows who hunt animals, who are big for blood sport, aren't like you and me. They're a shade less."

"I know, but—"

Bakinowski smiled. "I'm just trying to rule out some possibilities."

The lunch crowd at the Blue Bonnet was bigger than normal. With Mitch Brown's wife, the cashier, helping out at the tables, Mitch, with the smells of clean cooking clinging to him, emerged from the kitchen. His shirt, baker's white, was scrawled here and there with food stains, like notes to himself.

"Guess what?" his wife said, balancing plates of chicken pot pie. "TV people are doing interviews. They're supposed to be coming here next."

He was not interested. Craning his neck, he said, "I still don't see the chief."

When he had been appointed chief, the daily in Lawrence ran a profile on him, blew his picture up big, called him "personable and progressive," and mentioned his degree from Northeastern, his year in Vietnam, and the death of his wife. A drunken youth from Andover, driving his father's brand-new Buick with the gas pedal floored, had struck Elizabeth's Bug broadside. The youth had climbed out with the customary abrasions and contusions. That had been fifteen years ago last month. There were days when it seemed a hundred years ago and nights when it might have been yesterday.

He still lived in the same house, and sometimes, in the dead of an evening, he glimpsed her in another room, but always a shadow instantly carried her off. In the small hours he occasionally woke to find her only a breath away. If he did not move, the darkness held her there until dawn.

Such would have been the case now had he not stirred.

Andrew Coburn

Birds were making themselves heard through the half dark. Once awake, he could not drop back to sleep.

The house, which he had grown up in, was less than a mile from the green. It was more Gothic than Victorian and not in total repair, for he was a lummox with tools. When his mother had moved to Florida the house had become his. Elizabeth had had plans for it, but they died with her. Downstairs the kitchen and dining room were small and dim, with windows of dusty panes and peeling mullions. Floral wallpaper had long lost its bloom. In the living room he had installed a desk salvaged from the town clerk's office. It matched his one at the police station, which made him feel more there than here.

Upstairs were two bedrooms and a good-sized bath. After Elizabeth's death he had moved from the large bedroom to the small one, once partially furnished for the child they had never had.

He showered with his eyes closed until the water ran cold. Shaved, he patted his cheeks with witch hazel. Dressed, he watched the sunrise sign in another day while what was left of the night dripped off the trees. His thoughts were not of his wife but of Lydia Lapham. He felt stronger than ever that the bullet that had killed her mother had been meant for her.

When he stepped out the front door the sun was already swimming over the lawn. Clumps of unattended tiger lilies, rearing up foliage but not yet blossoms, cast the aura of a jungle. A robin flew out of its bedroom in a maple. Abruptly he stopped and scanned the street, as if he too were a possible target.

He checked in at the station. Meg O'Brien was the only one there, for the duty officer on the graveyard shift had left. Caught in the act of sneezing, she brought a tissue to her face. "Maybe this isn't the time to mention it," she said, wiping her nose, "but Mrs. Bowman rang up yesterday. Should I tell you what she called you?"

"I don't think so," he said with a cringe that evoked a memory of Arlene Bowman's mouth, a dash of violence in the smile. He began checking entries in the night log.

"Why can't you pick a nice girl," Meg said, "instead of fooling with those phonies from the Heights?"

"No lectures, Meg, please," he said and closed the log.

"Your hair's sticking up in back."

He groomed it with the flat of his hand. She had more to say, but he did not stay to listen.

He drove to the house of Lydia Lapham's aunt. Though still early, he knew she and Lydia would be up. The porch light was burning weakly in the sunshine, and the night officer who had spelled Sergeant Avery was dozing in his cruiser.

"You can go now," Morgan said, startling him.

The young officer snapped on his cap and squared it. "Should I come back tonight?"

"We'll see."

In the roses near the porch was a spiderweb in which a powdery moth was fastened like a miniature angel. Morgan thought of rescuing it, but was hesitant to interfere with the balance of life, which he felt was tentative enough. He meandered to the back of the house because he reckoned they would be in the kitchen.

"May I come in?" he said through the screen door.

No tears were in Lydia's eyes. They were all in her aunt's. Miss Westerly, her face crinkled lace that had aged overnight, was in her robe and quietly disappeared. Lydia sat at the table, near the raised window, with her hands embracing a cup of coffee that may have gone cold. Morgan doubted she had slept. In her wrinkled white uniform she looked like a private letter someone had tried unsuccessfully to steam open. The remote quality of her voice put a distance between them. "My parents are dead, Chief. Can you tell me why?"

"Not yet," he said quietly, wishing his presence was less bruising. He should have worn a suit and tie instead of a casual shirt and chinos. He should have worn real shoes instead of loafers.

"Can you tell me who?"

His jaw, taut with intention a moment ago, was loose. His feelings stretched to her.

"What am I going to do without them?" she said in a way

Andrew Coburn

her voice was never meant to sound. It could have come from a metal drum.

"You have your aunt. You have Matt."

"Don't tell me what I have," she said with increased tension. "I know what I have, Chief."

"Please," he said, "call me James. I might be the police chief, but I'm also your friend. Yours and Matt's."

"Mine and Matt's. That's nice, James. You couple us as if we were married. We're not." She pushed her hair back. "There's coffee on the stove if you want it."

He poured half a cup and dribbled milk from a pitcher. "It may not have been an accident," he said.

She chose not to hear, or not to understand. Her eyes slanted past him. "I froze, you know, when it happened. Maybe I could have saved one or the other. One might still be here."

"Nothing you could have done," he tried to reassure her.

"You don't know that. You're not a medical man."

She spoke in anger, and he felt her attention slip away, well beyond his jurisdiction. Standing tall, he drank his coffee in the silence that rose between them. When he tried to break it, she stopped him with the pure blaze of her eyes.

"I can't answer any of your questions, James. Not now. I have too many of my own."

Miss Westerly reappeared in one of her better housedresses. Her bright lipstick, hurriedly applied, was a red claw over her grief. "Can't this wait, Chief? She's in no condition."

"Yes, of course. Naturally." He rinsed his cup out in the sink and left it there. Lydia surprised him by rising from the table and moving with him to the screen door. She even stepped outside with him. Clouds had taken some of the sun away, and the air was a shade cooler. They heard thunder, loud enough to give her a start.

"My father used to say that's God pocketing his change," she said distractedly. "As a little girl I believed it."

"You need some sleep," Morgan said. "Let me call Dr. Skinner to give you something."

"Was the bullet meant for me?"

"I don't know."

She smiled. "I wish I could remember the moment before my birth. That's what I wish the most."

"Why the moment before?" he asked. "Why not the moment itself?"

"I think the moment before would answer questions."

"What questions?"

"The ones I don't know to ask," she said.

When Morgan returned to his car, he found Matt Mac-Gregor sitting in it. MacGregor was in uniform, though not on duty, and his cap was in his lap. He had not shaved and, like Lydia, probably had not slept, which distressed Morgan, who wanted him presentable, clear-headed, effective, not only for the investigation but for Lydia as well. MacGregor's voice was shaky. "Did you talk to her?"

Morgan settled in. "A little."

"She doesn't seem to want me with her," MacGregor said, raking his fingers through his short hair.

"She's in shock."

"Time like this you'd think she'd need me most."

"Time like this all rules are thrown out."

Morgan ran the car onto the road and drove slowly, avoiding the town center. From the distance came rumbles of thunder but no sight of rain. Sitting rigidly, MacGregor fixed his stare as he might have a bayonet.

"You had somebody sitting shotgun. Why?"

"Probably unnecessarily. But why take a chance?"

"You could've asked me to do it."

"You might've shot anybody in sight," Morgan said and turned left onto a street vaulted by maple trees. Mailboxes stood on posts meshed in ivy. MacGregor stared through the windshield with violent concentration.

"Where are we going?"

"Nowhere," Morgan said and went left at a fork. The road narrowed and curved past the Girl Scout camp and straightened as it approached Paget's Pond, which lay flat and undisturbed some five miles from the center of town. It was

Andrew Coburn

where he and his wife used to take winter walks with their dog, a shepherd Elizabeth swore was wolf. Certainly the size of the animal and the blunt shape of the nose were lupine, but the rest was gentleness. Morgan slowed, swerved, and parked near the pond.

"You're right, this is nowhere," MacGregor said, which irked Morgan, but only for a moment.

They left the car, followed a path, and sat opposite each other at a weathered picnic bench in sight of a No Swimming sign. The air tasted of new needles on the pines. A haze blurred half the pond, which Morgan fancied as the juncture between now and then. He said, "I thought you might've come up with something by now."

"You mean something I done could've pissed somebody off?" MacGregor crimped his brow. "Nothing big. Only little things."

"Tell me about 'em."

MacGregor's voice was an official drone. He had dispersed nighttime gatherings of youths drinking beer behind Pearson Grammar School, rousted couples making out in the cemetery, busted the Barnes boy for possession of marijuana, threw a hammerlock on Lester Winn, who was beating on his wife again, and just the other day . . . "You listening, Chief?"

Morgan was watching two squirrels, one pursuing the other. A breeze loosened the cooler air roosting in the pines and brought down stray needles. "Just the other day what?"

"I ticketed Thurman Wetherfield for speeding. If he hadn't given me lip, he'd have got only a warning."

Wetherfield was a firefighter feigning disability and cheating his estranged wife out of proper child support. For a mere second Morgan considered the duplicity of the man's character, its two thin sides. Then he watched the sun return and spread a net over the pond. As a boy he had skimmed stones here. No Swimming the sign said, but he had swum. "Anything else?" he asked.

"Yeah, but it was more than a month ago—that hot day in late April, remember, got to be eighty."

"Broke a record," Morgan said, remembering the day well,

especially the afternoon in the prideful home of the Bowmans, where casement windows overlooked a swimming pool and Arlene Bowman's terry robe opened on two estimable legs certain to coerce him into a state. He had suspected she was trouble, but at the time it hadn't mattered. "Tell me about that thing with Junior Rayball."

"Hell, that was more than a month ago. I told you about it."

"Tell me again."

"I responded to a call from the high school," MacGregor said with elbows planted on the table. He gave Morgan a picture of girls in sweaty T-shirts competing on the playing field, kicking a ball from one end to the other, their school letters undulating across their young chests and the sun shimmering off their healthy legs. The snake in the grass was Junior Rayball, undersized and unemployable, who had been warned in the past. Teachers had shooed him away. "This time he had his pants off," MacGregor said. "He was in the weeds on the sidelines, thought he couldn't be seen."

"You chased him."

"Ran him down," MacGregor said, giving Morgan an image of Junior flopping breathlessly on the ground like a caught fish gulping air when it wanted water. "Grabbed him by the scruff and gave the girls a laugh. Marched him bare-ass back to his pants while he kept his hand over his dicky."

"You didn't bring him in."

"Didn't see the sense. Figured he learned his lesson."

"Still think that?"

"I know what you're getting at, Chief, but I think you're stretching. Where would a poor little bastard like Junior Rayball get an F-1 sniper's rifle? And where would he get the guts?" An expression of pain, frustration, and relief passed simultaneously over MacGregor's face. "I've got to be honest with you, I'm not at all convinced the shooting has anything to do with me."

"Nor am I," said Morgan, gazing at pine tops glued into the sky. A pink spider no bigger than a pinhead, the sort that occupies lilies, was crawling on the picnic table. MacGregor

Andrew Coburn

spotted it and was about to squash it with a finger. "Let it live," Morgan said.

He drove MacGregor back to Miss Westerly's house, where for a single second they glimpsed Lydia's face in a window. It could have been a length of bone. MacGregor flinched as if the shadow of a hand had passed over him. "I feel like I'm losing her," he said without inflection.

"I want you to stay with her, Matt. You're the best one to get her through this."

"What if she says no?"

"Tell her you're under orders."

"She looks through me, Chief. Honest to God, like I'm not there."

"I know, Matt. I'm worried too."

MacGregor slid out of the car like a man on a mission, but took only a couple of steps and looked back. "What are you going to do, Chief?"

Morgan put a scrambling hand into his hair and scratched a nonexistent itch. "I don't know. Maybe just drive around and think."

After three days of financial business in New York, none of it particularly satisfactory, Calvin Poole shuttled from LaGuardia to Logan and then rode in a limo to his home in the exclusive Oakcrest Heights section of Bensington, where prime woodland had been cleared for estate properties with great sweeps of lawn and varying flourishes of architecture, from Tudor and Georgian to Swiss chalet and California modern. Poole's was mock Tudor.

He was disappointed and inordinately annoyed when the cleaning woman told him that Mrs. Poole was out. He liked people in their rightful setting at the proper time. His life was bound to routine and security and to the hope that his investments were sound and the world was as it should be.

Upstairs in the master bedroom, he was glad to be home. On his flight to Boston he had suffered from a nervous stomach, and in the limo he had failed to relax. With pleasure he got out of his pinstripes and slipped off his shoes. He had an austere face and a straight figure. Golf was his game. Tennis used to be. His first wife had died of an aneurysm on the court.

In his shirttails he went to the wide window to breathe in the scented air. Gossamer clung to the sunshine that hung over the goldfish pond, and wood notes came out of a birch, a relief after the noise-filled heat of New York, where he had eaten too well at the Princeton Club while conferring with colleagues from distant points of the nation. He was president of the Mercury Savings & Loan in Boston, named after the god of money. His best money years had been a string of recent ones when a fool was in the White House. His contributions had helped put him there.

He deposited his cuff links on the dresser, folded his necktie in two to put away later, and stripped off his shirt. The intelligent eyes of his second wife gazed at him out of a photograph. The marriage was the sort in which each strove to blur the hues of the other and shade in something much different. The rub was that the outline of the old bled through the shading of the new.

By the bed he skinned off his high black socks, vigorously scratched a calf, and stepped on something chill, a nickel. Near it was another. Crouching, he traced an exploring hand over the carpet, probed beneath the fringes of the bedspread, and dragged up a snatch of bright orange material he first thought belonged to his wife. Seconds passed before he realized with cold certainty that the article was a man's.

He shoved it back under the bed and straightened, his heart pounding. On naked feet he stepped first here and then there, faltering each time, as if the room had altered. Things seemed no longer in their familiar frames, or he in his proper body. His flesh crawled. The wall mirror over his wife's dresser reduced him to a skimpy undershirt and white boxer shorts with a telltale stain. Having survived the utter despair that came with the loss of one wife, he was in no way confident he could survive the loss of another. He was sixty years old.

Moving from the mirror, he struggled for composure by forcibly setting his face hard, as if revealing too much emotion

Andrew Coburn

about anything, even in private, was poor taste and bad business.

Moments later his head popped out of a colorful polo shirt with an alligator emblem over the breast pocket. Light poured through his rise of white hair, which he patted down. When he plunged a foot into a pair of cotton slacks a noise started up in his head, haunting at first, then mocking. He likened it to an echo from an ancestral cave.

He was in his high-ceilinged study with a snifter of brandy when his wife returned. He heard her exclaim something about a shooting to the cleaning woman, then unload her parcels on the foyer table. He set the snifter aside when she entered the study. "Darling," she said, "you're home."

"Yes," he said and kissed her.

"Hope I'm not disturbing you," Chief Morgan said when Doris Wetherfield answered the doorbell with pins in her mouth. She was a seamstress working out of her home, her specialty bridal gowns, though alterations and repairs were her bread and butter. The new zipper on Morgan's fly was hers.

"What are you doing here?" she asked, the pins removed. "Why aren't you working on that horrible business with the Laphams?"

"The state police are on the job. They're the pros."

"Then what are you getting paid for?" she said with a wink. Her hair was a cushion resting lopsided on her head. Her face was angular, her neck long, and the rest of her was a lank line. Her children numbered five, one attending a community college and the rest in lower grades.

"Is Thurman in?" he asked, and her eyes sprang.

"You know damn right well he doesn't live here anymore."

"I thought you might tell me where he is living."

"With some woman or other, who knows? Who cares? What d'you want him for? What's he done, besides not providing for his family?"

"Nothing that I know of," Morgan said, aware that despite gross injustices she remained a loyal wife. He rearranged his feet on the step. "I was wondering if Thurman does any hunting."

"Hunting? Thurman? What are you talking about?"

"Does he own a rifle?"

"Christ, no. He doesn't own any kind of a gun." Her eyes, red from her work, turned suspicious. "Why'd you ask me that?"

Her breathing rose, his did too. He wished he had not asked her anything, for he was frightening her with a suspicion so flimsy he had merely wanted to blow it from his mind. His eyes shifted as hers dug in.

"Look here, Chief, he might be a worthless shit, but he's no God-damn killer."

"I know that," he said, aware of a flow of air carrying the sweetness of trees. A hawk threaded the sky.

"Then why'd you come here?"

"I shouldn't have." His eyes returned to her. "But something like this happens, you check everybody."

The fright left her face, anger remained. "Next time you need your fly fixed, see somebody else."

"Accept my apology, Doris."

"Too late for that," she said and shut the door on him.

He returned to his car, radioed the station, and told Meg O'Brien where he was but not where he was going. He drove north, away from old-fashioned front porches with fluted columns to a meandering rural road, where wood-heated houses stood prone to fatal fires. The last one, three years before, had taken two lives. He drove toward the edge of town, where the woods were dense, birds their loudest. Approaching a battered mailbox, he slowed the car. Nailed to a tree was a crudely hand-painted sign: BIKES REPAIRED.

This is where he should have come in the first place, he was convinced of it.

He ran his car into the woods along a gravel road that petered out fast. In a clearing was a frame house surrounded by weeds, stumps, and the carcasses of cannibalized bicycles. Raspberry canes flourished around an abandoned oil drum. Beyond the clearing was a vista of swamp and dead trees, lovely to look at, but Morgan did not let his eye linger. He climbed out of the car, careful where he stepped. Poison ivy was rife.

This was the womanless home of the Rayballs, Papa and Junior. The elder son, Clement, was in parts unknown.

Papa Rayball's pickup truck was nowhere around, and the small frame house, the roof in need of repair, looked lifeless. A dirt path led to loose steps, which under Morgan's weight creaked out a dark music. No one answered his knock.

He peered through a clouded window and glimpsed a refrigerator, a metal-top table, and a stove that stood on legs. Wall pegs accommodated coats, jackets, and caps left over from winter. Moving to the side of the house, avoiding the rusted blade of a shovel that had lost its handle, he peered through another window, this one raised atop its screen. This was Junior's room, he was sure, and he stepped away with an impression of must, mildew, and unaired bedding.

Making water near a woodpile, he felt the solitude of the place tighten around him. He returned to his car, sat in it with the window lowered, and watched a squirrel mount a stump and strip the scales from a pine cone. Dropping his head back, he decided to wait. Unarmed, he wondered whether he dare close his eyes.

Papa Rayball fought the heartless Boston traffic into the depths of the city and parked the pickup on a side street whose failure was reflected in shabby store windows. Papa slipped out first, then came Junior, who was eyed by black youths wearing head rags, sleeveless tops, and cutoff jeans. Junior stuck close to his father and whispered, "Bet they're on dope."

"Keep your eyes straight ahead," Papa growled.

"They might steal the truck."

Papa shook his head. "Soon as they see where we're goin', they won't bother it."

Crossing the sun-glazed street, father and son cast short shadows. Papa was pint-size and Junior no bigger. In his early sixties, Papa was knobby and gnarled and had combustible blue eyes that smoldered in his face. His hair was the dead head of a dandelion exploding into dust. Though he could not readily see it, Junior was his spit and image.

They entered a small hotel squeezed between larger buildings. The lobby was miniature and dimly lit, and the smell of disinfectant stirred in Junior a distant memory that did not quite emerge. The desk clerk, an extremely fat man with a pink face, greeted Papa with a knowing smile. "Figured you were due."

"Two rooms," Papa said. "This is my boy."

The clerk pushed the register forward. "Certainly, Mr. Richmond."

"That ain't our name," Junior said.

Papa frowned, and the clerk smiled. "How old are you, son?"

"Twenty-four," Junior said, picking nervously at his sleeve. He had on a denim jacket splashed with decals. Papa signed the register for both of them and paid out the money in grubby tens, fives, and ones, creating a little pile. The clerk produced keys attached to plastic tags. Junior whispered, "You ain't never took me here before."

"This place cost more." Papa winked at the clerk. "I usually take him to Lawrence. It's quicker."

"We got quality here," the clerk said, his eyes skidding to Junior. "Gals that will teach you something."

"Don't give him somebody's gonna scare him to death."

"We aim to please," the clerk said and gripped the telephone with a padded hand.

Their rooms, one next to the other, were down a narrow corridor on the second floor. The women arrived within five minutes. Papa's woman rode in on the waft of her own unsubtle cologne, and right away he liked the cut of her. Her hair dangled in braids like metallic coils, and her skin was burnt almond. He frowned to cover his excitement.

"What's your name?"

"Is that important?" she said.

"Wouldn't have asked, would I?" With his pants off, he had the hind legs of a dog, but the strut of a peacock.

"Inez."

"Sounds foreign," he said and with gimlet eyes watched her undress. Her body outshone all others in his memory.

"I'm homegrown, my little man. Homegrown."

Some twenty minutes later, from the bed, he pounded the wall and shouted through it. "How you doin' in there, Junior?" When he got no answer, he pounded it again, with vigor.

"We ain't started yet," Junior called back in a voice that did not sound wholly his.

"For Christ's sake, time's runnin' out. Don't waste it." Papa turned back to the woman, trailing a knobby hand over the smart curve of her abdomen. "I got another son ain't like that one at all."

Junior cried through the wall. "I'm gettin' there!"

A half hour later, father and son made their way along the corridor to the stairs. Junior, invigorated, hooked a thumb into the waist of his jeans and, swinging his free arm, imitated his father's gait. "I ain't ever had a black gal before."

"Black, white, it don't make no dif'rence," Papa said, stopping at the stairs and patting his pockets to make sure he had not left anything behind. "Long's you get it off."

"You ever bring Clement here?"

"Clement didn't need to be brought."

"Maybe I can bring myself sometime."

Papa's eyes flared. "You can't *never* bring yourself *no*where. Look what you did at the high school. Let yourself be made a God-damn fool of."

"I know, Papa."

"No, you *don't* know. Shit like that the chief uses against me, always has."

"Me that done it, Papa. Not you."

"That don't matter to him. Come on, let's go!"

They descended to the lobby, where once again the smell of disinfectant almost awakened something in Junior. The fat desk clerk was eating pizza and did not look up. In their path was a man trying to pass as a woman, his face hyperbolized with abundant paint and lipstick. Stiletto heels scraped the carpetless floor. The voice carried the rhythmic cadence of a Haitian.

"You ought to try me sometime, junior."

Outside, the sun pouncing at them, Junior said, "How'd she know my name?"

"I don't think he did," Papa said.

The loitering youths were gone. The truck was as they left it, except for a beer can someone had thrown into the bed. Farther up the street music shot out of a storefront church. Papa started up the motor, and pondering something, took his time pulling onto the street.

"I ain't seen a ballgame in ages."

"I ain't either, Papa."

"We're lucky, maybe we can get bleacher seats."

"You takin' me, Papa?"

"I just said so, didn't I?"

Papa turned left at the tail of the street and rejoined the city's hot traffic, fiery in its sound, eye-maddening in its confusion, which several times made him curse, especially when cabbies cut in front of him. He threw a look at Junior, who was fidgeting in his seat. "Keep an eye out for the Citgo sign. That's how I can find Fenway Park."

Junior wheezed, as if too much were going on, a question of whether he could juggle it all. Papa threw him another look.

"You gonna be sick, I'll turn around right now," he threatened.

"I won't be, Papa, I promise."

Chronicle aired at seven-thirty on Channel Five, opening with a shot of the village green and a sweep of the town hall, the Congregational church, and the ivy-matted library, outside of which the names of war dead were scored in marble. Then came glimpses of Tuck's General Store, Pearl's Pharmacy, and the Blue Bonnet Restaurant. A voice-over said: "This is the bucolic community of Bensington, where the old rubs against the new."'

The camera cut across the green to a bright backdrop of smart little shops selling gourmet foods, giftware, leisure equipment, and children's designer clothes. The sunstruck plate glass of Roberta's Ladies Shoppe looked like a slab of ice in which a svelte mannequin stood frozen in a summer frock. "It's a growing town, population seven thousand, with the biggest influx during the Reagan years. It has become home to investment bankers, brokers, captains of commerce, and sports superstars. Natives living in old Victorians sit on their rose-trellised porches and watch the Audis and Jaguars go by."

Scenes shifted through pristine woodland butchered to accommodate mock mansions flourishing balconies and cupolas like statements of the owners' worth. Ornamental ponds and swimming pools dimpled the grounds. "This is the exclusive section called Oakcrest Heights. Gerald Bowman, chief executive officer of the Bellmore Companies lives here. So does Crack Alexander of the Boston Red Sox."

The camera switched to the owner of the voice, Peter Mehegan, a veteran Boston journalist whose unassuming appearance made him look like a native of the town. An old-fashioned bell jangled overhead when he opened the door of Tuck's General Store. Glancing back into the eye of the camera, he said, "This is not a town where killing is common."

Randolph Jackson, who had grown wealthy selling woodland to developers, watched the program to the end. Ensconced in an overstuffed chair, he thrilled to the emphatic sound of his voice when Peter Mehegan interviewed him. He heard himself say: "Either case, an accident or cold-blooded murder, we want the guilty person caught fast. If it was an accident, he should face the music like a man."

Doris Wetherfield watched the program while sewing new buttons on a blazer, and Meg O'Brien taped it on her VCR in the event that the chief missed it. Chief Morgan did indeed miss it. He had long since quit waiting for the Rayballs to come home and was having supper in the lounge of a restaurant in neighboring Andover. The television over the bar was tuned not to *Chronicle* but to the baseball game. While settling his bill, he glanced up and saw Crack Alexander strike out.

Fred Fossey, who was wearing his VFW cap for no particular reason, tuned in when the images of Flo and Earl Lapham appeared on the screen. The Laphams were their younger selves, the occasion of their twenty-fifth wedding anniversary.

The editor of the local weekly had provided Peter Mehegan with the photograph. Fossey rose from his chair with eyes filled with feelings for Flo. Standing straight, he saluted Earl.

Dr. Skinner, who had declared the Laphams dead, was watching a movie channel. He liked old dramas of foreign intrigue, in which people were obliged to show their papers.

At the home of Lydia Lapham's aunt, the television murmured to a vacant room. Lydia was restlessly asleep in an upstairs bedroom from a sedative she had given herself, and Miss Westerly was making tea in the kitchen. On the unseen screen Peter Mehegan was interviewing Lieutenant Bakinowski, whose hair had been wet-combed into a crest.

"How is the investigation going, Lieutenant?"

"I'm not without leads."

"Have you a suspect?"

Bakinowski seemed to nod.

"Is the suspect local?"

"Yes." Bakinowski's eyes acquired a slight cast. "Beyond that, I can say no more."

The headlights of the pickup plowed through the dark of the dirt drive. The high beams swarmed with moths, caught the eyes of an animal, and illuminated stumps, raspberry canes, and the skeletons of bicycles. Moonlight whittled holes in the pines. Papa Rayball pulled up near the little house, killed the motor, and sat still. Peepers, nighttime birds, and frogs from the swamp made their noises. Eyes darting, Papa said, "Somebody's been here."

Junior squinted. He had a headache from the excitement of his day. With a shiver he said, "How can you tell?"

"I ever been wrong?"

Junior's headache felt like a nail in his forehead. "Maybe it was somebody wantin' a bike fixed."

"Maybe."

Junior went into the house, and Papa stayed outside to look around. The heat of the day was in the house and mixed moistly with the smells of male belongings. At the kitchen sink Junior thrashed his face with water and dried it in a towel that could have been cleaner. Then he drank water from a chipped mug that may have belonged to his mother. He had no memory of her, though vaguely he remembered playing with her clothes, which his father had stuffed into a box. Those were his memories: a few threadbare dresses, a sweater ruptured at the elbows, a frayed bra deprived of two of its catches, underpants with elastic waists robbed of their goodness. With no photographs to go by, he painted pictures of her in his mind.

Occasionally through the years he had dreamed of her crouching naked in the kitchen and had awoken with the suspicion that the dream might be grounded in reality. He never dared to ask his father. Nor did he ever ask Clement, who might have told him.

The only women in his life he could remember were his grandmother, whose breasts were dry biscuits hardly worth stealing a peek at, and his aunt, who was more interesting. She had a squirrel between her legs. Then his grandmother died, and his aunt went off to become a whore—that was what he heard Papa tell Clement. Then his aunt died, and Papa said, We're the only Rayballs left, just the men. Except he was looking at Clement, not Junior.

Clement was the hero of the family. Clement finished school; Junior left after the eighth grade. Clement went into the army and sent home a picture of himself in a jeep. Junior still had it. Clement had mysterious jobs and mailed money to Papa. Junior was unemployable, with eyes that seemed channeled inward except when they were charting the movements of girls and women. Clement was special; Junior was a piece of shit.

Still at the sink, he uncapped a new bottle of aspirin. He always saved the cotton, though for what purpose he could not say, the same way he could not tell why he kept having that same dream about his mother. Through the window he glimpsed a shape in the moonlight. One leg cocked like a dog's, Papa was taking a leak near the woodpile.

Junior switched on the light in his little bedroom, where Clement's army picture was tacked to a wall. The picture was a Polaroid that had faded Clement into a ghost. He sat on the edge of his unmade cot and made a face. The aspirin had left a taste. Kneading his brow, he wished he could pull the nail from it, and he wondered why he had been born instead of someone else, someone bigger and better, like Clement. Then he felt eyes on him. Papa had come in and was peering at him.

"I bet he was here."

"Who, Papa?"

"The chief. Sometimes I can smell him," Papa snarled.

Junior lifted his head, which felt swollen. "I don't smell nothin' dif'rent."

"That's 'cause you ain't had him breathin' in your face for twenty years," Papa said and stood motionless, on the alert, as if the chief might be lurking. Outside, insects were singing their loudest. Inside, a moth attacked the lamp. Papa glared.

Junior said, "You blamin' me?"

"No, I ain't blamin' you. You don't know how to be blamed."

Averting his eyes, Junior stared at Clement's ghost. When he was ten, he had eaten spoiled meat and nearly died. Clement, not Papa, finally took him to the hospital in Lawrence and saved his life. And it was Clement who tried to put sense into his head, but always the assortment of words were too clever for him. Always his skull tightened, and a rage built. That was when he used to hate his own brother.

He said, "I miss Clement."

"You got me. You got nobody else." Papa's eyes beat upon him. "You ain't even thanked me, what I did for you today."

"Thank you, Papa."

A while later, naked under a musty sheet, Junior fell into a restless sleep and dreamed of the roof lights of a police car spinning red and blue into the night. The colors battled each other, neither winning, every strike a miss.

At the lounge in Andover, settling his bill, Chief Morgan watched Crack Alexander, in the throes of a slump, hitless his last thirty at-bats, take a third strike and then slam his bat so hard into the turf that it splintered. Cursing the umpire, he was ejected from the game, which was already lost. Someone at the bar said, "There's a man trying to stomp his own shadow." With a deeper concern, Chief Morgan said, "That's a man who wants to take it out on somebody else."

He drove back to Bensington, into Oakcrest Heights, a little town within a town. Stone lions flanked the entrance to the grounds of Crack Alexander's residence. Lamplight led the way along a curving drive. Morgan's headlights snared a young rabbit, a cottontail that took fright and fled with giant hops over clipped grass. Its white behind could have been a baseball bouncing to the depths of the outfield.

He parked near the garage, three stalls, one containing a Rolls, another a Jeep Cherokee. The remaining stall was empty. The house was outsize, lavish for a childless couple. Morgan had once taken a dip in the indoor swimming pool, which consumed a wing. A bowling alley occupied a good portion of the basement. Lights burned in every window as a security measure. Morgan rang the bell.

In a glass panel beside the door Sissy Alexander showed a face of clear surfaces distinguished by troubled cornflower eyes. When she opened the door, the fatigue of anxiety tilted her posture, which did not surprise him. It was the reason he had come. Her lips reached out but uttered no words and offered no kiss. He said, "Did you watch the game?"

"Part of it."

"He didn't do well."

"He hasn't in a while." She spoke in a soft, semi-secret voice never louder than it had to be. Her nerves were wrung, yet she smiled. Her barley-blond comeliness appeared borrowed from an age when fashion favored fullness and roundness.

"When do you expect him?" Morgan asked.

"Hard to tell."

"If you like, I'll wait."

"I can handle him," she said, which he doubted. The first time he had met her, following her surreptitious call to the station, he had viewed a cut and swollen mouth and bruised arms. Her husband, outplayed by younger teammates during a miserable road trip, had vented his frustration on her, as if she had undone a portion of his virility. "He's not predictable," Morgan warned.

"Who is?" she responded, her mouth parting into a slow smile. "Who would have thought you and I . . ." Her soft voice tailed off, and briefly she took asylum in his arms, her body tense with overlapping feelings for the two men in her life.

"Don't be afraid to call," Morgan said, his mind flashing unevenly, at odds with the beat of his heart. The last time he had made love to her was on a bed of flowers, from which she had risen with pansies in her hair and Sweet William adhering to her backside. "I'll be at the station," he said.

"This late?"

"Yes."

She stepped back and drew herself up straight. "You're good to me, Jim."

"I want you to be good to yourself," he said.

He drove over a moon-drenched road to the center of town. The town hall was dark except for the lights of the police station, where flying insects filled the glow. The officer on duty, a cousin of Sergeant Avery's, said, "Meg O'Brien wants you to call her, Chief."

Morgan looked at the wall clock. "This late?"

"She said it wouldn't matter."

He went into his office, to his desk. Somebody had obviously used it. His pen lay out of its holder. Someone had used his yellow notepad and carelessly ripped away sheets, leaving tatters. The varnished wedge with his name on it was turned the wrong way. Bakinowski, he suspected.

Meg O'Brien answered on the first ring. Her voice was ominous. "Something's going on, Chief, I don't know what."

He pinched his eyes shut for a moment. "Give me a clue, Meg."

"Lieutenant Bakinowski's been asking questions."

"What kind of questions?"

"Crazy ones. They didn't make sense, not one bit until I watched *Chronicle*. Did you see it, Chief?"

"Should I have?"

"I've taped it, you'll see it. He has a suspect."

"What?" Suddenly he reassessed his darkest suspicions of Junior Rayball. "Who?"

"He hasn't said."

"Who do you think it is?"

"Matt MacGregor."

3

Chief Morgan and Lieutenant Bakinowski met for a late breakfast at the Blue Bonnet, where they sat at a corner table and spoke in low voices. Mitch Brown in his baker's whites stole looks at them from the galley window, and Agnes Brown observed them from the cash register. Their waitress, a plump, rosy woman who had worked the rush hour, gave off heat like a little wood stove as she served Bakinowski pancakes topped with melting pats of butter. A silver pitcher held the syrup. Morgan, who had ordered a muffin, tore the tab off a tiny container of grape jelly. Their coffee mugs steamed. "Murderers," said Bakinowski, "have to be damn careful today they don't leave behind something of themselves. A drop of blood can do them in, not to mention a shred of skin, a strand of hair, a trace of semen."

Morgan spread jelly, slowly. He had had less than a full night of sleep broken by a dream in which his wife did not quite appear, her image molded in indistinct clay.

Pouring syrup, Bakinowski smiled and said, "One of the conspiracy stories out of the Kennedy assassination is that the real killer in the book building jerked off before he put the president in his sights. The FBI proved the semen wasn't Oswald's, but Hoover and LBJ suppressed the evidence."

"First I've heard that," Morgan said without interest.

"You got a theory?"

"Kennedy is history."

"I'm talking about the Laphams." Bakinowski filled his mouth and ate heartily until the immobility of Morgan's face began to annoy him. "Did you hear me?"

"I did."

"What I'm asking is if you've got anything to share."

Morgan reached for his coffee. "Not offhand."

They stared at each other, Bakinowski with jaws moving with another mouthful. He had replaced his blue business suit with one of dim plaid that carried a tincture of red. A pattern of diamonds occupied his tie. "I think we can agree the shooting was premeditated, which makes it a double homicide. Shooting of the wife brought on the death of the husband."

Morgan concurred with a nod. The coffee was strong, and for the first time in a long time he craved a cigarette.

"Something else we might agree on, Chief. It shouldn't have been the mother. The target was the daughter."

"That was my feeling from the start."

"Our minds are running on the same track, that's good." Bakinowski, a fast eater, was cutting into more pancake drenched with syrup. His fork dripped. "Nine homicides out of ten, the perpetrator is family or friend, sweetheart, someone the victim knew well. In this case, the intended victim is an attractive woman, so we look to the husband. Lydia Lapham's got none, but she's got a boyfriend. That must've jumped into your mind right off."

"It didn't."

"You sure?"

"Positive. I know Matt MacGregor too well."

"I can understand where you're coming from, he's one of your own, but let me tell you what I got." Bakinowski hunched over his plate, his eyes emerging from their caves. "MacGregor and Lydia Lapham have been going together for years, right?

People are expecting them to get married, he's expecting it, he's pushing it. You know all this, but here's something you might not know. A week ago she gives him a final answer, straight out, and it's no, *never*, he's not for her. I got that from the hospital she works at—two sources, a nurse she's friendly with and a doctor she's dated."

Caught off stride, Morgan glanced away. He was not surprised that MacGregor, tight-lipped about personal matters, had said nothing. On the other hand, in view of the events, he felt he should have been told.

Bakinowski said, "I bet you didn't know that about the doctor."

The only other patron, a trucker, dipped a doughnut into his coffee and ate the wet. Morgan, whose gaze had landed on him, shifted it to the front window, through which he glimpsed a distant figure rising out of a shiny car. It was Arlene Bowman in the dazzle of a white tennis costume. He saw her, then he did not. She had moved quickly toward the cluster of shops. "Have you confirmed this with Miss Lapham?" he asked.

"I will."

"How about Matt MacGregor?"

"I'm saving him." Bakinowski speared the last bit of pancake and plowed roads through the syrup left on the plate. "I expect your help."

"What kind of help?"

"You tell him he's my suspect, tell him I've got more on him than I'm saying, stuff you don't know. Hint it might be a witness. Who knows, you play it right, he might confide in you. Either way, he'll be off balance when I question him."

"He's not your man," Morgan said and pushed aside his half-eaten muffin.

"If I'm reading it right, and I think I am, this was a crime of passion. Think of MacGregor not as a cop but as a man spurned by a woman."

"I don't buy it," Morgan said with the smallest twinge of

uncertainty. Damn it, MacGregor should've told him! "I know the man."

Bakinowski's smile was tolerant. "Who knows anybody's real nature? You and I, Chief, most of what we are is subliminal. That means we know damn little about ourselves, so how in hell can we presume to know somebody else?" The waitress had left the check. He picked it up. "My treat."

Lydia Lapham grew roots in her sedated sleep, which wanted to keep her there. She woke hard. Her feelings were unassimilated, unmoored, trembly, and for moments she had no idea where she was. Then she heard the telephone ring. Presently her aunt answered it.

Showered, dressed, she looked in the mirror and felt alien, a stranger to herself. She did not belong to her hair, to the look on her face, to the clothes she had put on. She tried to force her mind to play a game. Yesterday had never happened. In the afternoon she would leave for work, where immobile patients awaited her, where elderly men sought her smile because it put life into their own. It was the little things that mattered.

Downstairs, in the sunny kitchen, her aunt greeted her with a smile. "You slept a long time, dear. I'm glad." Not long enough, Lydia thought, not by a long chalk. "Let me make you breakfast," her aunt said, and she shook her head. Coffee was enough. Her aunt poured. "Someone named Frank from the hospital called. Wanted to know if there was anything he could do."

"That was nice of him," she said without interest.

"He's not here now, but Matt MacGregor spent the night outside in his car."

"He shouldn't have done that."

"He loves you, dear."

At the table she tasted her coffee, and through the screen of the window she heard the plaintive syllables of mourning doves. Flowers from a well-tended bed diffused a sun-warm scent almost unbearably sweet. "How long have you been up, Auntie?"

"Hours."

"You're doing better than I am, aren't you?"

The older woman had been busying herself at the sink. Clumsily she turned around. A spoon fell to the floor. "Not really, dear. I've lost my only sister. Now I have nobody except you."

Lydia looked beyond the crinkled lace of her aunt's face and saw the suffering. The next instant she was on her feet, her arms thrown out. Sobs long held in were let loose.

A half hour later, emotions under control, Miss Westerly donned gloves and went out to weed and water her garden. Lydia stepped into the living room, where she slouched down in a cushioned chair, her legs extended. The tears had drained her, had washed away the reserve of strength with which she had been functioning. Had her aunt not returned within a few minutes from her gardening she might have slept again.

"A policeman is here, dear. He'd like to talk to you."

"What policeman?"

"That lieutenant from the state police."

An image circulated in her mind, but she was not sure it was the right one.

"If you don't feel up to it, dear, I'll tell him to come back later."

"Tell him to come in," she said.

Waiting, drawing her legs in, she could not control her face, an unmistakable step to more tears. Several minutes later, drying her eyes, she heard the easy voice of a man.

"It's the fear of nothingness, Miss Lapham. It breeds in the night. It creeps over you at the funeral of a friend. It hits the young when a parent goes. I know, I lost my mother seventeen years ago."

His voice startled her because she had not heard him enter the room and had no idea how long he had been sitting in the chair opposite her. His uncanny blue eyes reached out but seemed to take in nothing. Suddenly she had things to ask him, but wanted to keep them simple. She wanted to know only what was so and what was not.

Andrew Coburn

"I have questions for you," she said.

"And I for you, Miss Lapham."

Chief Morgan cut across the grass in front of the town hall. A quick side step avoided bees drawn to a large shrub that had erupted into bloom overnight and was disgorging creamy blossoms. He strode along the side of the building and entered the police station with much on his mind. His nod to Meg O'Brien was perfunctory. Baring her teeth, she spoke in a low voice. "Matt's in your office."

"Have you said anything to him?"

She nodded miserably. "I shouldn't have."

MacGregor, sitting on a metal folding chair near the chief's desk, sprang up when Morgan entered. His head was poised rigidly, as if from a crick in his neck, the price paid for spending the night in his car. Red spots moistened a patch of his left shirtsleeve. He had scratched the arm too vigorously and drawn blood. "What's going on, Chief? Am I going crazy?"

Morgan closed the door and took a seat behind his desk. "You talking about Bakinowski?"

"Yes!"

"Don't get upset. Sit down."

MacGregor shook from a cataclysm of feelings, anger and fear among them. He stayed on his feet. "I'm a suspect, that's what it looks like."

"Bakinowski's shooting in the dark," Morgan said. "All he's got is a theory."

"What theory?"

Morgan, quickly, gave him Bakinowski's reasoning and, in a slower voice, added, "He sees you as a spurned lover."

"That's horseshit," MacGregor said, reddening. "We haven't broken up, we're just not getting married . . . yet."

"Bakinowski says it's more definite than that."

"What does *he* know?"

"I shouldn't have heard it from him. Why didn't you tell me, Matt?"

"Tell you what? That my girl said she didn't wanna marry

me?" The words were spoken in a gush of ragged breath. "I got my pride, for Christ's sake."

"This isn't the time for pride," Morgan said sternly. "What about this doctor Bakinowski mentioned? Was Lydia dating him?"

"That's garbage. The guy's somebody she knew a long time ago. Maybe there was something way back then, not now." Tippy on his feet, MacGregor sat down hard on the metal chair. His cheeks burned. "You think I'm not busted up over this? I loved the Laphams, the both of 'em!"

"Take it easy," Morgan said in a calming voice. "Let's try to clear this up fast. Where were you when it happened?"

"I was trying to call Lydia, I told you. I was on the phone."

"But where were you calling from?"

"I was home."

"Alone?"

"You know my mother spends every summer at my sister's place on the Cape. Yeah, I was alone."

"You parked the cruiser in the drive. Somebody must've seen it."

"I don't know, maybe, probably not. Christ, Chief, I can't believe this conversation."

Morgan's gray eyes focused on him. "If there was anything I should know, you'd tell me, wouldn't you?"

"I can't believe you had to ask me that." MacGregor's flush had gained control of his pug nose and gave him the look of a high school athlete demeaned by the coach. "I've been a cop eight years, you got me the appointment, remember? You name me one time I've let you down."

"You never have," Morgan said, remembering the appointment. The selectmen had favored another candidate, and he had pushed for MacGregor, who had an associate degree from a community college, a menial job in Lawrence, and a sickly mother he and his sister were supporting. He also had drive and spunk.

Morgan rose from the desk, MacGregor from the metal chair. "I'm sorry I had to put you through this," Morgan said, stepping around the desk. He patted MacGregor's shoulder. "But I had to get those questions out of the way."

"So what do I do now?"

"Nothing different. Go about your job."

"What about Bakinowski?"

"I'll handle him."

MacGregor tensed. "Before I was mad. Now I'm worried."

Morgan gave him a final pat. "Trust me."

Alone in the small fitting room at Roberta's Ladies Shoppe, Christine Poole treated her fingers to the silky feel of a black evening shift, one that Roberta had not recommended. It was sequined, trimmed in satin, and looked recklessly wearable, but she frowned when she tried it on. The frown grew as she turned this way and that in the triple mirror. A voice, startling her, said, "I could tell you some exercises to get rid of that belly."

The voice was engagingly raspy and unmistakable. Christine pivoted and said, "I'm comfortable the way I am."

"That's what matters," Arlene Bowman said. The dress she was holding was a mere slip, ink black, elegantly simple. She raised it against herself. "What do you think?"

"On you it will look wonderful."

Arlene Bowman, trim and compact in her tennis costume, was younger by five years, but it could have been ten. Her glossy blue-black hair, cut short, crowned a remarkable beauty of the sort that made men immediately search for impurities to render her human, endearing, approachable. Christine tended to accept her at face value. They knew each other, casually, from socials at the country club. Their husbands, involved in business deals, knew each other better.

"Christ, I should've checked this before," Arlene Bowman said, glaring at the price tag on the dress.

"Nothing's cheap here, even on sale," Christine pointed out.

"Trust Roberta to charge New York prices. Do you have money of your own, Christine, or must you rely on your husband?"

The question was a blunt trespass into bad taste but in no way detracted from the woman. Christine smiled. "As a matter of fact, I do have money of my own."

"My problem is I don't."

"My first husband left me well situated," Christine said before she could stop herself.

"Ah, what the hell," Arlene Bowman said with a sudden dismissive glance at the price tag. "I might even try that one on too, unless you plan to buy it."

A dressing stall was available, but Arlene Bowman's body was meant to be looked at, and there and then the younger woman shed her tennis togs. Her bra was slim and her briefs wispy. After a moment of hesitation, Christine hiked the shift that flaunted her complacencies and revealed underpants that stretched over her navel.

The raspy voice said, "We have a mutual friend."

"Do we? Who is that?"

"The police chief," Arlene Bowman said and slipped the inky garment over her head. Her face came out of it smiling and vivid. "James Morgan," she said.

"I wouldn't call him a friend," Christine said, fighting for composure. "He investigated an attempted burglary at the house a few months ago and now makes random checks."

"I met him under somewhat similar circumstances. Handsome devil, isn't he? Those gray eyes." Arlene Bowman ran smoothing hands over the black dress, which flowed over her like a liquid seeking vacuums. "He must be busy now with that shooting. Fancies himself a detective."

Christine hurried into her old blouse and skirt, unfashionable and comfortable; then she gave repairing touches to her hair while avoiding the triple mirror, in which Arlene Bowman was viewing herself, the black silk clinging to every move.

"What do you think?"

"Eye-catching."

"That means Gerald won't like it, but *I do*."

At that moment Roberta, who had been busy with another customer, swept into the fitting room. She was ungodly tall, with oyster white hair and a whip of a figure. Her breasts, almost visible through a sheer top, were flat, pale disks. Her voice barked. "How are my two favorite customers doing?"

"I think I may take this little thing," Arlene Bowman said, "despite the outlandish price."

"A bargain, Mrs. Bowman, believe me." Roberta's eagle eye attacked from all angles. "No alterations needed. Amazing."

Arlene Bowman looked over her shoulder as Christine prepared to leave. "We must get together soon and talk about our friend."

Christine stiffened. "Why would we want to do that?"

"I think it would be fun."

The pathologist from the hospital in Lawrence phoned in the autopsy report. No surprises. Flo Lapham, remarkably healthy for a woman her age, had died from a single gunshot wound that had shattered an artery. Earl Lapham had a diseased heart. The coronary, as suspected, had been massive. "Devastating" was the word the doctor used. Chief Morgan thanked him and clicked off. Moments later he left the station.

He drove slowly away from the green and down one of the older streets, shady and melancholy, bound by the past. Children had played there, grown up, and departed, leaving behind aging parents who talked of selling but probably never would. A woman in curlers, May Hutchins, hurried to the mailbox and returned the chief's passing wave with some embarrassment. The largest house was at the end of the street, Drinkwater's Funeral Home, distinguished by a veranda with trellised rose vines. This was where the remains of Flo and Earl Lapham would be delivered, rear entrance.

He turned left and a few minutes later pulled up in front of Miss Westerly's little gingerbread house, where the porch light still burned. He was winding his way toward the back door when a voice startled him. "We're here."

Lydia Lapham spoke from a wooden lawn chair next to one occupied by her aunt. Lydia leaned forward and scratched both shins, leaving chalk marks. Morgan said, "I presume you've had a visitor."

"Yes. He asked questions that were irrelevant, pointless."

"But you know what he was getting at."

She was slow to answer, and the flat moment of silence spread. Her eyes cast an unnatural light. Finally she said, "It was not Matt."

"Who do you think it could've been?"

"I don't know." Her voice had a skeletal quality. Rising from the chair, she looked coldly pure and inviolate. For a confounding moment Morgan suspected that were she to walk away, she would leave no footprints, no traces whatsoever. "But it couldn't have been Matt," she said. "He loves me."

"And do you love him?" Morgan asked and felt himself flinch. It was not a question he had intended to ask. He watched her take a breath, which drew her face closer to the bone.

"I have strong feelings for Matt, but they don't include marriage."

"And you told Matt that?"

"Matt hears what he wants to hear. In many ways he's a boy."

Miss Westerly, who had not stirred, seemed to have grown smaller in the chair. She gazed up as a polite child would. "Maybe I should let you two talk in private."

"It's all right, Auntie." Lydia's eyes, which were enormous, shifted back to Morgan. "Are you busy, Chief? Could we go for a little drive? I need to get away for a bit." Her eyes flew to her aunt. "Do you mind?"

"I think it would do you good, dear."

In the car, Lydia cranked the window down on her side and asked Morgan whether he would mind driving out of town. She did not want people looking at her. She wanted the anonymity of a highway. He drove toward Route 495 while she sat erect with her eyes on the white stripe, as if it were the single thing holding the road together. On Route 495 she dropped her head back, and he drove in silence faster than usual, well beyond the speed limit. They skirted little cities known for what they had lost: Lawrence its mills, Haverhill its shoe shops, Amesbury its hat factory. When the highway,

Andrew Coburn

nearing its limit, began swerving toward Interstate 93, he slowed dramatically and took the first exit ramp. From there he sought a back road for the return drive. He thought she was asleep, but her eyes fluttered open.

"You seem to have a nice life, James."

"I don't know about that," he said, his eye out his window. "It's not the greatest thing, a man my age still running around."

"Your wife died young. Car accident, wasn't it?"

"Yes."

"Tell me about it. About you."

"Why?"

"Why not?"

They were on a narrow road now that followed the meandering of the Merrimack River, along which the sun had fastened itself. "When my wife died," he said, "I almost left town for good. I wanted to go to another part of the world where it was already tomorrow."

"But you stayed."

"I stayed."

"Why?"

He swerved slightly to avoid cyclists on the road. "I don't know," he said with a vision of Elizabeth as a bride, a civil ceremony, a romantic elopement. She was not from the town. A college buddy had fixed them up. She was a blind date who became the love of his life and took to Bensington as if she had been born there. "I'll never know," he said.

A breeze carried the fresh smell of lumber with the essence of the tree still in it. People with money were having a large, rambling house built on a rise above the river. Lydia said, "I remember your wife was beautiful."

"Yes, I would agree with you."

"How long did it take for the pain to pass?"

"It never does, but you learn to live with it."

"I've heard that said." Irony corrupted the tone of her voice and the posture of her body. Then she tossed her hair back. "I had a little crush on you when I was a teenager. A lot of us girls did."

"Is that so?"

"You telling me you didn't know?"

"Maybe a little," he said, dramatically slowing the car where the view was ideal. "It's a great river."

"As long as you don't jump into it."

He gave her a fast look. "That's not on your mind, is it?"

"No," she said. "That would be as senseless as what happened to my parents."

Gradually the riverbank went high with brush, then turned woody. A groundhog fed boldly near the side of the road where the weeds were greenest. Morgan scratched an earlobe. "Matt mentioned he was trying to call you about the time of the shooting. Do you know what he wanted?"

"Did you ask him?"

"I meant to."

"It could've been anything." She was smiling in the wrong places, from nerves. "Why are you harping on this?"

That was a question he was asking himself. Perhaps he was trying to be totally objective and professional. "Lieutenant Bakinowski mentioned a doctor you dated."

Her chin went up. "They weren't dates. He's a friend."

"What's his name?"

"Do you need to know?"

"Probably not."

"Then I won't tell you." Her smile was back, inappropriately and without meaning. Then it died.

Morgan said, "I'll shut up if you like."

The sun slanted into her side of the car and ate into her face. Her eyes narrowed to nothing. "I've thought about it," she said. "I've thought about nothing else. It had to have been a cruel accident. A criminally careless thing." Her eyes came open, painfully, like moths fluttering to the light. "Unless you know something I don't."

"That's the trouble," he said. "I don't."

They passed an isolated weatherboard house, where a pleasant-looking woman—someone Morgan imagined would put out seed for birds—was watering the grass. Then the trees thickened into heavy maples and oaks. Eventually they approached the metal drawbridge that spanned the river and led back to Bensington. Lydia stirred.

"Can we stop? Walk for a bit?"

He pulled over into weeds growing through the gravel. She climbed out and hurried dark glasses onto her face against the sun's wrath. The metalwork of the bridge looked like the prototype of a medieval war machine. With a swift stride she moved well ahead of him, her legs stalks of light below the cut of her skirt. He caught up with her halfway across the bridge, where she had stopped to peer over the plated railing. The river was high, the current strong, from a previous week of rain.

"Something magical about water," she said, peering down. "Full of secrets, like people."

He was staring at her. A thrilling dash of sun was in her hair. Two buttons undone gave a hint of a fine woman. He could understand Matt MacGregor's feelings for her.

With her eyes still on the water, she said, "If I hadn't frozen, maybe I could have saved one of them. Possibly both."

"No," he said. "There was no hope. They were gone."

Her eyes turned on him. "You're not a doctor."

"I read the medical report."

"Doesn't matter."

All at once she wanted to return to the car, but her step now was slow, full of fatigue. A delivery truck gunned by them on the bridge, then a sports car overloaded with cat-calling youths. At the end of the bridge they moved into the shade and trampled weeds. Morgan stepped on a puffball and exploded a world, some of it powdering his shoe.

She said, "May I drive?"

"It may not look it," he said, "but this is an official car."

"Since when did you follow the rules?"

She drove reasonably, in silence, across the bridge. Bug stains spotted the windshield, which the wash from the wipers merely scummed. When they crossed the line into Bensington, she lifted her nose. A skunk lay dead on the road near the dirt drive where a sign on a tree said BIKES REPAIRED and the mail-

box read RAYBALL. The stink stretched relentlessly, death ex-
alting itself. Morgan silently reckoned the animal would lie in
state overnight and give itself to crows that would come at the
crack of dawn and pick it to pieces.

A few heads turned when they rumbled down a neighborhood street, for the car was familiar to many. Lydia peered
straight ahead through dark glasses, which she removed when
they reached her aunt's house. Instead of switching off the
motor, she turned to him with a stark expression.

"Do you think it might've been Matt?"

"No," he said.

"Why did I have to ask that?"

Morgan stared hard, aware of the slew of browns in her
hair, some gone golden. "To get it out of the way," he said.

The house, which stood not far from the green on Chestnut
Street, was pre-Revolutionary and harbored unused servant
quarters, fireplaces in the bedrooms, and a still serviceable
Dutch oven in the kitchen. Ceiling-high windows, which once
let in mammoth drafts, were now true in their frames. Much
of the house had been restored or redone after Randolph Jackson sold the virgin woodland that became known as Oakcrest
Heights. The most distinctive sound in the house was the
jingle-jangle of the front doorbell, an ingenious brass device
created by a reputed apprentice of Paul Revere.

The doorbell sounded now.

The caller was Lieutenant Bakinowski, whom Jackson
seated in his study, where a sun ray teemed with dust.
Through it Bakinowski said, "I thought it best we talk."

"Of course, certainly. I want to be kept up to date on
everything." Jackson plunked himself into a club chair and
scratched his fingers through his sandy hair, reassurance that
the bare spot on the crown was covered. The years had put
more of the Yankee into his looks but offered less stamina to
his attentiveness. He fingered his lower lip.

"It's about your police chief," Bakinowski said.

"I've known Jim for years. Fine fellow."

"I don't doubt that, sir, but not strictly a professional, wouldn't you agree?"

"I appointed him. Board votes the way I do, you see. And I can tell you this, he does his job."

"Yes sir, I'm sure he does, but we have a tricky situation here."

Jackson's gaze strayed to the family Bible, which solemnized the hand-carved pedestal on which it rested. One of his lesser forebears had made a marvelous living selling Bibles door to door. Illiterates had bought the book just to have it in the house. This was family lore with which he might have amused Bakinowski had the visit been of a lighter nature.

"The suspect, sir, is one of the chief's officers."

Jackson's unkempt brows shot up. "Christ, who? He doesn't have many."

"Matthew MacGregor."

"What?" The words took time to sink in. "For God's sake, you can't mean Matt. He and the Lapham girl are engaged, or almost."

Bakinowski put forth his suspicions and posited motives of rejection and jealousy. His voice was unmodulated and official-sounding, as if he were testifying in a courtroom, no notes needed. "MacGregor meant to hit the daughter, not the mother."

"I can't believe this," Jackson said, his day tainted. He had not meant to end it with heavy things on his mind. "I'm sure Matt can account for his whereabouts."

"Not adequately, sir. I've just finished talking to him. Some people don't ring true. Officer MacGregor is one of them."

With an air of discomfort, Jackson said, "What do you want from me?"

"Ordinarily I wouldn't ask for help, but Morgan is uncooperative. At best, he's protecting his officer. At worst, he's impeding an investigation."

"Jim wouldn't do that."

"We have a homicide on our hands. Since his authority comes from you, sir, I'd like his cues to come from you."

"Cues? What cues can I give him?"

"I'd take it upon myself to advise you."

Jackson glimpsed his wife's shadow in the doorway and suspected she had been listening for some time. In the next instant she swept into the room on fine large feet plugged into dainty shoes, introduced herself in a bright voice to Bakinowski, and instructed him to sit down when he half rose. "Would either of you gentlemen care for a refreshment?" she asked.

Bakinowski politely declined, and Jackson, casting devoted eyes on her, mouthed a silent no. Delighted that she was in the room, he swung a leg confidently over the other and settled more comfortably into his chair. "The lieutenant is a state police detective."

"How exciting." A perennial ingenue in her late forties, Suzy Jackson was ungainly in a paradoxically graceful way, amusing when she was of a mind, and difficult when it suited her. "You must have many adventures, Lieutenant."

"A few, Mrs. Jackson."

She took up a position behind her husband and laid a wifely hand on his shoulder, a gesture that always pleased him. He felt claimed. To Bakinowski she said, "Too much violence in the world, don't you agree?"

"No one will ever discourage man from violence, Mrs. Jackson, for it's the easiest reaction. If we could commit murder by simply willing it, people would be falling dead all over the world, which would be depopulated within a year."

"Goodness, I'd better not argue with a professional policeman," she said and idly rumpled her husband's hair, exposing the bald spot. "But I can tell you one thing right here and now, Lieutenant. Matthew MacGregor's not your man."

Bakinowski's eyes strayed in their deep sockets. "How do you know that?"

She smiled. "A woman knows."

Sitting at his desk, James Morgan perused an old report, one he knew almost word for word, and after all these years the words still gnawed at him. The victim was a twenty-three-year-old woman whose marriage had eviscerated her emotionally and spiritually. Morgan knew this because his predecessor, Chief Carr, had found her diary hidden in a box of sanitary napkins, the only place her husband might not have looked. The diary was confiscated for evidence but no longer existed, destroyed perhaps when the old chief was cleaning out his desk. Morgan slipped the report back into its dog-eared and discolored folder. The typewritten name on the tab was Rayball.

The year he had become a policeman was the year Eunice Rayball died under questionable circumstances. The morning Papa reported her missing he said he didn't want her back, good riddance to her, and ranted about infidelities, which were figments of his mind, rabid with jealousy from the day he married her. Morgan and Eugene Avery, wearing rubbers over their police shoes, found her facedown in a foot of murky swamp water, where she had lain three nights and three days no more than fifty yards from the house.

Everybody suspected foul play, but nobody could prove it. Chief Carr, questioning Papa relentlessly, got nowhere and called in the top investigator from the district attorney's office to take over the interrogation. The investigator, a former federal agent, sat on a corner of Chief Carr's desk and activated a tape recorder. Papa sat righteous and close-mouthed in a wooden chair.

"Said she was goin' for a walk, that's all I know."

"Good God, Mr. Rayball, at that hour of the night?"

"She wanted the air."

"And you say your sons were asleep at the time."

"The young one might not be mine."

"I've met him, Mr. Rayball. The little tyke certainly looks like you."

"That don't mean nothin'. Some of my jism might've got mixed in with the other fella's."

"It doesn't work that way."

"I know how it works."

"What did you think when your wife didn't come back?"

"Figured she met somebody on the road."

"But she didn't go onto the road. She went into the swamp."

"How was I to know that?"

"Give me the names of some of these other fellows."

"I don't know no names. She was too careful for that."

"Look at me, Mr. Rayball. Look at me closely and listen. It's been pretty well established you were the only man in her life."

"I know better."

"Why are you smiling, Mr. Rayball? Is this a game to you?"

"It ain't *nothin'* to me."

An hour later they let him go and watched him strut arrogantly out of the chief's office. The investigator, with a grimace, switched off the tape recorder. "The guy stands five-foot-five and talks six-foot-eight."

Chief Carr said, "He's not a whole dollar."

"One thing's for sure, he's got a twisted thing about women."

"No bruises on the body except what you'd expect from a fall," Chief Carr said, mostly to himself.

The investigator shot a look at Morgan, who stood obediently near the door with his cap in his hand. "What are your thoughts, Officer?"

"He killed her," Morgan said without hesitation.

Chief Carr settled in deeper behind his desk. "We all know that, Jimmy."

The reluctant ruling, convincing no one, was that Eunice Rayball, perhaps distraught, left her home in the night, traversed uncertain ground, tripped and fell, and died by accidental drowning.

Morgan never forgot the look of her when he raised her from the water, and he never forgot the weight of her hair when it slopped over his sleeve. Nor did he forget how he and Eugene Avery, after averting their heads, argued over who would stay with the body while the other radioed the station.

"Why does anyone have to stay?" Eugene asked.

"She's been alone here enough," Morgan replied.

Andrew Coburn

Eugene, whose seniority was greater by a month, left him standing there. He remembered how the sun shot rays through the sharp angles of a swamp maple and irradiated Eunice Rayball's remains.

Later, when Chief Carr was battling cancer and planning to retire, he said to Morgan, "It's not your triumphs you remember, Jimmy, but your failures. Not the rights you did, but the wrongs. That's the way it goes for most of us. Life's final injustice."

"I don't know any wrongs you did, Chief."

"I did a big wrong, Jimmy. I let Rayball walk."

"You didn't have a choice."

"If I was a different kind of fella, I'd have taken him into the woods and beaten the truth out of him."

Arlene Bowman lay supine on the padded table, and the masseur, a huge, unsmiling bald man with remarkable hands, took the stress from her shoulders but not the edge from her mood. Her dark eyes half shut, she said, "Take the towel off, Pierre, and tell me what you think of my ass."

"I've seen it before, Mrs. Bowman. It's OK."

"Don't you want to see it again?"

"I see posteriors all day, especially ones that aren't OK."

"Mostly women's?"

"Half and half," he said, his sure fingers working the cords in the back of her slender neck.

"Do you know the Pooles?"

"I do Mr. Poole at the club. I've never met Mrs. Poole."

"She could use you. Though of course you know, Pierre, it's illegal in this state for a masseur to do a woman."

"We won't tell, will we, Mrs. Bowman?"

"Probably not, but I should warn you that I'm a terribly vengeful sort. My husband is even worse."

His fingers rode up her nape, into her black hair where the curl began. "Your husband has complete trust in me. Otherwise I wouldn't be here, would I?" With knowing thumbs he kneaded the bone behind each ear.

"Christ, that's good," she murmured. "Do other women confide in you, reveal their fantasies, Robert Redford and Warren Beatty in bed with them at the same time?"

"Usually they just relax and enjoy. You don't ever relax, Mrs. Bowman."

"That's because I don't want my juices ever to ebb, my skin to sag. I don't want ever to die."

"You can delay practically anything, Mrs. Bowman, but death has the edge. It has time on its side." With outstretched fingers, his hands swept down on her shapely back and found the right muscles to move. "How's this?"

"Wonderful," she whispered, luxuriating under his care. Then she lifted her head and glanced over the curve of her shoulder. "Impossible to tell your age, you don't have a line in your face. How old are you?"

"Sixty-four."

"And what's your real name? It can't be Pierre."

"Dennis," he said. He removed the towel from her and stepped back.

"Well?"

"You're in perfect shape, Mrs. Bowman."

Ignoring the perfume of skunk, Chief Morgan reached furtively out of the car window and opened the mailbox. Among a few flyers was a thick ordinary envelope addressed to Papa Rayball, with an extra stamp to carry the weight. The envelope looked as if it had been worn in someone's back pocket before being mailed. No return address was given, but the postmark, partially blurred, read Florida, which told Morgan who the sender was.

He drove around the corpse of the skunk and turned sharply. The car clawed its way over ruts in the gravel drive and came to a rest beside Papa's battered pickup. The air rang with insects. The sun struck the pines and seemed to give each needle individuality. Climbing out, Morgan looked toward the house, but Papa's voice echoed from another direction.

"You want somethin'?"

Andrew Coburn

Papa was working beside the shed on an old three-speed bicycle, his tools scattered near his feet. The bicycle was upside down. He spun a wheel. Approaching him, Morgan said, "I brought your mail."

Papa's arms hung short, and his face went small, to the point that he looked like a bird of prey. "Against the law to go into the box."

"Thought I was doing you a favor."

"You ain't never done my family no favors and ain't likely you will." He took the mail without looking at it and jammed it into a back pocket of his rumpled pants, which once may have been part of a suit, though Morgan could not remember ever seeing him in one, not even at Eunice Rayball's funeral long ago. "You here about the old thing, or is it somethin' new?"

"The old thing is history," Morgan said.

"But it's still on your mind, ain't it? All these years nosin' 'round ain't got you nothin'." The tone of voice was pugnacious, and the small eyes, blue like the flame of a welder's torch, were shrewd and arrogant. "You and the old chief smirched my reputation."

"We were doing our jobs."

"If I believed in lawyers I'd've sued and be sittin' pretty now."

Summer sounds from the swamp competed in intensity. Cicadas were the loudest. Morgan said, "Where's Junior?"

"Don't know, off somewhere." Papa spun the wheel again. "You here about what he did that time at the school? MacGregor had no call treatin' him like he did."

"Officer MacGregor could've arrested him, probably should've."

"What good would that've done? Boy Junior's age got no authority over his pecker."

"He's no boy, he's in his twenties."

"But he ain't bright, so why make more of a fool of him? I know why MacGregor did it. He thinks he's you."

High in the pines the sudden squawk of a crow sounded like the dissonant hooting of a toy horn. On the ground a dry leaf flipped itself over like a live thing. "Tell Junior I need to talk to him soon as possible."

"What are you blamin' him for now?" Papa snatched up a small socket wrench and looked for nuts to tighten. Swiveling the rod of the kickstand, he wrenched one that did not need it. "He ain't competent to be questioned. He could say anything, think it's true."

"Straight answers won't hurt him."

"You ain't told me what it's about yet."

Morgan turned and, treading over flat weeds, returned to his car, where black flies sketched the air. A breeze brought him the smell of fern and a taste of the swamp. With a deliberate turn, he looked back at Papa. "Can he handle a rifle?"

"You know well as anybody I learned both my boys young. Clement, time he was ten, could shoot the eye out of a squirrel."

"How about Junior?"

Papa's gnarled face twitched, then was still. "You're trying to put things in my mind don't belong there."

"You got a rifle in the house?"

"Old one that won't work. You wanna look at it?"

Morgan climbed into the car and peered out the open window. "That's not the one I want."

"You wanna look up my ass?" Papa shouted. "Maybe you'll find it there."

Averting his head, Morgan radioed Meg O'Brien and asked what was doing. Nothing much. Selectman Jackson had phoned, no message. Her voice clawed through static. She was worried about Matt MacGregor. "You don't have to be," he told her. She was alone in the station, she said. Bertha Skagg, her relief, whose ankles tended to swell, had called in sick. "I'll be there shortly," he said.

"Where are you?" she asked with an edge.

"In the woods," he replied and switched off, for Papa had come to the car with a soft grunt and was staring in with the crack of a smile. Morgan twisted the ignition key. The motor sulked, then caught. "Something to tell me, Papa?"

Andrew Coburn

"We oughta be more partial to each other, you and me. We both lost a woman."

"You were never good to yours."

"You gonna hold that against me all my life?"

"Only what happened to her."

Papa's blue eyes blazed, his face caught fire, and his head lolled as if mere threads kept him sane. "You don't know I did it. You don't know anybody did it."

"I know she didn't do it herself," Morgan said and shifted the car easily into reverse. "Same as I know God didn't strike down Flo and Earl Lapham."

"Go home," he told Meg O'Brien, and she did, but returned shortly to her post with two chicken sandwiches, one for him, which he accepted gratefully. Since his breakfast with Baki-nowski he had put nothing in his stomach except a Milky Way. The call came while he was sitting at his desk. Meg, perversely, put it through without asking whether he wanted to take it. Christine Poole's voice was the coldest he had ever heard it.

"Have you mentioned me to Arlene Bowman?"

"Of course not." His sandwich went tasteless. "Why would I?"

"She knows about us. So does that woman working for you. How many others know, James?"

"None that I know of," he said, with no wish to speculate, for the town was full of eyes.

"This is humiliating."

"I never meant that to happen."

"But it has!" Anger and anxiety disfigured her voice. "Good God, what if my husband finds out? What do you think that will do to him? And how can I look him in the face, James?"

He was slow in responding, too slow, and abruptly the line went dead. Presently Meg appeared in the door and stood with formal rigor, her rupture of pony teeth showing. With customary forwardness she said, "When are you going to learn?"

"When are you going to quit listening in?"

"When are you going to stop fooling around in the Heights? There are solid unattached town women who've had their eyes on you for years. Want me to name a couple?"

"I had a marriage, Meg. Another won't take the place of it."

"Afraid to love and lose again, aren't you, Jim?" Only during intimate moments did she forsake his title for his name. They had known each other all their lives. In the several years after his wife's death, when he had shut himself off from any romantic life, she had occasionally invited him to her house for a light supper, always a chore for him. Their common ground was here at the station. Here she could speak her mind, and he could use his authority to shut her up.

Very quietly he said, "Let's drop it, Meg."

A few stray clouds, like lost sails, maneuvered through the brilliant Florida sky. On the white beach the child's shadow marked the hour. The woman's shadow might have been the minute. The child, a boy of no more than five or six, said, "That man's looking at us."

"He's looking at me," the woman said, taking her grandson's hand. "Ignore him."

Together they scuffed to the ocean's edge, which gently swelled, splashed, and foamed. In the heat of the off-season the beach was sparsely populated, enlivened only by the wing-beats of pelicans. The boy played in the surf, and the woman moved to deeper water. She was in her fifties, big but not fat, certainly handsome. Her bathing suit was the sort Esther Williams had worn long ago in the movies. Lowering her head, throwing her arms out, she made an arrowhead of her hands and floated forward. When she waded back to the boy, the man was gone.

Later, wearing a beach jacket over her wet suit, she sat alone in the patio bar of the hotel. Her table was smack in the sun, and her hair was drying into tight, natural curls. Her drink was more fruity than alcoholic. The man appeared from behind her and said, "May I?" She hesitated, then simply smiled. As he drew a chair the waiter, on cue, brought him a bottle of beer. Removing dark glasses, he said, "My name's Chico."

She surveyed him. "You don't look like a Chico."

His fair face beaten by the sun, he looked Yankee or German. His features were closely crafted, the planes precise and straight, the brow smooth, the nose shaved narrow. His weather-bleached hair, which had thinned, was combed straight back, which gave him a dated look, as if he too had watched the Esther Williams movies, though they were before his time. She judged him to be not much more than thirty.

"Do you often stare at older women on the beach?"

"When they look like you," he said and lit her cigarette with a lighter that flamed high. Beyond them sprinklers bathed a bordering lawn already as green as it could be.

"You're still staring."

"Do you mind?" He drank his beer from a frosted glass. A Swiss watch consumed his wrist. He had on a silk shirt, powder blue slacks, and alligator loafers, no socks.

"What exactly are you looking for, Chico, or should I assume the obvious?"

The waiter, serving another table, dropped a tray of drinks. The sudden smash of glass startled her but not him. His lusterless eyes did not blink or swerve from her. Here was a man, she mused, incapable of fear, only of madness. A practicing psychiatrist, she sketched a profile of a loner, quiet, monosyllabic, mostly unknowable, with no women in his life except disposable ones. He did not frighten her, but he greatly interested her.

"Are you staying here at the hotel?"

"I have a room," he said in a way that made it sound permanent. "What color was your hair when you were young?"

"Sort of blond." A hand supported her chin. "Why do you ask?"

"When I imagine somebody naked I want to get it right."

Years ago she had had a patient who physically resembled him, a seducer who planted strawberries on women's throats for their husbands to see. She interpreted the behavior as cruelty, but upon reconsideration saw it as a death wish and was not surprised when months later she read of his murder in the Miami *Herald*. Sipping her drink, she said, "That's good, Chico, very good. That would thrill some women."

"I know a place, if you like, we could go swimming in private."

"Why would I want to do that?"

"For the adventure."

"And do you plan to swim in the buff or keep on your underpants?"

"I don't wear underpants, never have."

She lightly crushed out her cigarette. "I'd think the material of your trousers would irritate your thing."

"I'm not circumcised."

"That would explain."

A boy in the uniform of the hotel came out on the patio, glanced about, and then wound his way to their table. "You have a telephone call," he said, and Chico rose. The boy, Cuban, smiled at her.

"Will you be here when I get back?" Chico asked.

"Of course," she said. "This is interesting."

She watched him stride into the hotel, shoulders squared, suggestive of the military, in which she could easily picture him serving. In his absence she smoked another cigarette and gazed off at flower beds in the shape of coffins, as if the hotel management had been killing off guests and burying the bodies. He returned with less of a stride and sat down without drawing in the chair.

"I'm afraid I have to leave."

"The call must've been a woman," she said with a smile. "Are you popular, Chico?"

He finished his beer. "You haven't told me your name."

"That's true. Tell me something instead: what brought you to my table?"

His eyes pondered her. Then he removed his wallet and produced a brittle snapshot, the colors dim, the edges smooth as silk from wear. The picture was of a woman, not old, not young, whose expression seemed set in the tragic tension of someone about to be hurt. She stared hard at it.

"It looks nothing like me."

"To me it does," he said and returned the picture to his wallet. "What is your name?"

She plucked one from the air. "Esther."

The same sun that scored Florida fired the roses that walled the front porch of Drinkwater's Funeral Home. Inside, his back to the two glorious caskets, the Congregational minister said, "Time softens sorrow, scatters it with the winds, but always leaves behind irreducible kernels. This is the human condition. The kernels we carry to our own graves."

The resonance of the minister's voice carried beyond the seated gathering to the standing overflow in an adjoining room, where Chief Morgan, a ghost of his own clinging to him, gently tried to shrug it off. Alone, he might have sought to embrace it.

Friends and neighbors seated closest to Lydia Lapham and her aunt felt elect, privileged, entitled. Most had known the deceased all their lives. May Hutchins, her hair an hour out of curlers, had shared her most intimate secrets with Flo Lapham when they were classmates at Pearson Grammar School. Malcolm Crandall, the town clerk, had been Earl Lapham's best friend in high school. He remembered Earl's first car, purchase price thirty dollars, an old Buick that snorted like a hippopotamus and farted clouds of oil.

"Let us pray," the minister said, and Doris Wetherfield, seated toward the rear, bowed her head. She had lowered the hem of the dress Flo Lapham was wearing in the casket.

Lydia Lapham's head was not bowed. Her ear would accept only one voice at a time, which at the moment was her father's, full of pride on that sunny day she had graduated from nursing school, the top of her class. She was no longer that person, she had shed skin too many times since, and now she sat with her aunt, the only family she had left. When her aunt began to sob, she gripped the older woman's hand. The minister, an austere figure in gray, said, "Amen."

Everett Drinkwater took charge, each maneuver scripted, his pale hand under Miss Westerly's elbow as she and Lydia rose awkwardly to their feet. Matt MacGregor, clumsy in an ill-fitting civilian suit more appropriate for winter, threw out an unneeded hand of support to Lydia, who appeared stunned by the crowd of faces behind her, more than she had anticipated or wanted.

Outside, Mr. Drinkwater and an assistant queued cars into a caravan that stretched up the street. Motors idled, headlights glowed in the sunlight, and pennants fluttered from aerials. The caskets would emerge later, their insides stripped of certain niceties, such as the pillows on which the heads of Flo and Earl rested. Randolph Jackson took the time to press the hands of people who every two years returned him to his selectman's seat. "A sad day," he said as a cat's-paw of warm air reshaped his sandy hair and revealed the bald spot. Then he climbed into his Audi, which still smelled new. His wife turned to him from fixing her face and said, "What if that lieutenant is right?"

He cast soupy eyes at her and frowned, which deepened the grooves in his spotty brow. He scrunched down behind the wheel in a way that doubled his chin and made a loaf of his belly. Then the side doors of the funeral home opened, and he straightened. "Here they come," he said.

At the cemetery, he breathed in air awash with the richness of the grass and the scent of potted plants in high bloom. Some of the grander tombstones carried ornate engravings that could have been diagrams for entering the other world. With the frown back on his face, he skirted the periphery of the crowd and surreptitiously approached Chief Morgan. He kept his voice low, his chin high. "I've heard some disturbing things about one of our officers, Jim. I hope to God it's not true."

At the double grave site, Fred Fossey, wearing the full regalia of the American Legion, removed the flag draping Earl

Lapham's casket, wrapped it into official folds, and presented it to Lydia Lapham, who was gazing into the crowd, picking out faces from the hospital. A doctor she considered a stout bottle of quack medicine with an imposing label stared back with eyes full of sympathy. Another doctor, whom she had expected to see, defied distance by seemingly planting his face in front of hers.

"Let me," Matt MacGregor said and relieved her of the unexpected weight of the flag, for suddenly she was very tired and queerly light-headed and suspected she could easily stretch out on air that would float her away. Then she felt MacGregor's arm around her, supporting her, for tears were gushing. "Ashes to ashes," the minister said and tossed dirt here, then there, from the ceremonial handful.

"I can depend on you to do what's right," Randolph Jackson said, moving closer to the chief. "I know you well enough for that."

Morgan seemed to shake his head. "The only sure truth you can say about a person is that he was born, lived awhile, and died. Beyond that, everything's open to argument."

Jackson shot him a wary look, but then relaxed, for he felt he understood. "Your wife's here, isn't she, Jim?"

"I hope not," Morgan said. "I hope there's a better place."

The crowd began to disperse. Jackson threaded his way toward his wife, and Morgan stayed in place with his arms dangling. He looked to his left, his right; he was alert like an animal. In a sea of sunshine the crowd was going one way and a lone figure another. He pursued it, first with a hurried step and then in a trot that quickened. The figure was rabbity, jerky, fleeing into the warmth of the day, with Morgan keeping pace for a while. Zigzagging, dodging tombstones, it began to give ground, but Morgan was losing wind. He stopped, took a breath, and brought a cupped hand to his mouth.

"Junior!"

He had his boarding pass in hand when a woman stepped in his way. She was a vigorous little creature in a tight top and striped shorts, with a touch of humor in the pertness of

Andrew Coburn

her nose. Her eyes were black olives. "On the go again, huh, Chico?"

She knew the name he went by, but not his real one. She was an undercover security officer at the airport, with training in martial arts and with a weapon in her shoulder bag. Two years before, she and a partner had detained him—indeed, she had flung him against a wall, spread him, and cuffed him—but later a phone call persuaded them to let him go, much to her chagrin.

He smiled. No hard feelings then and none now.

She glanced at his carry-on. "What have you got in there, something I shouldn't see?"

"Would you like to look?" he asked.

"What good would it do me?" She winked with rueful irony. "Have a pleasant trip, Chico."

Twenty minutes after he boarded the jetliner he felt it leave the ground, claw the air, and presently sock itself into a shaft of steel blue sky. Soon the hostess served him a mixed drink, which he sipped slowly. His seatmate was an elderly woman with a wispy look, as if a breeze had brought her in. Turning to him, she said, "I'm always tense the first ten minutes, then I get over it."

He nodded politely and rattled the ice in his drink. A man across the aisle thrashed a newspaper about as if surely something in it must be worth reading.

"I can tell you travel a lot," the woman said. "The way you sit, relax, take everything for granted. That's simply marvelous." Then her hands were busy, and soon she was showing him color Kodaks of her grandchildren. She was on her way to see them. "It's so hard to buy for them. I usually give them money."

"Money never hurts," he said.

"When you were little, what did you want most?"

He glanced off as if he had no recollections, no past. The man battling the newspaper wore a print shirt reminiscent of a commemorative postage stamp, which made him wary. He did not trust people who came across as both ordinary and absurd. "A Lionel train," he said, "but I never got one."

"That's a shame." Her voice tried to reach him. "Is it too late?"

"Ma'am, I can afford to buy a hundred of 'em."

"You're right," she said with a fullness of feeling. "It's too late."

He reached over and gave her hand an easy touch. "There was something else I wanted," he volunteered. "I wanted to live in a tree house, above the world."

She brightened. "Now you *are* above the world, several thousand feet, at least."

"That's right," he said and finished his drink.

They parted in New York, where she got off the plane and he stayed on. The man in the print shirt left behind the newspaper, and eventually he gathered it up, straightened the jumbled pages, and began reading. By the time the plane returned to its roost in the air, he was well into the account of an earthquake in another part of the world, the havoc devastating, as if God had unclenched a fist.

Junior Rayball took shortcuts through the woods, skirted wetland where frogs croaked among arrowheads, and took refuge under a tree behind someone's house during a sudden brief shower that left brilliants in the shrubs and grasshoppers chirring in the grass. On the road, the sun reheating him, he stripped off his denim jacket and walked freer in jeans wearing through the knees. He consulted a watch that lost time and picked up his step at the sight of workmen in a drainage ditch. Eyeing them furtively, he envied their employment. His last job had been at a Lawrence construction site, where he had worked less than a day and was deemed unsuitable. His recompense had been a cap adorned with the logo of the company.

Ahead lay Tish Hopkins's farm, which he approached with nostalgia. When Tish had kept cows he once shifted a manure pile for her, shoveling up wet clumps dripping with earthworms disturbed in their reverie. Tish would have given him more chores had Papa not grabbed him by the scruff and told him that no Rayball should shovel shit, *especially for no damn woman!*

He flung several long looks at the barn and then began running for no reason other than that Wenson's ice-cream stand, shaded by willow and oak, was around the bend. The percussion from a car whipping by at an ornery speed threw him off stride, but the maniacal screech of a jay spurred him on. His sneakers pounded the pavement, his hot breath gusted, and his heart beat big. He arrived at Wenson's with the smell of a small horse that had won a race.

He stood in a queue of children, big and small, with whom he felt of an age though not an affinity, and he colored deeply when two girls in their high-school years glanced at him knowingly and whispered. When his turn came he produced pocket money Papa had given him and soon, holding it high, was carrying a dripping cone to a bench under an oak where he could sit half hidden in the shade.

A van swung into the lot, doors slid open, and children crashed into view. Licking strawberry, his favorite flavor, he targeted girls who glittered and memorized this one's shiny leg and that one's spirited smile. When a young mother leaned over her child, his eyes became new coins and his ear honed in on the tunefulness of her voice. In his head rose a world of storybook the kind Clement had read to him. Then, detecting a footstep behind him, he stopped breathing.

"You shouldn't have run," Chief Morgan said.

He was no longer licking the ice cream, nor was he thinking. He was tightening screws and operating on nerves, which put fire in the roots of his hair. He wished he were wearing his cap.

"I'm not your enemy."

The chief's voice stayed behind him, disembodied. Letting out a whiff of breath, he crossed his ankles. His socks had vanished into his sneakers, where they heated his feet.

"What were you doing at the cemetery?"

The melt from the cone trickled over his fingers and down his palm. He let seconds march by before he spoke. "I got the right. My mother's there."

"Not where you were."

The cone was glued to his hand. He did not feel well; bubbles rose from his depths, warnings. "I wanted to see what was happenin'," he murmured.

"The Laphams are in the ground, Junior, but the dead come back to haunt. I know that for a fact."

"That's a ghost story."

"Doesn't your mother ever come back to you in dreams?"

"I don't remember her."

"But you dream of her, don't you?"

He dreamed of someone but was never sure it was his mother. She never came close enough to touch, never spoke, never showed the full of her face, only the drop of her hair, the same shade as his.

"I think there's something you want to tell me. Make it soon, Junior. Longer you wait, worse it will be."

"You sayin' I done somethin'?"

"That's for you to say."

The voice yanked at him as if he were a dog on a choke collar, and quickly he shook his head. Something in his stomach welled.

"Eat your ice cream, Junior."

He licked hard and sucked the melt from his fingers and lapped his palm. The cone was mush. When he looked over his shoulder the chief was gone.

Calvin Poole looked at his long pinstriped figure in the hall mirror and, stepping closer, focused on his face, especially his lips: thin, almost unrealized, as if they had never whistled a tune. He forced his lips into a smile when he glanced in on his wife, who was on the telephone. She gave a little wave of the hand.

Upstairs, he entered the master bedroom surreptitiously, as if traces of illicit conversation might be hanging in the air, but found only silence. He loosened his tie with a sense of fatigue, for he had got little rest lately. His head held too many thoughts, each an enemy of sleep. When he unbuttoned

Andrew Coburn

his suit jacket and loosened his tie, a small surge of hysteria rose in his breast.

It passed.

With his jacket still on, he lay athwart the bed and wondered what forces had brought him to this position in his life. As a youth, a solid student at Phillips Academy, he had read Wordsworth, *the world is too much with us*, and the line now wheedled back at him with all the irony of the intervening years. Then, unexpectedly, he slipped into a stunning indifference to the shape of his life.

His eyes closed.

No more than a few minutes later they fluttered open. Christine was in the room, a blur at first, then a whole person, with hair and face, needs and wants, with a capacity for loyalty as well as for betrayal. She leaned over him.

"You're home early," she said with a strain in her face, as if she were trying to read his eyes. "There's nothing wrong, is there?"

He turned his head from the late sun bombarding the windows. He was a white-haired sixty, but once he had been a child with a mother to tuck him in at night and make everything safe. "The real estate market is going rotten," he said in a voice younger than his years.

"Certainly it will bounce back," she offered.

"It's a corpse," he said. "It's beginning to stink."

"Banks usually ride these things out."

"We're eating loans."

She unlaced his shoes. "Big ones?"

"Big enough," he said. "And maybe a bigger one to come. Bellmore Companies."

"Bellmore?" The strain was back in her face. "That's Gerald Bowman."

"Yes," he said, experiencing a wave of distaste. Another human betrayal, though he blamed himself for that one. He should have been more prudent, more wary about joining the ride to easy riches. He shuddered over the magnitude of the loans to Bellmore and the unsatisfactory response from Bowman.

"Are you feeling all right?"

"Yes," he said.

She removed his shoes, shiny English leather, and with both hands began rubbing his stockinged feet, first one and then the other, something she had done often with her first husband, he suspected, but until now not with him. "Maybe you should retire," she said.

Sympathy, he realized, was what he wanted. It mitigated a sense of abandonment and a deeper one of aloneness. It lifted him slightly. "Who were you talking to on the phone?"

Her hesitation was the tick of a second. "Bowman's wife. I'm supposed to have tea with her tomorrow."

He was not disturbed, merely curious, for all events in his life now seemed elliptical and vaguely ironic. "I didn't realize you two were friendly."

"I'll cancel out if you want."

"My problems with her husband don't extend to her."

"I'm not keen on going," she said.

"Then why did you agree?"

She gave a final rub to each foot and straightened. Her expression was tight and defensive. "The woman has a way about her."

With no warning, his head heated. He felt his chest constrict and his heart race. His knuckles showed white. He wanted to rise up and accuse her of the worst a wife could do. He wanted to batter her with questions. Who? Why? Why, damn it, why? Then a deeper emotion invaded him, the fear of losing her, the dread of aloneness in his final years.

"Calvin." She was leaning over him again, searching. "Are you sure you feel all right?"

His face gave away nothing, except his needs.

The last of the funeral guests had left Miss Westerly's house. She was clearing a buffet table, carefully setting aside bone china and relegating ordinary ware for the dishwasher. Outside on the porch Matt MacGregor, itchy and tense in his wool suit, stood close to Lydia Lapham, whose dark glasses raised a barrier, kept him from her. "Just tell me you don't believe it," he said.

"Of course I don't," she said. "You didn't need to ask."

"I was pretty mad when you told me you didn't want to marry me."

"I understood."

He wanted to be cleansed of suspicion, but her voice, a soap that didn't lather, failed to reassure. When he attempted to stroke her arm, she winced away. "I'll always love you," he said quickly, "no matter what."

"Get on with your life, Matt. That's what I have to do with mine."

He wanted to tell of his pain, but hers was greater, which left him impotent, his arms dangling. Helplessly bitter, he said, "Bakinowski had no right questioning me. I'm a cop same as him." His bitterness hovered between them like an odor plugged raw into air, unabsorbed, ineradicable. "The chief tells me not to worry—trust him, he says. Should I?"

"Have you ever had reason not to?"

"No."

"Then why are you asking *me*?"

"It's like I'm losing everything."

Her eyes glided away from him. "You'd better go, Matt. I should be helping my aunt clean up."

"Can I kiss you?" he asked and watched her hesitate before yielding up a cheek. "Never mind," he said and left.

"He was at me, Papa."

Papa, scrawny as if screwed together wrong, was taking a shower under a hose rigged up behind the house and equipped with a spray nozzle. He soaped himself vigorously between the legs, raising one knee and then the other. His testicles hung low as if coming loose.

Junior fidgeted. "Did you hear me?"

Papa, whose ear had soaked up every word, said, "He's always gonna be at you. You got my name." He soaped his penis, which was half hard, its head audacious. His pubic hair was reduced to a few skeins under the overhang of his small potbelly. "What kinda things was he askin'?"

"He asked if I dreamt about Mama."

Papa spat water. "You don't tell him nothin'!"

"I didn't, I swear, but it was like he was lookin' right in me."

"Ain't nobody can look in your head but me, you hear?"

"Yes, Papa, but he scared me."

"He don't scare me. He knows I don't take shit from no-body." Suds rushed down Papa's knobby legs, the bubbles iridescent in the sun. A moment later he jumped out of the spray and drained water from an ear with a knock on his head. "I know what he was doin'. He was fishin', but he didn't put much of a worm on the hook."

"What, Papa?"

"Nothin'." He swept up a scrap of cloth that once might have been a towel and began rubbing himself down. "I got news for you, you wanna hear it?"

"I do."

"Clement's comin'."

5

May Hutchins fed her husband breakfast, packed him a lunch, and sent him out the door without a kiss, which dismayed him. His full, rosy face looked back at her in confusion and hurt. A master electrician, he brought to his blue work clothes the shape of a pigeon and the vulnerability of a lapdog. Lifting his chin, torn from shaving, he said, "Did I do something, May?"

"You didn't do anything," she snapped. She was wrapped in a robe and bedecked in brushes of wire that looked like machinery, all her hair captured in it. "Not a damn thing!"

"Then what's the matter?"

"What's the matter? They buried a piece of me yesterday. They put my best friend under, her husband beside her. That's what's the matter. What else do you want to know?"

After he drove off in his shiny panel truck, she regretted her words, for she hated hurting him, but her grief and anger were overwhelming. In the bathroom she yanked out her curlers and, with venom, ripped a comb through her sprung hair, which was reddish at the ends and gray at the roots. In the bedroom she relinquished her robe for a housedress and gave a passing glance to the frock she had bought on sale at

Roberta's. With a chill she realized she could never show it off to Flo Lapham.

In the kitchen, minor annoyances got on her nerves to the point of anguish: a cabinet door that would not close properly, an ant in the food cupboard, a recurring ring of crud around the tap fixtures in the sink. Hands trembling, she reached for the telephone and rang up Reverend Stottle, the Congregational minister, whose house was behind the church. Delirious with relief that she had caught him in, she immediately began telling him of her intense feelings of emptiness and panic. Her voice broke. His was unperturbed and assured. "There's terror in all of us, May, and consciously and otherwise we spend our lives trying to keep it in check."

She reeled. "I see. Well, thank you, Reverend, for sharing that lovely piece of information." She was ready to smash the receiver down, but his voice stayed in her ear.

"We must face life, May. But first we must know what it is."

"I know what life is," she came back at him, "I've always known. It's a job you go to each day. Sometimes you call in sick and finally, Reverend, you call in dead."

"May, this doesn't sound like you."

"That's what I've been trying to tell you," she said and clicked off.

Ten minutes later, with a cup of steaming coffee, her voice still unsteady, she was back on the phone. On the other end was Ethel Fossey, who was glad she had called. Ethel had something to tell her. "You won't believe it, May. It's bizarre."

Listening with a bruised ear, she sipped her coffee, burned her lip, and calmed herself. "No, I can't believe that," she interrupted. "A rumor like that shouldn't be repeated. Where did you hear it?"

"Fred told me. He heard it at town hall."

"Good God!"

"You know what they say, May. It's usually the husband, or in this case the boyfriend. They were breaking up, did you know that?"

"Lydia wasn't the one shot."

Andrew Coburn

"Fred says it might not have been meant for her. At least that's what he heard."

"Does he believe it?"

"He doesn't want to."

May shuddered. "This is nonsense."

"I told you it was bizarre."

A while later, with crosscurrents of feelings and an enervating nostalgia over her younger days, she sat at a drop-leaf desk and began a letter to her mother, who lived in a Florida retirement village. Her mother was in her eighties and in marvelous health. *Dear Mom*, she wrote and asked herself, "Do I want to live that long?" In a nice hand, copperplate, she gave an account of the funeral, the flag on Earl Lapham's casket, the starkness of poor Lydia's face. *It's good Earl went too*, she wrote. *He wouldn't have lasted without Flo.*

When she finished the letter she realized with a bit of a shock that her handwriting had become almost childlike. She addressed the envelope with decided care and with a lick took the full taste of the stamp, which she pounded into place, her fist the hammer. Then, before tucking the letter inside, she added a postscript. *Terrible rumor going around about the MacGregor boy—too vicious to repeat.*

It was after she had sealed the envelope and poured herself another cup of coffee that her thoughts turned to the whole MacGregor family: Arthur MacGregor walking out without so much as a good-bye, leaving poor Luella spinning like a toy, with her daughter, Diane, just entering her teens and Matt still a boy. Then poor Luella worked at some little job in Lawrence till her health went—her heart, she said, though it seemed more like her spirit. But by that time Diane had married well, someone outside the town, and Matt was nearly a man.

Handsome boy, Matt, pug nose and all. He had mowed lawns and delivered papers. He had delivered hers. He had been good at high-school sports, she remembered, his picture in the paper more than once and then again when he became a policeman. Some people—although come to think of it, it may only have been Ethel Fossey—said he had sucked up to the chief to get the appointment. If so, so what? Sometimes it's the only way you get things.

What she did not understand, however, was what Lydia Lapham saw in him, for there had always seemed more to Lydia than to him. She, for one, had thought the girl would find herself some doctor, which would have pleased Flo. Unlike others in town, she was not surprised that Lydia and Matt had gone together for so long without marrying.

She let her coffee go cold and went outdoors. Waving to a neighbor, she strode down the front walk to leave the letter for the postman. Ropes of sunlight hung from the trees across the street, where children were setting up a lemonade stand. It was another fine day—meant to be enjoyed, she told herself. But when she lowered the lid of the mailbox, a wasp flew out and a chilling thought struck her. *What if? What if?* Her mind raced back into the past and tried to dredge up any occasional streaks of cruelty the boy might have shown. *The father was a queer fish, why not the son?*

Junior Rayball woke hard with crusted eyes and threw off the army blanket with a shiver of excitement. He moved quickly, a human monkey in droopy underdrawers, and peered through the window in hope of seeing a car in the yard. He saw only the pickup, which was shrouded in a morning mist that etherealized the pines.

He padded into the kitchen, where Papa was drinking coffee and eating a slice of bread smeared with blackberry jam. With disappointment breaking his voice, Junior said, "He ain't here."

"He's here," Papa said in the midst of a chew. "He just ain't here direct." Papa winked. "He ain't like us. He sleeps late."

"Where is he, he ain't here direct?"

"Some motel. He flew into Boston. You and me, we ain't never been on an airplane, have we?"

Junior saw hope. "But he's comin'."

"Said he was, didn't I? You got your story straight?"

"Yes, Papa."

"You're in enough trouble as it is. You don't wanna go wanderin'."

"Can I tell him you and me went to Boston?"

"Yeah, you can tell him that."

Smiling, Junior stood crooked and scratched a naked shoulder. The crotch of his drawers were permanently pee-stained, which never failed to annoy Papa, who took a sudden hot swig of coffee. "What's the matter, Papa?"

"You'd think by now you'd learn to shake it first."

Junior stepped to the table, looked into the jam jar, and reached for the bread. Papa's voice was a bark.

"Don't touch nothin'. You ain't washed yet."

Junior slunk back, color in his face. Then he stood straight. "Clement comes, don't talk to me that way."

Chief Morgan ordered scrambled eggs and a hot bun for breakfast. Mitch Brown came out of the kitchen to serve the order himself and cast a questioning glance at Matt MacGregor, who was with the chief. "Sure I can't get you something, Matt?" Mitch asked. "Coffee?"

MacGregor shook his head. He was not on duty, but he was in uniform, in a way that seemed defiant. The blue shirt was stiff with starch, and the polished shield on his breast glared. His hair was creased, his forehead reddened where his cap had snugged the skin. Drinking the chief's water, he said, "Word's got around. People are looking at me funny."

"You're imagining it," Morgan said and glanced at other tables. Malcolm Crandall, the town clerk, averted his eyes, and Fred Fossey, his mouth packed with food, raised his newspaper. At a window table two women, longtime employees of the library, employed their napkins with rapt care.

"You told me to trust you," MacGregor said, suspicion and jealousy in his tone. "Then I heard you took my girl for a ride. What was that all about?"

"It was a chance to talk." Morgan stopped eating. "What else would it be?"

"You know."

"No, I don't."

"Yes, you do."

MacGregor was pitched high, Morgan could see that. He resumed eating. "I'm not going to get into that kind of game with you, Matt."

"I'm sorry," MacGregor said and studied his thumbs, the nails bitten. "But this shit going on, it's not fair. I'm the cop, the good guy, and Bakinowski's trying to make me the heavy. You haven't heard the latest. He wants me to take a polygraph."

"Take it."

"It's an insult, God damn it."

"Take it," Morgan advised, "and get him off your back."

"You don't understand, Chief. Nothing's going to get him off my back until the real guy comes forward—or we catch him. Do you know what scares me, Chief? That we might *never* catch him."

Morgan stared at him closely, aware of a void between them. "Hold on, Matt. I've been going about this in my own way. Thurman Wetherfield, I know, wouldn't have done it."

"I told you that right off the bat."

"Let me finish. The answer's with the Rayballs, and I'm working on it, my own way."

MacGregor, who did not look reassured, drank more water. "All these years you've been trying to nail Papa Rayball, everybody knows that, and nobody's gonna buy it."

"Let me worry about that."

MacGregor slapped his cap on and yanked the visor as if to hide the rest of his thoughts. Then he was on his feet. "Face it, Chief. We're not the big league, we're semi-pro."

"Where are you going?"

"Where am I going? I got nowhere to go. I got a cloud over me."

Morgan watched him leave and then finished off his eggs. He was eating the remainder of the bun when Fred Fossey approached with the newspaper furled tightly under an arm. "I don't believe it, Chief. I thought about it for a long while and I don't believe it for a minute."

Andrew Coburn

"What don't you believe?"

"What I heard about Matt." Fossey leaned toward Morgan with wisdom in his eyes. "Besides, he just proved his innocence."

Morgan pushed his plate aside and used his napkin. "I'm not following you, Fred."

"He was guilty, he'd have paid for your breakfast."

A gas pain gave Sergeant Avery a travesty of a smile. Shifting his weight, he loosed air and hoped Meg O'Brien would not get wind of it. She was taking a call from May Hutchins, whose voice was loud enough for him to hear. Wasps were building a hive in her mailbox, and one had nearly stung her. Meg advised her to buy a certain spray at Tuck's, but she wanted help and asked specifically for Sergeant Avery, who tried to slip away. Meg's voice spun him back.

"She's waiting for you."

"What for?"

"You heard. Stop at Tuck's for the spray. She'll pay you for it."

"Get somebody else."

"There's nobody else." She stared at him. "You all right?"

He was plugged up, packed in like walnut meat, but he was not going to tell her that. "I'm fine," he said and, slapping his cap on, headed for the door.

"Eugene."

He pivoted heavily, assigning Meg a mean streak. "What now?"

"Treat her right. Something's bothering her more than wasps."

In the cruiser he farted to his heart's content and then drove around the green to Tuck's General Store, which had lost its crackerbarrel look and now resembled a superette. While buying an aerosol can of Ortho Hornet & Wasp Killer, he exhausted his eye on Sissy Alexander, the ballplayer's wife, who was buying feminine products. The only bribe he had ever taken in his life was from her husband, whom he had stopped for running a stop sign the year the Alexanders moved into town. The bribe was an autographed ball, one of several Crack kept in the glove compartment of his Rolls.

Outside, he watched Sissy Alexander drive away in her Jeep Cherokee, a Red Sox sticker on the back window. The sight of her had keyed him up and gave him a lighter head, and climbing into the cruiser he wondered whether stories he had heard about her and the chief were really true. He hoped not, out of respect for Crack.

May Hutchins's street stretched narrow under a canopy of trees, mostly maple, some oak. Elms and chestnuts had long vanished. He ran the cruiser into the Hutchinses' drive, climbed out, and waved to children selling lemonade. As he approached the open mailbox, spray can in hand, May Hutchins came hustling down the walk, which took him aback. She did not look herself without curlers.

"Forget the wasps," she said. "There was only one."

"You got me over here for one wasp?" Chagrined, he flourished the aerosol can as if he might spray her with it. "What am I supposed to do with this?"

"Take it back," she said.

"What did you get me over here for, May?"

She had him by the arm, a daunting grip for a woman not all that big. "Let's talk," she said and maneuvered him over the grass, away from mums and marigolds, to the side of the house, where a large maple quivered with life. Leaves quaked. A bird flitted out, and a squirrel tested a branch.

"You can let go of my damn arm," he said and rubbed it.

"What's going on, Eugene?" Her eyes were arrows. "It wasn't any use asking Meg O'Brien, she protects you guys."

"What's that supposed to mean?"

"It means I want to know what's going on." Anxiety shot color into her cheeks and deepened her voice. "Did Matt MacGregor have anything to do with what happened to the Laphams?"

"Jesus, May!" He reared up in defense of the department, in loyalty to the uniform, though his needed a press and some letting out. "That's an ugly thing to ask."

Andrew Coburn

"Just tell me."

"You know Matt well as I do. He's twenty-four carat."

"Sometimes we don't know people as well as we think."

Sergeant Avery gave a hitch to his pants. "I don't know who's telling you this stuff, but it's not worth listening to."

"Flo was my friend."

"Matt's mine."

"If it wasn't him, who was it?"

Sunlight tore through the maple. Leaves blazed. "Only one fella's going to find that out," Sergeant Avery said, "and that's the chief."

Lieutenant Bakinowski had three suits in his working wardrobe: business blue, dim plaid, and steel gray. Today he had on the gray, which gave him a wise and unyielding look. He and Chief Morgan shared a bench on the village green, where a drowsy quiet prevailed. Brushing a sleeve, he said, "I've learned something about MacGregor. He's got money in the bank, more than forty thousand."

Morgan tilted his head. "That much?"

"He had almost fifty, but a few weeks ago he drew out five. Where's a cop get that kind of money?"

"There's an easy answer," Morgan said.

"I'll take an easy answer the same as any other kind."

"His father died four years ago, left behind a good insurance policy. His mother shared the proceeds with him and his sister. His father bought the policy years ago from Earl Lapham, Metropolitan Life. Maybe you can make something of that."

"I see irony, is all." Suffering slightly from pollen, Bakinowski delivered a large handkerchief to his nose and blew. "Any idea why he drew out five grand?"

"Ask him."

"He'll tell me to go to hell. That's where we're at." Bakinowski seemed to smile. "I was expecting help from you, but I'm not getting it, am I? Your boy won't even take a polygraph."

"Ask him again."

"Would it do any good?"

"It might," Morgan said, watching two girls in straight-legged jeans cross the green, all the confidence of youth in their strides. "You may have guessed, I have my own theory."

Bakinowski showed neither surprise nor curiosity. He gave his nose another blow and put away the handkerchief. "You talking about the Rayballs?"

"You've heard of them?"

"I've heard you got a bug up your ass about the old man. Something about his wife's death—how long ago, twenty years?"

"I don't deny I think he killed his wife."

"Some say it's an obsession with you."

"I don't label it."

"I don't want to hurt you, Chief, but if you want people to take you seriously you got to be serious yourself."

Morgan's face was set hard. "Do you want to explain that?"

"Sure, if you want me to." Bakinowski looked up at the sky, an infinity of chalky blue. "I've heard people say when you can't sleep at night you count women's arses."

"You've got a big mouth."

"I'm just repeating what I hear. Some folks think you're a hero for putting something over on the big newcomers in town. They say the women lie with you in their garter belts and with their rich husbands in their bed socks. That true?"

Morgan stirred. "Why don't you take it for what it's worth?"

"I hear it everywhere. A fellow at the Blue Bonnet says you put your face in so much pussy you got a hairball in your stomach."

Morgan's estimable jaw was clenched. He rose slowly to his feet and for an instant seemed on the verge of yanking Bakinowski along with him. Instead he moved his eyes. Nearby, compliments of the Bensington Garden Club, was a rockery of flowers, the many varieties responding to one another, vying for attention and competing for glory. "Flowers remind me of women," he said, "do they you?"

Andrew Coburn

Bakinowski tossed an arm along the top of the bench. "What's it take to get a rise out of you, Chief?"

"Why should you want to?"

"I'm trying to get you to talk. When you're with me you got little to say and less to offer. That's aggravating."

"You have my theory."

"MacGregor told me all about the thing at the school. The motive doesn't fit the crime. Even if it did, it wouldn't wash. This Junior Rayball, he's slow, right? He doesn't think complicated. He wanted revenge, he'd go for MacGregor himself, not the girlfriend. Am I making sense to you?" Bakinowski sighed. "I see I'm not. You got the bug up your ass. You want, I'll grill the Rayballs myself."

Morgan shook his head hard. "The old man would spit in your face, and Junior would sink into his shell."

"So what are you telling me?"

"I'll handle them my own way."

"What way's that, Chief? You playing a *High Noon* sort of guy? Let's say you're right, I'm wrong. Or let's say you just plain piss the Rayballs off. They're like hillbillies, right? Worst scenario is you getting shot up in a bang-bang."

Morgan's gaze returned to the rockery, where a butterfly was flaunting its beauty. Pointing, he said, "See those lilies, the batch of creamy white ones. Like fashion models, aren't they?"

"I'm trying to talk sense, you give me flowers."

"And those pink lilies. They could be debutantes surging out of their green gowns."

"I wouldn't know about that, Chief." Bakinowski rose from the bench and buttoned his suit jacket, which was tailored to accommodate his weapon. "Unlike you, I don't have pussy on the brain."

Morgan crossed the green alone, the day's heat creeping up on him. His car was parked near the library. As he approached it, Orville Farnham, who operated a family insurance agency, greeted him, immediately mentioned the weather, and commented on the state of the economy. Farnham carried a face never at rest, the contours shifting, the creases tightening or widening, and he talked loud as if he did not want his real thoughts heard. Finally he said, "How's the Lapham case going?"

"We're expecting a break," Morgan said.

"Hope it comes soon. Otherwise rumors get out of hand. You hear all kinds of crazy things."

"You know what rumors are worth, ille."

"I do, Chief. Worth no more than dog spit on a french fry." His face grew full with his voice, and abruptly he slapped Morgan's arm. "I'm with you a hundred percent. We all are."

Morgan climbed into his car, which the sun had heated. Quite sharply he was aware of his own breathing and the heaviness of his face. Sometimes he wearied of being a cop and of trying to see through people. He wanted things to be as they seemed. From the dash came a crackle and then Meg O'Brien's voice: "You there, Chief?"

He activated the speaker. "I am."

"I've been trying to reach you."

"Anything important?"

"Lydia Lapham," she said.

Arlene Bowman did not serve tea. She poured sherry and said, "This is to make you relax. You're stiff as a board."

"Am I?" Christine Poole said simply and accepted the sherry without protest. She had dressed for the occasion only to find Arlene Bowman looking absolutely stunning in designer jeans. The room they sat in held exquisite things, porcelain, crystal, the finest of furniture, and at the same time conveyed comfort and casualness. A battered book lay open on a window seat. The ghost of a water stain lurked in the gloss of an end table. Christine, deciding on the spot not to play games, said, "Whatever may have been between James Morgan and me is over."

Arlene Bowman, sitting in a plush love seat with her legs curled beneath her, smiled. "Why do you feel you had to tell me that?"

"It's why you asked me here, isn't it?"

"Not entirely. Our husbands know each other quite well. Why shouldn't we?"

"I don't know. I'd like you to tell me."

"For openers, you're an intelligent woman. I like intelligent women. Bring two together, the world becomes bigger. Do you believe that? I do."

The sun flared against the high windows, a torch on the glass, but the room was cool. Potted plants thrived. Christine sipped her sherry and set her eyes upon a handsome black-and-white photograph, framed in silver, of two children, a boy and a girl who looked as if they had not been born but dreamed up. Perfect features, pleasing smiles, the boy as beautiful as the girl. "Gorgeous youngsters," she said. "Obviously yours."

"And Gerald's. I give him credit, or blame, as the case may be. They're now in the turbulence of adolescence. Both are at Phillips, Exeter, not Andover, and for the summer both are in Outward Bound, which Gerald says will straighten them out. Tell me about your children."

She had two sons from her first marriage, one studying for the bar exam in New York and the other with the Peace Corps in Kenya. She did not mention that her elder son had his father's features, which put joy in her eyes but a needle in her heart.

"And where are you from originally, Christine?"

New York, she told her. Her father had been a litigation lawyer in one of the city's larger firms. The sherry was making her voice lazy. "That's how I met my husband. My first husband. He was Dad's protégé, and Dad brought him home to dinner."

"From the stuff of that they used to make movies," Arlene Bowman said. "My father took his life in the comfort of a Cadillac in a closed garage, the motor running."

"I'm sorry."

"Don't be. It was a cowardly thing to do. I was at Wellesley at the time, senior year. I married Gerald soon after graduating. I knew he was going places."

Christine had a clear image of Gerald Bowman from socials at the country club. His grooming was correct in each particular, his manner whispered privilege and power, his polish was of a boardroom table, and his gestures seemed guided by inside information. She remembered him snapping fingers at a waitress.

Arlene Bowman was on her feet. "I shouldn't," Christine said but relinquished her empty glass.

Over a second sherry Arlene Bowman said, "Marriage is a funny business. The woman's a sponge soaking up her husband's acrimony and her children's fussing. I've tried to avoid that role."

"Your view of marriage isn't exalted, is it?"

"I've never believed a man would bring magic into my life. Money, yes. Status, comfort, a certain degree of affection—but magic, no."

"It depends on the man," Christine replied, loyal to a memory, to a phase of existence when she had cooked everything in wine and bought coffee by the bean.

"Tell me about him, that first husband of yours."

The memory burned as old feelings reasserted themselves. Her tongue loosened. "He died after lovemaking. My arms were still around him. I thought he had gone to sleep. Then I knew. I can't describe what the weight was like. To this day, when Calvin's on me, I feel like an open grave."

"Good God," Arlene Bowman said in a low voice.

"No man since has managed to touch the right chord in me."

"Not even James Morgan?"

Leaning back in her chair, she was amazed, even appalled, at what she was telling this woman, which did not stop her. "He's come the closest," she confided.

"To the chief." Arlene Bowman spoke with only faint irony in raising her crystal glass, the sherry fluttering. "He's handsome enough, quite virile, but not really our sort, is he? I wonder why we should have bothered with him."

"I'm not sure I know what you mean by that." She was fully aware but unprepared to defend him.

"Then I'll let it ride."

She lifted herself from the chair and gave quick tugs to her summery white dress of scaled silk. Her legs were steady; it was her head that worried her. "I really must go."

"I like the dress."

"Thank you."

They walked together to the foyer, where she paused to apply lipstick, the shade long ago popular. Their eyes met in the mirror. "You're an attractive woman, Christine. You'd be even more attractive if you lost some weight."

"I know that."

"Do you play tennis?"

"I'm not in shape for that."

"Then let's get you in shape. Are you free tomorrow morning?"

She hesitated. "I'm not sure. Why?"

"Don't ask," Arlene Bowman said. "I'll pick you up at nine."

She felt her blood run quick when she stepped out into the burn of the afternoon. Day lilies lit the air, a robin flew off and evaporated in the heat. Stepping into her car, she had a vague suspicion that she had been manipulated, entered into a game yet to be explained, the rules negotiable. She drove away with a wary sense of adventure.

The day before, after landing at Logan, he had rented a car and driven up Route 93 to the town of Andover, the outskirts, where he checked into a motor inn and out of habit used a false name. He spent the greater part of the evening in the bar, where the lonely, the unfaithful, and occasionally the desperate hung out. He sat knee to knee with a woman at a miniscule table that accommodated no more than their drinks and an ashtray. She was naive with men, always sticking her face up to be kissed and deceived. Her mouth hardened into a smile that would last the evening.

Later, in his room, he numbered the lines in her face and found them all beautiful. She admired his tan and asked where he had got it. "The beaches of the world," he told her with an importance he usually denied himself.

She puzzled over his name. "You don't look Puerto Rican," she said.

"I'm gringo," he told her.

"Are you married?"

"Yes."

"You don't wear a ring."

"No."

"What's your wife's name?"

"Esther," he said.

With her hand on his chest, she said, "I'm not usually like this."

In the morning, he phoned room service for breakfast, which awaited her when she emerged from the bathroom with a washed-out look, chaste and convalescent. She opened her purse with a veiny hand and discovered a brand-new hundred dollar bill folded lengthwise.

"What's this for?"

"For you," he said.

That was when she went hysterical.

Outside her parents' ordinary little house, her house now, Lydia Lapham waited in her car for Chief Morgan. The street was quiet, tree-shaded, property lines marked by friezes of barbered shrubs whose berries drew birds. Next door a curtain twitched: a neighbor was watching. Taking a deep breath, she yearned for the old coherence in her life, when no one infringed upon her unless she allowed it. Finally the chief's car pulled up behind hers.

They met on the sidewalk. She wore no makeup. Her hair was swept back and tied, which left her face explicit. Her heart beat rapidly inside a body that seemed dead. She said, "I wasn't sure whether I needed permission."

"You don't," Morgan said, gray eyes resting on her.

"And I didn't want to go in alone."

They moved toward the house. On the front door was an Off Limits sign, red letters on white pasteboard, posted by one of Lieutenant Bakinowski's men. Morgan tore it off. Lydia used her key. The door opened, and Morgan said, "Are you sure?"

She stepped inside, and for a second or so her senses teetered, her mind threatened to tip. She heard from somewhere, perhaps upstairs, an echo of her mother's warm, plump voice. She threw a look back at Morgan, but he seemed aware only of creakings and hums natural to a vacant house. The little hallway was stuffy.

"You'd better leave the door open," she said and stepped past dead flowers pluming a vase. Each step was forced, her eye sweeping one room and then another. Nearly all the furniture, prudently selected, dated to the early years of her parents' marriage. She had grown up with it: the faded brocade of the living room set and the ornate edges of the wall mirror, the massive mahogany of the china closet that seemed too much of a burden for the dining room, the indestructibility of the kitchen table with its old-fashioned cutlery drawer. Her mother could never understand why such drawers had been done away with, and now neither could she. She returned to the hallway, gave another look at Morgan, and said, "Please, wait here."

Upstairs, she passed by her own bedroom and entered theirs, which was stifling. Quickly she raised a window. The sun streaked her parents' bed, the same one with which they had begun their marriage. On her mother's writing table were two pages of notepaper, an unfinished letter in her father's hand. It was to a man in Michigan, an old war buddy with whom her father had maintained a correspondence through the years but had never managed a reunion. She lifted a page to her cheek as if the warmth of her father's hand might still be on the paper.

She opened a cedar chest and raised her mother's wedding gown, like lifting a mist, but against her face it was dry and scratchy. With reverence she replaced it and approached the closet. When she withdrew her mother's best Sunday dress, a breeze ruffled it, as if the wraith of the woman were in it.

In the bathroom, after dashing her face with water, she

peered into the glass and felt anonymous and pure. She dried her face in a thick towel, like a child who has been playing hard. Then she returned to the chief.

"I needed to know if I could stay here by myself. I can."

He looked doubtful. In the immediate period after his wife's death, he had avoided his house, entering it only at odd day-time hours and spending most of his time at the station, where he slept in the cell until Meg O'Brien got on his case. "It may be too soon," he said.

"If I don't do it now, I might never," she said, revealing darknesses in her face, also a determination.

He wondered whether she might reassess her feelings about MacGregor, if only to add a voice to the house. He doubted it, sensing in her a strength lacking in him during his greatest grief. He also doubted MacGregor would try to come over. Too much else was pressing on Matt and tightening him up.

"Besides," she said in a lighter tone, "my aunt and I are starting to get on each other's nerves. She's a dear, but she talks to herself on the toilet."

The chief smiled. "Good a place as any."

"And Reverend Stottle's been coming around. I can't re-spond to him. He tells me that the same God that invented life invented death. Then in the next breath he says maybe God got life all wrong."

"Maybe he's going through a crisis of his own."

"I have no time for him—and no faith in my own reality, let alone God's."

She had a few things in her car that needed to be brought in. The chief helped her. In the kitchen a shaft of sunlight quivered with dust. He raised the window and killed a moth planted on the screen. She lifted a carton of milk from the refrigerator, sniffed it, and poured it into the sink. Crumpling the carton, she looked at him in a way that told him it was time for him to leave. Concern marked his face.

"This is my home," she said. "I'll be all right."

He kissed her cheek. "You need only pick up the phone."

Alone, she stayed at the sink and once again slapped her face with water to reinforce her anonymity. Then she made herself gaze out at the back lawn and at the dark green of the woodlot. A quick glance at her watch told her it was the same hour of the afternoon that the shot had rung out. In the sunshine two aluminum lawn chairs faced each other, each occupied by a ghost.

Papa Rayball sent his younger son to his room and stared across the table at his elder son. Clement looked everything like his mother, but Papa saw only himself in him. The dark brown hair had thinned a little but not enough to matter. He was still lean like a hoe handle, and his features were blades. "You must be gettin' a lot of sun," Papa said.

Clement stared at the stove. He had a memory of his mother fussing with saucepans, steam lifting the lid off one. The memory hurt him. He said, "I think you'd better tell me more about why I came all the way up here."

"It ain't pretty."

"I've already figured that out."

"Junior's my burden, you know that. He wasn't born bright like you. I don't even know for sure he's mine."

"For Christ's sake, Papa, don't start that again."

"Can't help what I've always felt in my bones." Papa lowered his voice. "We can't talk here. He'll listen, he's got ears like a rabbit."

They went outside, where the heat felt like a noose around Clement's neck. It pained him to be back. He had hoped never to return. There was a time he had hoped to send for Junior, but that idea had faded.

Papa, with paternal pride, said, "You look good, Clement. You look like a real man."

They ambled away from the house, went into weeds, and stood under a swamp pine, which disturbed a squirrel whose chattering rose from a low branch to a high one. "Let's hear about it," Clement said.

Papa scuffed the ground, then assumed an air of stiff right-mindedness and began unraveling events in a murderous monotone. He spoke at length, his face alive, incandescent, his heart throbbing. "It don't matter what Junior done, Mac-

Gregor had no right treatin' him less than human." A snap came into his voice. "I ain't condonin' what Junior done. I'm just explainin' what worked up to it."

"Tell me exactly what he did," Clement said from a dark, deadpan face, and Papa's voice went low and flat, dry and intense, each word carrying its own charge. Clement peered up at the pine for the squirrel and thought of that moment of mindlessness when a hunter, or an assassin, squeezes the trigger. When Papa finished, he said, "Who showed him how to work the weapon? It's not easy."

"He figured it out himself."

"The weapon was worth thirty-five hundred dollars."

"You didn't pay no thirty-five hundred for it. I bet you didn't pay nothin' for it." The air was growing sultry, with mosquitoes on the attack. Papa swatted one and left blood on his cheek. "I did right heavin' it, didn't I?"

"I'm just telling you what the thing was worth," Clement said, feigning a small anger to conceal a great one.

"I got one thing to say," Papa said with the trace of a scapegrace smile. "The little shit got two for one."

For moments Clement did not trust himself to speak. He batted the air behind his head and then spoke out of a formal face. "You never should've let it happen."

"I never saw it comin'. He's always talkin' about doin' somethin' and never doin' nothin' 'cept pick his nose, you know that."

"This time he fooled you."

"Don't blame me. He was little, you brung him up more than I did."

"Don't give me that crap, Papa. And don't tell me anything more about him not being yours, OK?"

Papa's eyes went small. "You was always my favorite. You gonna blame me for that?"

"I blame you for a lot of stuff, Papa, maybe Junior least of all."

"You talkin' 'bout your mother now? That what you tryin' to hit me with?"

"I'm remembering you didn't want to pay Drinkwater for a coffin. You wanted me to make one out of scrap wood."

"Why put somethin' bad into somethin' good—that was my thinkin'. 'Sides, you know what she was."

"Let her rest, Papa." His face softened. He did not want to argue. Some memories hurt his skull, those of his mother the most. He said, "How's it stand with Junior?"

"It ain't as bad as you think. Only one botherin' him is Morgan, and he's only goin' on guess. You remember Morgan, don't you? He's chief now."

"I remember him."

"I know his game. He's gonna work on Junior, play it cozy with him. You know how he does it, he tried to work on you 'bout your mother. Tried to make it seem I done somethin' to her she done to herself." Abruptly Papa slapped his leg and looked triumphantly at his hand. "Every skeeter I kill is full of blood. They're livin' good here."

Monarchs busied themselves on milkweed. Clement remembered catching one and giving it to his mother, who told him to let it go. "What do you expect me to do?"

Papa rose up on his toes. "You can fix him. You can fix him good."

"How am I going to do that?"

"He's got a weakness. Women."

"Remember the time you took me to the hospital, Clement? Time I ate the rotten meat?" Junior spoke from his pillow in the dark of the little room they had shared as children. A scrap of moonlight clung to the screen in the window, through which came the ringing of peepers. "You saved my life."

"The doctor did, not me. All I did was take you."

"I'd've died, you didn't."

"Maybe." Clement sat on a stool with his back against the wall. The luminous hands of his Swiss watch told him the time. He had promised to stay in the room until Junior fell asleep, which he feared would be a long time coming. Junior's voice was full of raw energy.

"I had a whore."

"That's nice, Junior."

"Papa took me. She was black. His was too."

Clement sighed inwardly. "How was it?"

"Papa rushed me."

Clement rose from the stool and stood at the window, where he breathed in the scent of the pines and smells from the swamp. When he detected murmurs from his childhood he felt trapped inside his mind. "Next time," he said, "go alone."

"It was all the way to Boston."

"Can't you drive?"

"Sure I can, but I ain't got a license."

He looked at his watch again as night air bathed the quiet of his face. An owl hooted high in the pines. Gently he said, "Did you really shoot that woman?"

There was an immediate creaking of springs as Junior shifted about as if something were being exacted from him. The pitch of his voice rose. "Papa don't want me to talk about it."

Clement did not push. He suspected a sickness welling in his brother's stomach and, worse, the possibility of a fit. The silence that grew between them seemed feminine. It floated. It held secrets. Clement turned from the window. "Papa's right," he said. "You shouldn't talk about it."

Reassured, Junior said, "I still got the picture of you in the jeep. Did you see it on the wall?"

"I did."

"It don't have the same colors anymore. I have to look hard to tell it's you."

"It's me," Clement said and moved toward the door.

"I ain't sleepy yet!"

"You're not ever going to fall asleep long as I'm here."

"Why do you have to go to that motel? Ain't this better?"

"I've got a room. It's paid for."

"Papa says you ain't like us anymore."

The darkness had faded a little, and contours were returning to the sparse room. Clement discerned the glitter of his brother's face, which was probably feverish. "I have my own life now, Junior."

"When am I gonna have mine?"

"Aren't you happy?"

"I was happy when you was here."

"Aren't you happy with Papa?"

"It ain't the same."

Clement felt a hand squeeze his heart, and he moved closer to the door with a heavy foot, his body a stiff line. He remembered his brother as a baby burdened with an overplus of affection and bestowing drooly kisses. Anybody could make him laugh except Papa, who never took to him. "I'll be back tomorrow."

"Early?"

"Probably."

"Best time of day is when the dew's on the grass. Remember you used to say that?"

He was remembering too much, which irritated him. He did not want to be dragged back into a life best forgotten, best left in a box with all the pieces that could cut him. He was outside the room now. "Go to sleep."

"Clement." The voice was tentative. "Do you still think of her?"

He was stealing away, angry with himself, angry over dredging up images he felt were no longer a part of him. Outside the house, away from the ruined step, he rose up on his toes, drank the dark air, and killed a mosquito on his arm. Junior's voice wheedled through a screen.

"Clement."

"*What?*"

"I love you."

Stretched out on the sofa, James Morgan read until his eyes gave out. Too lazy to kill the lamplight, he placed the open magazine over his face and fell asleep breathing in the shiny scent of the printed page. When the telephone shrilled, he came awake as if someone had flung water in his face. He stumbled to answer it, first over his shoes and then over himself.

"Hello!"

There was no immediate response, and he waited, expecting the worst. It came. "Is this Chief Cock?"

He cringed. "Don't do this, Arlene."

"Do I have the wrong number?" Her throaty voice had strength, body, and insinuation. "I wouldn't want to make a mistake."

"What purpose does it serve?"

"Perhaps I have the right number but the wrong man."

He regretted the relationship, good only at the beginning, different, dangerous, and ever after hectic, demanding, frivolous. He had hoped it was over, cleanly done with, all wishful thinking. "Tell me what you want."

She said, "Are you the formidable police chief of Bensington, protector of the common good?"

Her voice was unnerving, part of her weaponry, as effective as her beauty. Once, in the ruffles of silken sheets, she had woken him with a harsh whisper in the shell of his ear: *Don't say a word. My husband's home.* A lie he believed. Her husband was in Europe on business. She had simply wanted to see whether his reaction would be worthy or cowardly. It was an uncertain mix of each.

"Look," he said, "if you want, we'll meet. We'll talk sensibly."

She was no longer on the line.

Clement Rayball drove his rented car to a house three streets from the heart of town and parked on the sidewalk, the front bumper nudging a hydrant. The street was heavy with shadows from a density of trees on each side of the street. Slowly he walked over moist grass in need of a cut, approached a lit window with a half-drawn shade, and peered in. Light from a lamp sluiced the solemn face of James Morgan, who seemed just a little older than Clement remembered him. Sharp eyes and an extra sense heightened by military training told him that Morgan was alone. He moved around to the front door and rang the bell.

The door opened on the second ring. Always he had felt a sense of inferiority in Morgan's presence, and he felt it now, faintly. Some things are never lost—all rooted, he reckoned, in childhood. Nasty business, childhood. He said, "Remember me?"

"Sure I remember you," Morgan replied in his stocking feet. "You haven't changed that much. Do you want to come in? If you don't, the mosquitoes will."

He stepped just inside the door and planted himself. The light showed up wear in Morgan's face, which at another time he might have considered an advantage. For a physical moment their eyes locked.

"Stories about you have drifted back, Clement. One is you deal in drugs."

"In Miami everybody deals in drugs."

"Then I heard you deal in women."

"Could be a little of both."

"How about guns?"

"Wherever there's a buck."

Morgan had an easy smile. "You must be doing well."

"I have good years, bad years. Yours must be all the same."

"This one's an exception." The smile remained. "When you went away I figured you'd never come back. 'Course, you never had reason till now."

"My father called me," Clement said with a hardness creeping into his voice, which could not be helped. His entire boyhood impinged on him.

"Papa's a short length of fuse that lights up."

"I know what my father is. It's my brother I'm concerned with."

"You have cause."

Clement had the answer he did not want but would have been surprised had it been otherwise. Fatalistically he accepted it, as he had accepted a lot of other things in life, and drew up his shoulders to leave. "I don't want to hurt you. You understand that?"

"And I don't want to hurt you, Clement, but I can't let another Rayball get away with murder."

"We've got nothing more to say."

He opened the door and stepped outside. The darkness offered anonymity but not safety—basic knowledge derived from his military training and later exploits in the warmer regions of the Americas. He felt Morgan's eyes on him as he headed toward his car. When he reached it, Morgan called out to him.

"I wish it were different."

He did not bother to reply.

6

At the waterline of sleep, where reality and dreams vie for attention, Lydia Lapham heard a car pause on the street and then creep on. That was at midnight. At three she woke short of breath, her heart racing, and was convinced she was dying. The silliest thought consumed her. Never again would she wash out her pantyhose and droop them over the shower rod to dry. Then her breath returned, and her heart caught hold of itself.

At six she was up. At seven, her aunt called, concerned, anxious. Lydia gave assurances that she was all right, which Miss Westerly was hesitant to accept. "Auntie, believe me." In a mirror she was aware of the dead calm of her face, a perfect match for her voice.

When Chief Morgan called a few minutes later, she said, "I'm going back to work." She sipped her coffee and heard him say that he thought that was a good idea. "I'm just a little uneasy about it," she admitted. "People will probably hammer me with kindness."

"For a while," he said.

"Did you drive by the house last night?"

"Yes."

"I thought so. Your car has its own sound."

At nine, with another cup of coffee, she phoned the hospital and told her supervisor that she would be reporting in for the evening shift. Advised that she should take her time, she said, "It is time," and asked about certain patients. Two had been discharged, one had died.

At the kitchen table she prepared a list, houseplants to replace those that had perished, fresh curtains for her bedroom, new locks for the doors, groceries of the convenient variety. Her mind wandered, first to Matt MacGregor and then to a man to whom she had not denied herself in nursing school. She had been nineteen. His name was Frank, a doctor, married. At the time it had seemed the tragic drama of her life. Now it seemed trivial.

In her bedroom she sorted through a dresser drawer of memorabilia, much of which she intended to throw out, but she found herself preserving the bulk of it. She read through high school test papers on Shakespeare. One question asked for the number of times Caesar's assassins had stabbed him. Twenty-three. She had gotten it right. Her notebooks from nursing school revealed a hurried hand, in parts unreadable. The stakes of t's were left uncrossed, the points of j's and i's undotted; n's, u's, and v's were one and the same. Doodlings on the margins were hearts pierced with arrows. At the end she threw away only snapshots of her and Matt taken randomly through the years when she was trying to convince herself he meant everything to her.

She made herself lunch, ate half, and was clearing up when the doorbell rang. Surreptitiously she glimpsed Reverend Stottle through a window. Instantly she shrank back and let him ring and ring. Finally he ceased. His voice came through the door.

"No one feels his parents have the right to die."

Matt MacGregor drove to Route 125 and followed it into Andover to the state police barracks, a brick building that flanked the entrance to a state forest. He parked in a visitor's space and climbed out with a scowl. He was in casual dress except for his sturdy shoes and the police belt in his jeans.

Inside, the young, crisp-looking trooper behind the desk gave him a cursory glance. "I'm expected," he said and felt color rise into the pug of his nose. "The name's MacGregor."

"You the officer from Bensington?"

"That's right."

He was ushered along a corridor and around a corner to a secluded room, where a small man in a summer-weight civilian suit was waiting at a table, his feminine hands lightly clasped. MacGregor instantly disliked the look of him, too neat, too meticulous. He was like the cleanest of cats. MacGregor half expected him to lick himself.

Rising, the man proffered a hand. He was from the Massachusetts Institute of Technology. His voice was treacle. "Sit down, Officer MacGregor. Relax."

MacGregor sat down, but he did not relax. He did not like a room without windows. Nor did he like the machine he was looking at. It looked medical.

"Have you ever taken a polygraph before?"

MacGregor shook his head. "First fucking time."

At the health spa at the country club Christine Poole stepped out of her frock and cringed at the sight of her flimsy underpants, which she never should have worn. They were much too small. The waistband had twirled itself into a cord well below the curve of her abdomen and the rest of the garment had shriveled into the crevice of her bottom. Quickly she donned a pink sweatsuit and hurried into the main area, where groups of women were exercising in a forceful atmosphere of good health. Arlene Bowman, a sweet figure in black tights, was waiting for her.

"Do only what you can," Arlene advised in a way that sounded like a challenge, which she immediately accepted. Arlene sauntered off to an advanced group, and she joined a squall of wide-bodied women trying to touch their toes and settling for their knees. With supreme effort, outdoing them all, she reached her shins, which flushed her face and revved her up. She felt ready to run a mile, scale a small mountain. With great heaves she brushed her ankles and paid the price.

An hour later, girded by a towel, she sat in the sauna and tried to ignore what the weight of her head was doing to the knot in her neck. The twinge in her back forced her to sit ramrod straight. Arlene, enjoying the vapors, her eyes closed, said, "This was only your first day."

"Maybe my last." Her hot skin was moist and pink, reminiscent of a shrimp peeled of its glassy pane.

"Where does it hurt?"

"Everywhere."

Arlene opened her eyes and smiled. "If our friend could see us now."

She did not want to respond but did. "Why would he want to?"

"It would make him wonder."

"Why should we care?"

"No man has the right to take advantage."

"I'm not sure he did."

They kept their voices low because other women, barely visible in the clouds of steam, were sitting beyond them, acquiescing to the wet heat rolling against them. Arlene mopped her face with a towel smaller than the one wrapped around her. Her eyes stood out. "Actually, it was his attitude. The son of a bitch thought he was saving me from something."

"Such as what?"

"Myself, I imagine. The arrogance of him."

Christine experienced a small inward shudder, for she had entertained somewhat similar thoughts about him, a man on a mission, a cop protecting marriages by seeing women through trying times. Always, when he was taking his leave, she had felt fully serviced but only half understood. Yes, the gall of him!

Arlene said, "This may come as a surprise to you, but he was my first extramarital affair. I wanted adventure. I wanted a lover who'd do anything for me, take all kinds of risks to be with me, but his biggest concern was that my husband would find out."

Floating through Christine's mind was a memory of lying in his arms and vaguely suspecting that she could have been anybody, any mock damsel in distress. "It was not that way with me," she lied.

"Maybe you expected less. By the way, are you still seeing him?"

"I broke it off, I told you that."

"He won't be grieving," Arlene said and swabbed the back of her narrow neck and the tops of her straight shoulders. Peering through the vapors, she discreetly directed attention to a woman who was sitting by herself. "Do you know who that is?"

Christine glimpsed a topknot of blond hair and scathingly white thighs that were beautifully big. "I have no idea."

"Sissy Alexander. Does the name mean anything to you?"

"Should it?" she asked and then got the drift. "I don't need to know all his women." The pain in her back streaked into her shoulders when she inadvertently moved. Her neck throbbed. With panic she said, "I don't think I can get up."

Arlene rose, breasts visible in the top of her towel, and extended a slim hand. "Do it slow."

She made it to her feet and out of the sauna and then into the privacy of a shower, where she found some relief under the needle spray, which she was reluctant to leave. Afterward, wincing with each wipe, she used the towel on herself but left her hair to dry on its own. The trial was getting into her underwear and dress, a slow and tormenting struggle. In her white pumps her feet were tippy. When she emerged in public she saw Arlene near the water cooler, waiting for her, ready for travel.

"Feeling better?"

"I'm afraid not," she said.

"Don't worry, I've got just the thing for you. His name is Pierre."

When Thurman Wetherfield had worked for the fire department, he had smelled of smoke even when he had not been near a blaze in months. Now he smelled of hard drinking. His breathing was a wheel sharpening a knife, and his hair, most of it a memory, was the color of cold ash. Perched at the bar of a Lawrence tavern he punched out his cigarette and ignored the man seating himself nearby. His eyes were on pictures on the wall behind the bar, poster-bright drawings of contemporary Boston ball players. Rattling the ice in his empty glass, he felt the man smiling at him.

"Remember me, Thurman?"

He gave a slow look. "Yeah, you're the Rayball went away. Army, wasn't it?"

"Special Forces."

"Yeah, but there wasn't a war."

"None we were supposed to be fighting," Clement said and, peeling a bill from a roll, motioned to the bartender. "Give my friend whatever he's drinking, a Miller for me."

Thurman lit another cigarette and said, "You still in those Special Forces?"

"I've been out awhile."

"You look like you done well. Nice watch. Those alligator shoes you're wearing?"

"You can get them handmade in Florida."

The bartender brought their drinks, and Thurman took his without thanks. "I'm doing all right too. I got a gal here in Lawrence. We live together." He rattled his rye and took a solid taste. There was a shaker of salt on the bar. He sprinkled some in his palm and licked it. "You better not flash that roll of yours on the street, you'll get knifed. City's half spic."

"They won't bother me. I speak the language."

"Far as I'm concerned, that's against the Constitution, but each to his own. I'm broad-minded."

Clement ran a thumb around the rim of his beer glass, then decided to drink from the bottle. "I heard you left the fire department."

"Wasn't never much of a department. Six permanents, the rest volunteers. I got out on disability."

"I helped you put out a fire once. I think it was one you set."

Thurman tossed him a suspicious look, which quickly broke into a smile. "Never no proof of that, and it don't matter anyhow. Too much time gone by." He shook more salt in his

Andrew Coburn

hand and gave it a good lick. "You just wander in here, or was it on purpose?"

"I asked at the firehouse. Fellow there mentioned a few places you might be. Before that, I saw your wife. She didn't know where you were."

He winked, man to man. "That's how I want to keep it."

"She says she sews for a living."

"Good money in that."

"She didn't look like she was living in luxury."

Thurman's noisy breath came out crooked. "She's got her life, I got mine."

"I can understand that," Clement said, glancing away. There were only two other customers, both sitting half hidden around the curve of the bar. The bartender was making himself an Alka-Seltzer. "I've been away a long time, Thurman, I need someone to fill me in. You've always had a handle on things, right?"

"Sure," he said importantly. "Firehouse you hear every-thing, but I don't get there much anymore. What do you want to know—something about the shooting?"

"That doesn't interest me. We've got a police chief to take care of it."

"Morgan's too busy chasing ass," he snorted with gravel in his voice. The cigarette burned his fingers, and he put it out. "He goes after the rich bitches in the Heights."

"You're kidding."

"Hell I am," he said and used hot fingers to tick off the names of women, here a rumor, there a fact. Then he pointed to the pictures on the wall and singled out the ball player with the biggest smile. "You know who that is, don't you?"

"I saw him play exhibition in Florida," Clement said with only mild interest. Something had altered in his face.

"He lives in Bensington. While he's shagging flies, Morgan's scoring on him at home."

"One of those other names you mentioned, was it Bow-man?"

"Yeah, wife of some big shot. She's a real looker, kind you see in magazines."

"You know the husband's first name?"

"No, but I heard he's rich as God. He runs corporations." Lifting his glass, Thurman drank up. Lowering it, he was surprised to see Clement slipping off the high chair, leaving behind a couple of small bills on the bar. "You going? Is that all you wanted to know?"

"It's enough," Clement said, turning away. Then he swung back with a queer smile. His hand shot out and gripped Thurman's wrist, unpared nails digging in. "A man should take care of his woman."

The grip was steel. Clement let go, still smiling, and left. The bartender came over and said, "What the hell was that all about?"

"Beats the shit out of me," Thurman said, nursing his wrist. Skin was torn, the bone felt bruised, perhaps cracked.

"Better put something on it."

"Whole Rayball family's crazy," he muttered to himself and reached for the salt.

May Hutchins did a washing, mostly her own things, and then, instead of using the dryer, hung the clothes outside on the line for the hot, fresh smell of sunshine. An hour later from the kitchen window she glimpsed a stunted figure in the yard, which held her attention until she distinguished the face, an echo of the father's. She got on the phone without moving from the window. "Meg, this is May Hutchins," she said and explained the problem with less alarm than the day before when the wasp had nearly stung her. Twisting the cord around her finger, she said, "Don't send Eugene, all right?"

Outside, Junior Rayball was oblivious of May Hutchins's eyes upon him, and he did not hear the screen door open a few minutes later. He was drifting among her clothes, avoiding the float of an apron, which was too large and emotional for him, though he could not fathom the reason. It was another mystery to knock about inside his head. Instead, face first, he was driven to a frayed oyster white slip, the sight, feel, and taste of which was immensely satisfying, a hit to his senses. "Mama," he said.

Andrew Coburn

"I'm not your mother," May Hutchins said.

He could have run; he didn't. May's helmet of metal curlers glinted. With her hand on her hip, she fed his eye while a memory in his mouth melted before he could taste it. "I was talkin' to myself," he said.

"We all do that."

Her voice was unthreatening. A smile broke her face into warm, reassuring pieces. "My mother's dead," he said.

"We've all got sadnesses, Junior. I've lost my best friend."

"Did you know my mother?"

"Not to speak to. She didn't leave the house that much."

"Did she look like you?"

"No, she was pretty."

Her voice nibbled his ear, and he arched his back as though a hand inside his shirt had run a feather down it. "And she was younger," he said, though he was asking. He wanted reaffirmation.

"Yes, younger. Don't you have pictures?"

"They were all torn up," he said. "Papa didn't want her in the house anymore."

She began taking clothes from the line. He helped. Another smile crumbled her face. "You're not very tall, are you?"

"I got a hole in my height," he said. "That's what a teacher told me."

They were standing together, near a full basket of clothes, when Chief Morgan appeared. The chief stopped and stood still, seemingly outside the frame of Junior's attention. Junior felt safe and protected in the nearness of May Hutchins, especially when she swayed closer and put sweetness in the air. "He didn't do anything," she called out. "He just kind of wandered in."

"Is that right, Junior?" The chief came forward. "Just visiting?"

"That's all he was doing," May Hutchins said and shared a look with the chief, an understanding of sorts.

"Anything in your pockets, Junior?"

Nothing but a soiled nugget of cotton, which he produced and let fall. The chief took him gently but firmly by the arm, which did not distress him. Nor did the bark of a neighbor's dog when they stepped onto the sidewalk. Only when he got into the chief's car did his throat knot.

"You gonna arrest me?"

The chief started the motor on the first try and pulled onto the street. "No need for that. I'm your friend."

"You gonna tell my father?"

"Not if you don't want me to."

Junior closed his eyes when they passed Drinkwater's Funeral Home; he opened them when the chief took a left at the end of the street. With utmost confidence he said, "I don't have to talk to you. My brother's home."

"It's up to you, Junior, you know that."

He noticed that the chief, slouched back, drove with a light touch on the wheel, unlike Papa, who threw himself against it and gripped it fiercely near the top. He was not sure where they were going because the chief took turns that did not make sense. Houses took on airs.

"Know where we are, Junior?"

On one of the great lawns a man was practicing his golf swing. "Where the rich people live."

"I liked it when it was all woods. How about you?"

"It don't matter to me," he said and went silent. Listless one moment, he was restless the next. His fingers drummed on the worn knees of his jeans while the chief drove aimlessly, no rush. A crow came out of miles of sky and planed a field. The sun was burning big. Then the chief took a straight course, and his heart tensed. "You drive up to the house, Papa will know."

"I'll let you off before we get there."

There was still a way to go. "Why you drivin' so slow?"

"The both of us, Junior, we've been running uphill all our lives. It's about time we took a rest."

He could not remember running up any hills lately, but he liked the sound of the words. He liked the easy way the chief drove with a single finger on the wheel and an elbow out the window. He wanted to say something, but the sentence unraveled on him. The chief was looking at him.

Andrew Coburn

"Sometime, you and I, Junior, we'll talk about her."

"Who?"

"Your mother."

"I don't have one."

"You did once."

"You don't know anything about her."

"I know something about her. I'm the one who found her."

He was sweating under the arms and across the chest. His skin poured through his T-shirt. He was glad when the road narrowed and the scent of pines filled the car. His hand was already at the door when the chief pulled over and glided to a stop near the mailbox. He clambered out with a stumble and hesitated in the gnat-tormented air. The chief leaned across the seat.

"What is it, Junior?"

He spoke shyly, almost indistinctly. "Did my mother wear an apron?"

"I imagine she did," the chief said. "And I bet it was the prettiest one in town."

"No," Junior said. "It was plain."

Lydia Lapham was back at work. Her white uniform dazzled. Nurses huddled around a desk glimpsed her and swept forward with warmth and kindness, bestowing no more than she could handle. A doctor in a scrub suit started to pass her by and then stopped. In the old days when she was an operating room nurse, surgeons never had revealed hangovers. They knew she would tell.

"Nice to have you back, Lapham."

"It's where I belong," she said.

"But you're not in OR, are you?"

"I'm on the floor."

"Thank God," he said with a smile.

She greeted patients, introduced herself to new ones, read their charts, and took their temperatures. When the anorexic woman in Room 202 drooped an arm over the edge of the bed, a ring tumbled from her finger. "Let it lie," the woman said, but Lydia retrieved it, tightened it with tape, and returned it to the bony finger. Then she cranked the bed up and brushed the woman's hair.

In the room across the corridor she delighted the eye of an elderly man who had outlived two wives. His roommate, a frail youth suffering multiple maladies, closeted himself in the bathroom. When he came out she helped him back into bed, which proved a struggle, for he had little strength. His face bathed in sweat, he said, "I want to be normal. I want to pee yellow."

"You will," she said.

"That a promise?"

She swabbed his face. "A vital hope."

A few minutes later, somewhat light-headed from eating and sleeping erratically, she helped a lovely elderly lady onto a potty chair, where, undulant and slow, the fragile creature did her business. Back in bed, tethered to a mood, the woman said, "If only you could empty your mind the way you do the other."

Lydia tucked her in. "I know what you're saying."

"Do you?"

"Look at me."

The eyes were enormous. "Yes, you do."

She was in the corridor, still light-headed, when a doctor in a business suit swept toward her and reached for her hands. Had nobody been around he might have tried to kiss her. He had thick black hair cracked with gray, an agreeable face, and a gentle voice. "How are you?" he asked. "I mean, really."

How was she *really*? She didn't know. She said, "Fine."

They stepped aside for a male orderly pushing a cart of fresh towels that looked like shoveled snow. He had lost possession of her hands and was eager to get them back. She kept them out of reach. "Would it mean anything to you," he asked, "if I told you my wife has filed for a divorce?"

Once, ten years ago, it would have meant the world. "I don't think so," she said in a tone that did not convince him.

"I shouldn't have mentioned it. It's too soon."

"No, Frank. It's too late."

He was about to protest, gently, when a sound distracted

Andrew Coburn

them. The orderly had rushed out of Room 202 and, spilling towels, was gesturing to them theatrically. They raced along the corridor and into the room, he sprinting to one side of the bed and she to the other. There were mothballs in the anorexic woman's face. The eyes had rolled back. The body was already going cold, as if there had never been enough blood to warm it. He reached for the wrist but soon tossed it away and pressed an ear to the heart. Seconds later he began to pound. "Christ, she's my patient!" he said.

The body jolted with each slam. The woman smelled neither of life nor death but merely of the hospital. She smelled of serum shot through a needle, of alcohol rubbed into a sore place, of medication that had come up on her.

"It's no use, Frank."

He stepped back, and she lifted the woman's hand and held it for a moment. The ring, securely in place, seemed the biggest thing about the hand. The woman's hair, though lacking light, was neatly brushed.

"Well, she's at peace," he said.

"She's nothing now," Lydia said. "She's nowhere."

With big, tender thumbs Pierre worked the small of Christine Poole's back. His thumbs picked up pain and kneaded it away, surrounded a quivering ache and dissolved it. In his T-shirt and cotton trousers, he was a blur of baldness and white. His thumbs shifted and pressed deeper. "Right there?" he asked, and closing her eyes, she murmured, "Yes, right there." Presently his touch traveled to her neck and loosened the knot. His huge hands lifted her head and rocked it from side to side, a baby in a cradle. He worked on her for thirty minutes in all and left her feeling pleasurably altered. When she slipped off the padded table she grappled with the towel, unable to hide everything.

"It's all right, he's used to it." Arlene Bowman, unforgivably beautiful, spoke from a great wicker chair, where her denimed legs protruded. "We don't turn you on, do we, Dennis?"

"I thought you said his name was Pierre."

"Professionally it's Pierre. Right, Dennis?"

"It's whatever you want," he said.

Christine vanished behind a screen. He was gone when she reemerged in her dress and white pumps. Some of the ache reasserted itself but nothing like before. Through sunshine pouring in from the great windows Arlene appeared with freshly poured sherry, which they carried out to the immense patio, where they sat on a white stone ledge. They clinked glasses.

"I feel wonderfully weary," Christine said.

"Dennis is a lovely man."

"Doesn't he ever smile?"

"It would give him lines."

Christine looked over the ledge, where the flower garden was a marvelous confusion of colors clumping into one another. The blue bells of campanula smothered their foliage, primrose of pink and yellow appeared pampered and sulky, madonna lilies radiated purity, but theatrical red roses, lurid in the wings, hogged the show. She said, "Did you ever buy Morgan a present?"

"I don't recall ever buying any man a present."

"A little one. Quite personal."

Something clicked. "How did he look in them?"

"Ridiculous."

"I thought rather cute." Arlene's smile turned mildly curious. "How did you know?"

"I knew he didn't get them himself. Not his style."

"I was having fun with him. Poor man didn't know how to take me. I'm his mystery."

Furrows in Christine's brow deepened as she stared over her glass of sherry. The biggest butterfly she had ever seen alighted on a lily and shut its wings. "When you met, who made the first move?"

"He wouldn't have dared," Arlene said.

The butterfly's wings were straight up, chafing, meshing as gears with the sunny air. "Why did he bother with me when he had you?"

"He could never believe his good luck." Arlene spoke easily, comfortably, with some joy. "I wasn't real. You were."

　　　　　　　　　　　Andrew Coburn

"Yes, that makes sense." She spoke from a dry mouth and wet it with sherry. "You're beautiful, and I'm all over the place."

"We're fixing that."

"Thing is, he was good for me. I needed him, he knew it."

"Don't make him into a saint."

The butterfly flew away in the direction of the glittering swimming pool. Christine leaned sideways on the ledge, sniffed a rose, and pulled back, inebriated by the scent.

Arlene said, "Are you sure you won't see him again?"

"I may. I have something to return to him."

Arlene reached into a pocket of her jeans. "Then you might give him this."

"What is it?"

"A key to his house."

It dropped into her hand, more of a weight than she had expected. She clenched it. "I have the feeling you want to hurt him."

Arlene smiled. "Only till he says uncle."

Bertha Skagg, who had relieved Meg O'Brien, was a floral shape at the telephone. Lieutenant Bakinowski ignored her and strode into Chief Morgan's office, where he propped a buttock on the corner of the desk. "MacGregor took the polygraph," he said.

"And?"

"It was inconclusive."

"The mere fact he took it goes a long way," Morgan said.

"He was hyper, like he was on something."

"He wasn't in the best of moods is more like it."

"Still pulling for him, huh, Chief?"

"And you're still shoving."

"Police work is like poker, same strategies," Bakinowski said, tightening the knot of his necktie. "If you don't play aggressively you'll lose every time. When you're defensive the cards go cold on you. You'll squeeze every one and catch nothing except those times another player's sitting on a full house while you're overfeeding the pot. Cards have a will of their own and admire an aggressive player, show no respect for a timid one. You understand what I'm saying?"

"Yes, you're telling me you're going to push MacGregor to the limit."

"Without hard evidence, I don't have a choice."

"You're reaching," Morgan said. "*Grasping* is a better word."

"You see him up close, Chief. I stand back."

"What if you're wrong?"

Bakinowski slipped off the desk, his smile magnanimous. "I'll be the first to admit it."

Papa Rayball said he was worried about Junior and did not want Clement to go back to the motel. "Won't hurt you to stay one night here," Papa said. "You'll help settle him."

"What's the matter with him now?"

"You never know," Papa said. "Could be anythin'. I've had my hands full."

They were drinking coffee out of chipped mugs at the kitchen table, Clement with his shoulders hunched. In ten years he had acquired a false self that had all but buried the old one. He did not want it back. He did not want Papa's eyes boring in on him, practically reading his mind.

Papa said, "I've already set up your cot in the room. That'll please him, you bunkin' in with him."

Clement did not respond to him, holding in an anger undefined and undirected. Papa was too easy a target, like the mustached faces he had aimed a fast-fire rifle at in tropical places where the heat could drive you crazy and the insects could eat you at will.

"You ain't sayin' nothin'. Maybe you ain't happy bein' with us. Maybe you ain't a Rayball anymore. You somethin' else now, Clement?"

"I'm here, aren't I?"

"I see you, but I ain't sure. Maybe you think it was my fault what Junior done."

"He gets through this, let's make sure it doesn't happen again."

Papa's eyes burned. "I ain't done bad by him, considerin'

the odds. And you always babied him when I was trying to teach him things."

"Maybe you taught him too well."

"I ain't gonna answer that. I don't have to."

Clement rose and went to the stove, where his mother used to boil water, the kettle singing the only song in her life, Junior at her skirts, thumb in his mouth. He remembered her rising from a scrubbed floor only to have Papa track it with the rippled prints of his work shoes. Pouring more coffee, he said, "Everything all right with the money?"

"I've been cashin' the checks," Papa said, "if that's what you mean."

"Have you been putting aside what I told you for Junior?"

"Yeah, ain't likely I'm gonna cheat him."

"When you get a chance, let me see the book."

"They don't give books anymore, you get statements."

"I know what you get. The last statement will do."

"His name ain't on it if that's what you're gettin' at. He ain't bright enough to have a bank account in his own name. And you ain't his meal ticket, I am."

Clement carried his coffee mug to the window. Moth wings and bug bodies littered the sill; a spider crept through the debris. "I'm thinking about his future, Papa."

"His ain't ever gonna be dif'rent. Mine neither."

He had drunk too much coffee, and his bladder interrupted his sleep during the night. It was not until he returned from the toilet that he realized Junior was not in his cot. He slipped into trousers and a shirt and went barefoot outside, where he heard a branch fall from a distant pine and shatter its twigs on the ground. Tree frogs shrilled. He walked slowly and carefully, his eyes sweeping over moonlit weeds to a seated shape on a stump.

"What are you doing, Junior?"

Junior was sitting forward with his elbows on his knees, his eyes cast toward the deeper shadows where the pines mingled with the swamp. The moon was yellow. "Sometimes," he said, "I can hear her out there."

Clement crouched. "It's your head hearing things, not your ears."

"You comin' back makes me think of her more."

"Maybe I shouldn't have come back."

The darkness in the pines quivered in places the way water pulses where fish lurk. Junior said, "Did Papa kill her?"

"Nobody killed her," Clement said. "God took her."

Junior said, "I hate God."

7

The corporate headquarters of Bellmore Companies was a tower of steel and glass in downtown Boston. Bellmore holdings, scattered throughout the Northeast, comprised shopping malls, office parks, hotel complexes, and condominium villages. The prerogative and power of the chief executive officer emanated from a clear, quiet appearance and an undeflectable gaze. The high walls of his office pulsed with contemporary art. The carpeting had an aura of depth, as if the bodies of lesser men had disappeared into it. Beyond his desk Boston peered in through thicknesses of glass.

Seated at his desk, he did not look up when his secretary of ten years brought her face down to his. Sadness entered her kiss, for she had given up on possibilities. She received no acknowledgment of the steaming black coffee she had set before him, for he expected things without asking and took them without thanks. He had an ice-smooth personality, his true feelings frozen deep.

Without warning, he rose and stretched as an athlete might before picking up a bat or tossing a ball at a hoop. He was of medium height and neither thin nor fat, though his face had a boyish pudginess that rimless glasses stiffened. His dark blond hair was neatly barbered, his jaw closely shaved, and his intelligence honed by an inexorable will to excel. Lately, however, he had been using all his intelligence to maintain viability in a misbehaving economy, brought on in some measure by his own strategies and tactics. Resinking into his high-back executive chair, he said, "Pembrooke."

That was his secretary's surname. She was halfway to the door when she stopped and turned, composed and gracious, a smooth golden bun behind her head.

"Am I free for lunch?" he asked.

She returned to his desk, opened his calendar book, and flipped to the page on which she had written *C. Poole, Mercury Savings, 1 pm*. She read it aloud.

"Christ," he said. "That will be a bore."

Two hours later, Calvin Poole arrived twenty minutes early and waited more than a half hour in comfortable circumstances with a current *Newsweek* Pembrooke had provided. He lifted himself up with dignity when she looked back in on him and said, "Mr. Bowman is meeting with you in his private dining room. I'll take you there."

The dining room had a clubby look, dark oak, with early American paintings on the wall. Gerald Bowman greeted him briskly, a man's handshake, all business. Bowman, in charcoal gray, was younger; Poole, in pinstripes, was taller. Bowman said, "You look tired."

Lunch was sole smothered by a delectable sauce, with broc-coli heads and carrot slices on the side. The servings were of a size meant for men watching their weight, though Poole had no cause to watch his. The middle-aged woman who served them was eager to please, quick to anticipate a complaint, of which Poole had none and Bowman had many. He distrusted cutlery and glassware and saw spots where there were none. Poole looked for the salt until he remembered Bowman did not allow it on the table. He attempted small talk.

"Our wives have been seeing a bit of each other."

"Good that they should get together. I believe they both went to Wellesley."

"I didn't know that," Poole said.

"We share something."

Poole had gone to Andover and Harvard, Bowman to Boston University on a full scholarship. His air of privilege was acquired, his ambition was innate. From the day he had entered the business world he had been perpetually on the move for a higher salary, a better golf score, a drier martini, and a greater climax. The climax diminished in importance when money and power delivered a heftier punch.

"Don't you like the fish?" he asked.

"It's delicious." Poole's hand trembled when he lifted his water glass, which was of heavy cut crystal. "I'm afraid we share something else," he said. "A problem."

"Ah, yes," said Bowman. "The loan."

Two years before, a subsidiary of Bellmore Companies had begun building an immense shopping complex in western Connecticut, with Mercury Savings and Loan providing the lion's share of the financing and pumping in more money when urgency demanded it. Now the project was at a standstill, ninety percent completed and less than thirty percent occupied.

"The whole country's hurting," Bowman said philosophically. "We really should have learned something from the Japanese."

Poole kept his voice under control. "Can you at least resume the interest payments?"

"Very good fish," Bowman said as the woman cleared away their plates and replaced them with dessert, small portions of Indian pudding. "Thank you very much," he said with unaccustomed civility.

"Nothing has been paid for four months," Poole said.

"That long?"

"I wouldn't want to be forced to repossess the properties."

"I'm sure you wouldn't. What would you get—a dime on the dollar? This is crunch time for everybody, separates the men from the boys."

"I understand that." Poole's voice stayed strong and, to a degree, hopeful. "I'm sure we can work something out."

Bowman consumed his dessert with three spoonfuls. Poole did not touch his. The woman quietly disappeared. "I'm afraid in this instance we're both going to take a bath," Bowman said and called the woman back. "We'll have our coffee now."

"I could go under," Poole said starkly.

"Nonsense. The bank could go under, not you. And is that such a bad thing?"

Coffee was poured. Poole creamed and sugared his but did not trust himself to lift the cup. He looked at paintings on the wall. A fury of colors was in one, the blood of a sunset in another. He watched the woman linger and then leave.

"How old are you, Poole?"

"I won't outlive my wife."

"Take my advice," Bowman said. "Go with the tide."

"He's not in," Meg O'Brien said to Lieutenant Bakinowski and clamped her lips over her pony teeth.

"I don't need to see him," Bakinowski said. "I just want to look at the old Rayball file, the woman who drowned or hit her head or whatever. Mind getting it for me?" She hesitated, glancing over at Sergeant Avery, who was picking his nose. "I think he'd like me to see it," Bakinowski added.

Sitting at Chief Morgan's desk, he opened the dog-eared folder and read the reports slowly and carefully. He scanned the brittle newspaper clips, which carried no pictures of the victim. The only photos of Eunice Rayball were those taken at the scene and in the hospital morgue. He stared at them for some time but could get no sense of the woman. Death had taken everything. He closed the file, left it beside the chief's calendar block, and returned to Meg O'Brien.

"Tell me about Eunice Rayball," he said. "What was she like?"

"Nobody knew her that well," Meg said. "She didn't get out much. But a sweet thing, what we saw of her."

"Wasn't she from Bensington?"

"She grew up in Lawrence, St. Ann's Home. That's an orphanage. At sixteen she was working in one of the Lawrence mills. Papa had a job there, janitor or something. That's how they met."

"Are you talking about Ralph Rayball?"

"Everybody calls him Papa. He married her young and made her old."

"Why do you say that?"

"Just my opinion," Meg said with an edge.

Bakinowski looked over at Sergeant Avery, who was drinking root beer from a can. "That your opinion too, Sergeant?"

"What Meg says, I say," Sergeant Avery replied, wiping his chin.

"That's it?" Bakinowski challenged. "Nothing to add?"

Sergeant Avery thought for a moment. "She was pregnant when they married. Everybody knew that, except maybe Papa."

"Of course he knew," Meg said. "She was showing."

"Was it his?" Bakinowski asked.

"That's the queer thing," Sergeant Avery said. "Clement, the first, he never looked like any Rayball I knew, but Papa always favored him. It's Junior, the second one, Papa had doubts about, which is crazy. They're two peas in a pod."

"Junior is slow," Meg said.

"And Papa?"

"Ornery is what he is," Meg replied.

"And sharp as a tack," Sergeant Avery said. "My uncle used to play cards with him."

Bakinowski lifted a cuff and read his watch, then compared it with the clock on the wall, which was a minute more. "The chief seems to think that Rayball killed his wife," he said, looking at Meg. "What do you think?"

"On a possibility scale of one to ten, I'd give it a seven, but the chief knows more. He gives it a ten."

"I give it an eleven," Sergeant Avery said.

"I see." Bakinowski straightened and buttoned his suit jacket. "And who fired the shot that killed the Laphams?"

Sergeant Avery, squashing the empty root beer can, looked at Meg and deferred to her. She said, "I can tell you with certainty it wasn't our Matt MacGregor."

At the hospital cafeteria Matt MacGregor, out of uniform, got himself a cup of coffee and carried it to a back table where a man with salt-and-pepper hair was eating his lunch. "You don't know me, Doctor," MacGregor said, "but do you mind if I sit down?"

The doctor looked up from his soup, into which he had crushed crackers. "I know who you are, Matthew. I've seen you with Lydia often. Sit down."

MacGregor drew a chair, a light of noble purpose in his eyes. When he seated himself, heavily, the light faded a little, then reignited. "Long time ago, Doctor, I used to be jealous of you, you probably know that."

"A long time ago you might've had reason. Since then I've been jealous of you."

"I've known her since we were kids. Our first real date I took her to a McDonald's and stole a souvenir. The napkin she wiped her mouth on. That's how bad I had it for her."

"That doesn't surprise me," the doctor said and resumed eating his soup.

"I'm worried about her."

"She's a survivor."

"Somebody should be looking out for her, Doctor. I don't feel I got the right anymore."

"Look, Matt, forget I'm a doctor, all right? My name's Frank. We're two guys with deep feelings for the same woman, and we're both in the same boat. She doesn't want either of us."

The light in MacGregor's eyes flickered. "Is that the truth? She didn't leave me for you?"

"Ask her."

"I don't want to bother her anymore."

The doctor sipped milk from a straw, his gaze angling to a table occupied by a lone woman who apparently had been visiting someone. She wore her hair short, shaped like a mushroom, which emphasized the length of her neck. The back of her neck was shaved. Her earrings were the dangling sort.

"And I didn't want to bother you."

The doctor's eyes journeyed reluctantly back to MacGregor. "Life's too short not to get on with it, Matt. That's

Andrew Coburn

the best advice I'll ever offer, appropriate to everyone, including myself."

"She said something like that."

"Yes, she would."

MacGregor tasted his coffee and wanted no more. Rising, he said, "Don't tell her I talked to you."

"No reason that I should," the doctor said and managed to catch the woman's eye.

Chief Morgan slept late. He had been up much of the night cruising Lydia Lapham's neighborhood and peering at the fronts of darkened houses where people had gone to bed hours ago. He could have had his night officer perform the duty, but he saw it more as a mission, a personal obligation, a response to feelings he had not yet put into words and perhaps never would. Lydia, home from the hospital at eleven-thirty, did not put the lights out until three. That was when he parked near the house, rolled all the windows down, and listened to sounds of the small hours. The howl of a cat in heat mimicked the bawl of a baby.

Now he was in his own house and pulling himself from bed, running his hand over the stubble on his jaw. The first thing he did was phone the station to say he would not be in for a while. Meg O'Brien, with a razor in her wit, told him to take his time, Lieutenant Bakinowski was making good use of his desk. When she told him the reason he was uncertain whether to smile or grimace. He did neither.

He was showered and shaved and dressed in chinos and a striped shirt open at the neck when the doorbell rang. It was Christine Poole, a surprise, for she had never come to his house before. She was costumed in a pink sweatsuit. A headband gave her an Olympics look. She stepped just inside the doorway, no farther, and smiled, sort of.

"I'm returning these," she said, and he knew immediately what was in the clear plastic bag, which he accepted tentatively. "Mrs. Bowman thought you looked cute in them. My opinion was different."

"Not my style," he said.

"That's what I told her. You'll also find a latchkey in there. She thought you'd want it back." Her smile evolved into a shape more gentle than not. "You have eclectic tastes with women, James. Or are we all the same to you?"

He had an urge to touch her, but he did not. "Hardly," he said.

"How's your back. Has it healed?"

"Pretty much."

She touched him. "I regret nothing we've had together, absolutely nothing, but I'm glad it's over. It never would have led to anything, am I not right?"

"We'll never know."

"Tell the truth."

"Probably not."

"That's what I always liked about you, James. You never made false promises. The fact is you never made any promises at all, and you took only what was offered. But what you got was more than you deserved, which I don't hold against you, unlike your other friend." She moved back a step, with a more comfortable pitch to her voice. "Do you like my outfit? I'm on my way to becoming a new woman, one who doesn't need an extra man in her life for whatever spurious reasons that come to mind."

"I understand," he said.

"Yes, of course, you would—and you did your job, James. You aroused my large, dozing breasts. I know what you're thinking, it didn't take much. But now it's time for the rest of me to awake. I want to look in the mirror and feel good— all by myself, no need of you."

When she took another step back, he teetered forward. "Christine. You're a wonderful woman."

"Don't flatter me, James. I'm just a woman. But in some ways I'm stronger than your friend."

He walked her to her car, opened the door for her, waited while she started the motor, and watched her buckle up. On the seat beside her was a videotape of *Jane*

Fonda's Beginner's Workout. "We still friends?" he asked.

"We were never more than that," she said, putting on over-size sunglasses that consumed the greater part of her face. She looked out at him. "I can understand what attracted you to Arlene Bowman, but you must've known you were playing with fire."

"That's over and done with," he said.

"Then I must warn you. You may still get burned."

Lieutenant Bakinowski, driving slowly on the rural road, scanned mailboxes. Then there were none. Pines reared up on each side, and a crow flew across the road like a thrown boot. Then he saw a crude sign nailed to a tree, BIKES REPAIRED, and a mailbox bearing the name he was looking for. Gravel and ruts took him to a small, weathered house. He looked at wild raspberry canes and wished the fruit were ripe. He saw an abandoned bicycle that could have been the cadaver of the one he had ridden until it was handed down to a younger brother. Climbing out of the car, he peered through live pines to dead ones populating a swamp, which queerly gave him a sense of his own boyhood, mostly the mysteries.

"You lookin' for me?"

The voice startled him. He looked toward the doorway of the house and saw a character from the comic books of child-hood, a Yokum or a Snuffy Smith, a sawed-off creature in old clothes, with eyes as blue as any Polack's, bluer than his own. "Ralph Rayball?"

"Ain't nobody called me Ralph in years. People call me Papa." Bakinowski approached him, identified himself, and showed his shield. Papa, stepping aside, did not bat an eye. "Come in." Bakinowski maneuvered over a dilapidated step and entered a kitchen, where coats and jackets hung from pegs, a greasy stove stood on legs, and a younger version of the cartoon man peered up from his eating. "This is my boy Junior."

Bakinowski, whose mother had been reared in West Virginia coal country and had passed on stories, wondered whether any Scotch-Irish blood flowed through the veins of these two. His mother's younger brother, he had been told, had not gotten enough air at birth, and he wondered whether the same had been so with Junior. "Hello, Junior."

"Hello, sir." Junior ate with his face in the plate. Beans mixed in ketchup. He raised a glass, and his nose touched what he tasted, which looked like apple juice.

Papa said, "My firstborn, Clement, he's come up from Florida. He ain't here right now."

"Do you know why I'm here, Mr. Rayball?"

"Sure I know. Chief Morgan thinks my boy here did somethin'."

Junior spoke with his mouth full. "What'd I do, Papa?"

"Nothin'. You almost done eatin'?"

"Don't rush," Bakinowski said. His mother's brother had operated on a short fuse but never harmed anyone, died young, and had been buried in the coal country. He watched Junior wipe his mouth and carry his plate to the sink. The refrigerator made sounds like a human.

Papa said, "You go on outside so the man and I can talk— 'less you want him to stay."

"No, that's all right. You go on out, Junior." He watched him leave, pint-size like the father, in need of a haircut, his neck nappy.

"He's a good boy," Papa said. "Never finished school because kids picked on him."

Papa drew up chairs, and they sat opposite each other at the table. Bakinowski said, "I've heard it mentioned he's not a whole dollar."

"That's right. He's maybe seventy-five cents, but that don't give people the right, Chief included, to take advantage of him."

"Why would the chief do that?"

"He thinks we're trash, never liked any of us, but there's more to it than that. Maybe you've heard."

"Suppose you tell me."

"He thinks I killed my wife. That happened a long time ago. I've had to live with it."

"Did you kill her?"

"I ain't answerin' that anymore, I'm sick of answerin' it. Sick of bein' looked at for somethin' I never did." Papa pulled himself up in the chair. "But I'll tell you this. My wife used to meet somebody out on the road. I always had the suspicion it was him, but I never had no proof. He's a woman-chaser, you know."

"I read the former chief's report. Nothing in there about Morgan having known your wife."

"Ain't likely there would be. He used to kiss the old chief's ass—that's how he got Carr's job, plus suckin' up to the selectmen. He could say anythin' he wanted for that report. Carr would've wrote it that way."

Bakinowski looked toward the window. For a second he thought he saw Junior's shadow, but then he looked beyond the window and glimpsed him near a woodpile.

"But it don't matter no more," Papa said. "My wife's gone, I ain't never pretended I was sorry. Maybe that's why he never let up on me, on Clement neither. Tried to put words in Clement's mouth to use against me. Now he's trying to get at me through my youngest."

"Could he be right about him, Mr. Rayball?"

"*You* saw my boy. You tell *me* he shot somebody." Papa flumped a hand on the table. "You want some of that juice he was drinkin'?"

"No thanks, Mr. Rayball."

"You know, people don't call me *Mister* Rayball much. It don't sound bad."

Bakinowski rose, stiff in one knee. For the first time he felt the heat of the house. He loosened his necktie and opened his collar.

"You leavin'?"

"I thought I might talk to Junior first, alone. Do you mind?"

"Don't mind a bit. Just let me say somethin' 'fore you go. Morgan, he's thrown a lot of dirt at me, but I got an answer to that. You wanna hear it?"

Bakinowski nodded. He was tired. "Go ahead, I'm listening."

"You ever go fishin'? You ever dig for bait? The darker the dirt, the whiter the worm."

"I don't get the meaning."

"The meanin' is I ain't guilty of nothin' and neither is my boy."

Bakinowski opened the door, which had squeaky hinges. The screen was patched here and there, in some places left torn. Papa was at his elbow.

"Clement, he won't be here all that long. He's not permanent. Junior's all I got."

"I heard you didn't think he was yours."

"I reckon he is."

Bakinowski's arm brushed a torn part of the screen. He conjured up images of coal country girls precociously developed, the sort his mother had said got themselves in trouble. "Was your wife pretty, Mr. Rayball?"

"She was a slut. You asked, that's what she was."

Bakinowski stepped out into the sunshine, tramped over bright ground, and approached Junior, who was sitting on a stump with his arms wrapped around his knees. He was wearing a cap now. The name of a heavy-equipment company graced the front. Bakinowski pointed at the ground. "Isn't that poison ivy?"

"I never catch it. I can touch it, it don't do nothin'."

"Where'd you get the cap?"

"Place I used to work."

"Do you work now?"

"Not much."

Bakinowski crouched down for a better look into Junior's eyes. "I'm going to ask you something, and you just answer yes or no, OK? Did you shoot anybody?"

"No, sir."

He returned to his car while removing his suit jacket, which he tossed into the back. He gave a thoughtful look at the house and then a swift one as he drove away. It reminded him of a dented tin can with the label peeled off, which was how his mother with a bitter laugh had described the houses in the coal country.

Papa Rayball watched the car leave in a cloud of gravel, took a swig of apple juice from the jug, and with a liberated swing of his arms went outside to Junior, who was still sitting on the stump, the visor of his cap pulled lower over his eyes. "You did good," Papa said, standing over him. "You did real good."

Junior did not look up. His shoulders were slumped. He nibbled a nail.

"Did you hear me?"

Birds chanted. Junior said, "I heard what you said about Mama."

"You got big ears, always said that."

"Did you kill her, Papa?"

Papa slapped him in the face, savagely. The cap flew off. Junior rolled into the poison ivy. Papa shook a fist. "Don't ever ask me that again!"

Lying flat, Junior looked up with blotted eyes. "I betcha did."

In his room at the motor inn Clement Rayball phoned Florida, the hotel where he had a semipermanent residence, and got hold of the desk clerk whom he knew well. "I need a favor," he said. "Do you remember the woman I was sitting with in the patio bar the day I left. She still there?"

"Christ, Chico, you sit with a lot of 'em. What's her name?"

"I don't know her last name. Her first name might be Esther. Big, attractive woman, frosty hair, curly. She was there with her grandson and I guess her daughter."

"You're talking about Dr. Rosen. I forget her first name, but it's not Esther. She's a shrink, did you know that?"

"She still there or not?"

"They checked out this morning."

"Look in the phone book, see if she's listed. No, never mind. It's not important."

"Chico, when you coming back?"

"Soon, I hope," he said and rang off.

He went into the bathroom, brushed his teeth, washed his face, and slicked his hair back; then he looked at his watch. It was too early for what he had to do. He left his room and went to the bar, peering in before he entered. He did not want to run into the same woman. In his room it had taken him a half hour to calm her down, and the last look he had of her was haunting.

The bartender remembered him. "Miller, isn't it?"

"Usually," he said. "This time make it bourbon on the rocks."

Lieutenant Bakinowski phoned Chief Morgan from his office in the Andover barracks. "You got your story, Rayball's got his," he said. "Which am I to believe?"

"Believe what you want," Morgan said, "I don't give a damn."

"I thought that might be your attitude. I'm sorry to hear it."

"You got anything more to tell me?"

"I do, but I don't think you'd hear. You got a voice in your head twenty years old that drowns out everything else. I'm sorry for you, Chief."

The line went dead in Bakinowski's ear. He replaced the receiver and looked at the young detective who had come into his office to scan the Lawrence paper. "I'll give you some advice," he said to him. "Never trust a local cop. Every one of them carries baggage."

"That's what I was told at the academy."

"Then they taught you right," Bakinowski said and locked up his desk. On his way out of the office he snatched the newspaper from the young detective's hands and took it with him. Outside in the fenced-in parking lot he saw a Bensington cruiser parked near his car. Walking toward it, he said, "Something you want, MacGregor?"

MacGregor stepped out of the cruiser in full uniform but with nothing aggressive about him. His face was pale. "I took the polygraph, I want to know what more you want."

Bakinowski had rolled up the newspaper and was slapping it against his leg. "You're scared, aren't you?"

MacGregor spoke calmly. "I wish we could change shoes, then you'd know."

"I wouldn't be in your shoes for a million dollars. I'd cut my feet off first."

MacGregor did not respond. He climbed back into the cruiser and shut the door. He put his sunglasses on slowly, hanging his head one way and then the other in fixing the wire wings to his ears. His demeanor was quiet and controlled. Bakinowski stepped close to the open window.

"I knew you did it from the start. I smelled it all over you."

"You're wrong."

"That's right, I'm wrong. Florence Lapham fell dead of a mosquito bite, and her husband only fainted. Pretty soon he's going to dig himself out of the ground. Tell that to the daughter."

"She doesn't need me to tell her anything anymore."

Bakinowski pointed the newspaper at him. "I just want you to think about something. A yokel cop doing hard time. They'll tear you apart."

MacGregor drove away, and Bakinowski took a deep breath and felt better than he had all day.

As Reverend Stottle motored out of Bensington, the sinking sun shot red through the trees and lit every leaf as if burning heretics. He was on a mission of mercy. Mrs. Dugdale, the oldest member of his church, childless, widowed in her prime, lay dying in Lawrence General Hospital. He entered the unkempt little city with foreboding, for he knew failure. Never had he penetrated the inconsolableness of someone who had lost a mate, a child, or a parent. Untrained in marital counseling, he had made messes of several young couples' lives. But all these years he had tried to do his duty and had never shirked a responsibility. That surely was in his favor but did not prevent a shiver as he parked in the visitors' lot. Whose cold hand was that around his heart? The Devil's was hot, he had been taught. These fingers must be God's.

He did not need to ask directions to the room, though he paused near a nurses' station to get his bearings. An older nurse was mapping out patients to an aide. Anorexic was gone. Hemorrhoids was in 202 now, and Impaired Kidney was next door. Emphysema was sharing 213 with Diabetes. The nurse looked at him. "Can I help you, sir?"

No help needed, and he strode on, time was precious. The last time he had seen Mrs. Dugdale she had been propped in a wheelchair like a rag doll, and he had had to look twice to assure himself she was breathing. Entering her room, he saw that now she was buried in bed and wired to a glinting monitor whose jagged stream of hieroglyphics looked evil. No hope, he could see that.

"It's Reverend Stottle," he said, leaning over her, and she seemed to hear him. "Fear nothing," he said, aware that lately he feared everything. "You've had ninety-three long years, more than most people."

Her eyelids flickered but did not open. Her voice was feeble. She asked for the time.

"God is the dispenser of time, Mrs. Dugdale. If God ceases believing in Himself, all clocks stop. The whole universe ticks down."

Toothless, Mrs. Dugdale's face gathered around her mouth, where the pleats ran deep. Reverend Stottle stared at the intricate network of lines girding her throat. Emotion pressed him forward, putting words into his mouth.

"Nothing is deeper and darker than aloneness," he said, with thoughts of episodes in his own life. Mrs. Dugdale's lids shuddered, and he gathered up one of her tiny hands, a mess of bones gloved in loose skin speckled like a tiger lily. Touch was important. Sometimes it was the only way two human beings could connect. "Life, Mrs. Dugdale, is the light leading to the final darkness, where we shall each lie alone."

Her lids went still. He released her hand and stepped back. In the subdued light her face shone luridly. With another rush of emotion prickling his skin, he pressed a button on a cord and waited. Two minutes that seemed like twenty passed before the nurse who had spoken to him appeared.

"I think she's gone," he said.

The nurse pushed past him and bent over the bed. Her bottom was substantial, and the pink of her underwear blossomed through the white nylon of her trousers. He started to look away and then did not.

"No, Reverend, she's just asleep."

"Are you certain?"

"Quite."

He rode the elevator to the ground level and, around the corner in the lobby, went into the public lavatory. At the urinals he stood wedged between a burly security guard and a slender Hispanic and relieved himself with a dash of dignity he found lacking in them. Afterward at the double sink he splashed his hands with much ado when he saw that they were not going to wash theirs. Then, watching them leave, he wondered whether Jesus had always washed his. In those days feet got the greater attention.

He was on his way into the cafeteria when he saw a familiar figure on its way out. It was Lydia Lapham, stark and lovely in her whitest of whites. His eyes played tricks on him because she seemed no more substantial than mist over water. He stepped in her path, startling her.

"Lydia. We must talk. Soon." He felt in his own head what must be going on in hers, a terrible effort not to succumb to despair. With a moist grip on her slim wrist, he said, "Some things cannot be faced alone."

"Yes, soon," she said sharply and pulled away. "Not now."

Clement Rayball drove to the residence of Gerald Bowman, a great, fancy house but no grander than others in Oakcrest Heights, which surprised him until he remembered his reading of the man: self-righteous and self-denying, stiff in his thinking and dedicated to his causes. A tight ass. He rang the bell.

The housekeeper, who was on her way out, a pocketbook hanging from the crook of her arm, answered the door, and he smiled at her in a way that might have charmed a less haggard woman who had not been on her feet all day. He asked for Bowman, admitted he was not expected, gave no name, and argued, "I'm sure he'll see me."

"You'll have to wait here," the woman said and closed the door in his face. He waited, it didn't matter, he wasn't insulted. He turned around in the dying sunlight and breathed in the spiced air, which raised a memory of a squad tent with wooden sides and a concrete floor. His long-ago military training had been in Georgia.

Finally the door reopened, and the woman brushed past him, her pocketbook bumping him. In the doorway was Gerald Bowman, whose stare had the effect of an ice pick.

"What is it?"

"You don't know me, Mr. Bowman, but your name rings a bell with me. I used to do work for the government."

"So?"

"We had patrons. I thought you might've been one."

"I doubt it."

"I could be wrong."

"I guarantee it. What's your name?"

"Chico."

"You're right, I never heard of you."

Bowman started to close the door, and Clement spoke fast. "I've got something to tell you, confidential. You don't want to hear it, it's no skin off my ass."

Bowman's ice-pick stare went deeper. Then he let the door hang loose and stepped back. "You've got five minutes. Come in."

Clement was directed into a large room and told to sit. Bowman sat well away from him in a more comfortable chair. Drapes of heavy brocade both dimmed and cooled the room. Clement stared at a table whose cabriole legs tapered to elegant hooves.

Bowman said, "What are you doing in this town?"

"I have family here."

"I always figured guys like you didn't have any. All right, what do you want to tell me?"

Andrew Coburn

"It's tender," Clement said. "It could be something you don't want to hear."

"Don't play games with me."

"It concerns the police chief in town, name of Morgan, maybe you know him."

"I know we have one. Go on."

Clement's eyes shifted to the doorway and his head nodded as a woman stepped into the room. So this was the wife. Striking. Skin color was bone china, hair glossy black. He had expected nothing less. Her voice, wonderfully low, had body, strength, and insinuation.

"Yes, go on," she said.

"Are you sure?"

"Don't stop now," she said with huskiness.

His eyes were on Bowman. "The chief has a habit of stepping out of line with other men's wives. He's the fox in the chicken coop."

"My husband, I'm quite certain, has heard of the chief's recklessness."

"Yes, ma'am. I just wanted to be sure."

Bowman spoke from the confines of a frozen face. "Get out."

He rose with grace and a slight squeak from his alligator shoes. His bearing was military. "Don't feel too bad, Mr. Bowman. You're not the only one."

She was in her bedroom, where she had finished brushing her hair. Still sitting at her dressing table, where jewelry lay on velvet, she removed her earrings, golden teardrops with delicate engraving. When she rose, her body shimmered through her frail gown like light penetrating glass. Her stride into the adjoining bathroom highlighted the indisputable aristocracy of her legs. When she came out, he was standing there with a blue-steel .38-caliber revolver. His face had thawed. In his brow were lines drawn as if in hell.

"You know what I'm going to do," he said.

"No, Gerald, what are you going to do?"

He pointed the revolver at her, and she did not budge. He squeezed the trigger. In its own way the click resounded as loud as a shot would have.

"I knew it wasn't loaded," she said.

He lowered his arm. "One day it could be."

She approached him slowly, smiled into his face, kissed his cheek. Looking into his eyes, she pressed her hand to the front of his trousers, shaping her fingers to the outline of his penis as if it were a roll of bills. "Do you want to?"

"Yes," he said.

Much later he switched on the light and wrote out a check with a Mont Blanc fountain pen. The ink was sepia, which gave a timelessness to her name. This was a game they had not played in years. She looked at him from her pillow.

He said, "Why, Arlene? Tell me why."

"Happiness is other times, Gerald, never now."

He left the check in the light of the lamp and got to his feet. The ghost of his body lay damp on the sheet. He found his robe, colorful like a boxer's, and put it on. "How many others?"

"No others. Morgan used me. The way you use your secretary."

He let that slide and stared at her, his mouth a straight line. She lay uncovered. Her face was as fresh as soap stripped of its wrapper. Her skin was lucent between the ribs. He said, "So the chief's had himself a good time."

"You could say that. Before me it was the ball player's wife. Now it's Christine Poole, if you can imagine that."

"The man knows his business, does he?"

"I call him Chief Cock."

"You're pushing me."

"No, dear. You're asking. But you needn't worry. He may have more oomph, but you have your tricks."

Reaching down, he wrapped his hands around her narrow feet and squeezed. Her painted toenails glared as if he had drawn blood. "I don't want to hear."

"Then get even."

"With you?"

Andrew Coburn

"With *him*, you fool!" She kicked free. "Take away his job. Get him fired. Leave him naked."

Lydia Lapham got home from the hospital at eleven-forty and resolved to drink no more coffee, but soon she had a pot perking. It had been a stressful evening. The brief encounter with Reverend Stottle was upsetting, but the later arrival of a woman with razored wrists was unnerving, as if with mutilation the poor creature were defeminized, altered, checked. At eleven on the dot, as she was quitting her shift, she heard that Mrs. Dugdale had died, a blessing, but it unsettled her anyway.

In the living room she put on lights and drew the shades. On the coffee table was a slim volume of poetry she would never read. Most poems touched on things she did not want to think about. At the kitchen table, a window open to the noises of the night, she sat rigidly with her coffee until a muscle loosened in her back. On the table were the two pages of her father's unfinished letter to his wartime friend in Michigan. With his fountain pen she wrote a postscript. The words were black threads rising, dipping, curling, and looping. *He died with her*, she ended it.

Upstairs, trembling a little for no obvious reason, she began running a hot bath. In her bedroom was a pot of shasta daisies for replanting, a gift of sympathy from the hospital administrator. Undressing, she threw her uniform into a corner and then the rest of her things. Naked, she was frozen milk. Her nipples were wintry points. The sinister part of tragedy was the aftermath, the scouring of feelings, the trivializing of thought, for which her nurse's training had not prepared her. One could tear the head off a perfectly healthy flower and not feel bad about it.

She tilted the large dresser mirror, aiming it at the bed, which was tightly made. Lying atop the powder blue chenille spread, she regarded the shape of her legs, the size of her feet. With her eyes in the mirror, she lifted her knees and viewed herself as a lover might. The sight did not seem appetizing, but Matt, and Frank before him, had always found it so.

She took her bath and went to bed. An hour later, she was still awake. Clad in a sweater and dark trousers, she slipped out into the night. Trees were moon-washed. The night air pushed at her. She knew the car would be there. His head was tipped back. Chief Morgan was asleep. Some watchdog! She reached through the open window and touched his shoulder. He came awake instantly, his eyes full of false light.

"Come in," she said.

8

At the cemetery a large maple quivered with life. Leaves quaked. Birds flew in and out. And Fred Fossey stood with bowed head at the graves of Flo and Earl Lapham, no stone in place yet, only two markers, with a toy flag behind Earl's. "Bless you both," he said aloud, feeling the sun on his neck. The morning was hot, the sky as blue as the grass was green. The grass sent up its spiciest scents.

His gaze dwelled on Flo's marker. All these years in love with her, so much in love, with fantasy inherent in every thought he'd ever had of her. "You never knew, did you, Flo? Never for a moment. Or maybe you did. I bet you did. I hope so." He wiped the sweat from his neck with a handkerchief. "I'm sorry, Earl. That wasn't for your ears."

"You talking to yourself, Fred?"

May Hutchins, with flowers in her hand, had come up behind him. He was not embarrassed, not in the least—why shouldn't the world know? "I was talking to them both," he said.

May nodded with understanding. "They say the dead don't hear, but I wonder."

"They hear, but they don't answer."

The cut flowers in her hand were from her garden. She

crouched, ladylike, and lay them between the markers. The sun added fire to the curly red ends of her hair.

"I should've brought some too," he said, watching her rise. "Ethel's got some nice petunias. I could've brought those."

"Mine can be from both of us," she said with more understanding than he had realized, which touched him deeply.

"I'm not trying to slight Earl, but it's Flo I came to see."

"We both loved her."

"How did you know I did?" he asked, and she nudged him with an elbow.

"Hell, Fred, everybody's known that since high school. Flo once said to me if she hadn't married Earl she'd have married you."

The last part was a white lie that darkened as soon as she said it, but he appreciated it all the same. With emotion he looked down at Flo's marker, from which emanated a mournful indifference. He said, by the way, "Old Mrs. Dugdale died last night."

"Good Lord in heaven, I didn't know she was still alive. Who told you?"

"Ethel. She calls Drinkwater every morning to find out who's come in. That way she doesn't have to wait for the paper."

"God almighty, I wondered how she found out those things so fast."

"You take the telephone from Ethel's ear, you'll find she doesn't have a head, just pure Bensington air."

"That's not nice, Fred."

"You don't know the things I have to put up with."

"A major part of life is putting up with things, don't you know that?" Her elbow brushed him. "Could you move away for a while? I want to talk to my friend alone."

"I was just going anyway," he said, though he shuffled off reluctantly. On his way to his car, he passed the stones of Vietnam War veterans, whose battles, home and abroad, were over and whose ailments, physical and mental, were part of the soil. He also noted those who needed new flags.

Nearing his car, he glimpsed on the ground a flag honoring

one of the World War II boys, and he detoured to tend to it. Respectfully he returned it to the plastic holder and stepped back to read the name on the stone, which seemed to stand taller now as if it had risen a little out of the sod. The grave was that of Chief Morgan's father.

Taking another step back, he snapped off a little salute. From the maple a cardinal trilled, a jay squawked.

It was only a little after seven when crows woke Lydia Lapham with hysterical throat-clearing caws, as if a murderer were among them. She rose from her bed with too little sleep. Morgan, who had had less, was gone. Where was he? Her head couldn't tell her, and her nerves didn't want to know. A robe made her decent.

With the uncoordinated movements of broken sleep she stumbled past the dresser and knocked over a wicker waste-basket that contained the foil from a condom used twice and forsaken the third time.

The bathroom mirror showed her the state of her eyes and echoed the raggedness inside her head. A smile would have brought a small explosion to her face. Brushing her teeth, she remembered he had entered her with a sense of trespass and proceeded cautiously until she urged, "You can go harder than that, I won't break." After that, he had the snort of a bull, she the low of a cow. That was the way it was, the way she wanted it. Inadvertently, with his voice tangled in her hair, he called her Elizabeth, which didn't bother her in the least. Indeed, she relished being two sides of a spinning disk, flesh and spirit drawing on a common muscle the way darkness and light swing off the same hinge.

She brushed her hair and tightened her robe. She descended the stairs, expecting to see him in the kitchen, embarrassed by the prospect. Would his mouth fly open for a kiss? She hoped not. Would the healing qualities of his voice translate to the morning? She suspected not.

The old coffee thrown out, a fresh pot awaited her, along with a note written in his hurried hand with her father's pen. *See you soon.*

There should have been more than that, much more. She crumpled the note. With bitter anger she sailed to a window. His car was gone.

With her robe wrapped tighter than ever around her, she sat in the breakfast nook with her coffee and watched birds assault the feeder that dangled outside the bow window. The feeder was a plastic tube with a short perch and a hole that accommodated only smaller birds. A finch was at it now. The finch ignored her and fed.

The coffee gradually brought her back into existence, but she was still groggy. Her hands trembled. Her legs were not all that steady when she moved to the living room and let in light. With her head on one of her mother's fancy toss pillows, she stretched out on the sofa, where she napped an hour and woke partially restored. The telephone rang moments later. She scurried to it. It was he.

"Damn you," she said with joyful anger. "Damn you twice."

Eschewing the buffet, which reminded him of the military, Clement Rayball breakfasted in the formal dining room at the motor inn. The waitress gave him a dish of strawberries and a pitcher of cream for his cornflakes. His newspaper was opened to a story in the sports section. The Sox were back from a long road trip. Last night they had beaten Cleveland, Clemens the winning pitcher, three hits by Boggs. The only mention of Crack Alexander was that he was benched. A twisted ankle, it claimed.

At the next table a businessman was smothering himself in pancakes, his lips glittering. Clement glanced at him and flipped pages to the foreign section, where he read a lengthy article about Central America. He was halfway into another article when the businessman rose, billowing from his breakfast and tongue-lashing the waitress, little more than a child, for delaying his check. Closing the paper, Clement caught the man's eye. "It takes only a little effort to be good to people."

"I pay for service," the man snapped back.

"No," Clement said. "You pay for the privilege of being served."

The waitress, red-faced, scooted off, and the man said with satisfaction, "She knows she's not getting a tip."

"That's all right, I'll double mine," Clement said.

The man wheeled by him, then turned back from a safe distance. "What are you, a communist?"

"A Boy Scout of America," Clement replied with irony that flew over the fellow's head.

Several minutes later he left the dining room and stepped into the growing heat of the morning. The sun had much color. The sky might have been Florida's. Before slipping into his rental car, which was squatting in the heat, he opened all the windows. By the time he crossed the line into Bensington, the windows were shut and the air conditioner was heaving a chill breath.

In Oakcrest Heights he drove past the Bowmans' house and several others and cruised between stone lions into a curving driveway. The house was magnificently pretentious, quite suitable for a millionaire ball player. Two of the three stalls were open in the garage, exhibiting a Rolls Royce and a Jeep Cherokee. He stopped when he spotted a husky, bare-legged man jogging the perimeters of the extended front lawn. He climbed out, waited awhile, then walked toward him. They met on the grass.

"Something you want?"

"I've been a fan of yours for years," Clement said. "I was worried. I read in the paper you got benched, bad ankle."

"It's OK, just sore." In the heat Crack Alexander's thinning hair lay misdirected on his head, like spill from a bottle. He looked older than his pictures, and bigger. He stood well over six feet, superlative in voice and manner. He lifted his T-shirt with a huge hand and mopped his face.

"We're all pulling for you," Clement said.

"I ain't worried. No reason you should be."

Inside the man's bluster, Clement had heard, was an ulcer that wouldn't heal. "You've been having some tough luck lately."

"Everybody has that."

"Especially on the road, I mean."

"I'm home now. It'll make a difference."

Clement toed the grass, which was unnaturally bright, alien under his feet. "You must have one of those chemical trucks doing your lawn."

"Yeah, a guy comes, but we're not gonna have it done anymore. The wife says it turns the worms purple, gives 'em cancer."

"Yes," said Clement, "those road trips can be grueling. More ways than one."

"What d'you mean by that?"

"You know."

"No, you tell me."

Clement gazed toward the house, and Crack did too. Clement shrugged sympathetically. "While the cat's away, the mouse plays."

Something bad and big came over Crack's face. Clement stood his ground.

"You want to know the guy's name?"

Sissy Alexander, who seldom used much makeup, sat at her dressing table and tried to paint happy thoughts on her face. It was an old trick performed in high school when she had been the subject of little ditties flattering only in disrespectful ways. Always, no different now, she gave too much and received in return too little.

She rose in one of her favorite dresses, white, flouncy, and ruffed, in which she was a magnolia blossom, not a little unlike herself at age seventeen, when she had married Crack and traveled the bush leagues with him, at times believing in him more than he believed in himself, knowing from the first time he laid hands on her that stardom was built into his body. That was when she was all puppy fat and baby talk, when baby talk was the lingua franca of their life together.

At the high window overlooking the front grounds she saw him jogging along the far edge, competing against himself and the growing heat of the morning. Gone was the long, loping stride with which, with such splendor, he had made it to the bigs. The bigs: that was a world apart from any other. There he had joined deities in form-fitting livery and dug his silver cleats into turf as shiny as brand-new money. And there, from her privileged box seat at Fenway, she had felt a part of the play, certainly part of Crack's graceful pursuit of a ball in center field, his glove big enough to snare an owl. So too, with Crack at bat, was she aware of the sex symbols of the opposing catcher, who, armored and masked, squatting, wiggled insinuating fingers in his spread crotch. She joined the ecstasy of the crowds rising into screams from a single swing of the bat. The fair youth trotting the bases like a god and doffing his cap to the multitudes was Crack. She felt on her own bottom the congratulatory slaps he received on his.

The umpires were priests with the power to send players to heaven or hell, except for Crack, whom they could merely relegate to purgatory, where he stayed no more than a day. He was in his prime, he was at the glorious beginning of his career and almost at the zenith. Already his agent was bargaining for super dollars, no amount too outrageous to ask for.

She bathed and bubbled in the thrilling backwash of his success. She knew all his teammates and called them by nickname. Dewey, whose glove was golden, she had a crush on and blushed whenever he spoke to her. Yaz was a prima donna, though so was Crack, even more so. She was a little afraid of Pudge Fisk but never took her eyes off him when it was his turn to hit. She adored the way he always stepped back a moment from the plate to size up his wood. Everything was sexual, and she had to admit that, especially the way Crack went for his crotch when behind on the count.

Some players she had been uncomfortable with. Oilcan Boyd was one, a poor black youth overwhelmed by potential stardom that never came. She had avoided him, but that was because she had been stupid then and hadn't known that blacks were people, which was something that Crack had to learn too, though he was slower to do so. She misunderstood the moodiness of Jim Rice, another black, until she realized that his home runs roused only half the reaction of Crack's.

It was a time of her life—and eventually Crack's—never to be repeated. She stopped accompanying him on road trips when he decreed that her job was at home, though they had no children and apparently never would have any. This house in Bensington was meant to mollify her over what she was reading in the papers, especially Norma Nathan's column in the *Herald*: colorful anecdotes about his carousing.

His slide came gradually, inexorably, and preyed upon him. Too many young new faces on the field. Pudge was long gone, laboring in Chicago, where Crack had two girlfriends. Yaz, whose stubble was gray, was in his last year. Jim Rice, either striking out or tapping into double plays, was on his way to oblivion. Crack, who expected to inherit Yaz's mantle of team captain, found himself increasingly frustrated by young pitchers who suckered him with sliders. That was when he began taking his slumps out on her.

She could tell by his face when she was in for it. Nothing pleased him, not his breakfast, not his shirts from the laundry, and especially not the condition of his scrapbooks, for which she was responsible. When he lost his temper, he used his hands, though only once had he hit her with his fist. Something must have told him that he could kill her with that.

She still stood at the window, though he had jogged out of her view several minutes before. Her nose pressed the glass until he reappeared, jogging with a heavier step and less grit, as though he were caught between two seasons, his body adjusted to neither.

She was about to step away when she saw a car curve up the drive and come to a stop. A man got out. She had no idea who he was, but she watched carefully as he met her husband on the grass, which he scuffed as if he too were a ball player, though she knew he wasn't. Her animal senses at work, she knew something wasn't right. When the man swung his eyes toward the house, she pulled back.

She went down the stairs on slow feet, one burdened by a blister. In their young days Crack would have kissed it better. He would have given her flowers stolen from a neighbor's scant garden, and each would have taken pleasure in the undoing of the other's buttons. But all that was gone, and all that was left was her helplessness and his rage and impotence.

She hiked through the house, paused for a moment at one of the cupboards in the gleaming kitchen, and then went out a back door, into the sunshine, and onto a carpet of grass, where each day she bought the friendship of birds with scattered bits of bread, which in her childhood she would have mushed up in milk for breakfast.

Several minutes later she heard him tramping in the house. She heard her name called and did not answer, but stood very still, waiting for the birds to come. She did not turn around when he came out the back door. She did not want to see his face.

"You and me," he said, "got something to talk about."

After his phone call to Lydia Lapham, Chief Morgan kneaded his brow. His mind remained with her. He agonized over the obscurities of their sudden and impetuous relationship. Too much was up in the air, beyond his range of vision and beyond even his willingness to understand, though he knew he had not meant to sleep with her. Nor had he meant in any way to interfere with the relationship, though broken, between her and MacGregor. His guilt was keen. Yet he also knew that, having been given the opportunity, nothing could have stopped him. Her nearness had inspired feelings long dormant and resurrected formidable memories of another life.

His chair creaked with a shifting of his weight. He was tired. His gray eyes were dust balls, which he barely raised when Meg O'Brien looked in on him and said in a private voice, "Reporter from Lawrence to see you. He wants an update on the investigation."

"You handle it," Morgan said.

"I can't. I don't know anything about it."

"Eugene out there? Have him take care of it."

"Are you serious?"

"I'm serious."

A few moments later Sergeant Avery, who had quietly farted, said, "Fire away."

The reporter, young and neatly dressed, started to speak and then stepped back disconcertedly and riffled blank pages of a steno pad as if he had forgotten his questions and needed more light to read them. "We've heard rumors a Bensington police officer is a prime suspect in the shooting."

"Pure bullshit!" Sergeant Avery shot back. "You can quote me."

"No, you can't," Meg O'Brien shouted from her desk. "Pure rubbish is what he said."

"Right," the reporter said, glad to give her his attention.

Sergeant Avery cleared his throat while letting out more air, hot and disturbing, disturbing because he felt no relief and feared he had soiled himself. "Any more questions?"

The reporter put his pad away, his smile small, and cut the interview short. "I guess I got enough for now."

The reporter went out the door, and Sergeant Avery disappeared in the direction of the lavatory. Meg O'Brien sat at her desk with an impassive face and waited for him to return. On a notepad she jotted down personal chores to be done, though never enough to keep her outside life busy. She had survived cancer, come to terms with the passing of her only brother, and recognized that her job was her whole life, which did not displease her. She could no longer imagine a better one.

Tired of waiting, she lifted herself up and went into the chief's office. He was deep in his chair, his eyes closed. "You're not sleeping, are you?"

He shook his head. Lydia Lapham continued to move in and out of his mind at will. His stomach made sounds like a drumroll. Without opening his eyes, he said, "Everything go all right?"

"Everything went fine," Meg said. "Eugene shit himself."

After a few holes of golf, Calvin Poole lowered his niblick and swabbed his neck with a linen handkerchief. The heat of the morning shimmered. In the distance it glared. Sticking the club back into the bag, he said, "I'm sorry, the sun's too hot for me. But it was nice of you to ask me."

"It was a bad idea," Gerald Bowman said and put away his club. "Come on, we'll have something cold in the bar."

In the motorized golf cart, Bowman was the driver, Poole the sunstruck passenger. Each wore raspberry trousers. The cut of their jerseys was the same, only the colors were different. Since receiving Bowman's early telephone call at home, Poole had been waiting to hear something miraculously encouraging about the outstanding loans.

A boy took the cart from them, and they entered the Bensington Country Club through the large rear entrance. The lounge was cool and deserted. They sat at a small mahogany table, where the bartender brought them orange juice chunky with ice. Poole drank his up almost at once and listened while Bowman spoke obliquely about people popping up on one's doorstep, faceless debris from the past. He failed to follow until Bowman made an unmistakable allusion to banana republics, and then he remembered that Bowman had once touched him up for a secret contribution, a sizable sum from the coffers of Mercury Savings & Loan to help fund an effort as much political as military, which had seemed right at the time. Now he wondered whether it was coming back to haunt him. Everything else was.

Bowman was now talking about something else, which again perplexed him. It had to do with women, their wiles, their intricacies, their peculiarities, which eventually put him on guard. He raised his glass. He needed a refill. The bartender, arriving promptly, poured from a pitcher, rattled it, and left it there.

"Hard to live without them," he said lightly.

"Almost as hard as living with them," Bowman said. "Your own wife, Poole, how well do you know her? I'm talking, *really*."

The orange juice was no longer vital. He had drunk too much too fast and put his glass aside after one weary sip. Through the window that ran the length of the far wall he glimpsed golfers motoring in from the green.

Bowman said, "You know, don't you?"

He recognized one of the golfers, Randolph Jackson, who

had once asked him to serve on a town board. Commitments on his time had prevented it, a pity because he would have brought professionalism to bear.

Bowman said, "Do you know his name?"

With no mask of toughness to hide his feelings, he looked away and remembered a childhood in which comportment and restraint had been among the things that mattered. A high reward for dignified behavior was a brisk pat on his head from his father, shrewd, staid, and proper, an old-fashioned Yankee banker, perhaps the last of the lot, though he, the son, had striven to fill the shoes.

"It's our rinky-dink police chief," Bowman said. "James Morgan. The kind of man who leaves his pawprints on a woman."

He remembered intruding into his mother's dressing room, he could not have been more than six or seven. Even in only her underwear she managed to look prim. A gentleman, she told him, always knocks first.

"It doesn't bother you, Poole, a guy screwing your wife?"

"It bothers me," he said. "It bothers me most that you should know."

Calvin Poole left soon after, and Gerald Bowman motioned to a familiar figure in the bar. Randolph Jackson, florid in golfing colors, patted down his hair and lumbered forth with a huge smile. Bowman was the force that had turned Jackson's woodland into Oakcrest Heights and in large measure changed the character of the town. They shook hands.

"Always good to see you, Mr. Bowman."

"Sit down," Bowman said.

Jackson sat with a thump and smiled broadly, some gold in his back teeth. "I thought that was you out there. You quit early."

"I didn't. Poole did."

"Was that Calvin Poole with you? I thought it was, the white hair. A fine gentleman."

Bowman said, "Your police chief's fucking his wife."

A number of seconds passed before Jackson responded. "My God, I didn't know that. If you want, I'll talk to Jim, tell him to stop."

"Your chief's a joke."

"I've known him for a long—"

"You've had a shooting, two people dead. You've got a clown in charge. What are you going to do about it?"

Flustered, Jackson said, "He's only technically in charge. The state police are really handling the investigation, and I've been somewhat involved myself."

"Get rid of him." Bowman finished off his orange juice and got to his feet. "You'd be doing yourself a favor—and me."

Matt MacGregor was home. Unshaved, wearing cutoff jeans, he was sitting on the front porch with a can of beer and his feet propped against the rail. His eyes were closed. In his lap was a pocket transistor tuned to old songs his mother might have been listening to were she home. Julie London had cried him a river, and now Peggy Lee, who could suckle lyrics, was singing a love song he had not heard before. It made him want to die. His eyes shuddered open when a voice said, "Could you use my help, Matthew?"

Out of a wash of sunshine Reverend Stottle emerged the mysterious way a photograph comes to life, from faint to clear. MacGregor killed the music and lowered his feet. "I don't need your help."

"Could you use God's? I'm his deputy."

MacGregor swigged beer. "Tell God to get the state cops off my back. They take turns driving by the house."

Reverend Stottle was also unshaved. His rumpled hair was gray and his stubble white. Otherwise he was neat. "I've heard the vicious stories, Matthew. I believe none of them."

"And tell God I want my girl back. Other than that, I don't give a shit about anything." He took another swig. "You want a beer?"

"No, Matthew. Oil to anoint my feet, yes, but we'll skip that. Do you want me to edit your message?"

"Do what you want."

Reverend Stottle leaned his backside against the porch rail. His eyes were packed with goodness. "You need care. Is your mother still away?"

"I talk to her on the phone. I don't tell her anything. Don't you."

"One should talk. This is a trying time for you and Miss Lapham."

"I wouldn't make good listening." He crumpled the can. "What the hell kind of life is this, Reverend? I'm a pariah in my own town."

"I believe in other lives, Matthew. This one, I'm sure, is only a first draft."

"Yeah? I got your word on that?"

"I could be wrong."

"Then you're giving me guff." He turned his head away. "What am I listening for?"

"I'm older than you, Matthew. I belong to an age when milk arrived in a bottle, the cream at the top. I know that men climb mountains so they can walk along the edge of the world." Reverend Stottle paused for a moment because he had too much spittle in his mouth. He spoke in worn words. How many times had he said them before? Sometimes he felt he were deep in the stuff of someone else's dream, playing a part not of his own making. "When the Enola Gay dropped its bomb, before you were born, Matthew, we became the first people in history to know with certainty that continuity is not a given, the world could end tomorrow."

"Let it," MacGregor said.

Reverend Stottle watched MacGregor rise from his chair and totter on legs as muscular as a football player's. He would have been proud to have him as a son. He and Mrs. Stottle had daughters grown and gone, married and settled, not here, other places. California was where youth went. He said, "You're not morbid, are you? Don't be morbid, Matthew."

"I'm sorry, Reverend, I can't listen to you anymore. My head hurts."

He was losing him. The boy was slipping into the house. "You shouldn't be alone."

"Then find me a woman," MacGregor said.

"What happened to your mouth?" Clement asked and sought a closer look, but Junior pulled away. The lower lip was cut and swollen, as if a tooth had gone through it.

"I fell."

"Is that what happened? You fell?"

Junior nodded. He pointed. "Over there on the stump. I was talkin' back, Papa hit me."

"He hit you that hard?"

Junior shrugged as if surprised Clement were making something of it. "He always does when I don't do right."

"Damn him!"

"It don't matter, Clement."

"It matters to me."

Clement went on into the house, where Papa was eating crackers from a box and sardines from a can. He ate ruthlessly, as if punishing the food. Clement looked away and waited until he finished before sitting down. Papa said, "You done anything about the chief yet?"

"Don't ask questions," Clement said. "I'm taking care of it."

"What's the matter with you? You got a hair across your ass?"

He folded his hands together on the table. He was not going to speak, but then he did. "Why did you hit him?"

"Who you talkin' about?"

"You know who I'm talking about."

"You talkin' about Junior?"

"I'm talking about Junior. You hit him."

"Someone's gotta do it."

Clement spoke from the dusk of his feelings. "Don't do it again."

"Don't tell me how to bring up the boy." Papa's damaging little eyes bored in. They insinuated. Like insects they laid their little eggs beneath the skin. "Don't you try to get between us."

"I'm not trying to do that."

"I'm the one does for him."

Clement did not trust himself to speak again. He went into the cubbyhole of a bathroom, which was never clean and had lost its wallpaper. He used the toilet quickly. When he came out, Papa was not in the kitchen. Through the window he saw Junior and heard Papa.

"Don't you never *never* go against me, you hear?"

He saw the look on Junior's face, doglike obedience, and stepped back from the window, from a relationship in which he had only a peripheral place.

Clement returned to the motor inn, bought a pair of swimming trunks in the gift shop, and used the pool. Back and forth, three times, he swam the length of it and then sat in a chaise in the burn of the sun and watched the women. The young ones in string bikinis were striking, but the older ones, showing less, impressed him more. None, however, seemed approachable or readily available. He returned to his room and changed back into his street clothes. A few minutes later he entered the bar.

"Miller, right?"

"Right," said Clement.

The bartender served up a bottle and said, "Milly told me how you stood up for her. That was nice of you."

"Who's Milly?"

"The kid who waits on tables in the dining room."

Clement shrugged. "I figured she was somebody's sister."

The bartender went away and came back with that day's edition of the Lawrence paper, which he opened up and folded back. "By the way, remember that woman you were chummy with here?" Clement nodded, and the bartender turned the paper around and pointed, "That's her."

The name meant nothing to him, and neither did the thumbnail picture until he looked at it closer. With a chill he scanned the story, which was scarcely more than an item. The woman, who was from Andover and believed to have been depressed over a recent divorce, had slashed her wrists the evening before. A neighbor had found her and summoned an ambulance. He pushed the paper away. He knew the color had left his face.

"Don't feel guilty about anything," the bartender said. "She was in here 'most every night, fair game to any guy had an eye for her. Something was wrong with her, I knew that right away."

"That's the problem," Clement said. "I did too."

The bartender put the paper out of sight and ran a wet cloth over the bar. "A lot of these women come in here, they're a button hanging from a thread."

Clement left his beer untouched and returned to his room.

Calvin Poole sat with a copy of the *Wall Street Journal* in his lap. From his chair on the veranda he watched a cardinal flit like struck matches through the nervous leaves of a birch. When his wife appeared, he did his best to rearrange his face into a healthier mold. She said, "Anything wrong, Calvin?"

He shook his head. She had her exercise togs on. She always seemed to have them on now. She had not eaten all day, except for a graham cracker to take the nick out of her hunger.

"It's the bank, isn't it?" she said, dropping into the chair beside him. "How bad is it, exactly?"

"Not all that bad," he said and wondered whether he might go to prison. Bowman wouldn't, he was sure of that, but he himself might, and he wondered whether unconsciously he welcomed betrayal, whether his life were tailored into perfect fits for failures.

"I think you're fibbing," she said.

The cardinal flared up and away. It vanished into the blue in a bulletlike way only birds can do. Wondrous creatures, he had always felt that.

"You don't have to worry about money," she said. "We have plenty, you know that."

"I've never touched yours," he said. "I don't intend to."

"Don't be foolish. It's ours."

"It was your husband's."

"You're my husband."

His head went back a bit, her voice a pinprick each time she spoke. He wondered whether she had ever truly loved him. Always the ghostly stuff of her first husband had littered their closets; even the outlandish orange skivvies might have been his. Though now he knew otherwise.

"What do they say about me behind my back?" he asked. "That you're married to some white-haired old fart?"

"Hardly," she said with surprise. "What makes you think that?"

Inside information, he wanted to say. Hot from a trader's mouth. His hands were clasped in his lap, over the *Journal*. He said, "Perhaps I'm feeling my age. I'm no youngster, am I?"

"Nor are you doddering."

"No complaints?" he asked.

"None, my dear."

Now her voice lay gentle on the air. That was nice. "I golfed with Gerald Bowman this morning," he said.

"Did he have anything positive to say?"

Poole shook his head. "Nothing worth repeating."

It was nearly dark now, many shadows in the room. Clement Rayball had been mulling over what all along he had known he would do. He left the motor inn and drove to a hospital in Lawrence, where the receptionist asked whether he was a relative. A brother, he told her. He rode the elevator with a man holding flowers and wished he had brought some. In the corridor a heavy female patient with her gown open in back was a peep show. He averted his eyes. Seconds later he danced out of the way of a young black man maneuvering a gurney. His mind moving too quickly, he strode past the woman's room and had to retrace his steps.

She lay quite still, her eyes closed, sharing the room with no one. Her wrists were bandaged big, but except for IV feeding she was not hooked up to anything, which he took as a good sign. She seemed sound asleep. When he moved to read the chart at the foot of the bed, her eyes opened. She looked at him clearly, starkly, and he could tell that she did not remember him, not at all. It should have relieved him of something, but it did not. He whispered, "I'm sorry, so sorry."

Her eyes closed.

"Visiting hours are over." The voice came from behind. A nurse, protective of her patient, edged him to the door. Her presence was commanding. "She shouldn't be disturbed. Are you a relative?"

"A friend," he said with a look at the plastic name tag pinned to her uniform. Even if he hadn't looked he'd have remembered her. "You're Lydia Lapham."

She recognized him. "Clement Rayball. You were a year behind me in school. You went into the army."

"That was a while ago." His voice deepened. "I'm sorry about your parents."

"Thank you," she said with no inflection. She was, he noted, much more attractive now than in high school, where they had had little to do with each other. They had passed in the corridors and on the stairs, that was about it. Matt MacGregor, he remembered, had been her boyfriend even then, or at least he had assumed so. She said, "How long have you known my patient?"

"Not long," he replied.

"We've had her here before. Pills, I remember. I try not to be emotional over patients, but I'm not always successful."

"Is she going to be all right?"

"No one can answer that. But is she going to live? Yes."

He felt the release now, the burden sliding from his shoulders. "Thank God," he said.

She said, "If there is one."

Randolph Jackson's stomach was upset. He brought a tumbler of warm milk to bed with him, propped his pillows, and sat erect with his legs stretched deep under the covers. A sultry night breeze blew in on him. His wife lay with her back to him. His light was on, hers was off. He sipped his milk and tried to lift his mind clear of emotions that would keep him awake. "Suzy," he said but did not get an answer. "Not asleep, are you?"

"I will be, soon as you turn off the light." She liked her eight hours, which she frequently stretched to ten. She felt it kept her young. "How long are you going to be?"

He polished off the milk, scratched his scalp, and switched off the lamp, which put the bed in a pale swash of moonlight. As he sank under the covers, she shifted about with a rumble. She was facing him now, half her head buried. He lay still a number of moments and then, abruptly, said, "Jim Morgan has been having an affair with Calvin Poole's wife."

Her voice came awake. "Who's Calvin Poole?"

"A banker who lives in the Heights."

"Heck, that's not news. Jim Morgan bangs all the women over there."

"You don't know that."

"You don't know he doesn't." She pressed a big, warm foot against his ankle. "All I have to say is, lucky gals. He's a hunk, you know."

A terrible thought occurred to him, which almost brought the milk up on him. "Has he ever banged you?"

"No, damn it."

He lay quietly, listening to the peepers. He wished now he hadn't drunk the milk. "I may have to get rid of him."

She was nearly asleep. "You know best, dear."

Lydia Lapham stayed well past her shift, for late in the evening the woman with the cut wrists had wanted to talk, and she sat by the bed for nearly an hour and listened to things that did not necessarily make sense. When she stepped out into the night, her head felt like a balloon. She drove out of Lawrence incautiously, striking potholes, running lights. Earlier there had been a moon, but now clouds covered it. Entering Bensington, she heard stupendous thunderclaps. No rain fell. Approaching her street, she told herself she did not care whether Morgan's car was there or not, better that it not be. It was.

She parked behind him and strode past him without a word.

Andrew Coburn

At the front door she took her time fitting the latchkey into the lock. When she did not hear his footsteps, she swung around and called out, "Do you need an engraved invitation?"

She left the door open behind her, and within minutes she had heaved off her uniform and was in a big sloppy robe, her most comfortable one, which was in need of laundering. When she stepped into the kitchen, he was sitting at the table.

"I won't be staying long," he said. "I'm going home and make myself something to eat."

Her feet were bare. She scratched one foot with the other. "Didn't you have supper?"

"I missed it."

She beat up an omelet and fed him. When he finished, he carried his plate to the sink and began rinsing it. She rose up. When he turned around, she put her arms around him.

"Guess what?" she said, half in anger. "I think I love you."

"I know," he said.

"How do you know?"

"Cops know everything."

◄ ◄ ◄ **9** ► ► ►

Sunday broke hotter than Saturday and was more humid.
The red maples flanking the Congregational church were
resplendent in the sun. Inside the church, the pews mostly
full, the air was close, and men were removing their jackets.
May Hutchins and her husband sat two pews away from Fred
Fossey and his wife. Eugene Avery, a bachelor, sat with his
sister, who had a tic. Few people from Oakcrest Heights were
there. They went to Andover, where there was a variety,
where Catholics had two houses of worship, Jews a temple,
and Episcopalians held their noses up.

"Good morning," said Reverend Stottle from his place of
authority. He appeared badly shaven, a noticeable cut on his
chin, and his austere suit, neat yesterday, was less so today,
as if the heat had wilted it. "We have lost a sister," he said
with resonance and an eye that seemed to sweep in everybody.
"Ida Dugdale has gone. But for the aged and sick, life becomes
an indignity. Worse, a mockery. How easy, then, to leave it."

Fred and Ethel Fossey traded glances. Everett Drinkwater,
sitting erect with his wife, did not move a muscle. He had
made arrangements for Mrs. Dugdale at a crematorium in New
Hampshire, her written wish.

"A greater loss, however, still hangs heavy on us," Reverend Stottle continued after a significant pause. "The loss of a man and wife, a cherished mother and father, our dear friends the Laphams."

May Hutchins's lace hankie went to her eyes, and nearby Fred Fossey bowed his head while Ethel, fanning her face, noticed that Matilda Farnham had on the same dotted dress she had worn the previous Sunday. The reverend was taking long pauses, and Ethel used the opportunity to let her eyes roam. "I don't see Lydia Lapham here."

Fred whispered, "You don't see Matt MacGregor either."

"That doesn't mean anything. He never comes to church much. And the chief, he never does."

Reverend Stottle said, "Some time soon, next Sunday perhaps, we must ask ourselves why God endows some women with beauty and denies it to others. This morning we will simply note that to Florence Lapham God gave much beauty and to Earl the privilege of serving her."

Doris Wetherfield, sitting with four of her five children, looked confused. Malcolm Crandall, the town clerk, mopped his high forehead with the cuff of a sleeve. May Hutchins returned her sodden handkerchief to her eyes.

"I believe that when our sister Florence was struck dead, her husband Earl chose to follow her. In light of this, sisters and brothers, I say that when the killer is caught he must be charged with only one crime, not two. We must be fair."

Feet shuffled in every pew. Lydia Lapham's aunt, Miss Westerly, appeared to faint. Randolph Jackson, sitting in his usual prominent place in the front pew, turned to his wife, who whispered, "Maybe the chief's not the only one you have to get rid of."

Reverend Stottle raised his arms. "God bless you all. I'm cutting the service short."

There was a silence as he strode down the aisle to the doors. Then pews began to rock as people struggled to their feet. Miss Westerly needed help, and old Dr. Skinner was there to provide it. Bertha Skagg, whose ankles had swollen in the heat, required the arm of Doris Wetherfield's eldest son. Fred Fossey spoke out of a red face to Ethel. "What the hell was that man raving about?"

Outside the doors in a blaze of sunlight, Reverend Stottle waited to shake people's hands, but many pushed to one side to avoid him.

"We'll talk about this later," Randolph Jackson said to him in a stern tone for others to hear, but the reverend's eyes were fixed on Suzy Jackson, on all that well-fed goodness and bigness. His eyes waxed. She was another one whom God had favored. "Soon," Randolph Jackson added strongly.

He smiled. "Yes, Randolph, soon. God willing."

Eunice Rayball placed bread on the table, a warm loaf, and with a popping sound opened a jar of raspberry preserve. With a gleaming butcher knife she sliced two slabs from the loaf, one for him and one for her. She smeared jam onto both slabs, more on his than hers. Then they ate, mother and son.

Junior woke from the dream with a cry, with anger, for he wanted it never to end. It was a dream he had never had before, and it was the first dream in which he had clearly seen her face. It was pretty.

He got out of bed and in the hot sunshine pouring through the open window slipped into his worn jeans. He put on a fresh T-shirt but the same socks, for he had run out of clean ones. It was his job to do his and Papa's washing, but he did that on Mondays, not Sundays, and afterward draped everything on berry bushes. Sunday, Papa said, was the Lord's day of rest—and his too. Papa always slept late on Sunday, sometimes until noon. He did not disturb him. He did not even use the toilet. He put his sneakers on and tiptoed out the house and peed in the woods.

Then, taking his time, he followed footpaths through pinewood that gave way to hardwood and then back to pine and brush. When they had been boys, Clement had told him that these were Indian trails, but later Papa told him they were made by people with nothing better to do than spy on birds. Some even picked up owl shit and saved it as if it were packed with secrets. All it did, Papa said, was tell you what the damn old owl ate.

He picked up his pace. He could walk anywhere, anytime, and never get lost. He always knew where he was by the sun, which Clement had taught him, and even when the sun wasn't out he had a sense of things. And always he felt safe because Clement had told him there was nothing in the woods that could hurt him, except maybe poison ivy. But even that didn't bother him.

He crossed a narrow road, no cars in sight, and plunged into woods of maple and oak, where there were no paths and the sun didn't always reach through the trees and where the bramble could throw thorns at you and other bushes could sprinkle you with little pickers that traveled up your pant leg like bedbugs. But he moved with immunity, for he had been through here too many times to count, ever since he was old enough to wander on his own. Had he not been on a mission he might have had fun with himself behind a tree and then put himself away still drippy. Instead he pushed on, sure of foot and deep in purpose.

He passed through a meadow and avoided looking at the woodlot into which he and Papa had snuck and Papa had gone down on one knee to put the pieces of the rifle together, and then had thrust it at him whole and said, "Go ahead, you think you can do it." It was too heavy and smelled of oil and was not like anything he had ever aimed before. He wished now he had never seen it, never smelled it.

He made his way to a street and walked under shade trees, houses on each side. A Yard Sale sign was nailed lopsided to a power pole, and a few cars were stopping. He scurried along. When he neared two girls playing hopscotch he started to smile and decided against it when they stuck their tongues out.

Soon he passed the big white church, where people were filing out in their best bib and tucker, some in a hurry. With anxiety mounting, he raced across the green, scattering birds, and trotted across the street to the town hall. His feet slowed considerably when he made his way around the side to the police station. His heart began banging when he stepped inside. A woman with big teeth looked up from what she was doing and said, "I know you. You're Junior Rayball."

"Yes, ma'am," he said, and his voice startled him. It was stronger than he had thought it would be.

"What can I do for you?" she said.

"I want to see the chief."

"I see. Can you tell me what it's about?"

"My mother," he said.

They slept late. Lydia Lapham would have slept even longer had Morgan not risen first and taken a long shower. The sound of the water came through the wall. He returned tracking wet, a towel slung around his neck. He used a hand as a fig leaf. "You don't have to hide it," she said from her pillow.

He looked into eyes that still craved sleep. The left side of her face was blotchy from the way she had lain on it. Her dreams, he suspected, had been bad. "I hope you don't mind," he said, "I used your father's razor."

"I don't mind, and he wouldn't either." When he retrieved his underwear from the floor, she advised him where he could find fresh. He looked at her questioningly. "Good God, James, he's not ever going to wear them again."

He looked deeper into her. "Am I already getting on your nerves?"

"It's not you, it's me. I don't know exactly who I am anymore. I used to be Matt's lay. Now I guess I'm yours. Am I?"

"I wouldn't put it that way."

"Am I as good as your ladies from the Heights? Or are you just being kind to me, James?"

"This isn't you talking. What's wrong, Lydia?"

"Nothing's wrong. Nothing's real. Not even you."

Dressed, also wearing her father's white socks, he went down to the kitchen and made coffee. It seemed his job now. He wondered about breakfast, which he never ate anywhere except in the Blue Bonnet. He suspected she ate none. The telephone rang while he was watching the coffee perk down.

Andrew Coburn

She was ensconced in the bathroom, where undoubtedly she couldn't hear it. He planned to let it ring, but it got on his nerves.

"Hello," he said and heard Meg O'Brien's voice. She told him she had been trying everywhere to reach him. He said, "How did you know I was here?"

"I took a chance, I don't know why, call it intuition."

"Is that the truth?"

"No," she confessed. "Ethel Fossey saw your car parked there. She phoned the station about something else and happened to mention it." The voice dipped, assuming authority with solemnity. "Should you be there, Jim? Should you really be there?" When he did not answer, she said, "What about Matt?"

"You're leaping to conclusions."

"Won't he?"

"Why are you calling, Meg?"

"You had a visitor, but he wouldn't wait. He did for a while, but got jittery."

"Who? Do you have a name?"

"Sure I have a name. I didn't have to ask, I knew who it was."

She was milking it all the way, for all it was worth, and he said, "OK, who was it?"

"Junior Rayball."

His heart jumped, and his stomach took a chill. "Where is he now?"

"I don't know."

He mounted the stairs, slowly at first and then rapidly, stumbling on the top one. He rapped on the bathroom door. "I have to go."

"There's a john downstairs," she said through the door.

"I have to leave."

The door opened. "I heard you the first time."

They ran into each other in Tuck's General Store, where they were picking up the Sunday papers. Arlene Bowman had the *Times* in her arms, Christine Poole the *Globe*. The store was crowded. People who had just gotten out of church were buzzing among themselves as if something unholy had gone on. Arlene nudged Christine with her shoulder and said, "Let's get out of here. I want to talk to you."

Outside, in the full strength of the sun, Christine said, "I've lost two pounds."

"That's great," Arlene said. "But you might have more to worry about than your weight. Have you had a visitor lately?"

"A visitor? I don't quite follow."

Balancing the bulky *Times* in one arm, Arlene gave an impatient swipe to her hair. "A visitor. To your house. Like a man."

"No."

"Has your husband?"

"Not that I know of. I don't know, why?"

"Then maybe you have nothing to worry about. Depends on Gerald, what he does."

Christine, who attended Christ Episcopal in Andover but had not gone that morning, had on a yellow dress. The sun tickled her bare shoulders and was melting her makeup. "Can you tell me what you're talking about?"

"I'm talking about a man who came to the house, someone Gerald apparently knows, from the town. He mentioned you, not by name, but it was obvious. You and the damn old chief."

She faltered. "Me and the chief?"

"You and the chief. And me too. What I'm saying is he spilled the beans to Gerald."

The *Globe*, an unwieldy bundle bigger than the *Times*, nearly slipped from her grasp. Her throat was parched. "They played golf yesterday. Calvin. Your husband."

"Did they? No repercussions?"

"Nothing." Her eyes flew here, there. On the green a man aimed a camera at children who did not want their picture taken. "No, he said nothing."

"Nothing? Then maybe you have nothing to worry about. The chief, however, that's another matter."

"What do you mean?"

"Gerald. I've never heard him speak in any tone but neutral. What I'm saying is he never gets mad, he gets even."

Christine hurried away, still struggling with the paper. Parts slipped away, then most of it. She stopped to gather up the loss. A man rushed to help her. "My name's Fossey," he said, smiling. "I handle veterans' affairs."

She left him with the ad inserts and the comics and rushed to her car. She was struggling with the door when Arlene called to her over the roof of a Mazda sports coupe. "I can handle my husband, Christine. If it comes to it, can you handle yours?"

As soon as Chief Morgan came to a bumpy stop near the house, Papa Rayball appeared bare-chested in the screen door. Before Morgan could switch the motor off, Papa shouted, "What d'you want? I got nothin' to say." Morgan silenced the motor, opened his door, and stuck a leg out. Papa hollered, "You can't come in. I ain't dressed. I ain't even pissed yet."

"Where's Junior?"

"I ain't seen him. He goes off." Papa scratched his chicken chest. "You wanna talk to anybody here, you talk to Clement. He's handlin' our business now."

"All right," Morgan said. "Tell him to come out."

"He ain't here. He lives better than us. You wanna talk to him, go check the motels. He's wearin' his fancy watch, maybe he'll give you a minute, though I ain't promisin'."

The screen went blank, as on television, and Morgan backed the car down the rutted drive to the road, onto which he spun quickly, with a squeal. He drove to stretches where he thought Junior might be walking and eventually to a lonesome one where pine rose up on one side and hardwood on the other. No luck. He cruised into the cemetery, past Eunice Rayball's grave, past his wife's, past the Laphams', and saw no one except Fred Fossey with flowers and flags.

Back on the road, a warning light flashed from the dash. He pulled over, climbed out, and raised the hot hood. The motor was a furnace, hissing hard and pinging loud. Teenagers in an open car worth three of his sped by with catcalls. The smart-ass driver blasted the horn. He returned to the wheel, radioed the station, and said, "I need help."

Meg O'Brien said, "Are you sure you called the right place?"

Lieutenant Bakinowski, sitting in his car in front of Matt MacGregor's house, stared out over a can of Diet Coke. He had been parked there for nearly a half hour. From the porch, his feet on the rail, MacGregor stared back over a can of beer with a malevolence that looted his boyish face of its better qualities. "I can sit here longer than you can," he said.

Bakinowski said nothing, nor did anything spring from his eyes, which he kept caged. He sipped his Coke as a boy flitted by on a bicycle. Next door a neighbor came out on her porch and stared with curiosity.

"You don't bother me," MacGregor said, flourishing the beer can. "I don't even know you're there. But I know what you are. You're just a fucking Polack, no brains. If you ever had any, they fell out your ass a long time ago."

Bakinowski's eyes started out of his head and then drew back. The neighbor woman retreated into her house as if some things were better left alone.

"You know what I heard about you, Polack? Not nice, believe me." MacGregor let out a harsh laugh. "I heard you blow dead dogs."

Bakinowski placed the Coke can on the dash. Reaching between his jacket and sweat-soaked shirt, he removed his snub-nose and, turning slightly, aimed it.

"Go ahead, Polack. We'll both go to hell."

He replaced the revolver in his hidden holster, smiled his sweetest, and said, "Guess who's sleeping with your girl?"

In the cemetery the sunlight stung, and the heat hung heavy. May Hutchins, with fire in her hair, came up on Fred Fossey and said, "We meet again."

"I saw you in church," he said.

"I mean we meet again *here*."

"This time I brought flowers." He had laid them all on Flo

Lapham's marker. "I brought flags for some of the guys. I already put 'em in place. Earl's got a new one."

May sucked her cheeks in. "Can you believe what that damn Reverend Stottle said?"

"I think he hit it on the head. I think Earl did choose to go. I know I would of."

"I mean about saying only one—"

"Let's not talk about it, May, not in front of them."

May fanned a hand near her face. "You got a hankie, Fred? Mine's sopping."

He reached into his pocket and dragged out a big one. "I don't know if I used it. I don't think I did."

"It's all right." She made it into a neat square and dabbed her throat and just inside the top of her dress. "I saw Chief Morgan on the road. His car's broken down."

"Didn't you stop?"

"He didn't want me to. He waved me on." Burning through her dress, the sun lit her plump knees. She sighed sharply. "I heard he's looking close after poor Lydia. Maybe too close."

Fred's eyes leaped. "Who told you that? Ethel? When she's right she's only half right, and when she's wrong she's all wrong. If the chief's doing anything, he's protecting the poor girl."

"Everything's so fishy, Fred, you don't know what to believe."

He stiffened. "We shouldn't be talking this way, not here."

They moved away, over the hot grass, toward graves where the occupants were too long dead to care, no interest in anything. May said, "Here's your handkerchief."

"You keep it."

She winked at him. "We keep meeting like this, I ought to bring sandwiches."

He winked back. "And some lemonade. The real stuff. Not from the mix."

"What would Flo say?"

"She won't tell on us."

* * *

Felix from Felix's Texaco picked up the chief's car, and Meg O'Brien picked up the chief. Meg drove an old Plymouth with a radio in it just like a real police car, a fishpole aerial quivering in the air. Morgan was surprised to see her. "Where's Eugene?" he asked.

"He never came back from church. He's still got a bug."

"Who's minding the store?"

"Bertha came in to rest her feet. But she doesn't think she'll be in this evening. Do you want me to take her shift?"

"Not if you don't want to."

"I don't want to," she said, "but I will. You don't have to thank me. I can always use the extra money."

"What extra money?"

"I was joking."

Morgan sat straight, on the alert, for Meg tended to drive in the middle of the road. The good thing was that she was driving slowly. She wanted to talk. "People," she said, "not just Ethel Fossey, noticed your car parked all night at Lydia Lapham's, last night and the night before."

A crow feeding on the road flew away. The heat in the car was enervating. Morgan, trying to concoct a response, came up dry.

Meg said, "She's always been Matt's girl, I don't have to tell you that."

"I know," he said. "But she's not seeing him anymore."

"James." Her voice was a reprimand, the tone censorious. "You took advantage."

It was a thought that had nagged him. "No," he said, "I don't think so. I hope not."

"She's not one of those Oakcrest Heights women. She's one of us, James. Don't hurt her."

He stuck his elbow out the window and let the heat hit his face. Harder on him was the pressure of Meg's eyes. "Watch the road," he said as a car came up from the opposite direction. They missed it. "You know how you're always telling me to settle down?" he said. "I think I could with Lydia."

"You're older."

"Fifteen years. Is that too much?"

"I don't know. Ask her. Then ask yourself."

"She was friends with a doctor. I checked up on him. He's my age, and his hair's gray. Mine's not."

"There's your answer." She drove slower and kept to her side of the road, too much so, for the tires on his side crunched gravel. "Another thing," she said. "On the investigation. If you told me what you were doing, maybe I could help."

"If I knew everything I was doing, Meg, I might not be doing it."

They approached the center of town and began to make the swing around the green. Malcolm Crandall was talking with Dr. Skinner outside Tuck's, and two women from the Heights were entering Roberta's, which opened on Sundays from one to four. A door hung open at the Congregational church.

Looking at it, Morgan said, "Maybe we should seek guidance."

"In there?"

"Why not?" he said. "Unless you're still a Catholic."

She was a lapsed one, with little regard for priests, whom she considered black-bound volumes of misinformation. Ministers she ranked lower.

"I'll walk through that door when you do," she said.

Morgan, who had not been in a church since his wife died, said, "That means we'll have to wait till hell freezes over."

"Some of the paper's missing," Calvin Poole said from the patio. Christine was a statue just inside the house. She made herself move and went out to him. "The comics," he said, "and I don't know what else."

"They must not have packed everything in," she said, examining his face but not meeting his eyes. Then she did. "Is there anything you want to ask me, Calvin?"

"Ask you?" he said, and she felt herself drowning in her own words. His she hardly heard. He busied himself looking for missing sections. "Such as what, dear?"

"Has anybody been here? I mean, while I was gone?"

"No, nobody. You weren't gone long." He dropped the

thick classified sections beside his chair and kept the rest of the paper in his lap. "Who were you expecting?"

"Nobody," she said and let her bare arms hang loose. *He knew.* Everything in her sensed that he did. Or was she wrong? She did not want to step irredeemably over the line, for she was only beginning to realize how much this second marriage meant to her. Yet she could not go on this way. "Calvin!"

He hurled his face up from the business pages and presented a facade—formal, hard, inerrant—in which she read agony. *What have I done?* she thought and shivered. Scarcely hearing his response, she slipped back a step with an agony of her own and a face shot with embarrassment. "What is it?" he repeated.

A friend in common, a woman, had introduced them. The woman, an irrepressible classmate of hers from Wellesley, had confided in her ear: "He's a straight arrow, old school, wouldn't say shit if he had a mouthful." Later she and Calvin had exchanged deep looks, and each had seen comfort in the other.

"Are you feeling all right?" he asked, and she watched him lift a pant leg and scratch a hairless calf, which made him seem more vulnerable.

"A touch of the sun," she said quickly. "Maybe I'm going through the change."

"You're too young for that."

"No, Calvin." Her voice drifted as she moved back toward the house. "No, I'm not."

Chief Morgan borrowed Meg O'Brien's car and drove to Felix's Texaco, on the east side of town, near the line. Felix, who serviced many of the expensive foreign cars from Oakcrest Heights, was a master mechanic, humorless and direct, with a thin black mustache Morgan's grandmother would have associated with a snake oil salesman. Though it was Sunday, he had his two sons laboring in the stalls, one with a Mercedes on the lift. Morgan's car was still strung to the tow truck. He was wiping his hands in a rag when Morgan approached him at the pumps.

"That shitbox of yours," he said, "ain't worth fixin', but I'll fix it. You need a new radiator, and the fan belt ain't pretty. I bill the town, I don't wanna wait six months for my money."

"How long do you wait for the folks from the Heights to pay?" Morgan asked.

"Those rich bastards," he said, lowering his voice, "you gotta squeeze 'em for every dime. My wife says they're anal."

"When can I pick up my buggy?"

"Tomorrow if you're lucky, and you probably won't be. I gotta hunt up a radiator." He tilted his head. "See that silver-gray Mazda over there? The woman in it, she's waitin' for her husband, but she's lookin' at you."

The Mazda was parked in the shade of a maple, and the woman was Arlene Bowman. "Yes, I know her," Morgan said.

"Figured you did," he said slyly.

Morgan ambled over to her. Despite the heat she looked cool as spring water. Her door opened, and she got out. He remembered the morning they had met. She had showed him scratches on the lock of the outside sliders leading into the kitchen. She was sure someone had been trying to get in. Perhaps. Busy, she moved agilely about the kitchen in her tight designer jeans and spoke to him with her behind. The next day he came back on his own.

Her smile now was no different from then. She said, "That's my husband in there. He's telling the mechanic exactly what's wrong. He doesn't trust the boy to see for himself."

"I had a car like that, I wouldn't either."

"But you'll never have a car like that. By the way, he knows."

"Knows what?"

"What do you think?" Irony floated into her smile. "No, I didn't tell him. One of your townies did. I didn't catch his name."

There was a knock in Morgan's head. "Describe him."

"Thirty, thirty-five at the most. He had the eyes of a sniper. They go through you."

"Are you in trouble?"

"No, you are," she said with greater irony, her dark eyes

pinned to him. "My husband's of the opinion you don't know your place. He does have a point, doesn't he, James?"

"What are you telling me?"

"He intends to cut your balls off. Perhaps he already has, but you don't know it yet."

Morgan's mind raced. "Are you talking about my job?"

"Exactly. Take that away from you and you're a zero, a big nothing."

"As far as I know, Arlene, I'm still the chief, and I don't plan to step aside."

"You may not have a choice. Gerald's a powerful man in case you've forgotten."

"In a town like this, his power might not reach down."

"I wouldn't depend on that." Her eyes taunted. "Would you like to give me a farewell kiss, old time's sake?"

He glanced away. The day was brilliant, even the dust was bright. "You always did like to play it close, Arlene. I figured you were looking to get caught."

"Don't analyze me," she said. "You're not that smart."

Gerald Bowman came out of the stall, for a moment blinded in the blaze of sunlight. Morgan had never met him, had glimpsed him only from afar, though he had often gazed at the formal photograph of him framed and hung in the master bedroom. Arlene stepped slightly away. Her legs were tapers.

"One small thing, James. Something that's bothered me. How could you go from me to that old bag Christine Poole?" Then her face altered and brightened, and her voice rose. Her husband was upon them. "Darling, I don't think you've met James Morgan. He's our police chief busy solving murders, though obviously not at the moment."

Behind his rimless glasses, Bowman's eyes were lilac. His neat dark blond hair looked as if each strand had been individually barbered. Nothing moved in his face. His wife's smile went back to Morgan.

"Gerald has heard things about us. Perhaps you'd care to give him your side."

Morgan said, "I don't have a side."

"Get in the car," Bowman said to her quietly and walked

around to the passenger side. Opening the door, he spoke over the roof, "I once had a cat like you, Morgan. He didn't know enough to crap in the box."

The door closed, hard. Arlene opened hers and smiled with meaning. "It's what I told you, James. He thinks you don't know your place."

The car slid away, sharklike, through a rinse of sunshine. Felix, who had not moved from the pumps and had overheard bits and pieces, came over to Morgan. "My wife had a cat like that too, Chief. I made her get rid of it."

Randolph and Suzy Jackson had had dinner at the country club and were now driving around the village green. As they passed the town hall Suzy spotted Chief Morgan. "Go around again," she said, "there's the chief." He looked at her unwillingly. "You might as well get it over with," she said.

"Not now," he said. "Tomorrow."

"Do you want his resignation or not?"

"Tomorrow," he insisted. "It's official business."

"Don't be afraid of him, Randolph. Besides, I want to watch."

He drove past Tuck's and made the swing back to the town hall, where the chief was watching them. "You stay here," he said in an undertone and popped out of the car with a spring to his step, which faltered. "You got a minute, Jim?"

"Sure," Morgan said. Suzy Jackson smiled at him from the car, and he stooped forward. "How are you, Mrs. Jackson?"

"Fine, Chief. You're looking fit."

Jackson had him by the arm and ushered him closer to the town hall, almost to the stone steps. The evening air was buggy, sticky, skinned with heat. "I haven't told you this, Jim, but I've been getting calls. The other selectmen have too. Orville Farnham tells me he gets them every day."

"What kind of calls?" Morgan asked.

Jackson, who detested sticky situations of any kind, cleared his throat and gave himself a wider voice. "People think you're protecting MacGregor. If the boy is a suspect—and people have heard he is—they want to know why he's still wearing a uniform and carrying a weapon. It's a legitimate question, Jim. Myself, personally, I think a leave of absence would be in order."

"I can't do that," Morgan said. "He's getting socked with too much as it is."

Jackson looked around, looked back at the car, and rued the situation. He truly wasn't a man who asked for much: a breeze on his back in the summer, a warm house in the winter, and his meals brought to him on a tray when he had a touch of something. "This is hard for me, Jim. Sometimes I wonder what the reward is in being a town father."

"A little more than being a police chief. What are you trying to tell me?"

"Some of the people don't think you're doing your job, at least not one hundred percent. And then there's talk about, you know, those women from the Heights."

"If you hadn't sold all that woodland, we wouldn't have the Heights, would we?"

"Now you're treading into matters don't concern you, Jim. What I did with that woodland was for progress. A town that sits still dies." He rose on his toes, galled that he should have to explain himself. "The point is—"

"The point *is*, Gerald Bowman's been talking to you."

"He's a resident, he has the right."

"He also made you rich."

"Look here, Jim, I'm my own man, always have been." He felt his color rising, his exalted position in town questioned by one of his public servants. Morgan, expressionless, stared at him.

"How's your new Audi running?"

His face burned, and his dinner at the country club now lay heavy, a burden in his belly. Returning from a political dinner in Andover, three sheets to the wind, he had cracked up his old Audi at the bend near Tish Hopkins's farm. It had been the chief who pulled him out of the car, sobered him up, and drove him home no worse for the wear, though in the morning he warranted breakfast in bed. "You're taking this all wrong, Jim."

Andrew Coburn

"I'm trying not to."

"Take it in the spirit I'm giving it. Basically, I'm on your side, always have been." He cleared his throat again. "All I'm saying is that people want the town to get back to normal business. They want this Lapham thing cleared up."

"So do I," Morgan said without inflection. "Anything else you want to tell me?"

"No, I guess that's it. For now."

Morgan stretched his neck and waved an arm. "Good night, Mrs. Jackson."

Jackson watched him walk away and turn into the dark direction of the police station. *That's his home,* Jackson thought, *that's where he lives.*

When he returned to his car, his wife gave him a sweeping look. "You bloody coward, you didn't tell him."

"No, but I warned him."

As soon as Morgan turned the corner of the town hall he was confronted by Matt MacGregor, who was in full uniform, his service revolver slung low. "I heard it all, Chief. You played him like a fucking piano, like you do the whole town. You should do a concert on the green, charge admission."

"Keep your voice down," Morgan said, smelling beer on his breath. "Are you back to work?"

"Right. I don't want to use any more sick time." He pulled at the visor of his cap and gave a hitch to his trousers. "You're protecting me, that's what I heard said. And you're not going to take away my badge and gun. I've been socked with enough, that's what you said."

"And that's what I meant. Listen to me, Matt, can you listen to me?"

"I'm listening. Like I've been listening every day since I put on the badge. You say something, I jump."

"You're *not* listening."

"Go 'head, I'm listening."

"I think I can put it together. If I work it right, get Junior Rayball alone in a perfect place, I think I can make him admit Papa incited him into using the rifle. I think Junior's ready."

MacGregor staggered back a bit, and his eyes emptied. "You make it sound so simple, Chief. Life's never simple. Ask me. I can tell you." His voice snagged on something, then stumbled forth. "I thought I was going to have it all. Lydia would be my wife, and I even figured someday I'd have your job. That's a laugh."

"Don't count yourself out of anything, Matt."

"You giving me hope?" MacGregor said sardonically. Then he let out a belch, full force, which was what buddies of Morgan's used to do in Vietnam to show disdain for everything in sight, including themselves.

"Go home, Matt."

"I'm on duty."

"You're going home. That's an order."

Snapping to mock attention, MacGregor saluted. "Yes, sir. You're the boss, you're the commander. You're Sherlock Holmes."

They trudged along, Morgan in the lead, to the dimly lit parking lot behind the town hall. Morgan went to Meg O'Brien's old Plymouth, to the passenger side. He flung open the door. "Get in, I'll drive you home."

"Then where are *you* going?"

The Plymouth had a small knock in the motor. A single headlight affirmed the road, though Morgan could have driven it blind. This god-damn town of his. He knew every inch, where women still hung clothes on the line, where the young left their tissues and the elderly their tears, where his boyhood had ended with his father's death and his manhood had begun with his marriage, each spot marked sweet and sour. He glanced at MacGregor, whose smile was unsavory.

"I had you pegged, Chief. You got to her, didn't you?"

This was what he had been dreading. He had no defense and no explanation except a weak one. "It just happened, Matt. Neither of us planned it, that's the truth."

"I don't want the truth. The truth doesn't mean anything to me anymore. Give me a big fucking lie, make me feel better."

The response made him feel worse and even more so when

Andrew Coburn

he pulled up at MacGregor's house, where beer cans glinted in the uncut grass near the porch, where the light had been left lit for two days. A single can, squashed in the middle, stood cockeyed on the rail. He said, "Here we are."

MacGregor shoved the door open and got out, no argument, only a heavy grunt of exertion, which brought another belch, this one unintentional. He closed the door, but not securely. In a way that was almost graceful, he crouched down to peer in. "You're having what I had, Chief. Now you know why I'm nuts about her."

Morgan shifted into gear. "Good night, Matt."

"Want me to tell you what she likes best?"

The car fled. Too fast. He had not meant to push the accelerator that hard, and he slowed down. The night sky was brilliant. Every star seemed close. The lights were on at Lydia's. She must not have gone to work, or else she was back early.

The steps creaked. Instead of ringing the bell, he gave a light tap on the door and waited. Not long. She opened it and peered out at him. She was in the old robe, and her face was drawn, her streaky brown hair unbrushed. She spoke quietly and firmly:

"Not tonight, James."

The telephone, ringing insistently, woke him from a snoring sleep, and he battled a tangled sheet to free his legs and then, swinging out a blind arm into the dark, sent a little table lamp crashing to the floor. Moving on bare feet, he cut himself on shivers from the broken bulb. Senses battered, he clawed the wall in the passageway and produced a light that pained his eyes. Tracking blood, he groped his way into the vacant room, where the phone continued to shrill.

"Hello!"

A voice said, "Ready to clear your conscience, MacGregor?"

His eyes shuttered tight. "Fuck you, Bakinowski! Fuck you and your mother too!" Then he ripped the cord free and threw the phone against the wall.

◄ ◄ ◄ 10 ► ► ►

Chief Morgan woke early to another day of heat. Someone else was up early. A neighbor with a full-mouthed voice that jarred ears was calling her dog, a mongrel Morgan sometimes wished would run away and never come back. Had it been a shepherd he might have thought more of it, though he had got rid of his after Elizabeth's death. Happily, for years the animal had had the run of Tish Hopkins's farm, where it expired behind a chicken coop after a full life.

He made coffee and carried a cup out to the car. He still had Meg O'Brien's Plymouth. The mongrel, back, barked at him. Birds gusted from the neighbor's maple. It was not yet seven o'clock. Driving with purpose, relishing his coffee, he was doubly aware of himself and of the tiny beats in the misty air, of the vigor of the emerging green, of the ready-for-business appearance of every tree, from which light dripped like water. This was his day, he knew it!

He parked the car off the road, near the Rayball mailbox, and finished his coffee. Two swallows did it. Then he got out and, avoiding ruts, ambled up the gravel drive toward the weather-bitten house. He picked a berry on the way. A mosquito seeking a meal whined in his ear. He killed it.

Papa's pickup was there, Clement's rental was not, which

was what he had expected. Without the slightest sound he crept to the side of the house, to the window he knew was Junior's, and peered through the blighted screen, where he smelled broken sleep. Junior was awake. He had almost expected that too. "It's me," he whispered and watched Junior nod from the bed. "Where's your father?"

"Sleepin'," Junior whispered back, a willing partner in the conspiracy.

"Can you come out? We don't want to wake him."

Junior had slept half dressed, and it took him no time to put on the rest. He put naked feet into stinking socks and into frayed sneakers. Lifting the screen, careful of sound, he came out through the window. Then, without speaking, they slipped far from the house to the green shadows of pines full of bird clatter, where Morgan said, "What happened to your lip?"

"I hurt it."

"What do you want to know about your mother?"

Junior spoke as if with a taste of torment in his mouth, nothing to wash it out. "It was you that found her. Can you show me where?"

Morgan's composure was granite, though his eyes blinked. This was going too well. He did not want to spoil anything.

"Clement and me used to look, but we didn't know for sure where. We used to guess."

"I'll show you," Morgan said.

They slid off toward the swamp, with the ground quickly giving in to uncertainty. What once might have been a path heaved up roots, beneath which water began to sparkle. They stepped around a rotting stump emerald with lichen, a mysterious growth that was part one thing and part another. Were they there for something else, Morgan might have explained the chemical mystery to him, which is what he would have done with his own child had Elizabeth lived long enough to give him one.

Junior pointed. "We used to think it was there."

"No," Morgan said, though he was quickly realizing he had no idea where it was and that one place might be as good as another. Birds and insects decorated the morning silence, weaving their own kinds of words into it. Morgan's eyes roved. One spot looked likely, another less likely.

Junior said, "Clement said it was farther in."

"Not too far." The brush was rife with mosquitoes, which Morgan kept swatting. Junior stepped where it was quaggy and soaked his sneakers. After all these years, with new growth burgeoning and the old dying, it was impossible to tell where anything was. "Here," Morgan said.

Junior went down on his knees in the wet.

"No, not there," Morgan said. "I meant, here." And with an emotion he could not explain, a sadness that should not have been his, he watched Junior move on his knees from the wet to the dry. It was too dry.

"How could she of drowned here? There's no water."

"There used to be," Morgan said softly.

Junior whispered, "Mama."

Morgan said, "Do you want me to go away for a while?"

"No." He got up, his jeans plastered to his knees. "Now I know, I can come back by myself. I can even show Clement."

"You never knew her, did you, Junior? You weren't much more than a baby."

"I had a dream. I saw her face."

"She was a good woman, Junior." Morgan was measuring his words. Each one had to cut. "She never hurt anyone. Nor did Mrs. Lapham." As he spoke, Junior's eyes went down, where the ground had become sacred. "I don't blame you, Junior, not for what happened to either of them. I blame your father."

"Not for Mama. Mama did it herself."

"Are you sure?"

"I don't know how to be sure," he said. "I got no way."

Black flies appeared from nowhere and scratched the air. Morgan spoke through them. "Did you shoot Mrs. Lapham?"

"No sir."

Morgan spoke fast. "But maybe you were there. I mean, maybe. We're not talking for sure."

"Yes sir, maybe."

"Maybe you even had the gun in your hands. A rifle, wasn't it?"

Junior's eyes came up. "Yes sir, a nice one."

"Maybe you even had your finger on the trigger."

"A little."

"You heard the shot."

"I thought it'd be bigger."

A happiness flooded Morgan. A sweet epiphany. Everything he had figured was true, everything imagined was real. "You did it, Junior."

"No sir."

OK, he was simply going too fast. An easy remedy. He'd skip over this and come back later. He slowed his voice. "Where's the rifle now?"

"We threw it away."

"You and Papa?"

"Yes sir, me and Papa."

Morgan's voice went fast again, he couldn't help it. "Where?"

"I can't tell."

"But not here? You didn't throw it away here?"

"No sir."

"Maybe you threw it in Paget's Pond."

Junior's face reddened. "No sir, not there."

"Where, then?"

"I can't tell!" Junior said, and all of a sudden his breathing was disjointed. Simultaneously something clicked in Morgan's brain, something spoke to him out of his own bone and blood. He was looking not at a killer but simply at a boy who had never become a man, at a half-man who had been a stunted child. He was seeing, in another kind of epiphany, two sides of a human equation.

"You didn't do it, did you, Junior?"

The breathing was still harsh, raspy, not under full control. "No sir."

"Papa fired the rifle, not you."

"I ain't sayin'!"

"Tell me!"

"I can't!" Junior shouted and began sinking to his knees, this time involuntarily, his breath going, his eyes leaping. Then he was on his back, thrashing, turning another color, not a pretty one. Morgan was beside him in a moment and cursing himself. What in Christ had he done? What kind of bottle had he unstopped? He grabbed Junior and did what he could.

When they emerged from the swamp, insects shrilling in their wake, Papa Rayball was sitting on a stump and eating cold cereal from a cracked bowl. He was wearing an old red shirt with the sleeves hacked off above the elbows. Slurping from the bowl, he looked like a hunter who feasted on his game and relished the umbles. Morgan, anticipating rage, saw a smile, one almost of triumph.

"What've you been doin' to my boy? He don't look so good."

"He's all right now," Morgan said as Junior hung back.

"I don't know, I got my suspicions," Papa said. "Maybe you got so many women, you want boys now. You sure you're all right, Junior?"

"Yes, Papa."

"You know if the chief put his hands on you, you got a case against him. 'Course, it'd be your word against his, and yours ain't worth spit." Papa winked, with cunning in his open eye. "Ain't that right, Chief? Who's gonna listen to a retard? I mean about *any*thing?"

With a grimace of distaste Morgan said, "If you touch him, Papa, if you hurt him, I'll bring an assault charge. I'll also tell Clement."

"What do I wanna hurt him for? He's my boy, same as Clement, just that one's brighter than the other. Junior knows that."

With a parting look at Junior, Morgan turned and strode away, raising yellow dust when he reached the gravel drive. Papa watched every step with fiery blue eyes. He ate a little more from the bowl and heaved the remains into the poison ivy. When he looked at Junior, his face had darkened and contracted.

"What did you tell him?"

"Nothin', Papa. I had a fit."

"Good."

Matt MacGregor woke at nine. He would have slept until noon had the sun not shot through the window and struck him full in the face. He might have gone back to sleep were his cut foot not throbbing. He suspected bits of broken bulb were still in it. Sitting on the closed toilet seat, the foot propped on his other knee, he did his best to get the shivers out. Some he could not even see.

Shaved and showered, his head feeling no better than it should have, he dressed in civvies and told himself there was nowhere to go but up. In his mother's room, the bed unslept in since Memorial Day when she had left for the Cape, he picked up the telephone and shook it for damage. He did not want to think how he would repair the torn dent in the wall. "Jesus, Ma," he said aloud, "if you only knew." As he was leaving the room, the phone rang.

He snatched it up with glee. He had a whistle and was ready to blow it in the bastard's ear. But the voice was not Bakinowski's. He did not even recognize it at first. It seemed years since he had heard it. It was alien.

"All right," he said. "You say where."

Clement Rayball, breakfasting late, looked up from his *USA Today*, scowled, and said, "How did you know I was here?"

"How many good motels around here are there?" Chief Morgan said.

"What name did you ask for?"

"I didn't. I described you. You've got eyes like a sniper's, did you know that?" Morgan drew a chair. "Mind if I sit down?"

Clement folded away his newspaper and began eating his scrambled eggs and sausages. He used his cutlery in the European fashion, his fork in his left hand and his knife in his right, no need to put either down. "You want breakfast?"

"Coffee will do."

The waitress was already pouring.

"Thank you, Milly, a little more for me too," he said, and the young waitress obliged in a manner that verged on love. He said to Morgan, "Did you read the sports pages yet? Sox fined Crack Alexander for not showing up for yesterday's game."

"I read he's got a bum ankle."

"He was still supposed to be there. They fined him and suspended him. They don't need him, anyway. He's washed up. What do you want to see me about, Morgan?"

Morgan tasted his coffee. It was strong, fragrant, better than what he was used to. He took his time, for there no longer seemed to be a rush. "Junior and I had a talk. He's told me things, some things I knew all along. Now I need your help."

"You need my help, huh?" Clement pointed his knife. "You wired, Morgan? No, you're not that sophisticated. Besides, what good would it do you? What kind of help do you want from me? The kind that will put my brother away?"

"Junior didn't shoot Mrs. Lapham. Your father did." The waitress breezed by with a reassured glance that nothing was needed. "Did you hear me, Clement?"

"Did Junior tell you that?"

"It slipped out. It half slipped out."

"I don't believe it."

"Your father has killed twice. Now and a long time ago."

Clement slapped his knife and fork down on the plate but kept his voice low. "I don't want to hear a word more about my mother, you understand?" He reached for his coffee and composed himself. A shiver relaxed him. "Clement was my mother's maiden name, did you know that?"

Morgan nodded.

"It's all I've got of her. You understand?"

"Yes," Morgan said.

"Good, because we got nothing more to say." Clement snapped his fingers for the check. It came in an instant, with affection.

* * *

Too much heat burdened the air. The sky glared with more sun than needed. Papa Rayball got off the road and out of his pickup and breathed in the cool that hid in the pines. He hated summer and winter. He liked it best when the weather was neither, never too warm for a sweater or too cold to piss outdoors, which saved on flushing when the well was low. Junior, though, never flushed anyway, unless he thought hard about it.

Papa cut through the pines, through splashes of fern, to the rim of Paget's Pond, where dragonflies, as much at home on the water as in the air, performed for him. When he had been little, his folks alive, he used to bring a half loaf of Wonder Bread here for his lunch and fish with a pole made from a sapling. Never no butter for the bread, but that hadn't mattered. He looked at his watch, not a fancy one like Clement's, but it told him what he needed to know.

Ten minutes later, he heard the rustle of footsteps and did not bother to turn around. He could tell one man's step from another, the same way he could sniff a woman, no matter what color, and tell whether she was clean, safe to pay good money to. He said, " 'Bout time."

Matt MacGregor said, "This isn't smart."

Papa said, "Only smart MacGregor I ever heard of was your father. He left you money."

MacGregor, wearing an old shirt over jeans, picked up a pebble, cocked his arm, and skipped the pebble over the water. He had done it better when he was ten. "Nothing goes the way you want it to."

"Maybe you never knew what you wanted. 'Course, that ain't none of my business, like you made clear."

MacGregor picked up another pebble, but he did not skim it. He held it in his hand because it was warm. It was like half an egg. At age ten his mother had dropped eggs on toast for him—and if she didn't, his sister did. Always a woman to look after him. If you don't have a woman, what the fuck have you got? He said, "What are you smiling at?"

"People think the shooter missed, got the wrong one. Shit,

I ain't never missed in my life. I even had to shoot fast because she moved."

MacGregor brought the pebble to his mouth and took a little taste with his tongue. It was like tasting himself. He tossed it into the water.

"What did you think of *him* fallin'?" Papa said. "That was a bonus."

"I didn't ask for that."

"Like you said, you don't always get what you want."

"Chief's suspected it was you right from the start."

"We knew he might, and we knew it wouldn't make no dif'rence. He can't prove nothin'."

"You shouldn't have involved your kid. Junior. That was dumb. The chief's working on him."

"Don't matter. You tell Junior shit is candy, he'll eat it. He's not of a right mind. Chief knows that." Papa stuck out a hand. "I want the rest of the money."

"Not now," MacGregor said. "I've got a state cop breathing on me. He's been looking into my bank account. He sees another five thousand gone, he's going to want to know what I did with it."

"You sound scared. You scared?"

"I'm just telling you what's what."

Papa surveyed him with a sardonic eye. "You don't look so good outa your police suit. You look ordinary. Fact is, you look snot-nosed."

"For a little man you've got a big mouth," MacGregor said, strangely without rage, without even lifting his voice, as if Papa were no longer in the scheme of things but merely a player reduced to a minor role.

"Chief's pet," Papa said. "If he could see you now."

MacGregor's attention was elsewhere. From the far shore of the pond, where the woods were wild, scraps of sound from Girl Scouts floated over the water. He remembered that Lydia had attended the camp until she discovered boys, of whom he was the tallest. She said the handsomest. Pug nose and all. He said, "Don't push me, Papa."

"Why, whatcha gonna do? I'm not Junior you can grab by

the scruff. 'Sides, my other boy's home now. He could come at you ten dif'rent ways, you wouldn't know which."

"Threats don't bother me," MacGregor said.

"Jus' don't take too long gettin' me my money," Papa snapped back. "I did two Laphams, I guess I can do one MacGregor."

MacGregor turned and, with a limp, shifted from soggy ground to where it was sure. He looked back with the travesty of a smile. "This might surprise you, Papa, but maybe I don't give a shit."

"I'd like something different," Christine Poole said. "Something to please my husband."

Roberta, flinging back her oyster white hair, emerged from behind a little counter, where she left a cigarette burning. "We talking sexy or sedate?"

"Something tasteful. And I think I might drop down a size. I've lost a couple of pounds."

Roberta looked her over doubtfully and slid open panel doors, her trained eye at work, her fingers fluttering over fine dresses, dismissing many, picking a few, which she laid out on a table, one by one. "Let's see if we can choose from these."

They took them all into the fitting room, where Christine chose two to try on. Behind a screen she got into a stunning silky number supple in its cut, but a surfeit of belly flesh strained the material, which rode up on her hips. She came out with it draped over her arm. "I don't think so."

Roberta had another cigarette going. "I didn't either. And I have my doubts about the other one." She placed the cigarette between her lips and picked from the pile. "How about this one?" she said, draping billowing chiffon against herself, against a long boy's body on which anything would look good.

"It's not me," Christine said.

"But it's your size. Those two aren't." Roberta took the cigarette from her mouth. "Let's face it, Mrs. Poole, you're still a bit of a cow."

Christine's face fell.

"You're certainly not shapeless," Roberta added quickly,

"simply ungainly in the expected places, like most women."
She tapped Christine on the rump. "And you can't be ladylike
with that sticking out, can you? What you want is something
to give your derriere a gentle rise, not a dramatic one." Roberta
blew smoke. "Do we agree?"

"I've come here too soon," Christine said. "That's the
problem."

"Some bodies will always jut out in places," Roberta said,
retrieving dresses, "but there are ways to hide that."

Christine picked up her purse. "But not from your husband."

Papa Rayball, returning home, drove the pickup roughshod
over the ruts in the gravel and found Clement waiting for him.
Clement, who did not look friendly, stuck his face out of the
rental car and said, "Where's Junior?"

Papa stuck his face out of the pickup and said, "How the
hell do I know?"

"You'd know if you looked out for him."

"Don't tell me how to run my house!" Papa barked, but
then moderated his tone. "He was here when I left. He takes
a mind, he goes off into the woods, like when he was young.
You remember that, don't you?" Papa got out of the truck.
"You used to go lookin' for him, but you didn't find him unless
he wanted to be found. It's the same way now."

Clement ran a hand over his face. "Was Morgan here this
morning?"

"Yeah, he came sneakin' up here early and talked to Junior,
but Junior didn't tell him nothin'. Chief got him goin', and
he had one of his fits."

Concern overshot Clement's other emotions. "A bad one?"

"There ain't no good ones." Papa hooked a thumb in the
waist of his pants. "You got something on your mind?"

"I do," Clement said, "but it's going to stay there for a
while. At least till I see Junior. Then you and I might have
something to talk about."

Papa, holding his temper, smiled. "Father and son should
always talk."

Chief Morgan, fiddling with things on his desk, was racked with second thoughts. If Papa Rayball, a deadeye with a rifle, had been the shooter, how in hell had he missed Lydia and hit her mother? The mother's death made no sense. Only Lydia's would have devastated MacGregor and satisfied Papa's twisted sense of revenge. And having hit the wrong woman, why hadn't the old man fired again? He could not picture him panicking. Something didn't fit, he wasn't sure what, unless from Junior he had heard only what he had wanted to and read in everything else. And how much could he trust anything Junior said?

With a snap he sat up straighter. The question now was whether to continue following his instincts, which he felt had seldom let him down. Besides, too much had rung true in Junior's voice.

He stared at the telephone. Earlier he had called the fire chief in Lawrence, who had promised to call him back. Now he considered calling Lydia Lapham, though he was uncertain whether she was home or at the hospital. He called neither place, for he did not want to mention Papa Rayball until he had something more substantial. Nor was he confident that she wanted to hear his voice, though he ached to hear hers. He called Felix's Texaco.

"That was fast," he said when Felix told him his car was ready.

"I didn't want it hangin' around," Felix shot back. "It's an eyesore to my better customers."

"Deliver it, Felix. I got another job you can drive back."

To relieve tension, he went outside and paced the parking lot until he noticed people in the town hall were looking out at him. When Felix drove into the lot, he felt a mild letdown. The car looked worse for the wear, and drippings from a tree had left the windshield sticky.

"I wished you'd washed it," he said.

"And I wished I was born rich," Felix said, climbing out. "Here's the bill."

Morgan looked at it. "You're kidding."

"I never kid about money." Green-black strands of hair hung over his work-worn face. His thin mustache looked like a slick of grease. "OK, where's the junk you want me to drive back?" He looked around and saw it. "Jesus, not Meg O'Brien's car. The thing shouldn't even have a sticker."

"It's got a knock in the motor," Morgan said. "See what it is."

"You know what it is. She needs a new one."

"Maybe not. There's a headlight gone, better replace both before she kills herself. Bill the town."

Felix gave him a look. "You sure, Chief? You got enemies, something like that can hang you."

Morgan reconsidered. "You're right. Bill me."

Felix got into the Plymouth and cranked the window, which went down only halfway. "Am I supposed to fix that too?"

Morgan went back into the station, where Meg O'Brien, drinking root beer, looked up from her newspaper. "Good, now I've got my car back. Where are the keys?"

Sergeant Avery looked up from his paper. "And I don't have to drive you places anymore."

"Felix took your car," Morgan said. "You need a headlight. Don't worry about it, he's doing it free." He went into his office, and she followed.

Sergeant Avery shouted out, "How come you two always talk in private?"

Meg closed the door. "I have a telephone message from the Lawrence fire chief. He says you can do what you want. What's it all about?"

"Maybe nothing, maybe everything."

The sobriety of Calvin Poole's suit complemented a manner marked by reserve and restraint, which today had quickly stiffened into a facade. Ensconced in his bank, since the doors had opened that morning, were two federal regulators who, though unrelated by blood, looked like twins with their crisp red hair and close beards and pale, faintly freckled faces. They were interested in the dealings with Bellmore Companies. Though he had been polite, gracious even, and had put people and computers at their disposal, he remained sickened by the sight of them. He knew the questions they would raise, the answers he would have to give.

He avoided them. He confined his activities to his office, which was high up over Boston, with a vast window that overlooked infinity. After a while he stopped taking telephone calls because he did not trust the quality of his voice. He was quietly brutal to his loyal secretary, which appalled him. She knew the score and was only trying to comfort him. He would apologize later. He would dispatch flowers to her and Red Sox tickets to her grandson.

In his private bathroom he blew his nose and got snot on his sleeve, which he spent three minutes carefully removing with cold water, though a trace remained. He thought of his prep school days and remembered the classmate he had shunned for trying to show him dirty pictures. Given those pictures now, he would pore over them. He weighed the possibility of prison and wondered whether he would be treated differently, whether he would be put in with his own kind and not the others.

Midafternoon he could bear the bank no longer and left quietly by a private elevator. It was like walking away from a minimum-security facility, or sneaking off school grounds after curfew, which he had never done. He had obeyed the rules, respected the honor code. He had pored over no dirty pictures. He had held himself to a higher standard in the neurotic presence of that faculty wife whose penchant for boys was well known.

The street was heated and busy. People in the quick-stepping sidewalk crowd gave him the feeling that they were going nowhere except on and on. A man in pinstripes like his moved corpulently past him. Glass buildings blocked out the sun but held in the heat. He looked for a bar.

He liked what he found. Good old-fashioned heavy paneling, hunting scenes hung large, and tables that offered a degree of privacy. He chose the nearest. He stretched a leg and felt some of the tension drain out of it. The throb in his left temple lessened. The demurely dressed waitress, busy behind the bar, signaled that she would see to him soon. He smiled back, no hurry. Then a man came upon him.

"Do you mind?"

He did not have a choice. The man, who had carried his drink with him—straight scotch, it looked like—had already seated himself. A tasteless necktie hung tristfully, pining for a tighter knot. The voice was big.

"My name's John. What's yours?"

He did not know this man. He did not want to know him. He said, "Calvin."

The waitress appeared, and John said, "Give Calvin whatever he wants. It's on me. And bring another Cutty."

The waitress said, "Don't you think you've had enough?"

"Six hours from now I might have enough. Now, no." He laughed. He had a warm, full-blooded face, a manly nose, and a substantial mouth. "I've lost my job, Calvin. What d'you think of that? Twenty-two years with the same company, and I'm out on the street. I wasn't the only one. They let a bunch of us go."

Poole looked for a means to escape, but felt anchored. The leg that had lost all that tension now lay under the table like lead. The waitress was back and placing a scotch before him, which he did not remember ordering. She left nothing for John, who gazed up in wonder.

"Mama knows best," she explained, and he smiled with glee.

"Isn't she a cutie? We'll share yours, that all right, Calvin?"

Nothing seemed right, and yet nothing seemed really wrong. The world was simply going one way and he another. "Be my guest," he said.

"Everything's catching up, Calvin. That's the bitch of it. And I'm a little scared, I'm man enough to admit it. Some guys wouldn't. They'd pretend."

Somewhere in the bar, tuned pleasantly low, was music. Vera Lynn was in the midst of a medley that always stirred the heart. It brought back all those World War II movies and the bravery of the British.

"I wasn't always scared, Calvin. Actually, I was adventurous. I left home when I was sixteen, slept in cars, washed up in public rest rooms, ate where I could, worked where I could. Happiest time of my life." He appropriated the scotch. "I'm self-educated. I spent a lot of time in libraries beating the cold."

A serious student, Poole had also spent much time in a library, where that faculty wife had helped out on Wednesdays and Fridays and sat negligently on a step stool. He wished now that, like the British, he had been brave and risen to the challenge.

"I had a lot of jobs, Calvin, but eventually I got into insurance, learned everything about it from a real nice fella. Some people, you know, won't teach you anything, they hold back. They're afraid you'll take their job, but old Lapham wasn't like that. He wasn't so old either. Had a bad heart and retired before his time. Often wonder how he's doing."

The name meant something to him, but he couldn't figure out what. He also couldn't figure out why he was sipping scotch from a glass someone else had had his mouth on.

"My first wife, Calvin, she hung me out to dry in the divorce. My new wife, she's a pretty lady, but she's stepping out on me, not even hiding it. She says I can't cut it anymore. There was a time I could cut it with the best. Believe me."

He believed him. He even half liked him.

"She's young. You must've guessed that."

"Yes, I guessed that."

John's eyes were minnows swimming in one direction and then another. He tapped the table for another drink. "Calvin, my first wife was a peach. I betrayed her."

"Yes, I guessed that too." He had an extra sense, a third eye.

"The worst thing is not my marriages, not my job, but my cat. She died last night in the kitchen. I was in the living room and heard the death gurgles. Nothing I could do. Too late, Calvin, everything's too late."

The waitress brought two drinks, and John tasted his and said, "I told you she was cute." Poole tasted his. It was ginger ale. "You got the world by the balls, don't you, Calvin?"

"Not entirely," he said.

He was bothered by the smoke when John lit a cigar, but it did not stay lit. He drew his leg up and found some spring in it now. John went to the men's room. He could have left then, but he did not. He stayed for John, whom he felt he owed something.

The bar served light suppers, and they broke bread together. "My treat," Poole said. There was a new waitress now, less caring. They lingered over coffee, and then it was truly time to leave. "Six hours," John proclaimed. "I said six hours, didn't I?"

Poole rose on steady legs. John's, surprisingly, were even steadier, though he had managed to have another drink, a double. Outside, the day's heat clung to the evening air. Street traffic had diminished, but exhaust smells hovered. John said, "You OK, Calvin?"

"I'm OK. And you, John?"

"I'm tiptop."

"You're not going to do anything foolish, are you?"

"I know what you're thinking." John smiled his big smile. "I don't have the guts for that. And I'm not driving. I'm going home in style, a taxi." They shook hands. "You're a real gentleman, Calvin. See you around."

"He's dead," Poole said.

"Who's dead?"

"Lapham."

"Poor old bugger," John said and hailed a taxi.

Poole strode on, past the bank, which was closed, the regulators gone but sure to be back tomorrow. He must not forget to send flowers, tickets too. That faculty wife, he remembered, had done herself in on pills and top administrators had breathed sighs of relief. He breathed in the chill dank of a parking garage, his heels tapping a monotonous tune across a gruesome tier of concrete. He rode the elevator to his car.

On Washington Street, a traffic light smoldered too long and he drove through it. The dashboard with its printout of cold blue lights was vaguely threatening, as if the automobile

Andrew Coburn

were programmed to explode under certain conditions. He rode the ramp onto the Central Artery and as he made the swing onto Interstate 93, he caught a last full look at the city. Ribbons of lights from the bigger buildings gave it a packaged look. It might have been a fabulous toy wrapped in gold and black, what a millionaire might give to his mistress. It was where his father had made his money and kept it, and where he had made his money and lost it.

He was tired, he hadn't realized exactly how tired he was. He was glad to be going home.

Clement Rayball tracked him down, not in the woods, but, guided by inspiration, at Wenson's ice-cream stand, where he saw him licking a cone at a secluded picnic bench inside the shade of a willow. He approached him with an easy stride, with a smile, with nothing to upset him. There was leaf shadow on his face and strawberry ice cream around his mouth. He sat across from him and said, "Use your napkin."

"Just before you said, I was gonna." Junior smudged his mouth.

"I heard you had a fit."

"I did." Junior spoke cheerfully. "The chief took care of me."

"How's your tongue?"

"The chief untucked it. I didn't bite it. He's a good fella, Clement."

Clement propped his elbows and brought his hands together. Two girls were looking for a table. Junior stared at the peaks in their T-shirts. "Who am I, Junior?"

He smiled. "You're Clement."

"Who else am I?"

"You're my brother."

"Your blood brother. You know where Florida is?"

"That's where you are."

"When I go back, how would you like to go with me? You could live there."

Junior looked happy, then uncertain. "I don't know."

"Tell me what you don't know. We'll talk about it."

Junior looked bewildered. "I don't know what I don't know."

"Then just tell me what you think of the idea."

"I've always lived with Papa, I don't know any other place." Anxiety made him fidget. "Would Papa come too?"

"I'll tell you what, we'll talk about it later. All right?" The two girls had found a table in the dying sun, and now they were staring over ice cream, one with giggles. Clement scowled, and they turned their heads. "Do you know why I came home?"

"To see us."

"To make sure nothing bad happens to you. But I can't guarantee nothing will if I'm not here. Junior, don't pay attention to those girls. Pay attention to me. Did you hear everything I said?"

"Yes."

"Now I'm going to ask you something, and I want the truth. Did you shoot that lady?"

"No."

"OK, just relax, everything's fine. Now I'm going to ask you another question. Did Papa shoot her?"

Junior hesitated, but not long. "Yes."

Clement tightened his hands under his chin. He felt an unsettling breeze on his neck. It felt like somebody's hot hand.

"He did it for me, Clement. To pay people back."

Clement stared up into the willow. "If he did it for anybody, he did it for himself."

"Don't tell him I told."

"I won't. I promise." He pulled himself up and put on a smiling face. "You take care, I'll see you tomorrow."

Junior bit into the cone. "Clement, am I a retard?"

"Who said you were?"

"Papa. Is it good or bad?"

"It's neither. It's something some people are and some aren't."

"So I am."

Clement felt something pull at his head and hurt his heart. "What you are, Junior, is my brother."

Lydia Lapham did not ask him in. He brought himself in with all his spiritual luggage and his overly good face and parked himself in the overstuffed chair that had been her father's favorite. Wrapped in her robe, she returned to the sofa and, despite the heat, stretched out under a thin blanket. She had had a chill since morning.

"Matt needs you," he said.

She closed her eyes. "Please, Reverend, some things aren't your business."

"The boy is eating himself up over you, I've seen it with my own eyes."

He was talking MacGregor and she was thinking Chief, whom she feared might be another mistake in her life. Another Matt. Another Frank. Another waste of precious years.

Reverend Stottle sat straight in his chair, like Abraham Lincoln in his. "Gauge your own grief, Lydia, and consider that his might be every bit as great as yours. You have lost your parents, and he has lost his mate."

"We weren't married."

"Ah, but you were as mates, don't pretend you weren't."

"Again, that's not your business. I don't even want you here, Reverend."

"We're all God's creatures," he said with utmost patience. "We must look after each other. Matt has a duty to look after you, but you won't let him exercise it. You'll end up driving him into the arms of whores."

"Tell him to wear a rubber."

"I didn't hear that, Lydia. It passed right over my head. Your lips, as far as I'm concerned, remain sweet." He shifted his feet. He started to rise and then stayed put. "God's breath became the beauty of women. I've always believed that. That's why no woman is born without charm."

She opened her eyes. "That's too fancy for me, Reverend. I'm sorry." The room was dim. The sun had quit coming in. Her eyes closed again.

"We all have unworthy thoughts," he said in a tone of concession, "men and women alike. When I was a boy I wanted to become a tailor so I could run a tape measure around a woman's bust. My uncle, on my mother's poor side, was a tailor and regaled my father with off-color stories. My father repeated the stories to my mother to remind her of her humble origins."

"Your father must have been a winner," Lydia said in a drowsy voice that left a taste in her mouth.

"My mother," he went on, "was a wise woman. When I said dirty words she reminded me that God has big ears. When I threatened to run away she packed me a lunch and told me not to eat it all at once because it would have to last me forever."

His voice was an irritant. "Reverend, I'm so tired. Would you please *go?*"

"I understand. Go to sleep. I'll tiptoe out."

She pulled the blanket closer and nodded off almost at once, though for no more than a few minutes. Now, instead of fighting chills, she was sweating and tossed the blanket off. Opening her eyes, she saw shadows and her father's empty chair. The stillness of the house was too intense to accommodate even his ghost.

Switching on a light, scattering any ghosts that may have tried to intrude, she mounted the stairs and used the bathroom. On her way out her shoulder banged the wall. She used the light from the passageway to enter the bedroom. Reverend Stottle's clothes were on the floor, and Reverend Stottle was in the bed, the covers pulled to his chin.

"I've been waiting," he said, his face fervent with a calling.

She turned, descended the stairs, and reached for the telephone. After misdialing once, she rang up the station. Bertha Skagg took the call. The chief came on the line moments later.

"James, you'd better get over here."

Chief Morgan escorted him out of the house, guided him down the path, and walked him to the car with a firm grip

Andrew Coburn

on his arm. Reverend Stottle shivered. Abjectly he said, "Are you taking me to jail, Chief?"

"I'm taking you home. Get in."

The reverend slipped into the passenger side of the chief's car and gave a start when the radio crackled. Head bowed, he placed his hands between his knees. The chief settled in beside him and tried to start the motor, which took awhile.

"God damn you."

"Don't curse me, Chief."

"The motor, not you."

"I've been under stress."

"Obviously."

The motor roared. The car fled forward, and the chief clicked on the headlights, which shot out and froze a cat and caught the gold of its eyes. He sped around it.

"You won't . . . you won't tell, will you, Chief? I'm on shaky ground at the church."

The chief said, "I won't tell."

"My car's back there. People will know."

The chief took a corner. "I'll have it returned to you," he said and slowed down a little. So far, for the most part, he had avoided looking at his passenger.

"You're disappointed in me, aren't you?"

"That was my girl you were bothering, Reverend."

"Not your girl, Chief. Matt MacGregor's."

"*My* girl."

"Yours? Really? Chief, congratulations. When the time comes, the church is yours free, even the organist, and I'll do the marrying. A deal?"

Morgan looked at him. "Reverend, shut up." He ran the car around the green, swerved into the drive beside the church, and pulled up near the white house, where the Stottles lived. "Good night, Reverend."

Reverend Stottle slipped out, stopped short, and looked back in horror. "I think I may have left something there."

"Don't tell me."

"My underdrawers."

"That happened to me once."

Reverend Stottle's smile came out nervous and conspiratorial. "We're no angels, are we, Chief?"

Christine Poole may not have found a suitable dress at Roberta's, but she did come upon running togs that caught her eye in Donna's Sportswear. They were crimson with white reflective bands, and she bought them immediately, though the price was outrageous. She had them on that evening, when the sun was nearing its low, and jogged three miles along the byways of Oakcrest Heights. She would have done more had the air not been so sultry. Her late supper was cottage cheese on a leaf of lettuce.

She was not surprised that her husband was not yet home, for she knew that the regulators had been expected that day and were probably still there with their treacherous little calculators. She imagined they even wore eyeshades. Poor Calvin.

Later, the stereo providing the haunting theme music from *Once Upon a Time in America*, she stretched out with a magazine and read women's secrets of weight loss. At ten o'clock she became concerned and called the bank, but heard only a recording. At eleven the front bell rang. She opened the door and saw a broad-shouldered state trooper, whose summer hat was in his hands. Her mind raced. Poised in her crimson sweats, she felt like something said too loud.

"My husband?"

"Yes, ma'am. He was in an accident on Eye-Ninety-three."

"He's hurt."

"It was a bad one, ma'am."

"He's dead."

"Yes, ma'am."

11

◄ ◄ ◄ ◄ **11** ► ► ► ►

With Chief Morgan watching from the shore, two scuba divers from the Lawrence Fire Department spent the morning searching Paget's Pond and came up with nothing of interest. They promised to return after lunch for another try. Hopes still high, Morgan returned to the station. Meg O'Brien, eating at her desk, said, "Any luck?"

"Not yet."

She was eating homemade potato salad laced with onion and herbs. "Want some?"

Dropping into a chair near her desk, he took some. Sergeant Avery was at the Blue Bonnet, and they had the station to themselves. Morgan had briefed her on all pertinencies, which neatened his mind but did not soothe it. He took a swig from her can of root beer.

"I want him, Meg."

"I know you do." She passed a napkin over her mouth. "Are you sure he threw it in Paget's?"

"Of course I'm not sure! He could have buried it. There are miles of woods. When I was at his place yesterday I could've been walking over it."

His tone was sharp, and he regretted it. Meg rose from her desk to retrieve something of no significance from a table, her way of giving him time to pull in his horns. She was wearing no stockings, which revealed the veiny luster of her legs. She was no spring chicken. Christ, neither was he. She had to be fifty, at least, and what was he? Forty-fucking-six.

"Meg, I'm sorry."

"What are you sorry about?"

"Everything. Me especially." He finished off her root beer. "What do you think about when you wake up at three in the morning?"

"My ulcer. That's what wakes me."

"I didn't know you had one."

"A lot of things you don't know, but that's all right. You're not supposed to. Watch the phone, will you?"

She gathered up containers and cutlery from her desk and went into the lavatory to wash them out. He stayed seated and gave way to a mood. What if they don't find the rifle? What if they do? Can I connect it to Papa?

Meg returned and said, "You didn't ask me what I dream about."

"OK, what do you dream about?"

"A lover dying in my arms and leaving me an annuity." She sat down at her desk, poised unevenly as if her buttocks were of unequal balance. "You're right, water's the best place to throw something, but I wouldn't pick Paget's. It was me, I'd toss it in the river from the bridge at the West Newbury line."

Morgan studied her face. "Yes, so would I."

Clement Rayball drove to Lawrence. The place he was looking for, Sherman's Rod & Gun, was situated between a pet store with a sick parrot in the window and a woman's shop where the mannequins were gussied up to suggest accomplished whores. A bell rang when he entered the gun shop and did not stop until he stepped back and closed the door securely. Sherman was a gaunt fellow with pouched eyes and an embroidery of neck skin. Clement explained what he wanted, and Sherman, whose eyes stayed hooded, wheezed down, opened a low drawer under the counter, and came up with two heavy-duty handguns of the sort that cost serious money.

"Take your pick."

Clement said, "I don't want one to keep under my pillow forever. I just want one that works."

"You want a cheap-o."

"I don't want one that's going to break up in my hand."

Sherman returned the big handguns to their privileged place and produced a Saturday night special. Clement inspected it carefully, and Sherman said, "It works, don't worry."

Clement balanced it in his hand, opened and closed the chamber case, tried the trigger, and said, "How much?"

"Two hundred."

"I didn't hear you."

"One hundred. That's as low as I go. You want ammo?"

"I don't need much."

"I got a few loose slugs. I'll throw 'em in the bag. Got your permit?"

"Do I need one?"

"You sure do," Sherman said, and Clement peeled off a hundred-dollar note and laid it on the counter. Then he added two more.

"Do I need one?"

"You sure don't."

Reverend Stottle was in bed, suffering. Mrs. Stottle brought him broth, and he sat up so she could arrange a tray over his lap. The napkin was one of their linen ones. When everything was settled for him, he reached for her hand, which was always there to accompany him through strife. He could always count on her. "My Sarah," he said.

She felt his brow. "I'd say it's nothing more than a little touch of something." Her eyes went wise. "You haven't been up to anything, have you?"

He tasted the broth, letting the grease linger on his lips before licking it off. "God," he said, "gave all of us hindsight, but few of us foresight."

"That means you have," she said and went to the window

to raise the shade. A ceiling fan, whirring quietly, rearranged the heat in the room. "Who have you antagonized now?" When he did not answer, she said, "You'd better cool it if you want to keep your job."

"I had a dream last night."

"I thought so. You were tossing."

"I dreamed I answered a knock on our door and found Jesus lying on the step, dead of his wounds. Why would I have such a dream? What does it mean?"

"It means you shouldn't have eaten all those Oreo cookies before you went to bed."

He stared at her. She was a down-to-earth woman, someone to whom he could always return after his flights of fancy. He soaked a Saltine in his broth and ate it when it turned to mush. "All of us," he said, "are born in blood and usually die in a bigger mess. That's our beginning, Sarah, that's our end."

Her back to him, she was busy poking in the dresser, where he could see her face in the glass. She was no beauty, granted, but she had provocative features and had never lost her shape. When they were young she had dished herself up to another man before settling on him. A man unworthy of her. But that was years ago and ninety percent gone from his mind.

"Only Adam," he said, "came into this world pure. He had no belly button. He was God-made."

She shut the dresser. "And you have lint in yours, and a wonderful lady made you."

That was true, and it brought tears to his eyes. His mother, God rest her soul, had died last winter, a year younger than Mrs. Dugdale. He wished he had been there to do for her what he had done for Mrs. Dugdale in those short hours before death.

The telephone by the bed detonated.

It split his head and spilled his broth. His wife rushed forth and snatched it up before it could explode again. Her voice was clear and gracious, that of a reverend's helpmate. She placed her hand over the mouthpiece.

"Matthew MacGregor wants to talk to you."

He paled and gestured hard and fast. "Tell him I can't talk to him right now. Tell him I'm indisposed."

"He can't talk to anyone right now, Matthew. He's under the weather."

"Way under," Reverend Stottle whispered.

Her hand was back on the mouthpiece. "He says he's coming over."

Chief Morgan glimpsed Randolph Jackson leaving the Blue Bonnet and caught up to him on the green when Jackson paused to breathe in the scent of the grass and other growing things. His eyes were small, as if he had not had his required sleep. The chief said, "I'm expecting a break in the Lapham case."

Jackson looked at once expectant and dubious. He patted down his hair and waited.

"Two scuba divers from Lawrence are searching Paget's Pond for the weapon," Morgan said.

"That's where you think it is?"

"That's where I thought it was, and it might be, but since then I got a tip it's in the river, at the West Newbury bridge."

"So they're probably wasting their time in the pond. Where'd you get the tip?"

"From a wonderful woman," Morgan said.

"I hope she's not from the Heights," Jackson said with his eyes in the air and started to move on. Morgan stopped him.

"There's a problem, Randolph."

"A problem, Jim. Don't we have enough of those?"

"The divers are working the pond gratis, a personal favor from the fire chief in Lawrence, but if they come back tomorrow to do the river I might have to think about paying them."

"Well, you have a budget, Jim. Unless you're already in the red, which is usually the case." There was an edge to Jackson's voice. He was generous in many ways but never with money, his own or the town's, which he considered his own. "And you've always been a sloppy bookkeeper."

"I was wondering if we could come up with some creative accounting," Morgan said blithely, and Jackson gave out a wild smile.

"Do you know what my wife says, Jim? Do you know what Suzy says about us? She says you intimidate me. She says you do it by just being your damn self, like the whole town revolves around you."

"I didn't realize she felt that way."

"Well, this time I won't be intimidated. If you want to search that river, you jump into the water yourself. So there you have it!"

Jackson swaggered away in triumph, whacking down his sandy hair, though none of it was up. Morgan watched him for a while and then turned and left the green. Malcolm Crandall and Fred Fossey were standing on the town hall steps, and he quickened his pace to avoid conversation. In the station, Meg O'Brien gave him a grave look. Sergeant Avery was still not back from the Blue Bonnet and the station was quiet, but she said, "Can we go into your office?"

He went in first and plunked himself down at his desk, tearing off two bygone pages from his calendar block, which he seldom used. He preferred keeping things in his head. "So what's up?" he said.

"Christine Poole from the Heights, she's a friend of yours, isn't she?"

"I know her."

"Her husband was killed last night on Ninety-three. His car hit an abutment."

For a number of seconds Morgan did not react. Then he ripped another page from the block. "How do you know?"

"Ethel Fossey's been phoning people. I must've been last on the list."

He ran a hand across his chin. "Thank you, Meg. On your way out, close the door please."

Alone, he looked at his watch. The seconds ticked in his head. When they made a minute, he lifted the phone and tapped out a number, which rang and rang and, like many things in his life, went unanswered. He imagined her sitting

Andrew Coburn

alone, stone still, as if under an infernal spell; then he wiped the image from his mind and rang up Drinkwater's Funeral Home.

"Everett, this is Jim Morgan. Do you have Calvin Poole there?"

"Yes, we do. We got him in this morning. He's not too bad, considering."

"Is Mrs. Poole there?"

"Yes, she is. My oldest boy is helping her with arrangements."

"How is she doing, Everett?"

"Holding it all in. A lot of people do that."

"Yes, she would," Morgan said without meaning to, and the image of her alone returned, this time with her face stark and frozen. "Everett, she didn't come by herself, did she?"

"No, Chief, one of her sons is here. The boy flew up from New York. Also she has a friend with her. A Mrs. Bowman, I believe."

The image fled. "Thank you," he said and started to hang up. "Everett, don't tell her I called."

Too late. The line was dead.

Clement Rayball pushed himself out of his car and trod over grassless ground to where Papa was tinkering with a bicycle. He said, "You make much money doing this?"

"It adds to Social Security and what you give me. 'Sides, I do it only when I feel like it, keeps me busy." Papa spun a wheel. "I pick the bikes up and I bring 'em back. I give people service."

Clement glanced around. "Where's Junior?"

"He's off again. Yesterday he didn't do the weekly wash, and he still ain't done it." Papa wiped his hands in a rag and shook sweat from the tip of his nose. The heat was abrasive. "You messin' up his mind, Clement? I didn't ask you to come all the way back to do that."

"Why did I come back, Papa?"

" 'Cause this is family. You like it or not, you ain't got no other." Papa tossed the rag aside. "You wanna get out of the heat, we can go in the house. No, it's hotter inside. We can go over there."

They ambled to the taller pines, where the wet was sultry and bright greenery had been spored into existence overnight. The claw marks of some wild animal gave drama to the soft ground. Missing heads of wildflowers suggested a groundhog.

"You know, Papa, you always made me think Ma was no good. I grew up thinking that, even when she was alive. But in my heart I know the kind of woman she was, she was a good woman."

"A husband knows, a son don't."

Clement wore an expression of purpose, necessity, but it began to crumble of its own weight. He broke off a fern frond and ran his thumb and index finger down the length of it, against the grain, stripping it of its growth. "Junior never shot that woman, Papa. You did."

Papa was cool. "You been listenin' to lies."

"No, I've been listening to myself. Junior doesn't have it in him to shoot anybody. But you do."

Papa's cool was intact, with something like pride added to it. "You was always smart."

"Why did you do it?"

"For Junior. Someone treats him like shit, it's the same as treatin' me that way. It tells you what they think of all of us."

"So you tried to take MacGregor's girl out and hit the mother instead."

"She got in the way."

"I don't buy it."

"Then I ain't gonna argue it."

"For whatever god-damn reason you did it, why did you involve Junior? Why the hell did you bring him along?"

"Guess you ain't so smart." Papa's color rose high, only partly from the heat. " 'Case something went wrong afterward. Me, they'd fry. Junior they'd only put in a home or someplace. He might even be better off there. I ain't gonna live forever, and you ain't gonna want him in your fancy life."

"Junior was the hedge to save your own ass."

"Look at it how you want."

Andrew Coburn

"When I go back to Florida," Clement said evenly, "I'm taking him with me. I'll let you and the chief fight it out. That is, if he's still chief. He might not be."

A muscle jerked in Papa's face. "You want Junior, take him, but he ain't likely to go. He don't know how to spit without me."

Clement said, "I'll teach him."

Chief Morgan, anxious to return to Paget's Pond to negotiate the following day with the divers, slipped out of the station and hustled into the parking lot as a Rolls Royce crashed through a haze of heat and ground to a stop. Morgan recognized the car and the driver and said, "Not now. Sweet Jesus, not now." A door flew open, and Crack Alexander, quite tall, came out of the Rolls in a crouch. Morgan was six feet; Crack, erect, was five inches taller. His voice was bigger.

"Where do you wanna talk, Chief? You wanna talk here, or someplace else?"

Morgan gave a quick scan of the back of the town hall. No faces were in any of the windows, which dismayed him. He wanted the protection of witnesses. "Here's all right," he said.

"You're a cop, how come you don't wear a gun? First time you came to the house, you didn't have one then either. I was cuffing the wife around, remember?"

"I remember," Morgan said.

"That's when you first met me. And Sissy. Right?"

"Right."

"That's when it began, you and her. Right?"

Morgan said nothing. The space between him and Crack was negligible. He could see the fillings in the big fellow's teeth and the hair in his nose.

"Don't deny it, she's told me *everything.*"

Told him everything? Did that include the hours he never laid a hand on her but simply sat close while she related her life in a girl's voice? Did it include the few times he did make love to her and she invariably called him Crack? The time she said, *Crack likes to do it this way?* He murmured, "What do you want me to say?"

"I don't want you to say anything. I want you to look at me."

He *was* looking at him, but they were within a circle too tightly closed. He was seeing large pores, an old scar over one eye and crow's-feet beneath it.

"What do you see?"

The longer he looked the less intimidating he found him. Gone was the muscularity that had suggested barbells and metal stretching devices. In its place was a vague bigness.

"What you see is a has-been. It took you and Sissy to tell me something I wouldn't admit to myself. How old are you, Chief?"

"Forty-five," Morgan said, knocking off a year.

"I'm thirty-seven. In baseball that's two years past retirement."

"Don't tell Nolan Ryan that," the chief ventured.

"Nolan Ryan's a pitcher playing with an artificial arm, like Tommy John did. I'm a hitter. They don't give hitters artificial eyes. Wade Boggs, he's got the eyes I had. 'Course, he's a lousy singles hitter. I always stroked the big ones. Shit, I was young, they compared me to Williams."

Morgan sensed the circle widening. Air blew in. The Rolls had been left running. The throb of the fine-tuned motor could have been the hum of a human heart.

"Fact is, I can afford to retire. Kind of money I made, I got nothing to worry about."

Morgan said, "I'm sure you don't."

Crack's squared shoulders gave in a little. The aggressive stance sank into a lesser attitude. "When I found out about you and Sissy, I was gonna beat her to a pulp, but the strength went out of me. It was like she wasn't really there but gone from me. I didn't want to lose her."

"I can understand that."

Crack gave him a knowing look. "Forget what you two did together, I don't care. All the gals I had, they didn't mean anything to me, and you didn't mean anything to her. I got her word for that."

"She's all gold," Morgan said, which Crack took the wrong way, with pride.

"She's a real blonde, not one of those others. But I'll tell you something more important you didn't know. I might be going out of the bigs, but I'll always be her hero."

Morgan wanted to say something, but his brain stuck. Then it unstuck, and he said, "Any chance of getting one of those autographed balls like you gave my sergeant?"

Crack grinned wide and, stepping back, reached into the Rolls. "Here, have two." Then he gave a sweeping wave to the town hall. In each window was a face.

Tish Hopkins's square-cut gray hair bobbed in the sun. The heat did not bother her. She was a tough old bird, perhaps a little younger than she looked, and still lean as cable wire. With the death of her husband, too many years ago for her to think about, she had lost one of the deeper meanings of her life, but her essential self prevailed. The farm was not all that it once was, but she had steadfastly refused to sell so much as an acre, which put her on the wrong side of Randolph Jackson when he was selling his woodland to a developer and wanted to work her acreage into the deal. All the cows were gone except an old thing not worth the bother, but she kept it for sentimental reasons and for the manure, which she could still shovel with strength and enjoyment. With the same enjoyment she fed her hens, prime layers, and gathered their eggs, frequently placing one against her cheek as if it were precious. That was what she intended to do now, gather eggs from one of the coops, but a shadow near the woodshed snared her eye and proved to be alive.

"Who's there?" she said, and Junior Rayball sidled into the open with a sheepish smile. Her eyes crinkled and narrowed. "I haven't seen you in ages," she said. "I could say you've grown but you haven't."

He shuffled closer, wearing a cap with stitching on the front, and scuffed up some dust. She remembered him sitting on a shitpile and eating sultana raisins from the box, a treat from her cupboard.

"What are you doing here, Junior? You come to give me a visit after all these years?"

"I'd've come a long time ago," he said, "but I didn't think you'd want to see me."

"Not want to see you? I've missed you, boy, didn't you know a simple thing like that?" She watched him beam the way he had when she had praised his handling of a pitchfork, awkward as it was, and she remembered his looking at her with the eyes of a pup caught peeing on the rug the time he had tried to go home with an egg in his pants and it broke in his pocket. *Don't have to steal, all you have to do is ask.* "You come for anything special or just to say hi?"

"I might go to Florida," he said.

"That so? Who's going to take you, you go?"

"Clement."

"I heard your brother was back."

"He came back to see me."

"He was always a good boy. Quiet, always quiet, I remember that. Florida sounds nice, Junior."

"I might not go. Depends."

"Depends on what?" she asked and was aware of the sudden tenseness in his posture, as if he had another egg in his pocket.

"On if you might let me come back to work for you like I used to," he said.

"I got a boy working for me, part-time. One of the Wetherfields, Floyd, you know him? He's putting himself through community college." She watched Junior's face begin to flatten into itself, and quickly she said, "He's not smart like you were when it comes to chores. You were the best."

"I just thought I'd ask," he said, "in case."

"Never any harm in asking. You want to come in for a drink of something cold?" she said, but he was already backing off, raising dust, perhaps feeling the heat of the sun, which would have been in his eyes had it not been for the visor of the cap.

"I gotta go."

She watched him break into a trot and then into a run, and she wondered whether she'd been wrong not to have found

Andrew Coburn

something for him to do. Poor bugger, he had always gotten in the way, the short time she'd had him.

Reverend Stottle got himself out of bed and waited for Matt MacGregor on a piece of wrought-iron garden furniture. Mrs. Stottle's garden shrilled too many colors. The reds, of which there were many, screamed. The oranges blared, and the several varieties of yellows whined. The music, he noted with melancholy, had been in the irises, cool blues and touches of bishop's purple, and in the sweet William, pinks and whites, which were gone or nearly gone.

Mrs. Stottle called from a window. "Would you like me to serve something when Matthew comes?"

"No, dear, I don't think he'll be staying long," he answered back with a slight cough. A jay flew toward a treetop as if on a secret errand—or perhaps for an assignation, a supposition that added to his apprehension. The possibility that MacGregor was coming to redeem his former girlfriend's honor had grown into a certainty.

When MacGregor arrived he felt an instant flood of relief, for the young man's face revealed no murderous intent. On the contrary, it bore the mark of a choirboy in need of guidance, of a father's firm hand, which made the reverend's world seem right and proper again. God was good.

"Nice of you to see me, Reverend."

"You didn't give me much choice," he said with a smile to show he held no ill feelings but was there to serve.

MacGregor sat down hard on metal, framing himself against roses that looked preoccupied with their own overly red beauty. He was shaved, which he had not been the last time Reverend Stottle had seen him, and he was dressed neatly in casual clothes. Only his voice was haggard. "Do you know what it is to love a woman?"

"Mrs. Stottle and I have been married an appreciable number of years. I do believe I know what it is to love a woman."

"Love her so much you'd do anything to keep her?"

Reverend Stottle pictured Mrs. Stottle with a suitcase in

hand at the open door and himself on his knees begging her to stay, which he had been prepared to do the night before. Thank God the chief was a brick and spared him such nonsense. "Yes, Matthew, I believe I do."

"That's how I was with Lydia."

"She may not be all you thought she was," he said, recalling her cold anger with not a word spoken as the chief hustled him out. A tic in MacGregor's face alerted him, and swiftly he added, "But I can't think of a finer woman, with the possible exception of Mrs. Stottle."

"I thought afterwards, after the thing, she would need me more than ever."

"Yes, the terrible thing," he said. "And I would have thought the same, indeed I would."

"You know what I'm talking about."

"Indeed." But the intensity of the young man's eyes caused him to avert his, briefly, for a splurge of scarlet phlox got on his nerves. Mrs. Stottle had a green thumb but no eye for coordinating colors.

"I knew one was enough. The key was the mother. All I had to do was twist it."

He felt that he had missed something, but it did not matter. The boy was spouting wind and relieving his innards. A good minister, he had been told in Bible college, must learn when to hold his tongue, at times even to bite it, lessons in his salad days he had been slow to learn, his rash, eager lips more likely to issue a solecism than a kindness. What was the unpleasing nickname his colleagues had given him? He'd rather not remember.

MacGregor said, "I knew the father had a bad heart, and I knew how close he was to the mother. I knew he wouldn't last long after she went. What surprised me was he didn't wait a minute."

Reverend Stottle perked up. "I spoke those very words, more or less. If you had been in church Sunday, you'd have heard them."

"It went better than it was supposed to. Rayball never knew he'd be popping one, but I'd be getting two."

He realized he was missing more than he thought. It was the damn flowers. Those acid yellows had no business in the garden. And Rayball. What did Rayball have to do with the price of sugar?

MacGregor said, "Her mom and dad gone, I should've had her in my arms that night, crying her heart out. Mine forever. Instead she's shacking up with the chief." He stopped himself, as if some things he could not think about. His breath went in. "Last minute I wanted to stop it, I called to warn her, but nobody answered. It was too late."

"What was too late?"

He looked deep into Reverend Stottle's face. "You *don't* know what I'm talking about."

"Not entirely," the reverend conceded, though the reference to Chief Morgan was certainly clear.

"Best laid plans, Reverend. You know what they say."

"Yes, I do, but I still don't understand."

MacGregor rose with a lightness he had lacked until now. "You think about it, Reverend. It'll come to you."

With a mild sense of relief Reverend Stottle watched him leave and then strode from the garden, glad to leave it, pleased he had done his duty. As he opened the side door to his house he remembered, with distaste, the nickname: Shit-for-Brains.

Chief Morgan waited on the shore of Paget's Pond for the scuba divers to finish the futile search. His sleeves were rolled to the elbows, and his forearms were red from scratching mosquito bites. The heat had ushered in a whole new generation. Behind him came footsteps.

"What's going on, Chief?"

"A hunch that's not working out," he said.

Lieutenant Bakinowski stood beside him. "They looking for the weapon?"

"Yes, but it's not there."

"Save yourself some time. Ask MacGregor where it is."

"You're ruining a good cop," Morgan said. "He's not showing up for duty."

"I can understand why. I'm breaking him. I'm wearing him

down. It's a damn crude way I'm doing it, but you left me no choice. You gave me no help, and neither did Jackson. I went over your head, you know. It didn't work. That's what I like about these god-damn little towns. Everybody's got a finger up the next fella's ass. You got yours up Jackson's, MacGregor's got his up yours."

Morgan took a breath, held himself in, and swatted his arm. "I have nothing to say to you except leave MacGregor alone."

"Yeah, I'll leave him alone. I'll hand him to you on a plate and you can cut him up any way you want." Bakinowski turned away and after a few steps looked back. His voice was calm. "I've been doing homicide too long not to know a killer when I see one. And you, Chief, you're plain wrong."

"Not wrong, just mixed up," Morgan said. "I had the wrong Rayball, is all."

"You want to explain that?"

"Yes, when I bring him in on a plate."

The evening seemed sultrier than the day had been, no movement in the air. The air in the station was clammy. Bertha Skagg's thighs stuck together, and her feet swelled. "I can't take no more of this," she said, and Chief Morgan sent her home and took her place at the phone with its modest array of buttons, two of which were meaningless. He punched an outside line and fingered in Lydia Lapham's number, which rang through. Then he called the hospital, but she was too busy to talk. He had the impression she did not want to. After a long hesitation, he rang up Christine Poole's house, expecting to hear the son's voice, but it was Arlene Bowman's.

"How is she?" he asked.

"How do you think she is?" There was a pause. "Are you asking yourself how much you had to do with it? You'll never know, will you?"

"I understood it was an accident."

"If you believe that, you must be great friends with the tooth fairy. Services will be private, so you needn't worry about attending."

"Are you handling arrangements, Arlene?"

"She has a son here, but he's no help. Her other son is in Africa with the Peace Corps, he's sent regrets. Calvin had children of his own, but they're not here yet. So, yes, I'm helping out. Does that bother you?"

"I hope she can't hear any of this."

"Of course she can't. And let me assure you, you're least in her mind. You may not even exist."

"Thank you, Arlene," he said and quietly disconnected.

A half hour later, Meg O'Brien came through the door with sandwiches and two cans of root beer. The sandwiches were cream cheese and olive, with a side wrapper of dill pickles. She said, "I knew Bertha wouldn't stay."

"I've got bad news," Morgan said, immediately biting into the sandwich she had slid his way. "The divers aren't coming back tomorrow. One's got commitments, and the other's going on vacation."

"Just as well," she said, passing him a pickle. "That was only a guess of mine about the river."

Morgan made a space between his finger and thumb. "Meg, I'm this close to getting him."

"Good," she said. "For Matt's sake."

Papa said to Junior, "You look at me when I talk!"

"I am," Junior said, his sneakered feet hooked on the rungs of his chair. He and Papa were at the kitchen table, around which the heat of the day was hovering for the night. Sweat dripped from Papa's nose.

"You don't let Clement fill your head with Florida, you hear?"

"I ain't said yet I'm goin', Papa. I'm jus' thinkin', like he told me."

"What you thinkin' with? *This?*" Papa rapped his own head. "You ain't got nothin' in there. I'm the one does your thinkin'."

Lowering his eyes, Junior placed his hands on the table and played with his fingers. "Would you miss me, Papa?"

"Ain't a question of missin' you. It's a question of what

---

you're gonna do on your own. Clement, he ain't gonna have no time for you down there, he's got his own life. You'd be like shit on his shoe."

"He wouldn't of asked me, he didn't want me."

"*Now* he wants you, later he won't." Papa snorted, the sweat flying. "You don't know how to do nothin' without me, when you gonna learn that?"

Junior lifted his face, with some fight in his eyes. "Lots of things I do you don't know about."

"Like goin' behind my back, that what you mean?"

Junior flushed and said nothing. His fingers were at play again, with Papa watching him closely. A bug beat at the screen in the window. Then Papa rose from the table, his voice softening.

"I'm gonna watch some TV, you wanna watch it with me?"

Junior shook his head.

Chief Morgan drove through the warm thickness of the night to Lawrence. He left his car in the Emergency lot and, entering the hospital, filtered into a waiting crowd of mothers with crying children, men with fierce wounds, and youths with their eyes glued to their hundred-dollar sneakers. A nurse bellowed a name. In some ways the area had the accusing air of a courtroom. He found quiet in a corridor and sought direction from a woman worker in sagging support stockings. At a nurses' station he was advised to try the cafeteria.

Lydia Lapham was sitting with a doctor. He guessed who it was. The gray in the man's hair pleased him. "Can I talk to you?" he said to her.

The doctor rose as if on a command from his scrotum. "I was just leaving."

Morgan sat in the vacated chair and pushed aside the empty coffee cup, which rattled in its thick saucer. "How are you?"

"I'm fine."

She did not look it. Stark minimum makeup put her face closer to the bone and made her eyes enormous, forcing them to shift for themselves. Her frazzled uniform looked like milk hesitating between fresh and sour. "Was that your friend?" he asked.

"Don't tell me you're jealous."

"I don't have the right to be."

"But you are," she said.

"Yes."

"That's interesting." A few white threads dangled from a sleeve, like thistledown. "Tell me more."

He pushed the doctor's cup farther away and said, "Was the other night something that happened and won't happen again?"

"I don't know what it was. I've been pondering it. I'm a little afraid of you. Who are you?"

"I'm starting to ask myself that."

"You're not Frank. You're certainly not Matt, and I'm not the wife you lost. They say you still carry her around."

"Not like I used to. Not as much."

"I hope to hell I don't look like her. Do I?"

"No."

"That's something." She had a little coffee left. She drank it. Two nurses smiled at her in passing. "I don't want to make any more mistakes with men. What bothers me is that I'm fair game. The Reverend Mister Stottle showed me that."

"Did *I* take advantage?" he asked.

"No, James. But could it have been anyone if it hadn't been you? That's the question in my mind."

"I'd like to think no."

"I would too." She looked at her watch and rose. Quickly she freed the back of her uniform, which was sticking to her legs. He was conscious of her down to the tips of her toes. He felt her in his nerves. She said, "My mother used to say I looked like a bride in my whites. Do I still?"

"Yes," he lied.

"I have to go," she said. "Thanks for dropping by."

Mrs. Stottle joined Reverend Stottle in the study, where they enjoyed late after-dinner coffee flavored with chocolate, a particular favorite of the reverend's. His brow was faintly troubled. "Do you remember, dear, our first parish in Rhode Island?" She did. She remembered it well. She had been some thirty years younger. He said, "The ladies' garden society kept the grounds beautiful, but I noticed something sinister. The magnolia blossoms lasted less than a week, the same with irises that bloomed later. Day lilies gave a show of longevity but only because they staggered their wealth. In reality everything was over in a wink. That's the way it is."

"And always has been," she said.

"Of course, we have heaven to look forward to."

"Heaven, I suspect, is filled with happiness too horrendously consistent to enjoy."

"I was thinking of Mrs. Dugdale, poor dear. Heaven is where she is, certainly not hell."

Mrs. Stottle tinkled her cup, paper-thin china, in the saucer. "Hell is hard labor and heaven no work at all. Which is worse?"

"Purgatory," the reverend said. "But of course we're not Catholics."

"Even they don't believe in it anymore. How are you feeling?"

"Better."

"I'm going to bed," she announced.

"Yes, I'll follow," he said, but settled a little more comfortably in his club chair, which had accompanied him to all his churches. On the wall hung a photograph of his graduating class, the cream of their generation, he liked to think. Then, for an hour, he listened to Beethoven and entered the depths of the music.

When he crept into bed, his wife was asleep, snoring ever so lightly. He stole back portions of the top sheet that belonged to him, a theft that occurred nightly, a sin of less importance than the colors of her garden. Then he laid his head on his pillow, contented.

Twenty minutes later, waking abruptly, he exclaimed, "Oh, my God!"

His voice bit through Mrs. Stottle's sleep, and she lifted her head. "What's wrong, Austin?"

"Matthew is going to kill somebody. Maybe himself."

"What? Don't talk nonsense. Why would he do that?"

"I *know* why."

Matt MacGregor ate a meal and listened to his mother's music. Peggy Lee sang "Say It Isn't So" with a mellow seductiveness that affected his stomach. Perry Como's "Prisoner of Love" churned it. The pain was bearable, in ways enjoyable. He could not imagine his father having shared with Mom what he had shared with Lydia, the kind of kisses that wallowed into the deeper ones and led to the antics of porno films. Hidden in his room was an old Polaroid of Lydia posing in a wet T-shirt. His mother never would have done that, nor would she have stood for his father whispering explicit things in her ear. That was a different generation.

He cleared up, stacked the few things he had used into the dishwasher, and put away the milk. The house had one and a half bathrooms. The half bath had been his and his sister's. Ducks, frogs, and sunfish still provided the motif. In the mirror he absorbed his own cankered smile in memory of a father whose face he scarcely remembered but from whom he had got his pug nose and nothing else.

Stepping back, he shucked off his shirt to look manly. He looked more than manly. He was a cop. Flexing an arm, he made a muscle. He had more than muscles, he had firepower.

Bare-chested, he phoned Lawrence General Hospital and, adding depth to his voice, asked for Lydia. He was transferred to a person who said she might be in the cafeteria. Would he like her to call him back? The impersonal tone of the voice, vaguely patronizing, kicked up a memory of Mrs. Lapham, whose dream was that Lydia would marry a doctor. He, Matthew MacGregor, was not up to her mark.

"Sir."

An old anger moved a muscle. The old bitch never knew that Lydia had fucked around with a doctor already married and that he, Matthew MacGregor, had waited in the wings until she came back to him, damaged goods, which he received willingly, no complaints, no recriminations.

"Do you want Nurse Lapham to call you back?"

"Not necessary," he said and banged the phone down. Even old man Lapham had considered him scrub, not varsity. It was not until the past year that the two of them had started worrying that Lydia would never marry and began favoring him.

He turned up the radio. Sinatra was beating out "I've Got You Under My Skin," which stretched his anger. He climbed the stairs heavily, each thinly carpeted step sending up a discordant note of music, and entered the larger bathroom, where an old-fashioned tub clawed the floor and his mother's best towels hung from a rack. The mirror flashed at him, and he menaced himself with a look. His eyes waxed. The lines around his mouth were ugly.

He clumped into his boyhood bedroom in half mufti, and minutes later reappeared in full uniform, armed for bear. The handgun was unauthorized, a Magnum. He poised himself in the doorway of his mother's bedroom, which was almost consumed by a four-poster for two people. His father had left so long ago he was no longer sure the man had ever existed. A framed photograph propped on the dresser was the only evidence. He aimed the Magnum. His hand jerked, the picture exploded.

He descended the stairs with a lighter step and a vision. The entire length of Lydia's body lay suddenly in his mind as if he were two persons and the other were with her now, having his way, taking his due. When she lay flat, her belly went in and her ribs came out. Then the vision darkened and altered. Not he but the chief was having his way. Whirling, knocking over a table lamp, he faced the old piano, tuneless now, that his sister had played dreadfully and he not at all. He fired two shots into it and struck chords drawn from the depths of the earth.

His heart pounded, overdriven. His eyes were lightning bugs. In the heat of his head Lydia rose, turned her back on him, and mocked him with the bold slash of her rump. The chief crazed him with a fatherly smile. He fired again, shat-

Andrew Coburn

tering his mother's only heirloom, a vase, and blowing a hole in the wall.

His chest heaved. Through a roar he heard Peggy Lee crooning, "Where Can I Go Without You" and saw the singer's gold-trimmed eyes and felt the breath of her red mouth. The words struck him. Lurching, Lydia in his head and the chief in his sights, he tripped over the lamp. His free hand leaped out to break the fall, but his gun hand, doubling in, detonated. In an instant, ugly and irrevocable, the shooter became the shot.

◄ ◄ ◄ **12** ► ► ►

Meg O'Brien took a call from Mrs. Ingersoll, a neighbor of Mrs. MacGregor's, anger in her voice. "He's got his radio going full blast, and he's shooting off firecrackers or something. Sounds to me like he's wrecking the place."

"I'll call him," Meg said with hidden alarm.

"You'd better do something! What's his mother going to think, she comes home?"

Before Meg could do anything, the other phone shrilled, and she grabbed it. It was another voice fraught with urgency. The night sergeant, who had been watching and listening, motioned to the chief, who was coming through the door. "Something's up," he said, and Morgan swept forward. Her face a bulge, Meg thrust the phone at him.

"It's Reverend Stottle calling about Matt. I'm not sure what he's saying, but he's scaring me."

Morgan took the phone and ordered the reverend to calm down. The night sergeant whispered to Meg, "What's up?" She said, "Matt, God damn it. Matt." Morgan barked into the phone, "What makes you say that?"

Meg picked up a newspaper, furled it, and clutched it. Then she stood stone still until the chief put the receiver down. His face glittered from the heat. "I know Stottle's batty," he said, "but—" Her teeth scraping her voice, Meg told him about the other call. He said, "I'm going over there."

"I'm going too."

"What's going on?" the night sergeant asked.

"Nothing," Morgan said. "At least that's what I hope."

The night sky was bright over the parking lot, with a great tide of stars speckling the unknown. Backing out, Morgan almost hit the sergeant's car, but on the street he drove more reasonably. Shadows of teenagers wavered on the green. "He's probably had too many beers," Meg said in a small voice. "I bet that's all it is."

The MacGregors' house was lit. They could hear the music. Next door Mrs. Ingersoll appeared at one open window and her husband at another. Mrs. Ingersoll shouted, "He's quieted down, but he's still got that damn radio on." Morgan ignored her. He told Meg to stay in the car, but she climbed out and dogged him to the front porch, where moths militarized against them. He rang the bell.

"Jim, he probably can't hear it."

He tried the door. It was unlocked. "Stay here," he said and went in.

The stench of cordite was strong, which for a moment stopped him in his tracks. Then his shoes crunched over broken bits of pottery. He saw the radio, an old Stromberg-Carlson, and killed the sound. His scalp prickled when he saw the fallen lamp, which was still burning, and glimpsed blood on the carpet, a smear here and an accumulation there. Meg was behind him, half a fist in her mouth.

"Get out of here," he said in a whisper. "Radio in for an ambulance."

"Where is he?"

Breathing in the sickened air, he felt inner beads unravel. His head hummed as his eyes sought room for doubt. "Do as I say, Meg."

She obeyed, and he stood still with formal rigor, though he was not absolutely sure his feet were on the floor. From the shadows of an overstuffed chair came a voice he hardly recognized.

"I'm here, Chief."

"I know you are."

MacGregor was sprawled deep in the chair. He was corpse-faced, like Andy Warhol. His uniform shirt was gore. His smile seemed someone else's. "Not scared, are you, Chief?"

What Morgan should have seen first he saw belatedly and feared for his life. But the bloodstained hand that held the Magnum, despite an agony of effort, lacked the strength to lift it. The voice was all ache and irony.

"I can't do nothing right, can I?"

With caution, dreading enlightenment, Morgan crept closer. "Reverend Stottle called. What was he trying to tell me, Matt?"

"You don't have the guts to hear."

"It's time I did."

MacGregor coughed blood, producing a fine burst of sparks but leaving his smile intact. "I want to see her face when she finds out."

"Finds out what, Matt?"

"I know her better than you. It'll break her. It'll crack her up."

Hearing footfalls, Morgan glanced over his shoulder at Meg, who kept her distance. Then the air altered, and he knew MacGregor was gone, though the face did not look truly dead. The eyes were half lidded in an intently thoughtful way as if the final details of death still needed ironing out.

"Jim, is he?"

Morgan, still staring down, said, "It would seem so."

Nobody got sleep. At six in the morning Chief Morgan returned to the station. At quarter to seven Meg O'Brien went over to the Blue Bonnet and brought back coffee and dough-nuts for everybody, using her own money, for none was in the kitty. All uniformed officers of the Bensington Police Department—once six, now five—were there. Sergeant Avery, whose eyes were red-rimmed, threw an arm around his cousin, who was nearer Matt MacGregor's age. Despite her ankles, Bertha Skagg was in. Somehow she had heard.

Andrew Coburn

In his office, exhaustion written on his face, Morgan stood at the open window and drank in the morning air. Then he returned to his desk to consume the coffee but not the doughnut Meg had brought him. She sat nearby. The door was closed. "Someone will have to call his mother," he said. "I can't."

Meg said, "You have to."

Morgan tore a page from his calendar block and wiped up a coffee spill from his desk. "It had to have been an accident," he said. "No man would have shot himself that way on purpose."

Meg said nothing. Cords stood out in her neck as if all her strength were situated there. Her eyes were simply spots in her face.

"Most of the blood was near the knocked-over lamp, that's where he must have done it."

"What difference does it make where he did it? He did it."

"I just want it clear in my mind."

Meg looked at him with much insight, all of it sympathetic, and said, "What you want made clear will take time."

"I don't want the guilt, but I've got it."

"Then you're choosing it."

Morgan's eyes grew large. "Meg, I saw it in his face. He wanted to kill me."

"Most sons do."

"I *wasn't* his father."

Meg picked at her blouse, which was sticking to her skin, to let in air. With some force she said, "What will you tell his mother?"

"As little as possible."

"Then I'll let you get to it," she said and rose. At the door she looked back. "It wasn't your fault."

Except for the pervading heat, the day was uncertain. Clouds wrestled the sun. Distant thunder faintly rumbled, but no hint of rain followed, though a silvery bird squirted like water through the pines. Clement hopped the ruined step and entered his father's house. "Where's Junior?"

Papa looked up from his cereal bowl. "You put Florida in his head, you shouldn't of done that."

"He talked to you about it?"

"I talked to him, told him what it'd be like. Told him he'd have to change the way he eats. Wouldn't want him shamin' you in front of your fancy friends. We figure you got plenty of them, livin' like you do." Papa scratched himself. "Also told him he's got only one papa, and it ain't you."

"You got your ways, don't you?" Clement said. "So where is he?"

Papa dug back into his cereal. "He got up early so I wouldn't hear him. He took the truck."

Clement was concerned. "Can he drive it?"

"He can drive good as anybody, but he ain't got a license. I go to Lawrence I see people can't speak English, but they got a license. You explain that."

"Aren't you worried about him?"

"He took twenty dollars from my pocket. That ain't near enough."

"Near enough for what?"

Papa smiled. "I know where he's goin'."

Chief Morgan made the call to the Cape. It was the daughter he talked to, Matt's sister, thank God. The mother would have gone to pieces as soon as he said the words. The daughter, mother of three little ones, had more control, could hold in what would come later. "What kind of accident?" she asked, and he said, "With his gun." Her voice went shrill. "Not that Magnum we begged him not to buy?" She could at least take temporary comfort in the fact that they had warned him. "Yes," Morgan said.

Afterward he faced the problem of telling Lydia Lapham and decided her aunt would be the best one to do it. After assigning Meg the task of phoning Miss Westerly, he left the station, tramped across the green, and headed for the house behind the Congregational church. Reverend Stottle, gaunt, something gone from his shoulders, was waiting. They sat on garden furniture under an intermittent sun.

"I want to know exactly what he told you," Morgan said.

Reverend Stottle appeared muddled, stricken, fissured. "He said so much and yet so little, sometimes as if I weren't there. As if I were already privy to the torture in his soul. The sense of it all didn't strike me till after Mrs. Stottle and I had gone to sleep. I don't know what woke me. Perhaps not a human hand. But it came too late, didn't it, Chief?"

Morgan spoke sharply, "From the beginning, tell me what he said."

"I've been going over it in my mind ever since. Matthew's face, his alien voice, his cold, ironic words, they're all in my hot head, Chief."

"Tell them to me!"

Reverend Stottle cleared his throat, raised his face, and began reciting dialogue like a radio actor with two roles, two voices, one of them MacGregor's, which he gave chilling and sardonic inflections. Morgan never interrupted and never took his eyes off him. His eyes blinked noticeably only when the name Rayball leaped from the reverend's lips in MacGregor's raw voice. When he finished the performance, for which applause would have been appropriate under different circumstances, Reverend Stottle wiped his embattled face and shuddered.

"Is it as diabolical as I think it is, or am I reading too much into it? Tell me I am."

Morgan said, "Son of a bitch, Bakinowski was right."

"Is there blood on my hands, Chief?"

"Maybe on a finger, but it's all over me."

"I don't think I missed anything."

"It was a confession, like you were a priest."

"If I were a priest, I could not have repeated a word of it. Praise my ancestors for being rabidly anti-papist."

Junior Rayball sped south on Route 93 with his body thrown close to the wheel like Papa's and hot winds blowing in from both open windows. Like Papa, he kept to one lane, no switching all around like those other drivers who swerved in front of him. Reaching Boston, he was not frightened by the soaring clamor of the Artery, for he had an animal's sense of direction and knew just where to get off and then which turns to take. He did not fight the traffic like Papa often did, he went with it and smiled when others honked their horns. Sometimes he honked back and waved.

He was put off now and then by the constant surges of traffic and almost sideswiped a taxi, but he kept his head and his smile and waved to a derelict who gave him the finger. The only thing that scared him was a motorcyclist varooming between lanes.

He found the street, those dirty old buildings told him so. Church music springing out of a store confirmed it. He parked almost in the same spot Papa had and did not worry about the truck because Papa had said it was safe there. He took a few steps and then hurried back to retrieve the keys. Maybe it wasn't that safe.

He entered the little lobby of the hotel, every bit the same as he remembered, especially the smell of disinfectant that, like the other time, stirred a memory that did not quite emerge. Then he was smiling into the fat pink face of the man who had called Papa by a different name.

The man remembered. "Richmond's kid," he said. "Where's the old rooster?"

"I left early," Junior said.

"That's OK, we start early. Black or white? Your father alternates."

He looked confused. Then he said, "The one I had."

"I don't remember the one you had, but I think your old man had Inez. She's not one of the early birds. I got something precious you won't have to make a choice, half this, half that, best of both. A real beauty is what I'm telling you."

The one he had had had purple shades in her skin, a different purple down inside her place. He waited for the key, which he remembered hung off a hunk of clear plastic with a number on it.

"Where's your money?"

He laid down two tens crinkly and worn from Papa's pocket, all that had been in it, which did not please the man.

"For that I can give you something looks like a woman, but he ain't in yet. Besides, he might not be in at all. He twisted an ankle on those high heels."

As if it had all been a joke, the man gave him a wink, which might not have been one. The fat face made it hard to tell. He waited.

"Thirty more you want the real thing."

Something was going wrong. "It's all I got."

"Full fare, no kid prices." A telephone was ringing. "Get out, boy, come back when you can do business."

He backed off, all the way to the door and stopped. He had got up too early and come too far not to get it. As the man talked, he edged toward the stairs. When the man half turned his back, he sneaked up them.

The corridor was narrow and smelled of that stuff. He tried to be quiet. He tiptoed and heard nothing from the rooms. He jumped when a door opened and a white woman who looked as if she had just got up ballooned out in a pink robe. Her face had a roundness that made him remember a girl in third grade who had climbed the play slide with a hole in her underpants. He was behind her on the rungs. The woman, both breasts visible, scrutinized him, and now he knew something for sure, he didn't like white. Black was better. The woman said, "You got money?"

He had the two tens back, but he wasn't going to spend them on her. Now she was looking at him in another way that reminded him of a teacher, first or second grade, he couldn't remember.

"I think you'd better go home," she said.

He crept on, turning a corner. He was looking for the rooms he and Papa had used, and he found them not by the numbers, just by where they were. It was Papa's door he stopped at, as if now he were going to take Papa's place. Quiet as he could, he twisted the knob and let the door swing open a little. A black woman was lying on the bed, and a white man was watching her touch the purple in her place. At first he thought she was only scratching herself. Then he caught the significance. The man's face was explosive, pitted with shot holes.

"Get out of here, kid."

"I ain't no kid."

But he backed off, took a few steps away, and flattened himself against the corridor wall. He wondered if that was what Papa had done, only watched, but he remembered the sounds heard through the wall. Then the man came out the door and said, "Little bastard."

He took the blow on the head, but he didn't fall, only staggered. The man had hit him with something metal, he didn't know what. It might've been a lead pipe drinking water's not supposed to run through anymore. Years ago a man from the town had told Papa to take theirs out, and Papa had told him to go to hell.

He found the back stairs and sat on the top one. Blood dripped down his neck from the back of his head instead of the front, where it hurt the most. He thought he would sit there until he felt better, but the hurting got worse and went into his stomach. He made his way down the stairs and, with deliberate steps, ambulated through an alley to the street, where he locked himself in the pickup and scrunched down deep behind the wheel. His cap lay on the other seat, and he put it on.

A questing homosexual man regarded him with curiosity and then with an urge to help, the kindness glimpsed and partly acknowledged, but the man moved on. Two prostitutes viewed him with amusement. One tapped on the window, but he ignored her. Later he lowered the window a crack. He needed the air.

When Chief Morgan returned to the station, Lieutenant Bakinowski was waiting for him in his office. Something was different about him, not only the new suit—a summer-weight French vanilla—but the eyes. They seemed too tightly set in their cages, as if something had driven them in for good. And he was not sitting presumptuously at Morgan's desk as he tended to do, but squarely in a chair, like a visitor. He said, "We've got to figure out what it means."

Andrew Coburn

Morgan dropped into the chair behind his desk. "You tell me what it means."

"I'm just trying to rule out the possibility he might have—"

"It was an accident. If you want to cut it fine, it might have been an accident meant to happen." On his calendar block Morgan scribbled "FLOWERS—2," underscoring the word and circling the number. Then he said evenly, "But we can't get into another man's mind, isn't that what you told me?"

"I thought I was in his, I still think so, I'm just not so sure now. I drove him pretty hard, Chief, things you don't know about."

"You don't need to fill me in."

"If he had planned it, left a note, we'd have a confession. There'd be no doubts. Tell me something, Chief, do you still think I was wrong about him?"

Morgan picked up the pencil again and toyed with it, breaking the point in the process. "It doesn't matter what I think."

"You're not holding anything back on me, are you?"

"What would be the purpose?"

"I don't know. It's your god-damn little town."

The words had a constricting effect on Morgan. The pencil was fixed in his fingers. A chair scraped. Bakinowski rose, straightened his suit jacket, and narrowed the knot of his tie, which was tastefully lavender, with some yellow.

"Too bad we didn't work closer together, Chief. Maybe it wouldn't have come to this."

"Who knows?"

"Maybe neither of us knew what we were doing."

"I've had the same thought," Morgan said tightly.

"But we're cops, for Christ's sake. We had to follow our noses."

"You're a cop," Morgan said. "I don't know what I am."

Rubbing his neck, Bakinowski stepped stiff-legged to the door. He was less himself without the swagger, or perhaps more himself. "I'll admit this to you, Chief. I wouldn't like to think I drove him to it."

Morgan waited until he opened the door. "He drove himself."

Junior Rayball came awake with a smile. He knew what that smell was now. It was Mama. Mama moving a mop and telling him not to step where it was wet. He heard the voice, he even saw the face, the same one he had seen so plain in the dream. A pretty face with strands of hair getting in the way. "Mama," he said, but not loud because boys were about.

He knew it was late because there was little light left in the sky and cars weren't jumping by every second. Clinging to the wheel the way a squirrel grips a tree, he drew him up and told the hurt in his head to go away. He was all sweat, and his legs were sticky. Though he had tried not to, he had peed himself twice. He didn't dare touch his head because it brought back the bleeding.

The same boys kept walking by the truck, back and forth, the bigger ones without smiles. The smaller ones made faces and banged the door. One even crawled into the bed but didn't stay. He closed his eyes and tried to bring Mama back, but she was gone, doing other chores, and he was sucking his thumb, which Papa hated but Mama didn't mind. He was special, she said, needed protectin'.

When he opened his eyes, two of the bigger boys were sitting on the hood and looking in at him, and one was scraping a knife across the windshield. He did what he knew Papa would've done. He turned the key on and roared the engine. Then, though it hurt him, he twisted the wheel as far as it would go and bounded onto the street. One of them stayed on longer than the other, and then that one fell, all his own fault.

His brain crowded his skull, but he wasn't scared. If he could get to I-93 he'd be all right.

Chief Morgan needed sleep, no doubt about it, but when he flopped onto the sofa, loafers kicked off, sleep would not come. His head stayed lit, and his thoughts came to sharp points over the Rayballs. Decisions had to be made, and he

　　　　　　　　　　　　Andrew Coburn

was making one on Papa, one that came much too easily. He lay with an arm over his eyes and then got up.

Little in the refrigerator was edible. Leftover clam dip sported fuzz, a banana stank sweetly inside its blackened skin, and something indefinable crept from a dish that had been pushed to the rear. He threw everything out except three bottles of beer, a carton of milk that still smelled fresh, and a can of Hershey Syrup he had punched open two mornings ago. Mixing chocolate with milk, he downed a glass of it at the kitchen window. Lights from his neighbor's house illuminated his backyard, where a raccoon, bold as brass, roamed at will.

The heat of the day had come into the house for the night, and he stripped off his shirt, tossing it atop the one he had worn two days ago. He yearned for the fall, when he could watch the Celtics play, root for Bird in his final years. Best was when the Bulls came to Boston. Bird was wonderful, but Michael Jordan was awesome, his body a vital force apart from the man. Balling up a flyer from his unopened mail, he threw a three-pointer at the wastebasket and missed. He considered a shower and instead snatched the telephone from the wall.

He called the Stottle residence and got Mrs. Stottle, who sounded shaken. "It's Chief Morgan," he said. "Am I disturbing you?"

"No," she said, "but the reverend's not himself."

"Neither am I, Mrs. Stottle. May I speak with him?"

Reverend Stottle came on the line with a voice that sounded in need of chicken soup. "Is there something more I can do for you, Chief?"

"Yes, there is."

"I can still hear Matthew's voice in my head. It will be there forever."

"That's what I'm calling about. I want you to pretend you were a priest. Your lips sealed."

"I don't understand."

"Yes, you do."

"Chief, I've told Mrs. Stottle."

"Then ordain her. You owe me."

Scratching his chest through his T-shirt, he made his way back to the living room and dropped into the easy chair, whose arms were frayed. It had belonged to his wife's mother and was among the many donations she had made to her daughter's venture in a marriage meant to last a lifetime. His eyes were closed. Sleep came. In a dream he and Elizabeth were feeling their way toward each other in the dark of an unfamiliar room. He could hear her steps, then her breathing, but the woman who slid into his arms was Lydia Lapham.

Lydia Lapham stepped out of her car in the white of her uniform. The moon, the sun's negative, hung ghostly, much of it missing. Her shadow, a scarecrow, followed her to the front door. She rapped lightly, stepped in, and called his name. She knew he was home because his car was in the drive. Her steps were tentative because she had not been in his house before. A light beckoned from the kitchen. He was not in it. He was in the living room.

"James," she said.

He was sprawled in an easy chair, his legs tossed out, his arms lying lean out of a T-shirt. He was unshaved and unshod. His sleep was sound. She prodded his stockinged foot with the scuffed white toe of her shoe.

"James," she said, and he came awake slowly and then all at once. He took a deep breath as if for a whiff of her. "Why didn't you tell me yourself?" she said.

"I didn't know how."

"So you left it to my aunt."

"It was the easiest way."

"You look like hell," she said.

"So do you," he said.

She batted back her hair. "I worked through my shift. It was a way to stay sane. Why did he do it, James?"

Morgan drew in his legs and sat erect. His brow was scribbled. He was pondering something, words that would not come out, though they might have had she waited for them.

"If you don't know, I do," she said. "I did it to him."

"It was an accident," he said.

"I don't believe it."

"All the same, that's what it was," he said calmly.

"You're lying."

He lifted himself from the chair, his legs shaky, and went into the kitchen. She followed him. His back to her, he made himself another chocolate drink, using the last of the milk, and raised the glass. "Shall we share it?"

"God, no."

"Want a beer?"

"Yes."

She drank from the bottle. She stayed standing while he sat at the table. With a start, she said, "Did you hear that?"

"Thunder. It's done that all day."

"God in heaven meeting Matt. He loved me, you know, very much."

"I know."

"And I did love him once, high school, puppy love in the backseat. And then, after Frank, he was still around, waiting, wanting. It was easy to fall back into something that was over. He was solid, dependable, not a bad lover, but he became an assault on my time, my attention, my moods. If I had not let it drag on and on, this might not have happened."

"That's not something to dwell on," Morgan said.

"Was it really an accident?"

"I'm not the only one who says it. The state police say it too, Bakinowski himself. That's what his report will read."

She scraped an unpainted nail down the bottle's label, and both she and Morgan remembered that that was what MacGregor used to do, invariably. She said, "I was sure it was suicide. Do you know what my first reaction was? Outrage. Pure anger and outrage for heaping guilt on me atop everything else."

"Don't feel guilt about anything, Lydia. You have no reason."

She belched softly. "Excuse me." Her eyes traveled. "Crummy house you have, don't you ever pick up?"

"I do it in spurts."

"Is this where we'd live if we got married?"

"Here or your place. Either would do."

"Neither would suit me." She put the bottle down. "Don't put stock in anything I say. I'm thinking out loud."

"I realize that."

"Summers usually fly by, but this one's pasted in place. I want it to end."

"I do too."

"James, who killed my mother and father?"

"Tomorrow," he said. "Tomorrow I think I can give you an answer."

During the night the sky convulsed, and the rains came, waking Papa Rayball, who had fallen asleep in a chair with the old black-and-white television blaring. "Little shit's not home," he said aloud, springing up and turning off the TV. "He's wrecked my truck is what he's done." He double-checked Junior's bedroom, but the cot was empty, which set him cursing and then worrying. He went into the kitchen and banged around and then carried a mug of apple juice to the screen door. Through the rain he saw the pickup.

He was going to throw on a jacket, but he was too angry to take the time. Water slobbered off the roof, which lacked a gutter, and splashed his neck and soaked the back of his shirt, which angered him more. The rain battered the pickup. Through a web of it he saw Junior behind the wheel. " 'Fraid to come in?" he shouted. "You got reason!" He yanked open the door, and Junior fell out.

Hunkering down to grab him up, Papa knew in the instant that what was in his arms was dying, and he wailed like a woman. Then he pleaded, "Don't, Junior. You're all I got. You're my boy!"

"No, Papa. I ain't never been your boy."

His eyes were open, and Papa squeezed him. He shouldn't have. It hurt him. The rain washed blood from his head and showed the split. Papa said, "Clement's not mine. It's *you* that's mine."

Junior's eyes rolled.

Andrew Coburn

13

It was early morning. Trees were awake, birds gossiped. Chief Morgan, staring out his kitchen window, finished up his coffee, black because the milk was gone. The nearly empty beer bottle stood where Lydia Lapham had left it. He had kissed her cheek, her ear, the dent in her temple, and she had stayed longer but not the night. He placed his cup in the sink and left the bottle where it was. When he stepped out the front door he heard the tinkling collar of the neighbor woman's dog, which had just deposited droppings on his lawn. From her porch the woman called out, "Come here, Buster."

Morgan called back, "There's a leash law, Mrs. Winkler."

She placed a hand on her hip. "Instead of worrying about a little shit on your grass, better you bring in a murderer."

"I intend to," he said, heading toward his car. "Maybe with my bare hands."

She stepped back, as if somehow she knew he was not joking.

He went to the Blue Bonnet for breakfast, he needed a big one, but ordered only juice, coffee, and one English muffin. The place was crowded, but the talk, focused on Matt MacGregor, was subdued. Morgan's statement, over his coffee, that it was an accident, no question about it, was neither disputed nor believed. Faces were friendly only to the point of politeness. On his way out, Orville Farnham, a selectman besides an insurance man, motioned him to his table and said, "Maybe now we can clear up that other thing."

Morgan said, "That's what I intend to do."

Farnham said, "You're a good man, Chief. Maybe too good for this job."

In his office, Morgan examined his revolver. The bore, he suspected, was pitted. He pictured the whole business exploding in his hand. Swiveling in his chair, his back to the door, he tried firing it empty. It jammed. He called in Meg O'Brien.

"You still carry that little gun of yours in your bag?" he asked.

She cocked her head. "What do you want to know for?"

"I need to borrow it."

"What for?"

"Just in case."

"What's the matter with yours?"

He pushed his across the desk. "Take a look at it," he said, and she picked it up and examined it.

"Jesus jumping Christ, I see what you mean." She went out and returned with her bag and took out her little gun, toy-sized and snub-nosed. "Before I give it to you, I want to know what you want it for."

"I plan a serious talk with Papa Rayball, just him and me, but he may have guns in his house. I don't want to stand there barefaced if he goes running for one."

Hesitantly Meg relinquished her little weapon, well oiled and regularly cleaned, shiny as a new nickel. "You haven't got much firepower there," she said, "and it's not too accurate, so aim at the body, not the head."

"Meg, I was in Nam."

"That was years ago, and this isn't Nam. Don't shoot yourself," she said. Her voice was nervous. "He's little, you could miss. Take Eugene with you. He's feeling better. He hasn't got his problem anymore."

"That's good, I didn't like his color," Morgan said. "But I

Andrew Coburn

don't need him." His eye went to the calendar block. "Could you do flowers for me? On one I'm a little late. You could have them sent to the house. Mrs. Poole."

"I was wondering if you were going to do that. First name's Christine, isn't it?"

"Yes." He was embarrassed. "It's proper, isn't it?"

"I don't know if it's proper, but I'll do it." She reached over and ripped the page off. "Before you go, Chief, could we sit here and talk awhile? About Matt?"

"Sure," he said, "I'm in no real rush. Funny thing, but I feel I've got all the time in the world now. How about some coffee?"

At the crack of dawn Papa Rayball drove to the motor inn in Andover and knocked on Clement's door. He did not tell Clement what was wrong, he merely said, "It's Junior. You gotta come." He drove back to Bensington in the pickup, a blood-soaked cap on the floor near his clutch foot. He was going to throw it out the window but decided it would be better burned. Clement followed several minutes later in the rental.

Papa stood waiting. The rains of the night had taken away some of the heat. The humid air was almost pleasant. When Clement got out of the car, Papa raised an arm and let it fall. "I've lost him, Clement. I've lost my boy."

Clement turned his face away for a moment. "What are you telling me, Papa?"

"He came back busted up. Someone must've done it to him at that whorehouse. He's dead, Clement."

Clement gazed over Papa's head. Pines beyond the back of the house looked unready for the world, as if a child had sketched them and applied too little crayon. "Where is he?"

"He's in his room. I put him there. I cleaned him up best I could. I changed his shirt, and I put clean socks on him. He didn't have any washed, so I gave him a pair of mine. Same fit."

Clement went into the house, and Papa followed. Junior was on the cot, where Papa had lain him out straight, brought the hands together, one over the other, and placed the folded army blanket over the waist and legs. The stockinged feet protruded.

"He was born broken, and he died worse. Not my fault, Clement. I brought him up best I could, same as I did you. But we had the whole town against us, the old chief and then this one. Ain't anyone ever been fair to us."

Clement stared at his brother. Traces of blood remained on the face, as if the thorns of roses had embraced it. Then Clement could look no more. He went into the kitchen and stood by the sink. Papa came out and stood by the stove. Neither spoke for a while. Then Papa did.

"I was layin' him out, I had my final words with him. Told him I was never 'shamed of him. Told him he was my flesh and blood."

"Like you never knew that, huh, Papa?"

"I wanna bury him here. This is where he belongs."

A streamer of sunlight transported dust. Peering through it, Clement saw a stunted and withered old man with a prehensile look. Peering harder, he remembered old stories his grandmother had told about Rayballs who had lived in the woods, shunned commitments, and wiped their snot on their wrists, scrappy and scrawny critters in daily danger of being mistaken by hunters for small game.

Papa said, "The way you're lookin' at me, maybe I oughta dig two graves. One for me."

"Maybe we should put him out there, with his mama," Clement said, pointing toward the window, the direction unmistakable.

"She ain't there."

"He thought she was."

Seconds later Clement was outdoors, and Papa was at his heels. Clement headed toward the woodpile, the top of which was sheeted with plastic. Papa said, "You're serious, ain't you? You can't dig there."

"You don't have to dig."

Papa grabbed at him. "I want you to promise me something. I got the name and address of that whorehouse written out.

You go there, Clement, you get the one who bashed him. You promise?"

With an air of fatality Clement said, "First things first."

Christine Poole sat by a tall window and looked out at the green grounds. The round ornamental pond glittered gold in the sun. Arlene Bowman said, "The scent is delicious." The voice did not bother her. It was simply there, like the furniture, the flowers. The flowers were on the mantel and two tables. "So many," Arlene said, "but none, I notice, from Morgan."

Christine faintly heard her. Her thoughts were on two men, both gone, one buried, the other cremated. She remembered how her first husband's death had emptied the familiar of meaning, had left the suits he had once filled hanging alien in the closet. Rooms in which his voice had vibrated gaped with silence. His favorite chair was hollow, his place at the dinner table vacant. The Persian carpet he had bought at a close-out still conveyed an imperishable quality of design but felt different under her feet. As it had been then with his death, so it was now with Calvin's.

"The nice thing, of course, is that you don't have to worry about money," Arlene said, moving away from the mantel. "That would add insult to injury."

She wondered whether in time she would confuse the two of them, whether they would slip into each other's clothes to play ghostly guessing games, with one tugging at her heart in the guise of the other.

"Money is the key," Arlene said. "My father killed himself over it, and Gerald is uncomfortable with men who make more than he does. He says money makes the man. Which is true."

Christine's composure teetered when Arlene moved into her line of vision. The woman looked ravishing, all lovely arms and legs in a little black dress that could have been inked on. At the same time, as Arlene drew closer, Christine felt something in herself dry up.

"It does something for women too. Keeps us fresh. I don't intend to grow old. I want always to be new. And you, Christine, no reason for you to grow old. We'll work some more on your weight. You've already lost some, I can see."

Arlene, hovering, was giving her all her attention, which became too much to bear, too much for anyone to bear. She rose from her chair, unsteady, unwell. "Would you excuse me for a minute?"

The carpet muffled her steps. Somewhere people were laughing, joking, exquisitely enjoying themselves, all ignorant of what lay ahead. A bride this moment might be tossing a bouquet. Enjoy it while you can, she thought. She entered the game room, where her elder son, throwing darts, haunted her with his looks. They were every bit like his father's.

She said, "Get that woman out of here."

Fred Fossey's eyes drank her in. She hadn't been fooling. She had brought sandwiches and a cold thermos of lemonade, real lemons, not from the mix. "I told you I would," May Hutchins said and handed him a paper cup. The sandwiches were roast beef, meant for a man. They sat facing each other on the grass near the markers, Flo and Earl's. Fred's face glowed. He was taking big bites and enjoying each.

"This is great, May. Honest to God, it's really great."

"Wasn't any bother bringing it. I thought it'd be fun." The red tips of her hair sizzled in the sun. "I saw you coming out of the library yesterday with a bunch of books. You must read a lot."

"I'm a student of military history, May. Right now I'm on the big wars, One and Two. 'Course, the Korean War's my favorite because I fought in it."

"Stands to reason. How's the lemonade?"

"Delicious."

"And the sandwich?"

"Even better. This is good beef." He stopped chewing and looked into her eyes. "When you saw me at the library, why didn't you holler?"

"Well, there's a time and place for everything. You got mustard on the corner of your mouth." She leaned forward and wiped it off with her pinky.

"Your hair looks nice," he said. "It's different from the last time."

"Really? I don't take much time with it. I know I'm not pretty," she said, lowering her eyes, and instantly he moved closer, spilling his lemonade. "Don't worry," she said, "there's plenty more."

"May, don't you know you're beautiful?"

Her voice went shy. "I guess I need someone to tell me."

His arm was around her, with one thing leading to another. His mouth moved from her cheek to her lips. He frenched her and felt her tremble. He was mussing the hair she had fixed so nicely. Her mouth fought free.

"What are we doing, Fred?"

"Everything." His hand was under her dress. Her legs were bare. "Have you ever done it in a cemetery, May?"

"Never." Then she was laughing, like a girl. "Not in front of Flo, Fred. We can't."

"Let her watch. Let her know we're both happy."

They were both laughing, joking, enjoying exquisite fun. "Earl's there too," she said.

"He knows what men and women do." He was having trouble with his trousers. The zipper was caught on the fly of his boxer undershorts, and he had to rip it clear.

"Oh, Fred, you're too big."

"Bigger than your hubby?"

"Much."

Then he was on her, and her hand was trying to make it right when a terrible rumble came upon them and then a roar. They leaped to their feet as a pickup truck bounced by with the face of a little man snarling at them. "It's that damn Papa Rayball," Fred hissed.

May was frantically brushing her dress. "I'm *so* embarrassed."

"We can finish it."

"No, we can't. Ever!"

Chief Morgan climbed warily out of his car. The pickup wasn't there, which meant Papa wasn't. Nobody was, he sensed it. All the same, he was glad he had brought along Meg's toy, which was a lump in his pocket, like a week's supply of small change. His eyes darting here and there, he tried to sort out what was making him uneasy. The woodpile looked the same and yet not the same. Things seemed altered, just a degree. The chorus of birds should have been reassuring, but a cardinal outdoing itself set his teeth on edge. Moving toward the house, he saw something small that had been burned on the ground, the ashes black. Cloth, he suspected. Going down on a knee, he detected a lingering stench that suggested a bit of plastic and something else, impossible to tell what.

The door had been left unlatched, and he stepped inside with his eyes absorbing everything in the cramped kitchen. A dripping water tap attacked his ear. Poking around, he saw a damp, blood-stained towel in the trash bucket and wondered what Papa had been killing. Years ago Papa had kept rabbits for eating, then shot them all when he got sick of the meat and they got out of hand.

He peeked into Junior's room. An army blanket covered the cot. Junior's old tattered sneakers had been tossed in a corner, the heels worn lopsided. He backed off, with no intention of searching for the F-1 sniper's rifle. He did not want to waste time looking for what wasn't there. What had disquieted him outside disquieted him more inside the house. He did not like the air, as if something, maybe the whole house, were going to blow up.

Back on the road, he drove randomly to give his mind a rest and his muscles time to relax. The road meandered, and the sky hurled down its brightness. Again, like Lydia, he wished the summer were over, no more dragons in his sleep, the little he was getting. Approaching the cemetery, he swerved fast as a car came out and almost hit his. The driver was Fred Fossey.

"What the hell are you doing?" he shouted, backing up.

Fred Fossey had slammed on the brakes and was now trying to restart the engine. "I'm sorry," he said out of a flushed face. "I was paying respects to Earl and Flo till Papa Rayball spoiled it all. He's in there barreling around in his pickup, like he's looking for his wife's grave and can't find it." Fossey got the engine started. "You want my advice, Chief, you oughta arrest the old coot."

Sounds came from the town clerk's office. Malcolm Crandall was alone in there, but he had grown into the habit of talking to himself. Quite distinctly, as Meg O'Brien was passing the open door, Crandall said, "Fuck them all."

"I hope that doesn't include me," Meg said, stopping in her tracks.

He reddened only for a second. "Our town's going to hell," he said. "It used to be nice and quiet, a pretty place to live, even with all those newcomers tearing up the woods, but now everything's bad. Flo and Earl Lapham dying like they did, and now Matt MacGregor killing himself."

"It was an accident," she fired back.

"We all know what it was," Crandall said. He had latching eyebrows, which in moments like this gave him a fierce look. "It's not hard to put two and two together. That state cop knew what he was doing, the chief didn't, or else he was covering up."

"You don't know what you're talking about, Malcolm."

"The hell I don't. The chief was here now, I'd tell him to his face. He's a god-damn fool."

Meg's sharp cheekbones almost came through the skin. "You want me to tell him that?"

Malcolm turned his back on her. "It's between you and me."

In the heat of the sun Papa Rayball stomped his wife's grave. His heels crushed the grass and cut the sod. "I know you can hear me!" His voice was terrible, like his face, which had caved in on itself. "He's yours now! You take care of him!" The sky blazed its bluest. His voice should have raised the dead, but it didn't. Exhausting himself, he stopped. That was when he saw the chief.

"Don't stop on my account," Morgan said.

Papa's face regained form. "How long you been there?"

Morgan had a hand in his pocket. "Anything wrong with Junior?"

"That's my business. And hers."

"She can't hear you. I'm the only one that can. And I'm going to put you away, Papa." Morgan's hand slid out of his pocket with Meg O'Brien's little snub-nose. "MacGregor told me everything."

"Seems to me I heard he shot himself. You tellin' me I'm wrong?"

"Before he did, he left a confession. I got you, Papa, it's all in writing."

The revolver was raised. Papa ignored it. It didn't much matter to him, and Morgan mattered only as an object of hate. "You got nothin'," he said, spittle showing. "You got pecker droppin's on a piece of paper."

Morgan gave a look at the ground. "Maybe I got her word too," he said, and Papa's eyes glowed with heat.

"Her? That tramp?"

"You killed her, didn't you?"

Papa grinned. He grinned the biggest he had in years, maybe ever. "Anybody around? Anybody hear us?" He gloated. "I'd do it again."

Morgan held the revolver steady as his eyes slid from side to side and then over his shoulder, which disconcerted Papa.

"What are you doin'?"

"Looking around for the rock I'll tell people you tried to hit me with."

"You ain't gonna do nothin'. You ain't the kinda man could kill a chicken. And that ain't a big enough gun, that's a cap pistol. I had one like it, I was little."

"You're still little, Papa. You're getting smaller."

"Big enough to stand up to you." Papa's voice challenged, his eyes baited. He was entering another rage, this one just as helpless but cold as ice, and Morgan watched and learned something, which took away will and purpose.

"I don't know what's happened, Papa, but I don't think I have to bother about you anymore." He lowered the revolver. "I think it's over."

"It ain't ever over," Papa said. Morgan pocketed the revolver and turned to leave, and Papa barked at him. "You were bluffin'! You were bluffin' all the time!"

"That's right, Papa, but you weren't. That was the rub." Morgan turned to leave again and stopped himself. "If I look for Junior, will I find him?"

"You leave him alone." Papa looked away. "He's where he wants to be."

Clement Rayball returned to the motor inn to shave and shower, put on a fresh shirt, and to pack. The packing took no more than a couple of minutes. His used underwear and socks he tossed into the wastebasket. He zipped up the bag and left it on the bed. He told the desk clerk he would be leaving that night and settled his account. The clerk said, "Thank you, Mr. Rodriques." At the bar he ordered a Miller. When the bartender served him, he laid down a hundred-dollar bill and a sealed envelope containing more than that.

"I'm checking out later," he said. "That's for you, the envelope's for her."

"Milly?"

"Yeah, tell her she's a nice kid, better than most of her customers."

"She'll appreciate it. She doesn't have much."

"More than my mother had at that age. Make sure she gets it."

Clement drank half his beer and left. The sun was white, the sky went on and on, like Florida's. He did not simply miss Florida. He yearned for it. He drove out of Andover, back to Bensington for the last time.

The death of Calvin Poole intensified the investigation into the Mercury Savings and Loan. The two red-bearded regulators brought in staff to help them winnow truth from fiction in complex loan agreements with Bellmore Companies and subsidiaries. One of the regulators said to his staff, "We're walking planks thrown across mud."

Gerald Bowman, whose contacts at the bank kept him

abreast of the investigation, conferred much of the morning with a team of lawyers, one of whom was a woman who annoyed him. He did not trust her judgment, nor appreciate her gloomy assessment. The others, the men, rendered cheerier forecasts, though by morning's end he distrusted their judgment too.

In the sitting room adjoining his private office he made love to his secretary. His love was translucent drops threading hair and beading the curve of her abdomen, for he was precautionary and quick enough to pull out at the agonizing moment. "Thank you," he said.

Attending to the golden bun behind her head, Pembrooke said, "It wasn't good, was it?"

"My mind's on other things."

It was like a poorly dubbed movie, the words ill fitting the movements of their mouths. She made herself decent, presentable, efficient. "I may be leaving you soon," she said.

"Another job?"

"Yes."

"It's time," he said.

An hour later he did something he rarely did. He left early for the day. On I-93 he had an urge to open the Mercedes up, to push it to the limit, but that was something he did only to himself and other human beings living in the closing decade of the twentieth century.

Entering Bensington, he drove beyond Oakcrest Heights to the country club, where he parked the Mercedes in a privileged space. His personal net worth, on paper, was the highest in the Heights, with the possible exception of that baseball player, whom he despised, a loud-mouthed ignoramus when he showed up here on the green.

The bar was quiet and cool, only one other patron. He took a table and soon had before him a glass of grapefruit juice chunky with ice. Leaning back, he said, "No need to sit alone," and a large man rose in the dim and ambled forth in a lightweight athletic jacket open over a spotless white T-shirt.

"How are you, Mr. Bowman?"

"Not bad, Pierre. Not bad at all. Yourself?"

Andrew Coburn

"Making a living," Pierre said. He was also drinking grapefruit juice, though without ice, which gave more for the money. His bald head looked polished, his smooth face free of any trying thought. "We don't usually see you here on a weekday."

"That's true." Bowman removed his glasses, fogged them with his breath, and applied a soft napkin. His defenseless eyes may have been born too soon. "Where do you live, Pierre, not here in Bensington?"

"In Lawrence, Mr. Bowman."

"That doesn't sound safe."

"I'm careful."

"Live alone?"

"I used to have a dog."

Bowman replaced his glasses. "To us, a dog is a lovable pet, a faithful companion with soulful eyes, but to the Oriental he's edible."

"Dining is relative."

"Everything is relative, Pierre, except the bottom line. That's where the real buck stops. I learned that at B.U. Did you go to college, Pierre?"

"I was a dropout. It was the sixties."

"The sixties, yes." Bowman smiled and sampled his juice. "That's when everybody wanted to learn to play the guitar, but very few did. I'm more a product of the seventies and an example of the eighties. We're all products of our times, Pierre."

"You think so, Mr. Bowman? I'd say we're products of ourselves."

"Everybody's entitled to his opinion," Bowman said with a wink, "but I agree only with my own."

The bartender sauntered over to see whether anything was needed. "Mr. Bowman? Dennis? Everything OK?" Everything was OK, to a degree. Bowman's eyes crinkled.

"What's this Dennis bit? I thought your name was Pierre."

"Dennis is my real name."

"We're all something we're not. It might not make the world move, but it makes it interesting." Bowman paused to smile.

He was lightheaded, as if the grapefruit juice were alcoholic. "You like your work, Pierre? You like being a masseur?"

"It has its moments."

"You like doing the women?"

"They trust me. They talk, I listen and never reveal a confidence."

"What does my wife tell you?"

"I never reveal a confidence."

Bowman laughed. "You're good. Tell me, professionally speaking, of course, what do you think of her ass?"

Raising his glass, Pierre considered the question. "I'm in the mood to speak personally."

"OK, go ahead."

"I like yours better."

Bowman looked away. Two customers had come in, and the bartender was busy with them. "I thought that would be your answer."

Glancing here and there, Clement Rayball walked through the house he had been raised in. His eye was quick and thorough, militarily trained. In the room he and Junior had shared as children, he snatched the Polaroid of himself from the wall and destroyed it. In the kitchen he tapped the face of his watch, which had stopped, but failed to wake it. A few minutes later he heard the pickup come into the yard.

He did not ask Papa where he had been. He did not want to know. He did not care. He sat at the table and drank Papa's apple juice. A mosquito whined, but kept its distance. "We got any family pictures, Papa?"

"No. I never saw the sense."

"None of Ma?"

"I burned those. You saw me do it, you were ten."

"Any of Grandma?"

"My ma?"

Clement nodded. His last memory of his grandmother was picking up kindling near the shack where she had lived. She had reverted to childhood and smiled at him from another century.

"I don't recollect any of her," Papa said.

"I got anything of mine here? Anything at all?"

"The rifle was the only thing, and you know where that is." Papa squinted. "What are you askin' these things for?"

"I'm leaving tonight. I don't expect to come back again."

Papa said nothing. He washed out a pan in the sink, which had been Junior's job. Clement stared at him and found him smaller. He tapped his watch again, without result. The battery was dead.

"I'm restless, Papa. I can't just sit here. I'm going for a drive, you want to come?" When he got no answer, he said, "Suit yourself."

Papa followed him out the door. "I'm comin'."

The digital clock in the rental told him the time, which was neither early nor late. It was just the time. The sun was still white, but the sky was now glass. Near a gully on Papa's side of the road a dead woodchuck awaited crows.

Papa said, "I been thinkin', it ain't right. Junior should be beneath the ground."

"He's all right where he is."

"She had better, he should have the same."

"Let's not talk about it, Papa."

"Where we goin'?"

"Nowhere in particular." He was approaching the bridge that connected Bensington to West Newbury. "This where you threw it, Papa?" He slowed down as Papa nodded and parked on gravel and grass, scaring up dust.

"Whatcha stoppin' for? Nothin' to see." Papa watched him climb out and sat tight. "I ain't goin' with you."

Clement walked onto the bridge and felt the breath of the river, the Merrimack, which had been clean only when the Indians had it. Through the metal rungs of the railing, he peered down. Last night's rain had given it life. It ran with authority.

"What are you stoppin' here for? I was farther down, I flung it." Papa's voice was right behind him and jumped ahead of him. With the strut of a game cock with the run of a henhouse, Papa went to the middle of the bridge and pointed. "Right here's where Junior and me got rid of it. He was 'fraid you'd be mad. I told him you'd be madder we didn't do it."

"You always told him right."

"I tried."

Two cars went by, one right after the other, and then there were none. Clement reached under his loose shirt and tugged free the Saturday night special. He stood directly behind Papa, who was peering through the rails to watch the waters rush. A gull with angry eyes, not unlike Papa's, planed the river.

"I ain't gonna turn around, Clement. You got somethin' you wanna do, do it. Just don't take all day."

The only man he had ever executed, a bullet in the back of the head, was a Contra captain who had given a nun to his men before killing what was left of her. Big stink about it later because the captain had been on the right side.

"I know what you got in your hand," Papa said. "Same as I knew back at the house you were only pretendin' you didn't care if I come. I *know* you. I brought you up."

"You want me to do it, Papa?"

"I ain't got nothing to live for. Like Junior, I ain't never been happy. Chief wanted to do it, better it's you." Papa gazed far out. "Only takes a second, then throw me in, no one knows."

Clement let his gun hand drop. He should've known he wouldn't do it. He wished the chief had, or God would. Papa spun around.

" 'Fraid? Then leave that thing with me and go on back to Florida."

Clement crossed his arms and hid the weapon in an armpit as another car went by. "I can't do that, Papa."

"Why not? I ain't your father."

"Maybe not, but I haven't known any other." Clement turned to leave. "You coming?"

"Not this time."

"I'll pick you up."

"I ain't goin'."

Clement trudged back to the car, slipped inside, and looked at the clock. The time now seemed significant. He had never known exactly when his mother died, only when he was told about it. He started up the car and coasted onto the bridge. Papa was standing in the same place.

"OK, Papa, last time. You coming?"

"No, I'm gonna suit myself."

"You always have."

"Ain't gonna change now, am I?" A mosquito flew into his ear, and he dug it out with his middle finger. "You take care of yourself, you hear?"

"Papa, what was your father like?"

"Like me."

"What was mine like?"

"Never knew him."

Clement drove on, into West Newbury, and soon came upon a weatherboard house, where a warm-faced woman was crumbling bread and tossing it to birds, mostly pigeons. Behind her a rock garden, freshly watered, vibrated. A short way up, he made a U-turn and, keeping a light foot on the gas, drove back to the bridge.

Papa was gone.

The eldest Wetherfield boy, Floyd, sat before Chief Morgan's desk. He wanted to be a policeman. Now that a spot was open with Officer MacGregor gone, he thought he might have a chance. "My mother said I should see you personally."

"How is your mother?"

"She's all right. Always working at that sewing machine."

"See much of your father?"

"Not too much."

"Floyd, it's too soon for me to start thinking about filling the vacancy. Too much else is going on." Morgan leaned toward the calendar block. "But look, I'll write your name here and keep you in mind."

"I want to be a policeman bad, Chief."

Morgan considered the face. It carried the strong good looks Thurman Wetherfield had once had before a nimbus of drunkenness circled him whether he was drinking or not. "How old are you, Floyd?"

"Twenty-one. I started college late. I'm putting myself through scraping chicken mess out of Tish Hopkins's coops. I don't mind. I want to make something of myself." He lowered his hot eyes and then raised them with twice the fire. "I want to be more than my father."

"Every boy does." Morgan mutilated a paper clip. "On your way out ask for one of those civil service forms. If Miss O'Brien's gone, ask the sergeant."

Floyd Wetherfield lifted himself up and stood taller than his father. "Do I have a chance, Chief?"

"Everybody has a chance." Morgan tossed the mangled paper clip into the wastebasket. "Well, 'most everybody."

Watching him leave, Morgan sat back. His eyes were unnaturally bright. He was afraid to close them, sure he would nod off. A few minutes later Meg O'Brien poked her head in and said something, but his ears were not receiving and his eyes were not focused. "I'm sorry, Meg. What did you say?"

"Someone else is here to see you, Clement Rayball."

Morgan showed no surprise. "Tell him to come in. Here, first take this."

She stepped forward and took back her little gun. "You sure you don't still need it?"

"Positive."

Presently Clement Rayball appeared, closing the door behind him. He looked different in a way Morgan could not put his finger on. Or maybe he looked more intensely the same, which was a difference in itself. At another time Morgan might have pondered the implications of that. Clement sat down.

"I'm leaving town tonight. I've got business in Boston tomorrow, and then I'm on to Florida. I did some dirt to you while I was here. I'm sorry."

Morgan waited. "Is that all you came to tell me?"

"No, there's a little more," Clement said. "You can write my father off your books. He's not around anymore. It was his choice."

Morgan's voice deepened. "Where is he, Clement?"

"Where he threw the rifle."

Andrew Coburn

"Then I have a fair idea where to look, unless you want to tell me exactly."

"He's not in a hurry to be found."

Morgan reached for another paper clip. "You didn't kill him, did you?"

"No, Chief, same as you didn't. Junior's gone too. It didn't happen here. It was misadventure in Boston, but he came back and died here. He's with his mother, where you found her." Clement reached under his shirt, where the handgun had been, and drew out an envelope, which he placed on the chief's desk. "That's the money to bury him. Put him next to where she really is."

"What about your father?"

"Like I told you, he doesn't want to be found." He watched Morgan's fingers try to bend back into shape what they had unbent. "I was a kid somebody dared me to swallow one of those. To this day I don't know if it ever came out."

Morgan threw the clip away. "So it's time for you to go back to Florida and be someone else?"

"You never forget who you are," Clement said with a cynical smile. "Dreams remind you."

"The trick is not to have any."

"Then you die."

"That sniper's rifle. That was yours?"

"Yeah, that was mine. I never should have left it there." There was a look on Morgan's face he did not like. "When I leave tonight, you're not going to try to stop me, are you?"

"I haven't decided."

He slouched easily in his chair. "Be careful, I know tricks you've never heard of. You can kill a man with your thumb."

"But I don't think you ever have," Morgan said.

Clement smiled. "You're right—not with my thumb."

"I want something from you," Morgan said in a suddenly stiff voice. "I want it in writing that Papa told you he shot and killed Florence Lapham. Also that he killed your mother. I'm sorry, Clement, but I know for a fact he did because he told me. In the same statement, write down everything you know about Junior's death. Then I want you to mail it to me from Florida, so it's like I'm learning about it for the first time."

"You've got it," Clement said quietly and picked himself up from his chair. "About my mother. I guess I always knew." He smiled again. "I guess we both know everything now, unless there's something missing?"

"Do you need to know?"

"Will it change anything?"

"No."

"Then I don't need to know."

Morgan picked up the envelope, weighing it in his hand as Clement moved to the door. "I suspect there's too much in here."

"No, there isn't. Give him the best."

Gerald Bowman had second thoughts even before he climbed out of his Mercedes, which he felt would not be safe. The street festered with activity. A man in a black shirt and tight jeans stepped out of a martial arts studio and gave the car a long look. Across the street, costumed in Spanish colors, was a man Bowman suspected was a drug merchant flanked by bodyguards. Nearby women paraded in and out of a body-toning salon. "Nothing to worry about," Pierre said, but he went through a dense moment of doubt.

Pierre lived above the martial arts studio in a tastefully decorated apartment, except for erotic artwork on the walls, which he ignored. He did not want to get into a discussion about it. The liqueur Pierre served was exotic, nothing quite like he had tasted before, and not entirely to his liking. The music was Wagner, but tuned low, which made it something other. They talked with quiet voices. His was strained while Pierre's came through pure.

"You're not comfortable yet, are you, Mr. Bowman?"

That was true. His eyes skimmed objects and returned to a wrought-iron piece of table sculpture that appeared to be a male figure swinging a baseball bat. Pierre was on his feet.

"Do you know the best way to relax, Mr. Bowman?"

He had never relaxed. Always the push to be better, supreme, not merely to be smarter than most but smarter than all, the cock of the walk. He had wanted the power to pull strings and make the world tilt his way. His eyes burned blue through his rimless glasses.

"What are you waiting for, Mr. Bowman?"

Stripped of his clothes, Pierre was pigskin. He was still dressed, and he stayed dressed. This was not what he had in mind, or if it had been, it wasn't anymore. How to explain?

"I can't do it. It's not you, Dennis. It's me."

Pierre had an erection and made it nod. "How do you know?"

All that skin—too pink and too moist-looking, hog hairs on the shoulders—was threatening, menacing. This was not for him, he wasn't that way. When Pierre stepped closer, he snatched up the statuette to ward him off.

"Put it down, Mr. Bowman. Nobody's going to hurt you."

He felt he was ten years old again and a bully was taunting him, humiliating him for his prissy ways. His father, who should've protected him, taunted him too. *Stand up to him, Jerry!* His father had never known his ass from his elbow. And had it been left to his father, he never would have gone to Boston University. His mother's push got him there.

"I didn't force you here, did I?"

"No, you didn't, Dennis." He was being humble and hated himself for it. And he hated this hulking bald man with no clothes on, whose erection had fallen.

"If you don't know what you are, how am I to know?"

He reached inside his suit jacket for his wallet, though usually there was little money in it, only major credit cards honored in most parts of the world. "Let me give you something."

"Keep your money, Mr. Bowman. I'm not a whore. You are."

He got out of there, descending narrow stairs, which shook with thumps coming from the martial arts studio, along with blood-curdling shouts of assault.

The Mercedes was safe and sound. The man in the black

shirt and tight jeans said, "Nice wheels." He went around him, stepping into the gutter, where a pigeon lay dead like the remains of someone's hurried lunch. The man said, "You must be a big shot."

"I am," he said.

It was dark now, and time to tell her. Chief Morgan phoned the hospital to leave word that he would see her later, but she was not there. He phoned her house, no response. Then, on a whim, he punched out his own number, and she answered. "What are you doing there?" he asked, an inane question. She was waiting for him. He asked how she'd got in, another silly question. Through a window.

Meg O'Brien was gone. He told Bertha Skagg that he was going home and did not want to be bothered the rest of the night, even if the station caught fire. Bertha, who tended to take things personally, said, "I don't smoke." Morgan, who always tried to be nice to her, though she got on his nerves, asked about her ankles, and she stuck them out. "Now don't you wish you didn't ask?"

He drove home with no sense of himself, only of Lydia. A sickle moon guided him. Stepping out of his car, he was amazed by the way stars used the night to defy time and space to make themselves known to someone as insignificant as himself. She met him at the door. He expected a kiss but did not fret when he failed to get one.

They went into the living room. He sat at his desk as if he were back in his office. She made herself comfortable on the sofa with her stocking feet drawn beneath her. She was in her uniform, for she had been to work and left early. Leaning sideways, she extended an arm and switched off the floor lamp. The only light leaked in from another room. Sitting back, she let the gloom eat up half her face.

"I'm ready," she said.

He went way back, to the very beginning, to Eunice Rayball, whose death mask he would never forget, and to Papa Rayball, who piled up hate the way Silas Marner bagged money. He jumped the years to the day Junior Rayball hid in the high grass edging the girls' softball field and Matt MacGregor grabbed him by the scruff. He moved to the tragedy of her parents and ended with Papa stomping his wife's grave. He did not tell her everything about Matt MacGregor. Maybe in ten years he would and then risk being hated for having held back. He told her he believed Papa was dead. He did not tell her how he knew, and she did not ask. He said nothing about Clement Rayball. She did.

"I saw him a few days ago at the hospital. I was looking at the son of the man who killed my mother and father. I'm glad I didn't know."

He watched her suffer a small death and slowly come out of it with tears. He moved from his desk and sat with her on the sofa. A warm breeze billowed the thin curtain. She sat in silence, and he did not break it. The night gathered around them and became a collection of summer sounds, all intimate. Finally she spoke again.

"Matt died with people thinking the worst about him."

He groped for a response but felt he would be absurd rendering any. She spoke of Matt's poor mother and sister, the ordeal of a funeral. She asked whether Matt would be buried in his uniform, and he said, "His mother may not want that."

In the kitchen was a small grocery bag. She had brought it. She began scrambling some eggs and sizzling bacon. Getting in her way, he prepared the coffee. She was out of her uniform and wearing one of his old T-shirts over her briefs, which covered little. Stepping back, he said, "You have the loveliest bum in Bensington."

"You've seen them all?"

"A few."

"You proud of that?"

"No," he said.

They ate together at his table, which in his mind he marked as an occasion, a memory he might take to the grave with him. Again, through a window, the night delivered its sounds and spread them around. She said, "Do you have a picture of your wife?"

"Many," he said. "They're packed away."

"You should bring them out, let them breathe. Then maybe you can."

The eggs were good, much better than his own efforts would have produced. The bacon was lean. She had given him the most. She lifted her coffee cup.

"One thing you really ought to do, James. Forgive her for getting killed. It's time." She lowered her cup, and he nodded. She said, "I thought that would throw you."

"No," he said, "there's truth in what you say."

The sheets on his bed were fresh. She had been busy. Laundry left on the floor had been tossed into a corner. Insubstantial in the half-light, she waited for him with her head in the pillow and said something that did not carry. Shadows figured her face. He breathed in what he could see. This time, he was sure, she would stay the night.

When he woke in the false dawn, she was gone.

Clement Rayball woke to a ring, compliments of the Ritz-Carlton. His room overlooked the Public Garden. Arlington Street throbbed with early traffic, the sidewalk with people hustling to jobs. One beautiful woman seemed to breed another. They were everywhere.

In the dining room he had English muffins and coffee at a corner table, where he looked out at businessmen who had forsaken power lunches for power breakfasts. The businessmen bored him, and he turned to the newspaper. The front page told him that Crack Alexander was hanging up his spikes. His horoscope advised him not to hold grudges. From a pocket he withdrew a scrap of ratty paper on which was scribbled the name and address of another hotel.

He found it without trouble and, though he did not know it, parked the rental in the space where his brother had spent some of the last hours of his life. In the hotel he described Junior to the fat man, who said, "No kiddin', that's your

Andrew Coburn

brother? Yeah, he came in, but he didn't have enough money, so he left. That's all I can tell you."

"He might've found a way back," Clement said and, snapping a crisp new bill, slipped the man a hundred. "Let me talk to the women."

"No trouble, is there?"

"No trouble at all."

"I got three early birds, that's all, only two today. Nice girls." He told Clement the room numbers, both on the same floor. "You might wanna try one. One puts on a show, good single act."

Clement, though unaware of it, retraced his brother's steps. The smell of disinfectant followed him up the stairs and invoked memories he swiftly purged from his mind. A white woman with sleep in her eyes remembered Junior, but little else. She blocked a yawn, tightened her robe, and said, "I had to look twice, I thought he was a kid."

A black woman said, "Yeah, my guy hit him. Is he all right?"

"He's fine," Clement said, with another note in his hand, as crisp as the first one. "Who was the guy?"

"His name's Sal. He makes book out of a convenience store around the corner. You won't miss him. He's got holes in his face." She tucked the money away. "Don't tell him I told."

"I won't," he said and started to walk away.

"It wasn't the kid's fault," she called out. "We get animals in here."

The store was no more than a hole in the wall, with a sign outside that said CORNER VARIETY and with an unaired smell inside. Girlie and macho magazines consumed a wall. Bread and milk appeared to be the major grocery items. The man behind the counter did indeed have holes in his face, as if he had survived debris from a shotgun. Clement said, "Hi, Sal, how you doing?"

Sal scrutinized him. "You a cop?"

"No, but yesterday you slammed my brother over the head. What the hell did you use?"

"That little turd was your brother?" Sal laughed. "Yeah, I

hit him. I was payin' to watch somethin', he was grabbin' a peek. Simple as that." Sal laid a plumbing pipe on the counter, the length of a baton. "He's a pervert. You got an argument about it?"

"No," Clement said. "Sounds like he deserved it."

14

It was a Saturday in September, a rather pleasant one after such an uncomfortable summer, which had ended with a drought. Autumn colors haunted the trees. Fleets of birds were already sailing south. The lilies that had exalted the paved path to the Congregational church had vanished, leaving behind forlorn stalks with empty prongs. Mrs. Stottle's garden, which had grown so riotously, was subsiding, withdrawing, which did not displease Reverend Stottle.

He was sitting in the garden with a notebook in his lap. He was mulling over what might perhaps be his last sermon, for it was clear that the board, Randolph Jackson in particular, wanted his resignation, which if not rendered soon would be forced from him. By his elbow was a glass of milk and a half-depleted dish of Oreo cookies. Earlier he had jotted down ideas on his napkin but later absently wiped his mouth on them, expunging them forever. He heard the sound of a car. Mrs. Stottle was home. He hoped she would not disturb him.

His fine-tip felt marker was poised over his open notebook. If this was to be his last sermon, it must sing in the voice of the ages. It must resound. It must reach a bellow. It must—Mrs. Stottle came upon him.

"Austin."

"Yes, my dear."

She was excited, her smile inordinately bright. "I went to plead your case to Mr. Jackson, but I didn't have to."

"I specifically told you not to," he said, reaching for a cookie. "Let God's will prevail."

"Mrs. Dugdale's is better. They finally found it. Her old lawyer didn't even know he had it. Excuse my French, Austin, but Mrs. Dugdale has saved your ass."

He bit into the cookie. "Please, Sarah."

"She left the church a bundle and named you sole authority over the funds until—and I'm quoting now—'until such time as Reverend Mister Stottle voluntarily retires.' Those were her words fifteen years ago, valid then, valid now."

He was impressed, but not all that much, and told himself he would not have another cookie. He knitted his brow the way he used to in Bible college when resolving never again to play with himself.

Mrs. Stottle laughed. "Sweet adorable bumblehead, I'm talking six figures."

He caught on. God, full of eternal goodness, had looked down upon him. God, who might mercifully grant a full house to a prayerful poker player accustomed to two pairs, had given him a royal flush. With this new hand, he said, "The question is whether I want to stay here or go to another parish."

"No other parish will take you, dingdong. You know that."

"I might simply retire."

"Your pension will be a pittance. Play that game with Mr. Jackson when he comes, not with me."

"He's coming here?"

"Yes. To ask you to stay." She leaned over and kissed him on the head. Then she was gone.

With a hint of rapture, his eyes smarted with happy tears. Breaking his resolution as easily as he had at Bible college, he snatched up another Oreo and poised the felt marker over the virgin notepaper. Inspired, he wrote, "Some of you may wonder what happened to the heads during the days of the guillotine. The answer is simple: God put them back."

* * *

Arlene Bowman played an hour of hard tennis with another woman from the Heights, who was a little younger and a little better than she, which gave the play more meaning. She felt vital. "We must do this again," she said to her partner, who had to hurry off to retrieve her small children from a lawn party at Pike School in Andover.

Strolling back to the clubhouse, tapping her racquet against her knee, she noticed a crowd on the links. The draw was Crack Alexander, who had a mighty drive. Some said he looked as good with a club as he had with a bat. Shading her eyes, she glimpsed Sissy Alexander, who was among his fawning admirers, and wondered what he wanted his wife there for.

Conspicuously leggy in her dazzling tennis whites, she entered the lounge and looked for a place at the crowded bar. She hoisted herself onto a high chair next to a man named Dick, who smiled at his good luck and greeted her by name. He had an overabundance of pampered silver-toned hair that could have been a crown of fur from a fine animal. His eyes were an uncertain blue. Perhaps they were gray, like the chief's.

"You look terrific," he said. His voice was enthusiastic, her response was not. A knee resting against hers, he told an off-color story, which did not amuse her. The man was an asshole. A past tennis partner, he had been trying to make her for months. "How's that husband of yours?" he asked.

"How's that wife of yours?" she replied, letting him pay for her drink. She enjoyed watching him get nothing for his money.

"I read in the paper he's in a bit of trouble."

"Nothing he can't get out of."

"This looks serious."

"If you look real deep into anything, anything at all, what you find is a joke. Have you ever looked deep into anything, Dick?"

"Yes," he said, his knee pressing. "Your eyes."

She finished her drink and left. She drove with the windows open, enjoyed the carnival colors of autumn, and let her hair blow. Oakcrest Heights looked especially beautiful. The road-side flamed with sumac and fire bush.

She stepped from her car and headed for the door. She was home early. She would be a surprise, welcome or unwelcome. Gerald had not been himself for a long while, a bear one day and a lamb the next. She left her racquet on the foyer table, where she sorted mail and saw nothing of interest. Stepping away, her eye caught a flash of color. She moved toward the sitting room, looked in, and froze. Her husband was wearing one of her dresses, one of Roberta's best.

Caught flagrante delicto, no moves to make, he smiled while attempting to conceal a ruptured seam. "How do I look?"

"Charming," she said and turned on her heel.

She sped back to the country club. She left her car in a space reserved for the handicapped and, walking fast, ran both hands through her hair. The lounge was still crowded, but Dick was no longer at the bar. He was sitting at a table with someone she knew vaguely, a dowdy woman from the Heights who was breaking out of her shell and trying to look pretty.

"Tell her to screw."

"Screw," Dick said, and the woman nearly fell over her chair in leaving.

Arlene sat down hard. "I need a drink."

Dick grinned. "Your turn to pay."

Christine Poole spent the morning at the Total Beauty Spa in Andover, where fabulous-looking women who did not look their age steamed and bathed her body, pampered her skin with oils, teased her muscles with infallible moves, unraveled her tensions, and reinforced her worth. Later she wriggled into her jeans. She had not dared to wear jeans in years. Then she slipped on her silk shirt and put repairing hands to her hair, which was a different color now, a shade she had always wanted to try. The manager, Leona, said, "You look fabulous, Mrs. Poole."

Before leaving, she gave a last look at herself in the wall mirror. Light lay furtively in her hair as if at any moment it might be shooed away. Her breasts were pronounced. She had lost weight everywhere but there, which she decided was not so bad. Swiveling sideways, she smiled at herself over the curve of her shoulder.

Back in Bensington, she stopped at Tuck's and bought a small container of salad at the deli section, which was a recent addition. The quaintness of the store was little more than a memory now. Returning to her car, she saw Chief Morgan ambling across the green and waited for him.

"How are you, James?"

He blinked and smiled. "Christine?"

"Didn't recognize me, did you?"

"You look wonderful," he said. Briefly he took her hand. "I'm sorry about your husband."

"I got your flowers. Thank you." For a moment her face was her former one. "They say it was an accident, but I know what it was. No one will ever convince me otherwise. But I'm not letting it get to me." She smiled. "Tell me about you. Is there anyone special in your life?"

"I guess you could say that. Problem is, she's not always there. She's in and out."

"Another one of those things, huh, James?"

"It would be easier if it were," he said.

"It's serious, then."

"On my part."

Her face hardened at the mouth. "What did you ever see in me?"

"You'd be surprised," he said.

"What did *I* see in you?"

"I don't know."

"I think I know," she said. "And you probably do too. It was my first husband. I talked about him enough."

"I gathered he was a terrific guy."

"He was terrific, but I made him out to be more than he was."

"Yes," he said, "we tend to do things like that, don't we?"

She went up on her toes and kissed his cheek. "Do you care who saw that?"

"No," he said. "It adds to my reputation."

"Good-bye, James."
"Good-bye," he said.

For his birthday, the tenth of September, Meg O'Brien had given him a handgun, a 9mm semiautomatic pistol, to replace his worthless revolver, which he had fired only once in the line of duty, at a dog frothing at the mouth. Sitting at his desk, he slid the massive pistol in and out of its shiny black holster and could not imagine aiming it at another human being. You needed both hands to steady it and a certain kind of brain to fire it. He slid it into a bottom drawer.

His birthday had been two weeks before. Lydia Lapham, vacationing in Bermuda with her aunt, had sent him a card with love and kisses, which was less than it sounded. Her handwriting was hurried, and she had neglected to include the zip in the address, which delayed the arrival. She was back now and had her house up for sale in a soft market.

Before that, in the midst of the August drought, he had attended a police conference in Chicago, where he sneaked off each day to watch the Bulls in preseason practice. He watched Michael Jordan and could not believe his eyes. Not once but several times he saw Jordan leap into space, defy gravity, and with absolute grace dislocate himself to make an impossible shot. Like a kid, he later stood in line for an autograph. When Jordan looked down at him from the heights, he said, "It's for my son."

Back in July, when people thought the heat would hold the summer in place forever, Papa Rayball's body was fished free of the Merrimack in Newburyport, near the mouth of the river. It was on its way to the sea when it washed up on a shoal and was discovered by a boater. Morgan tried to reach Clement Rayball in Florida but could not locate him. He used the money left over from Junior's funeral to pay for Papa's and tucked the receipts away in the event Clement ever wanted to see them.

Andrew Coburn

He did not have Clement's address, but he had his statement, which he made public the day he received it. It satisfied a lot of people in town because it meant that now Flo and Earl Lapham were laid to rest and others could go to bed at night without fear. Some felt shame for their insinuations about Matt MacGregor, whose sister established a thousand-dollar scholarship at the high school in his memory. Lydia attended the ceremony, but Morgan did not, for which some people faulted him. Most, however, agreed that he was not such a bad police chief after all and began joking again about his love life.

No one made much of Junior Rayball's death, especially since it appeared he had been assaulted not in Bensington but in Boston. The only one who grieved for him, as far as Morgan could tell, was Tish Hopkins, who came into the station wearing her overalls and boots and asked whether his killer would be caught.

Tucked in Junior's file folder was a crime clipping from the Boston *Herald*, which Morgan had inserted two days after Clement's visit. A man known as Sal the Face had been run down on the street moments after he had closed his convenience store for the night. The motorist, described as a deeply tanned Caucasian male, reportedly turned around and ran over the victim again. The car, which had been stolen near the Public Garden, was recovered near the Common. The organized-crime unit of the Boston Police Department was treating it as a gangland slaying.

Something had made Morgan read the article twice, simply a feeling, that was all, and after he clipped it out he slipped it into Junior's folder. As good a place as any.

He rose from his desk. Meg O'Brien was gone. She had left early to do some shopping in Andover, and Bertha Skagg, whose ankles had receded to near normal, had come in early but did not look pleased about it. She said, "Where will you be?"

"Blue Bonnet," he said.

Lieutenant Bakinowski joined him there, which was becoming a habit. The lieutenant was working on a case in Andover. A mother of three had been done in, and the suspect was not her husband but her father-in-law, with whom she had been having an affair. "You're not doing anything," Bakinowski said. "Maybe you'd like to work with me on it in your spare time."

"Not on your life," Morgan said.

"Too bad," Bakinowski said, lifting his coffee cup. "I could learn something from you, you could learn more from me."

They were quiet for a while, each with his own thoughts. Bakinowski had developed a noisy way of breathing. He said, "You've never met my wife. Why don't you come over for supper tonight?"

"No," Morgan said.

"Why not?"

"I'd be jealous."

When they stepped out of the Blue Bonnet, the air awaiting them was cool. Dark clouds looked as if they had been hammered into the sky. A woman was sitting alone in the passenger side of a Rolls parked nearby. "Excuse me," Morgan said and went over to her. Her blond hair was in a ponytail, accenting the wholesomeness of her face. "Where's Crack?" he asked.

"Around somewhere. I'm waiting for him. Guess what, I'm going to have a baby."

Morgan smiled. "Congratulations."

"Well, I'm not pregnant yet, but Crack and I are working on it practically every night." Her smile was that of a very young girl. Then it vanished into the woman's face. "Thank you, James. For everything."

"Everything's fine?" he asked. "Silly question. It must be."

"Crack's thinking of joining the professional golf circuit. People say he's good enough."

"I bet he is."

"He also wants to become more involved in the town. He might run for selectman next year." The little girl's smile was back. "He could become your boss. I bet he'd make you toe the line."

"That might not be so bad," Morgan said and started to ease away from the car. "He's coming."

She reached out and touched his hand. "Don't worry, James. He thinks you're the greatest."

Clement Rayball sat in the patio bar under the Miami sun. A moment of weakness had put him in a mood and led to the meeting with the man who was sharing his table. The man, a former army buddy now working out of Washington, had put on pounds and taken on the look of a state secret. He said to Clement, "I don't know where you're coming from, but it's not good thinking."

"It was just a thought," Clement said.

"You're not down and out, I know that. Sounds to me like you're looking for a home."

"Maybe I miss drinking army coffee out of a canteen."

"The president waves the flag, you gotta jump. You want that?" The man sat back. "You're going through something, let it pass."

Clement clasped his drink. "You're right, of course."

"Let the young guys do the fighting, Clement. We're too old, I'm too fat."

"You always did make sense."

The man looked at his watch, a Swiss one like Clement's. "Gotta go."

"Thanks for coming."

"Glad you listened."

He finished his drink alone and left. He drove into the heated parts of Miami, where the streets vibrated with zealots, exiles, smugglers, intriguers, junkies. Whores flashed their legs. It was a world of stucco and displaced Spanish, through which he passed without fear and approached cool, palm-fringed streets where the stucco houses were bigger and defended by walls. Then he entered an area of small professional buildings and parked in front of one.

He rode an elevator to the fourth floor, which was the uppermost. The elevator doors opened almost into her office suite. The walls of the reception room were the soothing blue shade of a robin's egg. The large potted plants were not over-whelming. The receptionist said, "She won't see you without an appointment."

He said, "But she might."

He went into her office, where she was smoking a cigarette and reading a journal that looked forbidding. Her tight curly hair had the frosty shimmer of moonlight and her tanned face the luster of women half her age. She removed her reading glasses.

He said, "My name's Chico. Actually it's Rayball—Clement Rayball. Do you remember me? We had a drink together."

"Strangely enough, I do remember you," Dr. Rosen replied easily. "You're the one who doesn't wear underpants."

"I lied."

"I see." She put her cigarette out. "I won't ask you how you found me. I suspect you have your ways."

"Doesn't everybody?" He took a chair. "So you're a shrink."

"That's what some people call us. What's your problem, Mr. Rayball?"

"What's your modus operandi, Doctor?"

"I try to recognize my client's essential contradictions and restore the balance, put him back on the beam, so to speak."

"What if he's never been on the beam, so to speak?"

"Then we work from scratch."

"That could take awhile."

"Yes, it could. And it would cost you money."

"Money's not my problem."

"What is your problem, Mr. Rayball?"

"Two problems. The little one is a lady named Esther. The bigger one takes telling."

She glanced at her watch. "All right, let's begin."

The sermon was written. Randolph Jackson had been and gone. Still in the garden, Reverend Stottle dropped his head back and closed his eyes. He should have enjoyed a pleasant catnap and instead had a nightmare in the afternoon's fading light. Jesus appeared in white robes that gradually darkened with blood the way red roses in the final flicker of day become the gore of the garden. But it was all right when he woke. A drop of rain touched his face like a child's tiny kiss, and Mrs. Stottle was smiling down at him.

"You'd better come in, dear."

Randolph Jackson returned exhausted from his visit with the Reverend Mister Stottle. He went up to the master bedroom, slipped off his calfskin loafers, stretched out on the bed, and listened to the rain. He was nodding off when his wife came home. He heard her call his name and mount the stairs. Her abrupt weight on the edge of the bed rocked him.

"That chief of yours," she said, "is up to his old tricks."

He rubbed an eye. "What tricks are those?" he asked and watched her remove wet pumps. Her hosiery was translucent blue.

"He was seen in front of Tuck's kissing some bimbo from the Heights, and I saw him myself with that baseball player's wife. I told you to get rid of him, you didn't listen."

"You're right, Suzy. One of these days."

She thrust an arm across the bed and leaned over him, her damp hair redolent of the rainy outdoors. "It's been a long time, do you know that?" Her eyes caressed. "Usually it's me that's tired."

He looked at her with great interest. "Suzy, you surprise me," he said and watched her dress come off. In a short while she surprised him more. "Goodness me," he said and reached down to stroke her head. With his other hand he tickled her bare back, the skin as pink and smooth as the day he married her. Playfully he said, "I hope you've never done this to the chief." Her lips popped off him, and she winked through her fallen hair.

"Only in my imagination."

The rain ran into the night. It was steady. It clattered on Chief Morgan's car, which was parked under a streetlight. The green gloom of the rain bloated shrubs, aggrandized trees, and obliterated the For Sale sign Lydia Lapham had authorized some weeks before. Morgan, relaxed behind the wheel, had listened to the news, stuff about a possible war, and now was listening to music, his fingers tapping to the melodic time-lessness of Peggy Lee's voice.

He glanced toward the house when the porch light went on. Then the front door opened, and in the next instant Lydia Lapham was running toward him in her sloppy robe under an umbrella, which nearly slipped from her grasp. She nearly slipped too. He did not begin cranking down the window until she banged on the glass.

"For God's sake, come in!" she shouted.

His look was undecided. "What have you got on under that thing?"

"Nothing."

"OK, I'll come in."